W9-BRW-172

PRAISE FOR DAVID GEMMELL

"I am truly amazed at David Gemmell's ability to focus his writer's eye. His images are crisp and complete, a history lesson woven within the detailed tapestry of the highest adventure. Gemmell's characters are no less complete, real men and women with qualities good and bad, placed in trying times and rising to heroism or falling victim to their own weaknesses."
—R. A. SALVATORE

"Gemmell is very talented; his characters are vivid and very convincingly realistic."
—CHRISTOPHER STASHEFF
Author of the Wizard in Rhyme novels

"Gemmell's great reading; the action never lets up; he's several rungs above the good—right into the fabulous!"
—ANNE MCCAFFREY

"Gemmell not only knows how to tell a story, he knows how to tell a story you want to hear. He does high adventure as it ought to be done."
—J. GREGORY KEYES
Author of Newton's Cannon

By David Gemmell
Published by Ballantine Books

LION OF MACEDON
DARK PRINCE
ECHOES OF THE GREAT SONG

KNIGHTS OF DARK RENOWN

MORNINGSTAR

The Drenai Saga
LEGEND
THE KING BEYOND THE GATE
QUEST FOR LOST HEROES
WAYLANDER
IN THE REALM OF THE WOLF
THE FIRST CHRONICLES OF DRUSS THE LEGEND
THE LEGEND OF DEATHWALKER
HERO IN THE SHADOWS

The Stones of Power Cycle
GHOST KING
LAST SWORD OF POWER
WOLF IN SHADOW
THE LAST GUARDIAN
BLOODSTONE

The Rigante
SWORD IN THE STORM
MIDNIGHT FALCON
RAVENHEART
STORMRIDER

Books published by The Ballantine Publishing Group are available at quantity discounts on bulk purchases for premium, educational, fund-raising, and special sales use. For details, please call 1-800-733-3000.

ECHOES
OF THE
GREAT SONG

DAVID
GEMMELL

BALLANTINE BOOKS • NEW YORK

Sale of this book without a front cover may be unauthorized. If this book is coverless, it may have been reported to the publisher as "unsold or destroyed" and neither the author nor the publisher may have received payment for it.

A Del Rey® Book
Published by The Ballantine Publishing Group
Copyright © 1997 by David A. Gemmell

All rights reserved under International and Pan-American Copyright Conventions. Published in the United States by The Ballantine Publishing Group, a division of Random House, Inc., New York. Originally published in Great Britain by Bantam Press, a division of Transworld Publishers Ltd. in 1997.

Del Rey is a registered trademark and the Del Rey colophon is a trademark of Random House, Inc.

www.delreydigital.com

ISBN 0-345-43232-0

Manufactured in the United States of America

First American Edition: December 2002

10 9 8 7 6 5 4 3 2 1

Echoes of the Great Song is dedicated with grateful thanks to Richard Allen, who—back in the sixties—showed me the way to popularity by breaking my arm. And to Peter Phillips, whose heroic appearance in another time of great danger prevented even more fractures.

Acknowledgments

My thanks to my editor Liza Reeves, test readers Stella Graham and Edith Graham, my copyeditor Beth Humphries, and to Alan Fisher for his invaluable insights.

Chapter One

And that was in the time before our time, when Tail-avar, the god of wisdom, travelled with Storro, Speaker of Legends, and Touch the Moon, god of tribes, to steal power from the magic fang of the Frost Giant. With a rope crafted from moonlight Tail-avar lassoed seven serpents of the sea. They drew his canoe across the Great Water in less than a day. When Touch the Moon saw the beast they had come to find, he fell to the floor of the canoe, and cried out to the Spirit of Heaven to grant them courage. For the Frost Giant was greater than mountains, its white back tearing the sky. The breath from its mouth flowed for many leagues as a cold mist across the water. Its claws were as long as the ribs of a whale, its teeth as sharp as betrayal.

from the Morning Song of the Anajo

Alone on an icy hillside, the wind blowing cold across the glaciers, Talaban recalled the first time he had heard the prophecy.

The Great Bear will descend from the skies and with his paw lash at the ocean. He will devour all

the works of Man. Then he will sleep for 10,000
years, and the breath of his sleep will be death.

The words had been spoken by a Vagar mystic; a
ragged man in clothes of filthy fur, sitting on the lower
steps of the Great Temple. Thinking the man a beggar
the young blue-haired Avatar officer had given him a
small silver coin. The mystic looked at it, turning it over
and over in his grimy hand. His face was smeared with
dirt and sweat, and upon his neck was an inflamed boil.
Had he been anywhere else in the city the Watch would
have arrested him, for no Outland beggars were allowed
in the streets of Parapolis. But the Temple was the ac-
knowledged center for the world's religions, and all were
free to gather here. Vagars, tribesmen, nomads, all journeyed to Parapolis. It was as much a political decision by
the Avatars as a spiritual one. For the barbarians returned to their homes and convinced their followers of
the futility of revolt. Parapolis, with its gleaming towers
of gold, and its powerful magic, was a symbol of invincible might.

Talaban watched the fur-clad beggar examining the
coin. The boil on his neck seemed ready to burst, and the
pain must have been great. Talaban offered to heal it for
him. The man shook his head, the movement causing
him to wince against the agony of the inflammation. "I
need no healing, Avatar. The boil is a part of me, and it
will leave me when it is ready." The mystic gazed down
at the silver coin in his hand, then glanced up at the tall
blue-haired soldier. "Your gift to me shows a generous
spirit, Avatar," he said. "Look around you, and tell me
what you see."

Talaban gazed at the colossal buildings at the center of
the capital. The Great Temple was a magnificent edifice,
roofed with gold sheeting and adorned with hundreds of

beautifully wrought statues of marble depicting scenes from a thousand years of Avatar history. The gilded Monument, a towering column of gold 200 feet high, stood beside it. Everywhere he looked Talaban saw the glory that was the Avatar capital: awe-inspiring buildings, great arches, paved walkways. And beyond them, breathtakingly serene, dwarfing all the incredible works of Avatar architecture, loomed the brooding presence of the White Pyramid. Three million blocks of stone, many of them weighing more than 200 tons, had been used to create this artificial mountain. And then the whole edifice had been faced with white marble. For a moment Talaban was lost in the wonder of it all. Then he remembered the question the ragged man had asked him. "I see what you see," he said. "The greatest city ever built."

The mystic chuckled. "You do *not* see what I see. You see what is. I see what will be." He pointed to the glittering Monument, rising like a spear towards the skies. It was a work of wonder, and golden spikes radiated from the crown set upon it. The gold of the crown alone weighed almost a ton. "The crown will fall when the whale's body crashes against it," he said.

"I have never seen a flying whale," said Talaban, amiably.

"Nor will you," agreed the mystic. Then he spoke of the Great Bear and its sleep of death.

Talaban was growing bored now. He smiled at the man and turned away. The mystic's voice followed him.

"The bear will be white. Gloriously white. Just like the pyramid. And you will be one of the few Avatars who will gaze upon it and live. And when you do your hair will no longer be dyed blue. It will be dark. For you will have learned humility, Avatar."

An icy wind whispered across the snow-covered hills.

Talaban's mind returned to the present. Pushing his fingers through his night-dark hair, he lifted his fur-lined hood into place, and stared out over the glaciers.

There was a time when he had hated the ice. Hated it with every fiber of his being. Yet now he gazed upon the cold and brittle beauty of the glaciers without rage. It surprised him that he could even appreciate the sunlight creating pale colors upon the ghost white of the glacier flanks, the faint blue of the reflected sky, the gleam of gold as the sun set.

So much was hidden beneath it, lost forever. His childhood friends, his family, thousands of works of literature and philosophy, all buried now. Along with his hopes and dreams. Yet despite what it had taken from him, the ice had proved too powerful for his hatred; too huge and too cold for his fury.

And now, as his dark eyes scanned the white mountains, his heart felt a curious sense of kinship with the ice, for his own feelings were now buried deep, as deep perhaps as Parapolis, which lay frozen beneath the belly of the Great Ice Bear.

The tall warrior transferred his gaze to the small group of men working at the foot of the ice mountains. From his vantage point on the hillside he could see them planting the golden probes, and setting up small pyramids created from silver poles. Golden wires were being attached to the pyramids, linking them together. Talaban could see the short, stocky figure of Questor Ro moving among the Vagars, issuing orders, barking out commands. At this distance he could not hear him, but he could tell by the impatient gestures that Questor Ro was putting the fear of death into his team. And the fear was very real. Questor Ro was one of the few Avatars who still, routinely, sentenced his slaves to be flogged for minor infractions. The little man was powerful within the Council, and it was by his influence that this expedition had been realized.

Would he be so powerful when they returned, Talaban wondered?

He had long since cast aside his optimism and considered the venture futile, but his orders were specific: bring Questor Ro and his Vagar team to the ice, protect them, oversee the operation, and return within three months.

It was the seventh team to attempt Communion in four years. Talaban had commanded three of the expeditions. All had ended in failure and he had no expectation of greater success on this trip. The prevailing opinion was that Communion was no longer possible. Questor Ro had argued against this, calling his colleagues "pathetically defeatist." His enemies, and there were many, had part sponsored the current expedition. Their aim was obvious to see Questor Ro humbled. This did not seem to perturb the little man.

Turning from the ice Talaban scanned the barren plain seeking signs of movement. Nomads still lived in the mountains to the east. They were a savage and fierce people. With only twenty soldiers under his command Talaban did not relish the thought of battle in this cold lonely place.

These icy lands, once so wondrously fertile, were full of peril now. The nomads were only one of many dangers. On the last expedition a pride of saber-tooths had attacked a working party, killing three Vagars and dragging off a fourth. Talaban had killed the beast as it mauled the Vagar. The victim had bled to death within moments, the artery in his groin torn open. Then there were the krals. Not since the first expedition had they been seen, but fear of them remained strong, and the descriptions of their ferocity had grown in the telling.

Talaban had never seen a kral, but witnesses told him of their speed and savagery. They were covered in white fur, like a snow bear, but their faces were almost human, though incredibly bestial. Three accounts described them as more than seven feet tall, with long upper arms. When they charged they dropped to all fours, and killed with talons and sharp teeth.

The last of the perils, but by no means the least, lay in the herds of tuskers, who roamed the forests to the east. Their shaggy hides protected them from the severity of the cold, and their tusks, some measuring more than ten feet, made them dangerous adversaries. Even sabertooths generally avoided the mammoths—unless they could isolate a stray.

The vast plain appeared empty. Talaban gestured to his sergeant, Methras, positioned on a hillside some 600 paces to the east. The man spread out his arms in a flat line, signalling nothing to report.

A movement out to sea caught Talaban's eye. At first he thought it was a ship, but then he saw the great back of a blue whale lift and dip, before the sea swallowed it once more. The mystic's words came back to him again. And now he knew that, as the tidal wave engulfed Parapolis, a whale had crashed against the Monument's crown, ripping it away. He wondered if the little mystic had survived.

Down in the bay, sails furled, *Serpent Seven* was at anchor. Even here in this gentle bay the huge black ship looked unseaworthy, her decks too high, her draft too low. Talaban sighed. Drawing his black woolen cloak around him he strode down the hillside. Three Vagars, waiting for the ship's boat, were crouched in the shelter of several boulders. They were wearing coats of white fur, and boots of sheepskin. Even so their lips were blue with cold. Talaban knelt among them. "Once there were vineyards here," he said, "and away to the north was a lake where the Avatar Prime had a palace. I swam in that lake as a child, and my shoulders were burned red by the sun."

"The lake is ice now, lord," said one of the Vagars, blowing into his hands. "Everything is ice now." His voice was toneless and he did not look up at Talaban.

"Two more days, and then we will sail back to the city," Talaban told them.

His words did nothing to lift their spirits and he moved away from them down to the water's edge. Chunks of ice were floating along the shoreline. Raising his arm he signalled the ship. Instantly the silver longboat was lowered to the surface.

Swiftly, without oar or sail, it glided through the water and Talaban could see the hunched, hooded figure of Touchstone seated at the tiller. Talaban shivered once more. The cold was seeping into his bones now. The three Vagars hurried down to the water's edge as the boat neared, then waited until Talaban had stepped aboard before scrambling over the side.

"Them's cold rabbits," said Touchstone, grinning, gesturing towards the shivering Vagars. Talaban smiled. Touchstone pushed back his fur-lined hood, shaking free his black braids. "Nomads are close," he said, tapping his nose. "I smell them."

The three Vagars tensed, and Talaban saw the fear in their eyes. At least they've forgotten how cold they are, he thought.

"How close?" he asked Touchstone.

"Half a day. Twenty riders maybe. Hunting tuskers they are. They be close to here tomorrow. By dusk maybe."

"And you can smell all this?" put in one of the Vagars.

"A good nose I have," said Touchstone with a wink,

stroking his long curved nose. He grinned at the man. "You see. Tomorrow. Come dusk."

Talaban raised his arm to signal the ship, and immediately the silver longboat began to glide backward out into the bay. Touchstone pulled the tiller arm and the craft swung towards the waiting ship. Talaban's gaze focused on the black vessel, with its high prow, and long, raking lines. The newly added masts were an abomination, but sadly necessary in these days of fading power. Fifty years ago there were seventy or more warships, sailing the oceans, mapping new lands, keeping the peace of the Avatar Prime. Now there was one, *Serpent Seven*, its power chest almost empty, its beauty scarred by the clumsy wooden masts hammered into its deck. Where once it had cleaved through the sea like a giant dolphin, now it labored like a sick whale, needing to keep close to the shoreline, wary of every wave that threatened to capsize it.

The silver boat drew alongside the huge vessel. Ropes were lowered. Touchstone tied two of them to the prow and stern. Talaban climbed the ladder to the central deck, responded to the salutes of three black-clad Vagar sailors, then strode on towards his cabin.

Once inside he doffed his cloak, unbuckled his sword belt and stood before the brazier of burning coal beneath the stern windows. Holding his hands to the heat he shivered with pleasure. Though he could tolerate it better than most men Talaban hated the cold. The quarter window was open, allowing fresh air into the cabin, and helping alleviate the stink of coal. Talaban gazed longingly at the crystal globes set into the wall. Once these had supplied either heat or light—indeed both if required—for the captain's cabin, but there was so little power left in the chest that Talaban did not dare activate them. Moving to his desk of polished oak he sat down, enjoying the luxury of the deep, padded chair.

Closing his eyes he thought again of the palace of the Avatar Prime, the burning sun, and the scent of nearby vineyards. Talaban had been happy there for a while, content to work on the maps he had so carefully charted the year before. It was the year that Questor Anu had been stripped of his rank. Talaban had been sent to question him, to decide if he posed a threat to the State.

The inquisition had taken place in Anu's home on the outskirts of the city. Anu, like all Avatars, eternally youthful, had welcomed him warmly, and they had sat in his garden in the company of a slack-jawed half-wit, who drooled and stared vacantly into space. The half-wit was an Avatar but, because of his condition, was not allowed blue hair or any other badge of rank. Talaban found his presence off-putting. It was made more disturbing by the contrast with Anu. He was a slender man of medium height, his features regular, his expression friendly. Yet there was about him an almost tangible radiance, a sense of unworldliness that was both compelling and unsettling. It was the kind of feeling Talaban experienced when climbing a mountain and looking out over the landscape of the world, a sense of awe and deep humility.

Anu smiled at Talaban's discomfiture. "Why does he disturb you so?" he asked.

Talaban returned the smile, and decided upon a course of honesty. "To be frank, sir, it is because I am here to decide your sanity. It seems curious to be doing so while in the presence of an idiot."

"An interesting point for debate, Talaban. What is it that makes a man an idiot? Togen cannot dress himself, and if left to his own devices would probably starve to death. He does not understand politics, and if I sent him to market he would become lost before he reached the first shop. And yet, tell me, Talaban, upon which science is our civilization built?"

"Mathematics," answered the officer.

"Indeed so. Now here is a riddle for you: Tell me the square root of 4,879,625?"

Before Talaban could even think of a method to supply the answer the half-wit spoke. He did not look up or change his expression. "Two thousand two hundred and eight point nine eight seven three two four five four five."

Anu clapped his hands. "And the square root of that, Togen?"

Again the half-wit spoke instantly. "Forty-point six nine nine eight."

"How does he do that?" asked Talaban.

"I have no idea. But he has proved immensely useful to me these last six years. So, is he an idiot or a genius, Talaban?"

"Apparently he is both. So let us put the question of his sanity aside and examine yours."

"As you will."

"You are preaching heresy, Questor. How do you justify your actions?"

"My actions require no justification. But let us return to mathematics. I have studied the science for almost eight hundred years. Through it I have helped the Avatar to achieve greatness through architecture, travel and commerce."

"No one is disputing that, Questor. I have used your star maps myself on my journeys. But that is not the point at issue."

"It is the very point. We have a thousand years of history behind us, Talaban. But what is before us? Catastrophe awaits. Based upon my studies I have concluded that the earth itself passes through a series of regular cataclysms. During such times the earth rolls, falls if you like. I have studied ancient records. Such an event almost certainly took place about eleven thousand years ago. It is my belief it will happen again some time in the next two years. With the help of Togen I shall narrow down that estimate. But we must prepare for the end of all we know—indeed of much that we love. Within a few years this little garden will be buried beneath a mountain of ice. If we do not make preparations then the civilization we have brought to this planet will pass from memory."

"I have heard of your predictions, sir. Such is your reputation that even Vagar mystics are now predicting the end of all things."

Anu shook his head. "Now it is you who are missing the point. Those same mystics were prophesying the cataclysm long before I began my calculations. Indeed, it was my fascination with them that led me to apply my knowledge and expertise to the question."

"But they go against prevailing wisdom, sir—and worse—against the views of the Avatar Prime himself. Can you not accept that you might be wrong?"

"I am not wrong, Talaban," he answered, sadly. "I would give all that I possess—my life itself—if it could be so. And I know what must happen. The sun will rise in the west, the seas will tip from their bowls, and not one stone will be left upon another." The Questor sighed, then gave a sad smile. "The Avatar Prime will either have me killed or declare me outcast. If it is the latter I will be stripped of my grants, my annuities, and my position. Even so I will continue to preach what you call heresy. I will take as many of our people as will travel with me and head north—far north. We have outlying settlements, and with the help of the Source, we shall survive the catastrophe. Whether there will be enough of us to rebuild our civilization I do not know."

Talaban had reported the conversation to the Council. Some called for Anu's death, but Talaban spoke against such a course. The argument was fierce and raged on for several hours. Questor Ro had been vehement in his calls for death, and such was the recommendation to the Avatar Prime. Happily he overruled the judgment and instead declared Anu stateless. His property was confiscated and he could no longer walk the streets of Parapolis. The former Questor had removed himself to the temple grounds, where he survived on gifts of food and clothing from the few friends who stuck by him. Here he continued to preach the coming catastrophe.

Within weeks Anu's dark prophecies began to be spouted among the populace. But they were derided by the Council.

True to his word Anu did refine his calculations, predicting the fall on the eighth or ninth day of summer in the eighteen hundred and third year of the Avatar Empire.

Two years and four months later, on the ninth day of summer, while taking *Serpent Seven* on a mapping expedition to the far north-west, Talaban had viewed the fall of the world. The ship was sheltering in a wide bay and his scouts were returning from a trip ashore. It was close to sunset. Talaban was standing on the high upper deck as the silver longboat cut through the waves towards the *Serpent*. It had been a good day, bright and fresh and cold. Melting ice floes still clung to the shores of the bay and a cool breeze whispered across the decks. The longboat secured, his men on board, Talaban turned toward his cabin door. The sunlight was almost gone, the clouds shining red and gold above the western mountains. Talaban paused to watch the last of the sunset. Suddenly the winds rose, a storm arriving from nowhere. Distant trees were bent by its force, and the clouds began scudding across the sky. The ship lurched. Talaban was thrown against the cabin door. A bright light washed over the *Serpent*. Talaban turned—and saw the sun rising again. He stood, lost in the wonder of the moment. From all over the ship came the sound of shouting, as men called for their friends to come and see the phenomenon. Then Talaban remembered the words of Anu. *The sun will rise in the west, the seas will tip from their bowls, and not one stone will be left upon another.*

Shading his eyes he stared into the west. The area they were mapping was a narrow strip of land, some 20 miles wide. On the other side of the mountains lay the ocean. A huge dark mass, like bunching storm clouds, reared up over the mountains.

. . . the seas will tip from their bowls.

The mountains were almost two miles high. The tidal wave beyond them was half as high again. And it was roaring towards the bay.

For the first time in his life Talaban felt the onset of fear-induced panic. It rooted him to the spot, and he stared horrified at the immense wave darkening the sky. For a dozen heartbeats he stood still. Death was coming, and he felt powerless to oppose its immensity. On the deck below him a man screamed in fear, and fell to his knees, covering his head with his hands. The man's terror touched Talaban like a cool wind. Forcing down his own panic he sprinted for the control deck and entered the inner sanctum. Swiftly he placed the power crystals into the black panels and spun the wheel. The black ship swung and sped out to sea. Her power chest fully charged, *Serpent Seven* was almost a mile from shore when Talaban swung her again, pointing her toward the towering wall of water bearing down upon her. At the last moment he turned her again, making an oblique angle. The colossal wave struck the ship, lifting the *Serpent* higher and higher, like a spear towards the sky, until it seemed the ship would be hurled through the clouds. Ferocious winds tore at the vessel, and several men who had remained on deck were sent hurtling to their deaths.

Still the ship climbed, Talaban urging every last vestige of power from the chest which lay at the heart of the *Serpent*. The ship slowed and began to topple. Talaban clung to the control panel and glanced through the port window. It was a dizzying sight. Miles below him he could see islands about to be swamped. If the ship capsized it would fall back down the wave and be buried beneath the roaring ocean mountain. Twisting the wheel once more he struggled to straighten the *Serpent*.

A crystal on the panel cracked. Another shattered.

And then the ship righted itself, and was sailing serenely behind the great wave.

The world he knew was gone—and he had survived.

As Touchstone entered the cabin Talaban opened his eyes. The tribesman gave a half-hearted salute then slumped down into a second padded chair alongside the desk. He was a short stocky man, round-shouldered and thick-necked. His greasy black hair hung in two braids, and, despite his two years as Talaban's scout, he refused to apply for Vagar citizenship and still wore his black tribal vest decorated with fingers of bone. He glanced up at Talaban, his green eyes shining with mischievous humor. "Them's running around like snow rabbits," he said, "digging into the ice. You think they find what they look for this time?"

Talaban shrugged. "They will or they won't."

"Buy a big house, farm maybe, with all that gold," said Touchstone. "Big waste."

Talaban found it hard to disagree. Driving gold rods into the ice was an expensive exercise, and so far it had achieved little. "These nomads," he said. "Will they fight us?"

Now it was Touchstone's turn to shrug. "Who knows? Them's tough boys. They'll fight if they see the gold. They don't believe in Avatars no more. They know your magic is dying. They know the ice killed the empire."

"Wounded it," corrected Talaban. "Nothing can kill the empire. We are too strong." The words were spoken by rote and even Talaban had long since ceased to believe them. "And you shouldn't verbalize such thoughts. I don't want to see you lying upon the crystals."

"Straight talk?" asked Touchstone. Talaban nodded. The tribesman leaned forward. "You Avatars are like elk surrounded by wolves. You still strong, but the wolves will tear you down. They know it. You know it."

"Enough straight talk, my friend. And now I have work to do. Come back in an hour, and bring the Questor with you."

Touchstone rose. "I bring food first," he said. "And more coal."

"My mother took less care of me than you do," said Talaban.

"Keep you strong," said Touchstone. "You die and promise not be kept."

"I always honor my promises," said Talaban. "And I have not forgotten." Touchstone looked at him for a moment, the green eyes locked to Talaban's dark gaze. Then he left the cabin.

Talaban took up his pen and opened the log, carefully detailing the day's work. As dusk deepened he lit a lantern. The beautifully painted walls of the cabin had been soiled with carbon deposits from lantern flame and coal over the years. Idly he wondered whether the ship felt a sense of shame at the loss of her power and prestige. You are a romantic, he told himself.

With the log entry completed Talaban stripped off his

clothes and moved through into the small sanctum beside his bedroom. He removed the three crystals from the velvet bag hanging by the window and placed them on the rug. Then he knelt facing the window and opened his arms wide. Taking a deep breath he drew on the power within. With his eyes closed he reached for the first crystal. It was pale and clear, like glittering ice. Lifting it to his forehead he slowly chanted the Prayer of One. His trance deepened and he felt his body relaxing. He became aware of knots of tension in his shoulders and neck. Gently he eased them. Completely relaxed now he laid the crystal down and reached for the second. This was a blue gem the size of his thumbnail. He held it to his chest, over his heart. The power of the blue seeped through his skin, entering the heart, invigorating the blood and flowing through his arteries and veins, filling them with strength. Lastly he took the green crystal, the largest of the three. This one he held against his belly as he chanted the Prayer of the Avatar Prime. This time the power flowed with more urgency, revitalizing his organs, healing and renewing them. The shock to his system was great, and pain flared from his kidneys and liver. But it passed and Talaban rose and placed the crystals once more into the black velvet bag.

The green was coming to the end of its energy, he knew. How long had it been since he renewed it? And what was stopping him? Pushing the thoughts aside he lit a second lantern and carried it to the full-length mirror in his bedroom. Leaning in close he examined himself. The skin of his face was tight and glowed with health. His body was lean, the lines of muscle sharp and clear in the lantern light. Only the eyes were old, he thought, dark and somber, brooding. Gazing into his own eyes discomfited him and he turned away from the mirror.

From the closet he took fresh leggings of black wool

and a shirt of silver satin. Then he pulled on a dry pair of boots and returned to his desk. Touchstone had left a plate of salted meat and some fresh bread. He had also replenished the brazier, which was glowing red. Talaban opened the rear door of the cabin and stepped out onto the balcony beyond. Cold air whispered against him, but this time it was pleasant, following the heat from the cabin. The Vagar team had left the glacier, but he could still see the silver pyramids glistening in the moonlight. And below the ice the energy of the golden rods silently sought the Great Line.

An elk surrounded by wolves. Touchstone's words drifted back to him.

The analogy was not quite correct. More like a dragon surrounded by lions. They feared his terrible fire and held back. He feared their fangs and their claws . . .

. . . and hoped they would not learn his fire was dying.

Chapter Two

Questor Ro was a traditionalist. His head was shaved, his forked beard dyed blue, and every day he practiced the Six Rituals of the Avatars for precisely two hours. His clothes were of dark blue, a shirt of expensive satin edged with silver thread, leggings of finest wool, and boots of blue-stained lizard skin. Around his waist he wore the silver-edged belt of First Questor, and he still carried the ceremonial scepter, despite the fact that its energy had been spent some twenty years before. Though oceans had washed away the Avatar Empire and ice had entombed its power sources, Questor Ro believed in maintaining standards. It was one of the many reasons he disliked Talaban.

He considered the others as he waited outside the captain's cabin with the savage Touchstone.

"Him's busy," said Touchstone. "Call us soon."

Questor Ro did not reply. In the glory days no savage would have dared address an Avatar directly. They would have approached on their knees, then touched their heads to the ground. Every address would begin with the words *Lord hear your servant*. In this way discipline was maintained, and lower orders understood their place in the world. Indeed, in the opinion of Questor Ro, they were far happier for it. Clearly defined borders of behavior were the cornerstone of any civilization. Talaban seemed to understand none of this, and allowed savages to address him as an equal. He had even journeyed among the barbarians, living in their squalid tents. Questor Ro shuddered inwardly. There was almost no doubt in his mind that Talaban had Vagar blood. Added to which he was young, barely two centuries old. He had not lived long enough to understand fully the need for maintaining fear among the sub-races.

But then his mother had also been well known for her fey behavior, refusing to have a child until her eightieth year, when she—despite her crystal-inspired youth—was close to becoming barren. It had been the cause of many rumors, and had brought considerable humiliation upon her 300-year-old husband. Most Avatar females lost the ability to carry children past the age of seventy, and few males past the age of two hundred could sire them. No, the consensus was that she had fallen pregnant during her travels. Few Avatar women made long journeys of any kind, and then only from necessity. She, on the other hand, had apparently travelled for pleasure, visiting the outer cities of the empire. Questor Ro could readily imagine what pleasures she had found among the vulgar races who peopled the cities. Soon after she returned she announced her pregnancy.

Her son's current behavior only served to fuel Ro's suspicions. Talaban was too close to the Vagars who served him. He was even popular, which was a situation no Avatar should achieve. Vagars respected discipline, they reacted best to fear. Popularity, as far as Questor Ro was concerned, merely showed weakness in areas of leadership. It surprised Ro that the General could not understand these obvious flaws in Talaban's nature. Added to this there was the fact that Talaban had never married. And since he was fast approaching the age when his seed would no longer be strong it was an added insult to the Avatar race. Every citizen should sire Avatar children. What future for the Avatars without them?

"Him's ready now," said Touchstone. Questor Ro had heard nothing, but the savage opened the door. He stood back as Questor Ro entered—which was at least something!

Ro stepped inside. Talaban was sitting at his desk, but he rose as the Questor entered. He moved round the desk to greet his guest. Like most of the warrior caste Talaban's movements were graceful, always in balance. The soldier towered over the short stocky mage. The two men opened hands in the Avatar greeting. Questor Ro bowed, halting the movement a few inches short of the required angle. Not enough to be insulting, but sufficient to show Talaban he was displeased. If the warrior noticed the discourtesy he did not show it, but returned the bow smoothly, offering the perfect angle.

"How is your work progressing?" asked Talaban. Questor Ro cast a glance at Touchstone, who had sat down on the floor by the door.

"It is not seemly to discuss such matters before inferiors," said Questor Ro. His slender hand tugged at the twin forks of his blue beard, signalling his rising irritation.

Talaban said nothing, but Touchstone rose and silently left the room. "Be seated, Questor," said Talaban, returning to his chair.

Ro glanced at a guttering lantern, then transferred his gaze to the cold crystal globes set into the wall. "I once journeyed to the western lands in one of these vessels," he said, sadly. "They were impressive then. No storm could touch them."

"Times change, Questor. Now how is your work progressing?"

"I expect better results by tomorrow," said Ro. "Our probes need adjustments—minor adjustments," he added swiftly, seeing the concern on Talaban's face. "We are not entirely aligned."

"Nomads will be in this area tomorrow," said Talaban. "We do not have much time."

"Surely that is why we brought soldiers," said Ro.

"Indeed it is, Questor. We have no *Avatar* soldiers. If the nomads come in strength we will be outnumbered ten to one. My Vagars are armed with conventional weapons only. They will not withstand a heavy assault."

"Of course they won't," snapped Ro. "I said at the start that we needed Avatars. On an expedition as important as this it is hard to credit that it could have been refused. Surely the empire would not have been weakened by allowing us true men and zhi-bows?"

"This was not intended to be a war party, Questor. The General was specific about that. Any complaints you have should be taken up with him upon our return. However, since we are speaking frankly, you should be aware there are fewer than fifty zhi-bows still in operation."

"Fifty? That is a disgrace," stormed Ro. "Why only last year the General assured the Assembly there were over three hundred such weapons."

Talaban leaned back in his chair. "Questor Ro, I am aware of your great skills, and I know you spend much of your time in research. But surely the eastern revolt did not entirely escape your attention. Six thousand tribesmen? The zhi-bows swung the battle, but most were exhausted. We did not have the power to feed them. Hence this expedition."

Questor Ro absorbed the information. "It did not escape my attention, as you put it, captain. Few events escape my attention. However it seems a criminal waste of resources to allow our main defensive weapon to be exhausted by one petty revolt."

"With respect, you are not a soldier, sir. Without the bows we would have been overrun in the east. That would have encouraged the other tribes to join in the revolt. The cities would have fallen." Questor Ro was about to argue, but Talaban raised his hand. "Enough of this, sir, for it is now history. Our task is to replenish the energies of the chests. Can it be done?"

"I need two days, captain. I believe Communion is near."

Talaban fell silent. "Do not tell me what you believe," he said, at last. "Tell me what you *know*."

The man is insufferable, thought Ro. He took a deep breath, calming himself. "Some of the rods have picked up faint emanations. I believe . . . I know . . . that with adjustment I can hone them to the pyramid. Once I have done so we will draw on the power and feed the chests."

Talaban's dark eyes fixed to Ro's gaze. "Be sure, sir, for I will have to risk the lives of my men and the security of this vessel. Be very sure."

"Only these facts in life are sure, captain: the sun rises and sets and lesser beings die. Give me two days and we will power the six chests."

Talaban looked long and hard at the smaller man. He did not like him, and had no reason to trust him. And yet . . . The power of one full chest would recharge every zhi-bow in the city and keep them charged for up to five years. The dragon would breathe fire again.

"You will have your two days," he said. "But get your men back to the ice tonight. They can work under lanterns."

Talaban stood on the balcony deck behind his cabin and watched the Vagar team scurrying about on the ice.

The bald blue-bearded figure of Questor Ro moved among them. "Make me smile, him," said Touchstone. Talaban considered the comment.

"He's a man from a lost time," he said, at last. "I both admire and pity him."

"He faces the wrong way," said Touchstone. Talaban smiled.

"For him the past is golden, the future barren. What else can he do but strive to recreate what is gone?"

"He could live. Now. Read the stars. Sire small sons."

"How old are you, Touchstone?"

"I took breath when the red wolf ate the moon. Twenty-four summers back."

"Questor Ro was more than four hundred summers old by then. And he had lived all those centuries in Parapolis, the greatest city ever built. He was part of an empire three thousand years old. Ships like these sailed the oceans without need of wind. No grotesque masts, no bulging sacks of filthy coal. And then, one day, the sun rose in the west, and the seas rushed up to greet it. Parapolis was engulfed, the people swept away. Those that survived, like Questor Ro and myself, journeyed back to Parapolis. But the stars had changed, the earth had tilted, and it was bitter cold. All the trees had died—frozen in a single night. In one day the invincible cities of the Avatar had perished. And every day since the land is buried further beneath the ice. One mathematician calculated that 90,000 tons of fresh ice a day gathers over the old empire."

"You want big truth?" asked Touchstone. "Avatar anger Great God. He struck you down."

Talaban shrugged. "I do not believe in gods. Unless I am one, of course," he added with a smile. "But I was talking of Questor Ro. He is older than I. For three hundred and fifty years he lived among great wonders.

No disease. No death. That is why he cannot let them go. Perhaps it is why none of us can let them go."

"No death, no life," said Touchstone. "We need it." Talaban knew what he meant. Man was part of the seasons, the youth of spring, the strength of summer, the aging wisdom of autumn, and the cold departure of winter. Hearts beating to the rhythm of nature.

"Easy to say when you are mortal," said Talaban.

"You have blue hair like him, once?" asked Touchstone.

"Yes. It separates us from ordinary mortals."

"You are not gods," said Touchstone. "Gods need no golden rods. And why you sire no sons?"

Talaban said nothing. Stepping forward he leaned on the rail. Several more lanterns had been lit on the ice.

"What you do about the nomads?"

"I will talk to them," said Talaban.

"Pah, talk! Them's fierce men. They fight. They kill. No time for talk, I think."

"I will speak in a language they understand."

Touchstone bared his teeth in a wide grin. Talaban returned to the cabin. Touchstone followed him, pulling closed the door. "I'll be with you when you talk," he said. "But now I sleep."

Alone once more Talaban moved to a long wooden chest by the wall. Inside, wrapped in black velvet, was an ornate weapon, golden in color, and shaped like a hunting bow. Gems of many colors adorned the grip. Talaban hefted the weapon and touched his thumb to a red gem just above the grip. Thin threads of light flickered, forming what appeared to be the strings of a harp. Talaban tuned his mind to the zhi-bow. The weapon was almost empty. No more than one bolt remained. He touched a white gem above the red and the strings of light disappeared. Setting the weapon down he considered the problem. He could take the bow to the *Ser-*

pent's chest and recharge it, but there was little power left there, and if he drained it none of them would survive the voyage back to the city. The Avatar *Serpents* were never seaworthy vessels in their own right. Only the power of the chests kept them afloat.

Dismissing the idea, Talaban removed his clothes and moved to the bedroom. Lying on his bed he could see the stars flickering through the curved window.

He had been far to the north-west when the Great Bear's paw had lashed the ocean, sending a tidal wave three miles high across the continent of the Avatars. But even 2,000 miles away, on the outer edges of the empire, the earthquakes had toppled buildings, and a terrible hurricane had swept across the land, ripping away homes, killing hundreds of thousands.

Many had thought it to be the end of the world. For much of the earth's population it was exactly that.

The five settlements on the Luan River had escaped with only minor damage, and loss of life that ran into hundreds. Talaban had sailed the *Serpent* across to the west, seeking sign of other colonies. But he found nothing. With the *Serpent* running short of energy he had returned to the twin cities of Pagaru and Egaru.

A mere 500 Avatars had survived the fall of the world—and only this many because the former Questor Anu had brought 200 with him from Parapolis.

Thinking of Anu brought back memories of the Vagar mystic. Talaban drifted to sleep with the ragged man's words echoing in his mind.

He will devour all the works of Man. Then he will sleep for 10,000 years, and the breath of his sleep will be death.

Touchstone sat on the floor of his cabin, lifted a small brown pouch from around his neck, and held it cupped in both hands. This was his medicine bag, and contained great magic. Through the soft hide of the pouch he could feel the curved fang of the first lion he had killed. It was entwined with a lock of Suryet's dark hair. Beauty and savagery, forever together. There was a tiny sea shell, and a small amount of earth from the belly of the great mountain. The shell allowed him to commune with the spirits of the sea, the earth brought him the scent of home. Lastly there was the feather flight from his first arrow. This reminded him that he was a hunter and a provider for his tribe. All that Touchstone loved was epitomized by the contents of his medicine pouch. His land, and the sea that washed its shore, his woman, his tribe, and his mother, the earth.

Softly he sang the Song of Far-away, knowing the music of his spirit would touch the dirt within his pouch and would thus reach the mountains of his youth. There the trees would pick up the song, and whisper it through their leaves until it reached the tents of his people.

Then Suryet would hear it sighing on the wind. She would look up, her deep, dark eyes scanning the blue, seeking sign of him. And she would know he was alive and that one day he would find her again.

Eyes closed he sang the song with feeling, repeating it twice more, his mind reaching out to Suryet, hoping for a glimpse of her.

Instead he saw a pillar of fire, surging up through snow and ice. Then it was gone. The vision troubled him, for he could not decipher its message. Ice and fire. It meant little to the Anajo tribesman.

Looping his medicine bag over his neck he tucked it into his shirt, and stretched out upon the rug. Touchstone did not like beds. Soft pillows made his neck ache.

He lay upon the floor, arms folded across his chest, and pictured again the wild hills and the hunts, saw once more the glorious day of his marriage, and recalled with ever-increasing fondness the first night with Suryet.

Two months later the Blue-hairs had landed in the Sacred Cove. Touchstone had been among the war band who fought them. They would have won, but for a black-haired warrior carrying two swords. His speed was terrifying, and he had stood his ground as others fled. As his comrades died around him Touchstone had hurled himself upon the warrior, seeking to bury his axe in the man's skull. Someone had struck him upon the head, and he awoke to find himself locked in an iron cage deep in the bowels of this ship.

The journey had been long, and Touchstone had been taken to a city of stone where, day after day, Blue-hairs had come to him, struggling to teach him their language. Months had passed. And he had learned. He had learned their language, and much more. He had learned to hate them.

They asked him many questions about his people, and whether gods walked among them. He answered them with lies and half-truths, until the bright day when he had been allowed to walk in the gardens. He had surprised them then, sprinting away and leaping to grab the low branch of a tall tree. Swinging up he had scaled the trunk and leapt the wall. Landing heavily, he twisted his ankle. Yet still he had escaped into the twisting alleyways around the castle.

Weaponless and injured he had sought a path to the sea, intending to steal a boat. He made it to the dock, and stood staring at the ships moored there. There were no small boats, no canoes. His heart sank.

A figure moved out of the shadows and he found himself facing the same warrior who had killed his friends. Touchstone tensed, ready to attack.

"I understand you have learned much," said the man.

"I make you dead," said Touchstone.

"Perhaps. But not without a weapon, and certainly not with an injured leg. Sit down on the wharf and I shall heal it for you."

There was nowhere to run, and with his swollen ankle Touchstone could not have escaped the man. He did as he was bid and sat down. The warrior knelt over him, then took a green crystal from his pouch, holding it to the injured limb. Instantly the pain began to subside. After several minutes the warrior rose. "Try standing on it," he said. Warily Touchstone did so. All pain had vanished. "Come, let us eat and talk," said the warrior, turning away from the tribesman and walking towards a dockside inn.

Touchstone had followed him. He still did not know why.

Inside the inn the warrior, Talaban, had ordered a meal of good red meat. Touchstone ate it.

"One day," said Talaban, "I shall return to the west. If you desire it I shall take you with me."

"Wife is there," said Touchstone. "Must return."

"There is a war coming, and no ships are making that journey now. But when they do you shall travel with them. This I promise."

"How long?"

"A year. Perhaps two."

"I steal small boat. Go myself."

"With good winds it will take you three months."

"It is so far?" Touchstone was appalled.

"Indeed it is. Added to which the western lands are immense. If a ship took you to the northern coast you could walk south for a year and still not reach your lands. That is if the ice did not kill you. Much of the world is covered by ice now."

"I think I steal boat," said Touchstone.

"May the Great God watch over you," said Talaban. Rising from the table he paid for the meal and walked away.

Touchstone had found a small boat. There was no paddle, but he soon mastered the long oars and began to row himself out to sea. Better to die attempting to reach Suryet than to live as a prisoner of the Blue-hairs.

Eighteen days later, dehydrated and delirious, he had been hauled aboard a black ship. When he awoke the tall warrior was sitting at his bedside.

"A valiant attempt, my friend," he said. "Now I think you had best accept my offer."

Touchstone had done so. But it had now been two years since his capture. Two long, lonely years.

"I will come home, Suryet," he whispered. "Wait for me."

But as he was falling asleep he saw again the vision of the pillar of fire. Unlike most of his visions this was impossible to read, for surely ice and fire could not exist in the same place. Pushing it from his mind, the tribesman slept.

Chapter Three

*And while the Frost Giant slept they climbed his
matted fur, ever higher towards the great jaws resting upon a mountain top. Each strand of fur was
thicker than a man's arm, and within the fur dwelt
demons, spirits of evil men, condemned to live for
ever upon the back of the Beast. Tail-avar carried
his bow of lightning, Touch the Moon his axe of
silver, but Storro had the greatest weapon of all.
He alone could find the magic fang and draw its
power.*

From the *Morning Song of the Anajo*

Questor Ro returned to the *Serpent* just before dawn.
He was exhausted, though not entirely discouraged. Six
times they had linked to the emanations, only for the
power to drift away after a few heartbeats. It was not
failure that exasperated him. Rather it was the tantaliz-
ing closeness to success. His cabin, as befitted a
Questor, was large and fitted with wide windows, and a
second door which led to a small, but private roofed
deck on the port side of the ship. When the *Serpent* had
been fully powered the cabin would have been considered luxurious, with its wide couches, deep chairs and
thick carpets. Now, however, the tall windows allowed

heat from the brazier to escape and the cabin was always cold. Questor Ro believed Talaban had this in mind when he had offered him these quarters back in the summer warmth of the port city of Egaru, the second city. Questor Ro would have been infinitely warmer in the smaller cabin, below decks, occupied by his Vagar assistant, Onquer:

Suppressing his irritation he added coal to the brazier. Then he practiced the first of the Six Rituals, seeking to ease away the bone-numbing weariness that exhaustion and intense cold had brought to his system. Sitting cross-legged upon the floor, head bowed, index fingers held to his temples, the little man chanted the Prayer of One. Concentration was difficult, and random thoughts and fears intruded on the prayer. Even so, the ritual brought him inner warmth. This was pleasant, but did nothing to alleviate the weariness. It hung on him with the weight of failure.

How his enemies would love to see him return in shame. Caprishan would, of course, feign sympathy, while hiding his gap-toothed smile behind his fat hand. Niclin would be more openly hostile. He would be the one to point out the incredible waste of resources, highlighting the fact that he had predicted such an outcome, and had only sponsored it because of the once-infallible reputation of Questor Ro. The others would fall in behind them and Ro's power on the Council would diminish rapidly.

It will not happen, he told himself. I will not allow it. The seeds of doubt sprouted even as he made this promise. He had been right to believe that his newly designed pyramids could link to the Great Line. They had done so. And with ease. But they could not hold to it.

Think, he ordered himself. The line could not be moving. The emanations were radiating from the White Pyramid some sixty miles away, beneath a mountain of

ice. It was a solid object, existing in one place. Therefore the lines of power should be straight and constant,
and, once found, form Communion. Yet it was as if the
source of power was constantly shifting and moving
like a frightened deer.

You are missing something, he told himself.

Questor Ro pushed himself to his feet. From a small
casket on his desk he took his crystals of white, blue
and green, and a glove of white lace. Lifting the glove to
his lips he kissed it, and thus began the second of the
Six Rituals. He would rather have saved the energy of
the crystals, but weariness was fogging his mind. Slowly
he drew on their power, feeling the birth of new
strength.

Then, holding the glove to his face he relaxed into a
trance, his mind flowing back through the valleys of
time. He pictured the park, and the grove of flowering
trees by the fountain pond. He saw himself sitting there,
Tanya beside him, the children playing nearby. The sun
was high and bright, the park bathed in the gentle
warmth of early autumn. He always summoned the
same image. It occurred to him then that there are times
when true beauty whispers past the conscious mind, invisible as a breeze. The day in the park had been pleasant. No more than that. He had smiled as his three
children played. He had kissed Tanya's hand. But his
mind had been working on a mathematical problem,
and he was anxious to return to his office and continue
with it. If only there had been a moment of prescience.
If only he could have guessed that for seventy years—
lonely, isolated years—he would summon that ancient
image like a man bringing forth his greatest treasure.

He had told Tanya of the mathematical problem.
"You will solve it," she said with utter certainty. That
certainty had invigorated him. It was one of the reasons
he loved her so dearly.

Now he faced an even greater problem, and she was no longer here to feed him with her faith.

When at last he opened his tear-filled eyes he was calmer.

Wiping away the tears he returned to the problem. The White Pyramid, buried below the ice, could not be moving. This was a certain fact, beyond argument. What then could explain the phenomenon? Moving to the window he rubbed the frost from the glass then stared out over the white mountains. His men were returning now, and a second team waited, shivering on the decks above. Soon he would have to join them. Questor Ro was not a fool. He sensed they could spend endless days seeking Communion. And he had promised Talaban results.

He tugged at his forked beard. The answer was there—if only he could find it.

Wrapping his cloak around him he left the cabin, climbed the spiral stairs and emerged onto the central deck. His second twelve-man team were huddled together, watching the return of the silver longboat. As he stood with them there came a sound like distant thunder and a huge section of ice toppled from a nearby glacier, striking the calm water of the bay and sending a large wave that lifted the longboat.

In that moment Questor Ro had his answer. Ordering the men to await his instruction he stood silently until the longboat was secured and his exhausted team were aboard, then summoned his assistant Onquer to his cabin. The Vagar was hollow-eyed, his lips blue. Questor Ro allowed the man to stand for a while before the small brazier of hot coals.

"It is not the power source that is moving," said Questor Ro. "It is the ice covering the land."

Onquer rubbed his thin hands together before the heat. "Ice moving, lord?" he said dumbly.

"Pour yourself a drink," ordered Questor Ro. With trembling hands Onquer lifted a blue glass decanter and poured spirit into a crystal goblet. Lifting it to his lips he sipped the fiery liquid. He shivered with pleasure.

"Yes, it is the ice," said Questor Ro. "It is brittle, and it moves. The pyramid is sixty miles away. Between there and here there are probably thousands of small shifts in the ice. We are like this ship, bobbing upon the bay. Constantly moving while staying in the same place. You understand?"

Onquer drained the drink. "Yes, I see, lord. But what can we do?"

"We need one mobile receiver linked to the others. Thus we can adjust our movement to match the shifts in the ice."

"This will take time, lord. More time than we have allowed."

"No, it will not. I will go below to the store rooms and begin to assemble the equipment. You return to the ice with the fresh team, and re-site the receivers. Place them closer together, each no more than ten units apart. Hold to the emanations as best you can. This time do not seek Communion, merely try to read the ebb and flow. How much movement is there, and between which points. You *follow*?"

"Yes, lord."

"Then do not delay," said Questor Ro, waving his hand towards the door. The exhausted Vagar bowed, then left the room. Questor Ro had all but forgotten him even before the door closed.

Karesh Var had been asked many times what made him a great hunter. Young men were fascinated by his success in killing tuskers. He answered none of their questions. Did they not have eyes to see his skills?

Could they not look at the scars he bore—the wicked cut upon his cheekbone, the ragged tear that had lost him half an ear—and realize that, though his youthful recklessness had placed him in many perils, he had survived to learn from his mistakes? The answer was, apparently, no. They watched him, tried to emulate him, and failed. And men, being what they are, called him lucky. They claimed he was blessed by the gods, and that he carried a secret talisman which drew the tuskers to him. Karesh found it all faintly amusing.

Idly he rubbed at the long vivid scars on his right cheek. A kral's talons had almost ripped his face away, but he had killed the man-beast with a dagger thrust to its heart. That incident alone had taught him to be wary and ever-patient in the hunt. Death lay waiting everywhere in this icy land. As to his skill with the tuskers, that was born from love, and the endless magic that sprang from love. Though he would never explain that to his followers. Let them learn themselves, he thought. Why would a man give away the secrets that led him to such glory among his people?

Anyway, they would have laughed at the notion.

Karesh Var loved the tuskers, and saw in them all that was good upon the cold earth. They were loyal creatures, fiercely protective of one another. They raised their young with endless patience, and they moved across the land with immense dignity, coupled with a lordly arrogance.

Leaving his twenty men seated around two campfires Karesh Var saddled his pony and rode out along the ridge. From here he could look down on the plain and observe the death ritual. His men were not interested in such spectacles. They had seen them before, the herd forming a protective circle around the dying mammoth, the great bulls pushing their tusks beneath the victim, trying to raise her to her feet. His men found it boring to sit out in the cold until the cow died. Not so Karesh Var.

Two days ago they had hit the herd, three riders moving in fast to taunt the fighting bulls, pulling them away from the rear. Then ten men on fast ponies had galloped in on the flanks, shooting their arrows into the victim chosen by Karesh Var. When they wheeled away Karesh Var and four others rode in, plunging their spears into the wounded animal.

Then they withdrew to wait. The herd moved on, two bulls flanking the stricken victim, seeking to protect her from further harm. But she was dying now, and all that was required of the hunters was patience.

As Karesh Var sat upon his pony and watched, the cow pitched to her side, her long trunk rising and falling, seeking perhaps to taste the air for one last time. Around her the bulls had ceased in their efforts to raise her body. They fell back, and the whole herd lifted their trunks and trumpeted to the skies. Perhaps it was a farewell song. Karesh Var did not know, but it touched him. Alongside her now two of the bulls gouged the earth with their tusks. Then the herd moved around the body in a slow circle before heading away towards the east.

Karesh Var watched them go, then rode his pony down the slope, dismounting alongside the massive corpse. Moving to the great head he placed his palm on her brow. "You died so that my people may live," he said. "I thank you for the gift of life, and I pray that your soul walks in the garden of all things."

His riders arrived within the hour. Two of them set about sawing away the tusks, which would later be transformed into buttons, bracelets, buckles and ornaments, many to be sold to the people of the eastern cities. The meat would be cut and salt-dried, the bones reduced to powder for medicinal remedies and animal feed. The skin would be dried and used in the making of boots, jerkins and other clothing. This one mammoth represented great wealth to the Zheng tribe.

The legendary Karesh Var had succeeded once more, and his people would survive the long winter in relative comfort.

One of his men brought him a bloody strip of meat. Karesh Var threw it over his shoulder and mounted his pony, carrying the meat downwind, hurling it out on to the snow. Saber-tooths, wolves and krals would have picked up the scent of blood long before now, and were probably already tracking the kill. The meat would give them something to fight over until the wagons arrived.

By mid-afternoon the wagons were loaded and the long trek back to camp began. No krals had appeared, which pleased Karesh Var greatly, and he had left enough meat behind to satisfy the saber-tooths. All in all this had been a good day.

The riders and wagons slowly climbed the mountain road. The sun was bright, though not warm, and Karesh Var tied down the ear-flaps of his fur hat. These last two years, since he had turned thirty-five, he had felt the cold more, though he told no-one—except his wife. She had made him the hat from rabbit fur. Karesh Var smiled. Most of the tribesmen felt he was foolish to have only one wife. But she was worth any ten women he had known. He was looking forward to seeing her again, when one of his scouts came riding down the trail.

"The black boat has returned, Karesh," he said. "There are Blue-hairs upon the ice."

It was nearing noon when the first of the six silver pyramids began to glow. Questor Ro, cold and exhausted now after hours upon the ice, saw it begin. At first he rubbed his tired eyes, thinking the glow merely a dreamlike symptom of weariness coupled with desire. He stared hard at the four-foot-high triangular structure, its interlinked silver poles wrapped in gold wire. Was it just reflected brightness he was seeing? Then he sensed the excitement in the Vagars around him. They too could see it, a halo of white light radiating from the structure. All weariness vanished from Questor Ro.

Beside him a slim Vagar was holding the small wooden box from which golden wires trailed to the snow, spreading out to link with each of the six pyramids. "Stand very still," Questor Ro told him. Moving alongside the man he carefully lifted the lid, holding it at an angle which prevented the Vagar from seeing inside. Two of the white crystals set into the mica were glowing brightly. The third was flickering with a soft gentle light. Questor Ro set the lid back in its place. A second pyramid began to glow, then a third.

The twelve Vagars stood in stunned silence as, one by one, each of the six pyramids began to radiate white light.

"Do not move," Questor Ro reminded the box-holder.

"Yes, lord."

As if obeying his own instruction Ro also stood still, excitement causing him to tremble. With an effort he swung away and summoned four of the Vagars to follow him to the waterside, where several boxes and a linen-covered chest were lying on the snow. From one box the Vagars took wooden overshoes which they slipped over their fur-lined boots. Then they took from their deep pockets long wooden thimbles, which they placed over their fingers and thumbs.

Carefully they unwrapped the white linen from around a rectangular chest, some four feet long and three feet wide. It was of black wood, heavily engraved with symbols the Vagars could not read. On each of the two longest sides three large golden rings were set into the wood.

"Be careful now," said Questor Ro. "Your lives depend upon it." Alongside the chest were two wooden poles, each eight feet long. With great care Questor Ro slid the poles through the golden rings. With this accomplished the four Vagars hefted the poles, lifting the chest clear of the snow. Questor Ro led them to a clearing at the center of the six glowing pyramids.

His heart was beating fast now. Ordering them to lay the chest on the ground, Questor Ro covered his fingertips with wooden thimbles and took up a length of golden wire. Taking a deep breath he approached the chest.

"Lord!" called out one of the Vagars. Ro was annoyed and swung towards the man.

"What?" he shouted.

"Your boots, lord. You are not protected."

Questor Ro glanced down. In his excitement he had forgotten to slip on the wooden overshoes. "Give me yours," he snapped at the man who had saved his life. The overshoes were far too large, and Ro was forced to slide his feet forward, rather than walk. He flashed a warning glare at the Vagars. No one smiled. Kneeling by the engraved chest Ro looped the golden wire over two bronze spheres on its front. The other ends he attached to the first of the pyramids. A low humming noise began to emanate from the chest.

Questor Ro raised his hands to the heavens. "We have Communion," he said.

"Praise be!" chorused the Vagars loyally. Ro knew they did not care. All they wanted was to be free of the ice, safe and warm in their cabins on the *Serpent*. It did not matter. This was what he had promised the Council. This is what he had fought for, risked humiliation for.

He had achieved Communion with the White Pyramid, buried now in an eternally frozen city. The line of power had been caught and held, drawn through the gold rods, swirling along the golden wires, and feeding the tiny diamonds that filled the silver poles of the pyramids. Here it was changed by the gems, filtered and re-energized to flow into the chest, the power stored in the mica, gold and crystal interior.

Removing the thimbles he dropped them into his pocket then pulled clear the white lace glove, which he lifted to his lips and kissed. Tears formed in his eyes, but he blinked them away. Such displays of emotion were not seemly in the company of Vagars. As if in cosmic punishment for his mistake, one of the pyramids flickered, the light fading. The humming from the chest was subsiding.

Fighting down his panic Questor Ro kicked off the overshoes and ran to the man holding the mobile receiver. "Move a little to the right," he said, trying to keep his voice calm. "Gently now! Seek the line!" The man edged to the right. Once more the pyramid glowed and the humming began. "Watch the pyramids closely," he told him. "If the light begins to fail try to find it again."

"Yes, lord. I am very cold, lord."

"We are all very cold," snapped Questor Ro, moving away. His assistant Onquer was lying on the ice. Questor Ro nudged him with his boot. "This is no time to be sleeping," he said. "On your feet!" Onquer did not move. Questor Ro knelt alongside him. Onquer's face was grey. "Stupid man," whispered Questor Ro. Summoning two Vagars he ordered them to carry Onquer to the silver longboat. "When you get him back to the ship remove his clothes and gently warm the body. Massage him with warm oils."

"Yes, lord," they said in unison. Both were glad to be leaving the ice.

For an hour the chest continued to hum, showing no sign of full recharge. Weariness had long since returned to Questor Ro, but he could not yet go back to the ship. The box-holder stumbled, then righted himself. For a moment only the lights flickered on the pyramids. Questor Ro trudged over to the man and relieved him of the box. "Go back to the ship," he said. "You are useless here."

"Thank you, lord," said the man.

Questor Ro stood with the box in his hands, feeling the gentle vibration of Communion. Some sixty miles away, buried beneath the ice, the Great Pyramid was even more closely linked to him now. And less than a mile from the pyramid was his home, and the icy, unmarked grave of his beloved wife Tanya and his children. Questor Ro sighed.

"If I could I would have died with you," he whispered.

Chapter Four

Karesh Var heeled his pony into a run and led his men out onto the plain. Far ahead he could see the outline of the black ship against the white ice and just make out the tiny insect figures upon the glacier itself. Why did they keep returning to the ice? What were they looking for? he wondered, as his pony steadily closed the distance between his riders and the coast.

Two years ago just such a ship had moored in the bay. Karesh Var and one hundred men had arrived as it raised its anchor and set sail towards the north. All the nomads found on the ice were holes, as if made by tent pegs. Nothing else. He and his men had dug around for a while. But there was nothing to find. It was perplexing.

As he neared the coast he slowed his pony, raising an arm for the twenty riders to follow his lead. Karesh Var's keen dark eyes scanned the ice. Only one Blue-hair could he see, a small figure with a forked blue beard. The others were ordinary men. Karesh Var was nervous. Legends told of the great weapons of the Blue-hair, bows that sent bolts of light into the enemy, opening great blackened holes in the chests of warriors, bursting asunder breastplates of bronze. They spoke of black swords that shimmered with lightning, swords that could cut through metal as a wire slides through cheese. Karesh Var had no wish to tackle a foe armed in such a manner. And yet, and here was the quandary, his young men were fighters. Indeed they loved to fight. They were, he had decided long since, men with little imagination.

"We would ride into Hell for you, Karesh," young Jiang had told him once. He had smiled and patted the boy's shoulder. The young were made for such futile gestures, for they believed in immortality. They were convinced—just as he was once convinced—that the power that flowed through their veins would flow forever. They gloried in their strength, and even mocked older men who could no longer ride as hard, or hunt as well as they. As if those men had *chosen* to grow old, or in some way had *allowed* age and infirmity to overtake them.

The young riders who followed Karesh Var wanted to attack the Blue-hairs, to destroy them and thus earn glory back in the village. Karesh Var would also like to destroy them, for had they not brought the world to calamity? Were they not the bringers of ice and fire? Even so he had no wish to lead his men into a battle that would end with the slaughter of his riders.

With these somber thoughts in mind he saw two men walking toward the riders. Neither were Blue-hairs. Karesh Var drew rein and waited for them. One was tall, his long dark hair tied back in a ponytail. He wore no armor, but a short sword was belted at his side and he carried in his left hand an ornate golden bow. Karesh Var narrowed his eyes. The man was carrying no quiver of arrows. He transferred his gaze to the second warrior. This one was shorter and stockier and held a small single-bladed axe in his right hand.

Beyond the walking men the single Blue-hair was still out on the ice. He was holding a small box from which dangled bright, shining wires. It seemed to Karesh Var that lanterns had been set upon the glacier, and they were shining brightly, and he could hear a distant hum, like a swarm of bees.

The taller of the two men had halted some twenty paces from the riders. The second man sat down upon a rock, and began to sharpen his axe with a whetstone.

The tall man drew his sword and lowered the point to touch the frosted dirt of the plain. Then, walking across the path of the riders, he steadily cut a narrow line in the earth. This done he sheathed his sword and took up the ornate bow of gold.

Karesh Var was an appreciative man. He had never envied his fellow hunters, even in the days when, as a young man, he could not match their skills. Instead he had watched them, learned from them. Now he appreciated the talents of the man before him. Faced with twenty fighters he had made no overt threat, and yet, with one simple action, had stated his intentions. He had drawn a line, created a border. The message was clear. Anyone who crossed it would face grim retribution. Karesh Var was a proud man, but not overly arrogant. He had nothing to prove to anyone. Some of his more reckless companions would have charged at the man, and he could sense the growing anger in the riders around him. Karesh Var sat his pony in silence, studying the two men. They seemed at ease, not at all nervous. Possible answers came to him. Firstly there might be warriors hidden close by who would rush out and attack if the nomads advanced. Karesh Var scanned the plain. Unless they had dug themselves holes in the tundra no such force could be seen. Secondly the men might be stupid, or unaware that the nomads hated the Blue-hair. They did not look stupid, and the line in the earth was a clever move. This left only one conclusion. They were at ease because they had no fear. They *knew* their weaponry could destroy the riders. Karesh Var smiled as a last alternative occurred to him. Perhaps they wanted the nomads to *believe* they were all-powerful. Perhaps it was all a bluff.

Karesh Var dismounted and walked to the line in the earth. Then he looked across at the tall man and opened his hands. The tall man's expression did not change, but he beckoned Karesh Var forward. The stocky warrior left his seat upon the rock and stood close by, axe in hand.

"Why do you come here?" asked Karesh Var.

"Because we choose to," said the tall man. His voice was deep. Karesh Var held to the man's dark gaze, and saw no give there. His eyes scanned the face. It was strong, the answering gaze direct and unafraid. The man was a fighter. Karesh Var could see that in every line.

"You are on my land," said Karesh Var, keeping his tone even, still trying to read the man opposite.

The man smiled. "Nomads do not own land. They move where they will, and settle where they choose. So it has always been. You take your tents and follow the tuskers. You own only what right of arms wins for you. Were I to kill you I would own your tent, your women, and your ponies."

Karesh Var was impressed. Not only by the man's knowledge, but by his calm. There had still been no threats. And the bow he held was not strung.

He decided to draw him out. "What was the purpose of the line in the earth?" he asked.

"Death is permanent," replied the warrior. "Unnecessary violence is abhorrent to me. Yesterday you made a kill, and the meat will feed your people. Yesterday was a victory over starvation and death. It would be wise to return to your tents to celebrate yesterday. For there can be no celebration found in today's possibilities."

"You think not? Perhaps I see it differently."

The man shook his head. "No, for you are a wise man. A fool would have led his men in a charge, and they would have died." He spoke in a voice loud enough to be heard by the riders.

"You believe you can kill me and all my men?" Now it was said, and Karesh Var found tension rising within him. His hand had remained close to his hunting knife, and he was poised for battle.

"Of course," said the man. His thumb touched a jewel on the grip of his bow. Instantly four strings of dancing light flickered into being. Karesh Var was impressed. He had heard of the terrible weapons of the Blue-hair, the bows that loosed lightning.

"An interesting weapon," observed Karesh Var, his hand now resting on the bone hilt of his knife.

"It is time for choices, nomad," said the man. "For I am growing cold." His voice had hardened.

"Indeed it is, stranger," said Karesh Var, dropping his voice and stepping in closer to the warrior. "However, you seem to be a man of some wisdom, so answer me this: if a war leader brings his men on a raid, and then leaves with nothing to show for it, how then can he remain a leader? It might be better for such a man to risk death in order to save face. Is this not so?"

"It is a sad truth," admitted the man. "You killed a mammoth yesterday. How long were its tusks?"

"Seven feet."

"My people also use ivory for ornaments. I will offer thirty silver pieces for the tusks. By my reckoning that is twice what you and your people would receive from trade merchants for your trinkets and brooches."

Karesh Var relaxed and gave a broad smile. Sharing out the silver would placate his men. "Agreed," he said, "on one condition."

"That being?"

"Though we have heard of them, neither myself nor

any of my men have seen weapons like the one you are carrying. Perhaps you would give us a demonstration."

The warrior smiled and Karesh Var knew he understood. His men would need some sign of the power they were facing, in order for the silver to fully placate them. The warrior took a step backward, spun to his right and lifted the bow. The fingers of his right hand stroked the first string. A bolt of white light flashed from the bow, striking a rock some thirty paces to the east. The rock exploded, sending a shower of dust and fragments into the air.

"Most impressive," said Karesh Var. "I will send two of my men back for the tusks."

Questor Ro saw the nomads arrive, and watched as Talaban and Touchstone strode out to greet them. Then he transferred his attention to the pyramids. He had more important matters to consider. Nomads came under Talaban's area of expertise, and Questor Ro wasted no energy considering them. Instead his mind returned to the problem of Communion. The second chest was almost full, the humming subsiding now. But it had taken almost seven hours. This was more than worrying, since the first chest had taken only three. Even allowing for the fact that some residual energy was left in the first chest—since it was the power source for the *Serpent*—such a time discrepancy was cause for alarm.

The White Pyramid had been buried below the ice for more than seventy years. Could its powers be fading already? That was a possibility rich with terrible implications, and Ro was not yet ready to consider such a calamity. Perhaps, he thought, the second chest, having been empty for so long, had developed a fault. He did not know. And this galled him.

He glanced back to see the silver longboat returning, carrying the third chest. It was also empty of power and could be handled without fear of harm. When the six Vagars carried it to the site he handed the box to the first then, placing the wooden thimbles over his fingers and thumbs, removed the gold wires from the second chest, applying them to the third. As before he carefully slid the poles through the golden rings and stood back as the Vagars lifted the second chest, carrying it to the longboat.

Questor Ro climbed into the silver boat and returned to the ship with the Vagars. Ropes were lowered and tied to each end of the poles. Then sailors began to hoist the chest to the center deck. Questor Ro scrambled up a rope ladder to stand alongside the sailors. "Careful now," he warned them. "Keep well back."

The chest cleared the deck rail and a black-clad sailor tugged on the pulley arm. The chest swung over the deck. One of the poles slipped and the chest lurched. Instinctively a sailor stepped forward and threw up his arms to stop the chest sliding clear. As his hands touched the black wood there came a tremendous flash of light and heat. Blue flames flickered over the man and fire exploded from within his body, bursts of flame erupting through his eye sockets. The sailors holding the ropes leapt back as the heat seared them. The chest fell to the deck, landing on one side. The burning man had made no sound, and his blackened body fell across the chest. The smell of burning flesh hung in the air, and the other sailors stood by, horrified. Questor Ro was furious. Taking a rope he looped it over the corpse, dragging it clear of the chest.

The Vagar team clambered aboard. They too stood in stunned silence, staring down at the body. Flames still flickered and his clothing was smouldering. "Move yourselves!" roared Questor Ro. The Vagars, their fingers once more protected by the wooden thimbles, righted the chest. Questor Ro replaced the poles and ordered the men to carry it to the rear of the ship. Here he examined the chest for any cracks or breaks. Finding none he watched as the Vagars placed it inside a larger chest lined with lead. This was then carried below to the store room.

Two blood-smeared tusks had been laid here, which brought a new flicker of annoyance to Questor Ro. This was also his workroom, and he was less than pleased to find them here. Most especially since they had been unceremoniously dumped upon his desk and blood had smeared upon several of his papers. "Remove them," he ordered two of the Vagars. "Put them in a corner somewhere. And clean the blood from them," he added.

"Yes, lord," said one of them, bowing deeply.

"And send for Onquer," he said. "We have work to do."

"Lord," said the man, bowing low, "I regret to tell you that Onquer died. He was dead before we reached the ship."

This was really too much. Questor Ro had spent eight years training the Vagar. Now he would have to find another assistant and waste valuable time initiating him in the rigors of research.

He said nothing more to the Vagars and made his way to his cabin.

Two chests were full, a third was in place. All in all, it had not been a bad day.

Chapter Five

The Frost Giant's mouth was open. Storro climbed between the white gates of its teeth, and found the magic fang. Casting a great spell he began to draw its power. The Beast stirred, but did not yet wake. It did not need to, for the terrible demons who dwelt upon it sensed the theft, and began to climb through its fur towards the thieves.

From the *Morning Song of the Anajo*

The coal oil lantern flickered, its light casting deep shadows upon the walls of the windowless Heart Room deep in the belly of the *Serpent*. Talaban watched the four Vagars carefully lower the chest into the carved recess at the center of the room. Once they had done so he dismissed them. As the door closed behind them Talaban moved to a panel beside the recess, which he slid open. Within were two small bronze wheels. He slowly turned the first. Two copper cups inside the recess inched towards the bronze spheres at the front of the chest. Talaban spun the wheel until the cups covered the spheres. The warrior could feel his excitement rising as his hands moved to the second wheel. This he turned two full circles. At the rear of the panel was a second, hidden recess. Talaban opened it. A long sheet of shining mica met his gaze. There were six deep indentations in the mica and in one a solitary white crystal glowed. Talaban opened the pouch at his side and from it took five more crystals, which he laid in the remaining indentations. Sliding closed the lid, Talaban took a deep breath—and gave a final turn to the second bronze wheel.

Instantly light flared from the two crystal globes set into the wall. Talaban's spirits soared. Blowing out the lantern he stepped into the corridor beyond, locking the door behind him. All along the corridor there was clean, bright light. Climbing the circular stair to the central deck Talaban leaned over the port rail. *Serpent Seven* was no longer bobbing in the bay. She sat, calm and proud, free of the pull of the sea.

Climbing to the upper deck he saw his sergeant, Methras, and a group of soldiers sitting by the port rail, staring up at the lights which had appeared all over the ship. The men were Vagars, and had never seen a *Serpent* under full power. Talaban summoned Methras to him. Methras bowed low. He was a tall slender warrior, fair-haired and balding. Despite the harsh race laws there was every indication that Methras had Avatar blood. Highly intelligent, he was the best Vagar sergeant Talaban had known. This alone would not have stirred Talaban's suspicions, but the man was also fully ambidextrous and this was the one trait that separated the Avatar from the other races. All Avatars had this advantage, and the allied ability to work simultaneously with both hands on different tasks. Talaban had mentioned the sergeant's skills to no one. To do so might have alerted the officers of the Council, and threatened the man's life.

"What a fine sight, sir," said Methras, pointing at the lights.

"Fine indeed," agreed Talaban. "Fetch axes and saws

from the store room and rid this ship of those damned masts."

"Masts, sir? Sails and all?"

"Sails and all," said Talaban.

"Yes, sir," said Methras dubiously.

"Fear not," said Talaban, with a broad smile. "The *Serpent* will sail faster without them. And I promise you there will be no motion sickness upon the return journey."

Talaban returned to his cabin. Touchstone was waiting for him there. The tribesman was sitting on the floor, his face tense, his eyes fearful. "What is wrong?" asked Talaban.

"Wrong? Nothing wrong," said Touchstone. "I am well. Very strong."

Talaban moved to his desk and sat down, gesturing for Touchstone to rise and sit in the chair opposite. The tribesman did so. "Speak," said Talaban. "I can see you are concerned over something. Was it the death of the sailor?"

"No. It is demon lights. So bright," admitted Touchstone. "No flame. Little suns in glass." When the lights had first flared Touchstone had screamed—a fact he would admit to no one. He had been sitting on the floor, but had surged to his feet in a panic. He had run into the door, then wrenched it open, flinging himself into the corridor beyond—only to find that the globes there had also filled with light. His heart had thumped like a war drum and he had difficulty catching his breath. Then a sailor had come walking along the corridor, seemingly unconcerned by the demon light. He had grinned at Touchstone and moved past him.

Still trembling, the tribesman had returned to the cabin. Steeling himself he approached a globe, staring hard into it. This had made his head ache, and for a while almost blinded him. He had retreated to the rug at the center of the room, squatting down and closing his eyes, awaiting the return of Talaban.

"There is nothing demonic about them, my friend. And you are quite right to call them little suns, for that is what they are. The power of the sun held in glass."

"How you trap sun?" asked Touchstone, seeking to appear only mildly interested.

"Everything traps sunlight," said Talaban. "Every living thing. We are all born of the power of the sun, every man, every plant. We hold the sunlight within us." Touchstone looked sceptical. Talaban rose from his desk and moved to a shelf on the far wall. From it he took a jar of sugar. Opening the lid he reached inside and scooped out a handful of white granules. This he tossed into the coal brazier. Instantly flames roared up. "The sugar stores sunlight. The coals released it, and it reverted to energy. The coals themselves were once trees, and filled with sunlight. When we light them we free them to return to what they once were. Fire from the sun. You understand?"

Touchstone did not, but it seemed that he should and so he nodded, adopting what he hoped was an expression of enlightenment. Talaban fell silent. Touchstone felt he should say something wise. "So," he said at last, "dead sailor was sunlight."

"Exactly. The power chests store energy. They must be handled with great care, and certainly never touched by human flesh. The sailor inadvertently drew power from the chest, and it released the sunlight within him."

"Why you need come to ice?" asked Touchstone. "If sun gives energy why not leave boxes in sunlight?"

"It is not quite that simple. Your axe is made of iron, fastened to a wooden haft. At some time in the past the wood was merely timber, the iron a lump of metal. Then an armorer was given the wood and the iron, and he fashioned them into an axe. In the same way the sunlight was—in effect—refashioned by the White Pyramid into something we could store in the chests. The pyramid radiated that power to all corners of the empire, so that wherever there were Avatar cities their chests could be replenished."

"How long this new power last?" asked Touchstone.

"If the chest remains in the ship, five years at the very least," said Talaban.

"Maybe you become gods again," said Touchstone.

"Maybe we will," agreed Talaban. "But I hope not."

On the morning of the third day a blizzard raged over the bay. Four chests had been recharged, but the process was becoming ever more slow—a phenomenon Questor Ro did not wish to examine. He feared he already knew the answer. One of his teams was still on the ice, seeking to recharge the fifth chest. Swirling snow and icy winds made their work increasingly difficult. Talaban, his zhi-bow recharged, stood with them. Touchstone moved alongside him.

"Air is bad," he shouted above the howling wind. "Must leave here. Now!"

"It is cold," Talaban agreed.

"Not cold. Bad. Death is coming." Talaban knew the tribesman's uncanny talents were rarely wrong. Ducking his head against the wind, he struggled across to where Questor Ro was kneeling by a flickering pyramid. "Back to the ship!" shouted Talaban. Questor Ro glanced up. He wanted to argue, but he knew Talaban was right. The weather was making Communion almost impossible to maintain. He nodded and began to unloop the gold wire from around the pyramid's base. Touchstone loosened his fur-lined robe and drew his axe from his belt, his green eyes squinting as he tried to see through the swirling snow.

A Vagar, working some 20 paces away, suddenly screamed and staggered to his left. Blood was pumping from a huge wound where his left arm had been. He lurched to his right, and then it seemed to Touchstone that the snow reared up and covered him. Touchstone hefted his axe and began to back away towards Talaban.

A huge form reared up at Touchstone. It was white, with long arms and a gray face. Touchstone saw sharp fangs in its maw, and terrible talons on the ends of its fingers. The tribesman threw himself to his left, hitting the snow with his shoulder and rolling to his feet. The beast was fast and bore down upon him again. A bolt of light struck it in the white fur of its chest. There was a flash and a huge hole opened in the beast, spraying blood and bone to the snow. More krals came running through the blizzard. Touchstone spun and sprinted back to where Talaban was standing calmly sending bolt after bolt into the beasts.

The panicking Vagars were running in all directions. Questor Ro drew his golden scepter and stepped up alongside Talaban. Touchstone glanced at him. The little man showed no fear. Touchstone's respect for him rose a little.

Three of the beasts charged forward. Talaban shot the first, the bolt hurling the creature back through the air. The second was almost upon him but Touchstone threw himself at it, ducking under the sweep of a taloned arm and hammering his axe into the beast's face. The blade sank deep. The kral staggered, then sent a crushing blow to the tribesman's side. His axe wrenched from his hand, Touchstone flew through the air, landing heavily.

Talaban shot the creature just as the third beast reared over him, but Questor Ro thrust forward his scepter, straight into its belly. Blue flame blossomed around the kral and its huge grey head exploded, fire bursting up from its shaggy neck.

Down by the waterside four of the creatures were slashing their talons into the bodies of dead Vagars. Talaban shot the first two. The others hooked their talons into two corpses, dragging them into the sea before disappearing below the water.

Touchstone struggled to his feet. His shirt was blood-drenched and he felt dizzy and faint. Stumbling to Talaban and Questor Ro he dragged his axe from the head of the dead kral.

The ground moved beneath his feet and he almost fell. At first he thought it was merely dizziness that had thrown him, but then he saw that Questor Ro had also stumbled.

"Get . . . to ship . . . or all die," he told Talaban. "Pillar of fire coming. Kill all."

Talaban helped him down to the water's edge. Only five Vagars remained alive. Talaban ordered them into the longboat, then helped Touchstone over the side. "Got to be fast," said Touchstone.

Talaban tossed his zhi-bow into the boat then glanced back to where Questor Ro was still trying to dismantle the wire from the pyramids. He ran back to the little man. "There is no time, Questor," he shouted. Ro ignored him. The ground heaved beneath them, throwing Talaban to the ice. Rising he moved behind Questor Ro, grabbing the man by his fur cloak and dragging him back. Instinctively Ro brought up his scepter. Talaban blocked it with his left arm then slammed a right cross to the man's chin. Ro slumped to the ice. Talaban hauled him up, throwing him over his shoulder. Then he gathered the scepter and made his way to the boat.

It glided across the bay. Still panic-stricken, the Vagars scrambled up the rope ladder ahead of Talaban. Touchstone followed, moving slowly and painfully. Talaban tied ropes fore and aft then, carrying Questor Ro, hauled himself up over the central deck. Dumping the little man on the floor he ordered the waiting sailors to weight anchor and climbed to the upper deck and the control cabin.

Placing his hand on the triangular gold plate set into the dark wood he twisted it to the left. Below the plate were seven symbols. A dull rumbling sounded from the glacier. Talaban did not look back at it. He lightly pressed the five symbols that controlled the lock and the door opened. Without pausing to close the door Talaban moved to a long black cabinet against the far wall. This too had a golden triangle, and Talaban opened it, his fingers flicking swiftly over the symbols within. The door opened. Inside was a long shelf covered by a glittering sheet of mica, with seven indentations. A velvet bag had been laid upon it. Talaban opened the bag, tipping the seven crystals within it to the mica.

A huge explosion came from the ice. Talaban glanced up. A colossal pillar of fire had erupted from the glacier, hurling massive chunks of ice into the air. Calmly he picked up a crystal and placed it in the third indentation on the mica. Instantly a faint blue light flowed around the ship. A boulder-sized lump of ice hurtled toward the deck, struck the blue light and bounced away. Talaban added two more crystals, replaced the others in the bag, then closed the lid. Red lava erupted from below the ice and the air became thick with steam. Molten rock struck the blue light and rolled down into the sea, like wine poured over the outside of a glass goblet. Talaban moved back to a large bronze wheel and spun it.

The *Serpent* glided through the lava storm untouched, as ice and fire rained down upon the sea around it.

• • •

Questor Ro stood on the small port deck of his cabin watching the fire raging upon the distant glaciers. His jaw ached from where Talaban had struck him, but this was not the time to think of revenge. That could come later. All he could think of now were the six silver pyramids filled with precious gems, and the gold rods that drew on the power. Ro had paid for these himself, and they had cost him almost half his not inconsiderable fortune.

Also there was the loss of the fifth chest. No one in the new empire could fashion them now, for the source of the special mica, found far across the western ocean, was closed to them.

A huge spume of fire roared towards the sky and a thunderous explosion followed it. Ro moved back inside, closing the deck door and slumping down into his chair. He had succeeded beyond the wildest dreams of his enemies, but for him there was only a sick despair.

What good were four chests if they could never be replenished? Their power would merely stave off the inevitable for a little while longer.

Ro rubbed his jaw, then poured a drink into a beautifully cut crystal goblet. Ro stared at it. The crystal was clear and clean, and he saw his reflection in a score of the facets. Idly he tugged at his forked blue beard, then drained the liquor. Ro was not a drinker, and the fiery spirit surged through him with raw power.

Resting his head on the high-backed chair he tried to plan a further expedition. In future they would have to journey closer to the center of power, traversing the ice. His heart sank, even as the thought came to him.

Krals, saber-tooths and nomads would make such a journey almost impossible.

Added to which, and this was the real reason for his despair, he knew now that the power of the White Pyramid was fading. Shielded from the sun it could no longer replenish its own energy, let alone power fresh chests.

Ro was tempted to refill his goblet, but he did not. Instead he turned his mind to the problem of Talaban. There was little doubt that the captain had saved his life back on the ice. But this could not outweigh the fact that he had struck a Questor, in full view of the Vagar team and the savage Touchstone. Perhaps even some of the sailors had seen it.

Had it just been the Vagars Ro could have sentenced them to death. But Talaban would never allow such a fate for Touchstone. It was a thorny problem.

He was considering the possibilities for revenge when Talaban arrived. The captain entered without knocking, which was his right but nevertheless galling.

"How are you feeling, Questor?" he asked.

"I am well. Thank you for saving my life."

"May I sit?" This, at least, was courteous, and Questor Ro gestured for him to take a chair. "I congratulate you, sir," said Talaban. "I did not have any faith in this venture, and you have proved me—and many others—wrong."

"A small success, captain. We lost one chest, and powered only four. But I thank you for your kind words. Did my Vagar team escape the eruption?"

"Most were killed by the krals, but five escaped. They were concerned for your health. They believed you had been struck down by the beasts."

"And you apprised them of the real situation?" asked Ro, mildly.

"I did not. I merely told them you had fought the krals and suffered an injury, but that you would be well. It does no harm for the Vagars to see the rejuvenating powers of the Avatar."

"But your man Touchstone saw you strike me?"

"No, Touchstone was badly injured by a kral. Six ribs were broken and his lung pierced. He was only semi-conscious when I carried you to the boat. I can assure you, Questor, that no one observed me strike you."

"Well, it is of no consequence, Talaban," said Ro, forcing a smile.

"I disagree, Questor. We are a minority people, and if the Vagars, or other tribes, witness us at odds with one another it would create an impression of weakness. I regret deeply the action I took but, as the alternative was to let you die, I felt I had no choice. However, on the more positive side, despite the loss of our equipment, the Vagars did witness you and me fighting the krals. They will carry the tale back to the cities, and further enhance the myth of Avatar superiority."

"Myth? Why do you say myth?"

Talaban smiled. "We are merely men, Questor. No more than that. But we need the myth in order to rule."

Questor Ro was not surprised by Talaban's heresy, but he feigned shock nonetheless. "You are losing your faith, Talaban. We were born to rule. And there is no question that we are superior to lesser beings. We are virtually immortal, and our knowledge is as far above theirs as they are above dogs."

"Precisely, Questor. Knowledge. That is all it comes down to in the end. We discovered the secrets of the sun's power. They did not."

"And that, in itself, proves our superiority," said Ro triumphantly. "I have lived with Vagars these last seventy years. I know what they are capable of. They can be loyal, and really quite bright. But they do not possess our insights. The Avatar is a different breed—a race apart. Take Viruk, for example. He embodies all that is strong in the Avatar."

Talaban fell silent. Ro met his level gaze. "Say what you are thinking, captain. Do you disagree?"

Talaban smiled. "It is good to see you well, sir. I must attend to Touchstone."

Rising, he bowed low, then departed.

Questor Ro sat at his desk for a while, thinking over the brief conversation. He had hoped Talaban would take the bait, and condemn Viruk. It would have been pleasant to have passed on the information to the Avatar warrior.

They were such dissimilar men. Talaban so cool and in control, Viruk wild and dangerous.

And quite insane.

Chapter Six

Of all the gods who walked the earth when the sun was young and not yet strong, the worst and best was Virkokka, the god of war. He dwelt within the Fire Mountain, dreaming dreams of death and pain. His face was fair, his manner calm, but those who saw his smile were those about to die. And on this day, when Virkokka left his place of fire, the world trembled, and all was changed forever.

From the *Evening Song of the Anajo*

Viruk lay very still, watching the riders as they moved out into the valley. There were thirty in the raiding group, and five wagons were being hauled slowly behind them. The wagons' wheels were cutting deep grooves on the dirt road. The raiders have done well, thought Viruk. His pale grey gaze fastened on the lead rider. He wore a bright red cloak, with a brooch of yellow gold in the shape of a sunburst at the neck. His clothes were of gaudily dyed wool, and he wore loose-fitting leggings and wooden shoes. His beard had been covered in red wax and jutted from his chin like a blood-covered tongue, which identified him clearly as a nobleman of the Mud People. Viruk smiled. The full tribal name was Erek-jhip-zhonad, which Viruk—and most Avatars—found impossible to pronounce, and, in translation, the People of the Stars—too pompous to consider. Hence the derogatory title bestowed by the Council.

The leader's men were dressed more simply, boasting no golden brooches. They wore breastplates of stiffened leather and carried long spears. Their hair was caked in a mixture of red clay and wax, giving the impression of poorly designed helmets of pottery.

Viruk glanced to his right. Outnumbered three to one, the ten Vagar archers awaited his command. To a man they all looked terrified. Viruk gave a tight smile and hefted his zhi-bow. It was black and unadorned, save for the two red crystals above the grip. Viruk had refashioned it himself. It seemed to him that the traditional zhi-bows were too complicated. Why have varying levels of power in the bolt? If a man was attacking you why merely knock him down and stun him, when you could rip out his chest and watch his blood spray out like a flower in bloom? Zhi-bows were meant to kill. And they did it beautifully.

The riders were closer now and well within range. But Viruk gave no orders to the hidden Vagar archers under his command. Equipped with only traditional bows and knives the men were sick with dread as the riders approached.

"Shoot when I do," ordered Viruk. Then he rose to his feet and strolled down the hillside to meet the advancing raiders. He was a tall slender man, his long yellow hair dyed blue at the closely shaved temples, and he wore no armor, sporting only a shirt of light blue silk, black leather leggings and grey lizard-skin boots.

The lead rider, a burly man, his face tanned nutbrown, drew on his reins and waited for Viruk to approach. His men hefted their spears and bunched alongside him, ready to charge.

"You have strayed from your lands, Mud-man," said Viruk, amiably. "In doing so you have disobeyed the General's directive."

The rider grinned. His front teeth were made of gold. "Your power is failing, Avatar," he said. "You cannot enforce your *directives*. Now give me your zhi-bow and I will let you live. I will send you back to your general with a message from the king, my brother."

"The king is your brother?" said Viruk, feigning surprise. "I suppose that makes you an important man among your people. A man not to be taken lightly. I'll tell you what we'll do. I will send a message to the king, your brother." His voice hardened, and his eyes grew more pale. "The survivors among your band can deliver it." Lifting the bow he sent a bolt into the rider's chest. It exploded with a fearsome sound, spraying blood and shards of bone over the other men. Terrified horses reared, pitching their riders. Viruk's thin fingers danced upon the strings of light and four more bolts thundered into the milling riders. One man's arm was torn clear of his body. Another's head fell to the ground and rolled toward Viruk. The Avatar warrior kept shooting. One rider spurred his horse into a charge. Viruk shot the horse in the head, stopping it dead in its tracks. The rider flew over the headless neck, landing heavily. He scrambled up, but an arrow took him through the neck and he pitched to the ground.

His Vagars had come from their hiding places now, and were sending a rain of shafts into the raiders. Within moments the massacre was over. The only living Mud People were the drivers of the five wagons. Viruk approached the terrified men, ordering them to climb down. They did so. The Avatar assembled them in a line.

Tossing his zhi-bow to a startled Vagar he approached the first of the drivers. Placing his left hand on the man's shoulder he leaned in close. "Such violence is dreadful, don't you think?" he asked.

"Yes . . . dreadful," agreed the man.

"Then you shouldn't have come," said Viruk, brightly, ramming a dagger deep into the man's chest. The victim screamed and tried to drag himself back from his killer. But the blade pinned him. He died and sagged against Viruk. The Avatar patted the dead man's cheek. "So nice to meet a man who doesn't outstay his welcome," he said. Dragging the knife clear he let the body drop. The other prisoners fell to their knees, and began to beg for mercy.

"What I need," said Viruk, "is a man who can remember a message. Can any of you sub-humans do that, do you think?"

The men glanced at one another. One of them raised a hand. "Good," said Viruk. "Follow me." Swinging away he glanced at the Vagar sergeant. "Kill the others," he said.

The remaining raiders scrambled to their feet and started to run. Three of them were cut down instantly, but the fourth was dodging and weaving and running so fast that none of the archers could hit him. "I don't know," said Viruk, laying his hand on the trembling prisoner's shoulder. "They are supposed to be highly trained archers. But do you think any of them could hit a cow's arse from five paces?" He shook his head. "Wait here."

Then he strolled back to the others, took up his zhibow and sent a light bolt through the man's back at almost 200 paces.

Returning to the survivor he gave an engaging smile. "Sorry to have kept you waiting." The man was still wearing his sword. But he stood stock-still, his eyes fixed to Viruk's pale gaze. "What are you staring at?" asked Viruk.

"Nothing, lord. I was . . . just . . . awaiting your orders."

"Was he really the king's brother?"

"Indeed, lord."

"Baffling. But then I suppose it doesn't take much to become royal among you sub-humans. Are you royal?"

"No, lord. I am a potter by trade."

Viruk chuckled and draped his arm over the man's neck. "It is always good to have a trade. Now, take your weapon," he ordered him, "and cut off the head of the king's brother. Then find yourself a horse and head for home."

"His head, lord? The king's brother?"

"The king's *dead* brother," Viruk corrected him. "Yes, the head. And be careful not to damage that ridiculous beard." He hesitated and stared down at the dead man. "Why do they do that? What is the point of having a beard waxed so stiffly? I mean how does a man sleep with a beard like that?"

"I don't know, lord. Perhaps he sleeps on his back."

"I expect that's it. Now, let us return to the task in hand. Cut off the head."

"Yes, lord." The man drew his sword and struck four blows to the neck of the corpse. Still the head did not fall clear.

"I hope you are a better potter than a swordsman," said Viruk, drawing his dagger and kneeling to slice through the last tendons.

Rising he swung to the man. "My name is Viruk. Can you remember that?"

"Yes, lord. Viruk."

"Good. Tell the king that if there is one more incursion onto Avatar farmlands I will ride into the pitiful hovel he calls his palace and cut out his entrails. Then I will make him eat them. Be so kind as to repeat that back to me."

The man did so. "Splendid," said Viruk, clapping him on the shoulder. "Now pick up that head. I'm sure the king will be glad to get it back. It will be something to bury, at least."

Walking back to the wagons he glanced into the back of the first. It was filled with sacks of grain. "What is in the others?" he asked his sergeant.

"Mostly the same, lord. The last wagon contains some plunder. But it is worth little."

"Well, take them back to the city." Then he strolled out to one of the surviving horses and stepped into the saddle.

"Where are you going, lord?" asked his sergeant.

"Just for a ride, dear boy. I fancy there may be a few more raiders close by. Wouldn't want to see you brave lads attacked on the way back, would I?"

Gathering his zhi-bow the Avatar galloped his horse away to the east.

"He's a lunatic," said the man standing beside the sergeant.

"Yes he is," snapped the sergeant. "But we're all alive. I'll settle for that."

The prisoner rode up to the sergeant. "Do I go now?" he asked.

"I should," advised the sergeant. "The captain can be very . . . changeable. He may decide he doesn't want the message sent. And then . . ." he gestured to the bodies.

Swinging his horse the Mud-man rode away.

Viruk felt energized in a way no crystal could ever supply. His body was vibrant with power, and the air he breathed tasted fresher and cleaner. Even the shoddy horse he now rode felt like a prime charger. Life was good today. Recalling with delight the expression on the leader's face as he loosed the first bolt, Viruk laughed aloud. He wondered what the man had felt in that one dreadful moment when he knew that his life was about to end in an explosion of fire and pain. Did he know regret? Despair? Anger? Did he wonder why he had spent so long grooming that ludicrous wax beard? Probably not, thought Viruk. His expression had been one of disbelief. Even so, the short battle had been wonderfully invigorating.

He imagined the river king's face when the messenger arrived with his brother's head. The man would be furious. It was likely he would kill the messenger—especially when he heard the message. Viruk hoped not. He had taken an instant liking to the little potter.

Viruk's action would not find favor with the High Council. They would call it provocative. But he didn't care. All-out war with the tribes was becoming increasingly inevitable. Every Avatar warrior knew it. Just as they knew the outcome.

Without the zhi-bows the cities would fall within days. Viruk hefted his own bow, checking the power. It was low. Perhaps five bolts remained.

Viruk rode on, crossing the rich farmland, ignoring the burnt-out buildings. The raiders had cut a wide swathe through the valleys. With only fifty zhi-bows left in the city most of the garrison troops had been withdrawn, leaving the farmers helpless against raids. Viruk did not agree with the policy. It invited the Mud People and other tribes to enter the corn valleys, disrupting trade and causing shortages of food in the five cities. But then Viruk had chosen not to be part of the policy-making team. He preferred life as a soldier-captain, free to ride the wild lands, fighting and killing. Now he almost regretted his decision. The Questors had given their short-sighted orders and Questor General Rael loyally saw them carried out. Rael should forget about tradition and strip the Questors of their power, thought Viruk.

But he wouldn't. Rael, for all his skills, was a prisoner to tradition, chained by a code of honor that had died with the tidal waves that destroyed the home world. He should have declared himself Avatar Prime. Then perhaps the outlook would have been less grim.

Viruk rode to the crest of a hill and looked down upon the walled village of Pacepta. The raiders had bypassed it to strike at lone farms, and Viruk, hungry now, decided to ride down and eat.

The guard above the gate looked frightened as he approached, but made no hostile move. "What do you want?" he shouted down.

Viruk drew rein and hefted his zhi-bow. Then he rode closer. "You have one more chance to ask that question properly," he told the young man. "If you do not I shall kill you."

"A thousand pardons, sir," said the youth. "My eyes are not good. I did not see you were a . . . lord."

"Open the gate, numbskull," said Viruk. The youth shouted a command to someone beyond the walls and the thick timber gates were dragged open. Viruk rode through. The buildings here were squalid and there was no tavern. Riding to the largest of the nearby homes he stepped down from the saddle and moved to the front door, opening it and stepping inside. A large man was sitting at a long table, upon which a large bowl of soup was steaming gently. The man held a chunk of bread in his hand and was about to dip it into the soup as Viruk entered. The man's small eyes blinked rapidly as he saw the Avatar. He dropped the bread and rose, his chair falling back to the floor. An elderly woman was kneeling by a fire stirring a pot of soup with a wooden spoon. She did not rise, but bowed from where she was.

"Welcome, lord," said the man, forcing a smile.

"You have bread between your teeth," chided Viruk, righting the chair and sitting at the table. "Fetch me food," he ordered the woman.

The man rushed away to the back of the house, returning with half a fresh-baked loaf and a dish of butter. The woman ladled soup into a clay bowl and placed it before Viruk. Then both the Vagars stood in silence as the Avatar ate. Finally Viruk sat back. "You have wine?" he asked.

"I will fetch some, lord," said the old woman, hurrying from the house.

Viruk looked up at the large man. He was beardless and bald, and his stomach bulged over the length of rope holding up his canvas leggings.

"When did the raiders pass here?" he asked the man.

"Yesterday morning, lord."

"They are dead now," said Viruk. Leaning forward he took the last of the bread and dipped it into the remains of the soup. Finishing it he looked up at the man once more. "I saw when I rode in you have only two wagons. Surely a supply village like this should have more?"

"Raiders took five of them, lord."

"The wagons were outside the walls?"

The man's face paled. Viruk could see he was toying with the idea of a lie. He gave him a cold smile. All thoughts of fabrication vanished from the man's mind. "No, lord. They demanded the wagons and we gave them."

"Upon whose order?"

"Our headman, Shalik. He said that five wagons was a small price to pay for our lives."

"Did he, indeed? Fetch him to me."

"Yes, lord. He had the best interest of the villagers at heart, lord."

"I'm sure that he did," said Viruk amiably. "Fetch him."

The woman returned with a jug of wine. Viruk tasted it. It was cheap, young, and remarkably sour. Looking up at the woman he ordered her to wait outside.

The large man reentered the building just as she was leaving. Behind him came an elderly man dressed in a full-length tunic of green wool. "You are Shalik?" said Viruk.

"I am, lord," he answered, offering a deep bow.

"Tell me about yourself."

"Little to tell, lord. I have been headman now for seven years, appointed by the General."

"You have a family?"

"Yes, lord. A wife, four sons, two daughters. We have recently been blessed with two grandchildren."

"How nice," said Viruk. "Now, you gave away five of the General's wagons yesterday. Would you explain the thinking that led to this deed?"

"There were thirty raiders, lord. They could have sacked the village. Instead I negotiated with them. At first they wanted all the wagons, but I am a skilled negotiator. They settled for five."

"And why do you think they needed these wagons?"

Shalik blinked and licked his thin lips. "To . . . carry goods, lord?"

"Indeed. Without the wagons they could not have plundered farms and settlements. As a result of your *negotiation* they filled their wagons with the General's property. Because of your *skill* they felt empowered to slaughter the General's workforce. Not so?"

"I was protecting my village, lord."

"Men make choices," said Viruk, with a smile. "Sometimes they are good choices, sometimes bad. You made a choice. It was a bad one. Now go home and cut your wrists. I will come by to examine your body before I leave. Go now."

Shalik threw himself to his knees. "Oh lord, I beg of you . . . spare me!"

The emotional display irritated Viruk, but he did not show it. "You aided the enemy, man. The penalty for such a crime is your execution and the deaths of your entire family. Do this small thing, Shalik, and your family can go on with their lives, secure in the knowledge that you saved them. For, if you are not dead within the hour, I will come to your house and I will kill your wife, your four sons, your two daughters and your grandchildren. Now be gone, before I regret my generosity."

The large man led the weeping Shalik from the house. He returned moments later.

"You are now the headman," said Viruk. "What is your name?"

"Bekar, lord."

"Well, Bekar, the next time raiders approach you will deny them any aid. Is that not so?"

"It will be as you command, lord."

"Good. Is Shalik's house better than yours?"

"It is, lord. He is a rich man."

"He is a dead man. His property is yours."

"Thank you, lord."

"Now send me one of the village whores. It has been a long day and I need the services of a woman."

"There are no whores in the village, lord."

Viruk stood and gave the man a broad smile. "You could become one of the shortest-lived headmen in history, Bekar. Is that what you want?"

"No, lord. I will fetch a woman immediately."

Chapter Seven

There were many things that Sofarita wanted to say as she stood in the doorway of her father's house. She wanted to look into the Avatar's pale eyes and tell him she loathed him worse than any plague. She wanted to ask him how he could consider rutting when a good man was sitting with his family, telling them he was being forced to kill himself. Yet she could not. For despite her pride, and an irrepressible personal courage, she knew that to anger this man would bring terrible retribution on others. Sofarita would have willingly spoken her heart to this man, even in the sure knowledge of death. Yet the Avatar, this slim young killer, would have no compunction about killing her entire family. Perhaps the whole village. To risk such a tragedy would be foolhardy in the extreme.

Instead she stood in the doorway, head bowed, hands clenched tight beneath the red shawl wrapped around her slender shoulders, hoping that the racking cough she had endured for the last three months would not ruin what chance she had of placating this man of evil.

Her father had chosen her for this distasteful mission because she had been married for two years. He felt his widow daughter would find the violation easier to accept. How simple men are, she thought. How little do they understand the nature of such violation.

Yet she had not criticized him. At twenty-two Sofarita could read the faces of men, and she saw in Bekar a terrible fear, and a great longing. He had been made headman and this, he believed, would bring wealth and security to his family. Yet it all rested on the charms of his daughter.

Sofarita thought him short-sighted. There would be no wealth, and precious little security for the headman of Pacepta. They were too close to the borders of the Erek-jhip-zhonad, and soon other raiders would come, followed by settlers who would either kill the villagers or force them from the land. The Avatars would be wiped out. Everyone knew that. The sure knowledge of it whispered in the movement of the wind-rustled corn. It could be heard in the fluttering of a sparrow's wing. But great damage could still be done to the Vagars in the death throes of the Avatar Beast.

The Avatar Beast . . .

She raised her eyes and looked at the man. His face was handsome, his yellow hair close-cropped at the front and sides, long at the back. At the temples the hair was dyed sky blue. He smiled and beckoned her forward. It was a gracious smile, full of warmth and friendship. But then, thought Sofarita, if evil wore an ugly face no one would yearn for it.

"Tell me about yourself," he said. The voice was light, but yet still manly. It was the voice of a bard or a singer. She looked into his pale grey eyes, seeking sign of the cold killer she knew him to be. There was nothing to be seen. The horror lay below the skin, behind the eyes.

"I am a widow, lord," she said, averting her dark gaze from him.

"And that is your life story? How drab. Did your husband teach you to be a good lover before he died?"

Anger flared in her, but she suppressed it, though her

cheeks burned red. Suddenly she coughed, the spasms rocking her. Bile and blood entered her mouth but she swallowed them down.

"Have I offended your Vagar sensibilities?" he asked her. "If so I apologize. Now close the door and show me your body."

As she did so she considered his question. Had Veris made her a good lover? Did a woman need a man to show her how to make love? But then, she reasoned, he does not mean what he says. To a man a good lover was someone who offered *them* the most pleasure. Veris had not *made* her a good lover, he had *been* a good lover. Something she believed this Avatar would never understand. Sofarita pushed shut the door, then turned and let her shawl fall to the floor. Beneath it she was wearing a simple dress of white wool, laced at the front with silver ribbon. She began to untie the lace. The Avatar rose, moving smoothly to stand before her. His nimble fingers took her hands and drew them away from the ribbon. Then he untied the dress, slipped it over her shoulders and allowed it to fall to the dirt floor.

His right hand slid over her belly. "You have borne no children," he said. "How long were you married?"

"Three months."

"Follow me," he said, and walked through to the back of the house and into the main bedroom. The bed was of carved wood, the mattress laid over wooden slats. He dragged back the blankets and knelt by the bed. For one insane moment Sofarita thought he was praying. Then he rose. "No bugs that I can see," he told her. Swinging toward her he suddenly slapped her face. It was not a hard blow, but it stung.

"Why do you strike me?" she asked him.

"For your impertinence," he told her, with a bright smile. "The correct answer was 'Three months, *lord*.' How did your husband die?"

Her face was hot from the slap. "He was gored by a bull, lord."

"How sad. Now get into bed." Sofarita did so, averting her eyes as he removed his clothing.

His lovemaking was assured and surprisingly gentle, and Sofarita did her best to make him believe that she was enjoying the experience. When at last he rolled clear of her she even reached out to stroke his cheek. His fingers snaked out and grabbed her wrist. "There is no need for further play-acting," he said, still amiable. "You did well. The tension is gone from me."

"I am glad I pleased you, lord," she said.

"No, you are not. You are glad that your father will not suffer."

Rising from the bed he dressed swiftly and walked back to the outer room. Sofarita lay for a while in her parents' bed, then she followed him. Lifting her dress from the floor she shook the dust from it and put it on.

"Shall I leave, lord?" she asked.

"No, sit with me for a while." She joined him at the table and he poured her a goblet of wine which she sipped dutifully. She felt the cough rising again, and took another sip of wine. "Did you know that you are dying?" he asked her, his voice bright, almost cheerful.

The words shook her. "You are going to kill me?" she asked.

Leaning forward he slapped her again. "How many times must you be told? Are you so stupid that a simple instruction, a small courtesy, is beyond you?"

"I am sorry, lord. Your words frightened me. Are you going to kill me, lord?"

"No, I am not going to kill you. You have a cancer in your chest. It has already covered one lung. How long have you been bringing up blood?"

"Some weeks now, lord." Deep down she had known the truth but had not faced it. Now she was forced to.

Her energy had been low now for months, and weight had been dropping from her despite the meals she consumed. She took a breath, seeking calm. It was a shallow breath, but all she could manage these days. Then he spoke again.

"Well, a man should always pay for his pleasures," he said, rising to tower over her. From a pouch at his belt he took a green crystal which he held to her breast. Pain pierced her and she cried out. "Sit still," he said. A feeling of warmth entered her belly, rising into her chest. It seemed to focus on the right side of her body, seeping deeper. Sofarita felt dizzy, but the Avatar's left hand dropped to her shoulder, steadying her. At last the warmth subsided.

"Take a deep breath," he said.

She did so, and to her delight her lungs filled with air.

"You are healed," he told her. "Now you may go."

"You have given me life, lord," she whispered.

"Yes, yes. And next time I see you I may take it away. Now go and tell your father I am well pleased. Tell him also to bring out Shalik's body so that I may see it before I leave."

Sadau, the potter, had no desire whatever to deliver the head of the king's brother. He had seen the bodies of those who had angered Ammon—bodies impaled outside the royal palace. Sadau had no wish to be impaled. As he rode to the first bridge across the Luan he halted his pony and gazed around. No one was in sight. With one heave he sent the head spinning out into the rushing water. It sank like a stone.

Relieved, he rode across the bridge and made his slow way home. All might have been well—save for his cousin Oris. Sadau made the mistake of telling him what had occurred. Naturally he swore him to secrecy. Unfortunately Oris told his wife, swearing her to se-

crecy also. By the end of the day every member of the
village knew—though they were all sworn to secrecy.
The last person to hear was the sergeant of the watch,
who reported the tale to his captain.

Four of the king's soldiers, dressed in red robes edged
with gold thread and carrying long swords and wicker
shields, arrived at Sadau's home at dawn the following
morning and the little potter was dragged from his bed
and hauled to the palace.

Sadau had never been inside the palace, and had only
ever glimpsed the king from afar, riding the Swan Boat
along the Luan at the time of the spring floods.

The soldiers said nothing as they walked. Sadau
trudged along beside them, glancing up, every now and
again, into the stern faces of his guards. "I haven't done
anything wrong," he said. But they did not respond.

The Red Palace loomed before him. High columns of
fluted sandstone skirted the building, which had been
constructed of mud-bricks from the red clay of the upper Luan. There were no statues around the palace,
though it was said that Ammon had commissioned two
likenesses of himself from the city of Egaru and these
had been covered with gold. Sadau was not thinking of
statues, however, as the soldiers paused before the huge
double doors of the main entrance.

Two of the king's guards marched down the steps to
take charge of the little potter. They were burly men,
dressed in tunics of black silk, over which they wore
breastplates of bronze. Upon their heads were long,
black conical caps of lacquered silk, emblazoned with a
silver star.

Sadau was led up the steps and through the doors. Inside there were lanterns set in bronze brackets on the
painted walls, and scores of servants moved purpose-
fully around the great hall. Nobles lounged on couches,

or sat on cushions, and the floor was covered with delicately fashioned rugs. At the far end of the hall was a golden throne flanked by two life-size golden statues, showing Ammon standing, arms folded across his chest, a stern expression on his androgynous face.

The royal guards pulled Sadau towards the empty throne then pushed him to his knees. He gazed up at the faces of the statues, seeking some sign of gentleness in the features.

A slim young man moved across the hall and sat down upon the throne. Sadau blinked and flicked his gaze back to the statues and then to the young man. There was no mistaking the resemblance. Sadau looked deep into the man's face. It was strangely beautiful. The eyelashes were darkened with lines of black ochre, the eyelids dusted with gold. The young man's hair was dark and long, the temples shaved close and stained with gold.

"You have a message for me?" he asked, his voice light. Sadau looked into his violet eyes and felt a shiver of fear.

"I was too frightened to deliver it, lord," he said, his voice breaking.

"Deliver it now."

Sadau closed his eyes. "The Avatar said to tell you not to raid his lands again."

"His exact words, potter. I require his exact words."

Sadau felt a hot flush in his stomach and sickness rising in his throat. He swallowed hard. "He said that if you raided his lands again he would ride into . . . into . . ."

"Go on."

". . . the hovel you call a palace and would rip out your entrails and make you eat them."

To Sadau's surprise the king laughed, the sound rich and vibrant. He opened his eyes and blinked. The king rose from the throne and walked to where the potter was kneeling. "And my brother's head?" he asked.

"I threw it into the Luan."

"And what do you think should be your punishment, little man?" asked the king. He was so close now that Sadau could smell the jasmine perfume he wore.

"Please don't impale me, lord," wailed Sadau. "Kill me cleanly. I did not mean to cause offense."

"Would you consider it justice if I removed your head and threw it into the Luan?" asked the king.

Sadau nodded dumbly. Anything was better than being impaled. "Send for the headsman," ordered the king. They did not have long to wait and a huge man strode down the hall to stand alongside the potter. Sadau glanced round and saw that the man carried a huge cleaver with a curved edge. The potter began to tremble. "Never delay a message to a king," said Ammon. "It is well known that kings have terrible tempers, and a great lust for blood. Now bend your neck."

Sadau began to weep, but he leaned forward, exposing the nape of his neck to the headsman. The king gestured and the cleaver swept up. Sadau could see its shadow stretching out before him.

The blade swept down. Sadau squeezed shut his eyes. The cleaver flashed through the air, but the headsman halted the blade at the last moment, allowing the cold metal to lightly touch the back of Sadau's neck. The potter fainted and fell forward.

"Carry him back to his home," said the young king, "and when he wakes tell him to beware of secrets in the future. Secrets are like grain seeds. You can bury them deep, but they always seek the light."

The first of the guards bowed low. "As you command, lord. But might I ask a question?"

The king nodded. The guard cleared his throat. "Why do you let him live?"

"Because I have the power," said the king. "You have other questions?"

"No, lord."

"Good. When you have returned the potter to his home fetch Anwar. Bring him to my apartments."

The soldier bowed. Then he and his comrade lifted the unconscious Sadau and carried him from the palace.

Chapter Eight

Anwar was teaching when the soldiers came. His six senior students were engaged in a complex building problem concerning weight and stress. Anwar had shown them designs for a building and they were working together to decide whether it was structurally sound. He knew they would decide it was not. It was at this point he would tell them it was a copy of the Museum building in Egaru. They would then have to recalculate their findings.

He enjoyed teaching and loved to see the minds of his students expand. The young were a constant wonder to him, with a seemingly limitless ability to make instinctive leaps of imagination. Their minds were not yet enclosed by the walls of tradition.

When the soldiers came Anwar felt a moment of irritation. Instructing the students to continue in his absence and write their conclusions upon their slates, he left the class. Throwing a cloak of red felt about his scrawny shoulders he walked ahead of the two soldiers and out into the sunlight beyond. The bright light made his old eyes weep. Squinting against the sunshine he moved on, away from the new university building. A chariot and driver awaited him. He clambered onto the platform. "Not too fast," he warned the driver. The man grinned, and flicked his whip above the heads of the two ponies.

The ride was mercifully short, and Anwar felt enormous relief as he stepped down before the mud-brick palace. He glanced up at it feeling, as always, a sense of distaste. It was clumsily constructed, ugly and square. The architects had shown little imagination.

A royal guard took him through to Ammon's apartments. The king was lying face down on a table, his naked body being massaged by a young slave. Anwar stood silently in the doorway. Ammon raised himself on one elbow and grinned boyishly.

"Good to see you, my teacher," he said.

"Always a privilege to be invited to your home, lord," replied Anwar. Ammon dismissed the slave boy, draped a cloak of heavy blue silk about his slender shoulders and walked out into the gardens beyond. Flowering trees filled the air with a heady scent. The king stretched himself out on the grass, beckoning Anwar to join him.

"How is life at the university?" asked Ammon.

"It will be better next year," answered Anwar. "And the year after. Some of my pupils are now more expert than the teachers. I shall appoint some of them to the university staff."

"Good. Knowledge is the key to the future," said Ammon. "I remember you taught me that."

"You were a fine student, lord. Perhaps the best I ever knew."

"Perhaps?" queried Ammon with a wide smile. "One never uses the word perhaps to a king. You are not a diplomat, Anwar."

"I fear not, lord."

Ammon glanced round, caught the eye of a waiting servant and summoned him. "Fetch cool drinks for myself and my guest," he said. The man bowed low and ran back into the palace. The king lay back on the grass, the sunlight bringing a gleam to his oiled skin. "One raiding party was wiped out by the Avatars," he said.

"As you predicted, sire. I take it your brother is no longer a thorn in the flesh."

"No. Sadly he died. What was interesting, however, is that the enemy sent only a small group of Vagars led by a single Avatar."

"Viruk?"

"The very same. Such a small response to our provocation. What does this mean?"

"They are weaker than they appear, lord."

"Indeed so. And yet I do not believe this is the time to strike at them directly."

"Might I inquire as to your reasoning, lord?"

The servant returned with golden goblets brimming with the juice of several fruits. Ammon thanked him and sat up. "Whoever strikes first—even if he wins— will be weakened. My army could—possibly—overrun the five cities. We would suffer enormous losses. How then would we counter an attack from our tribal enemies?"

"I find your reasoning sound, lord," said Anwar. "It would therefore be advantageous if our own enemies made the first attack."

"Precisely. And by a happy coincidence that it is what Judon of the Patiakes is planning."

"How can I be of assistance, lord?"

Ammon sipped his drink. "Our people in the cities must do nothing to aid Judon once the battle starts. Quite the opposite, in fact. They must assist the Avatars in every way."

"I will get a message to them. One of my agents is

leaving today, with gold to finance the Pajists. But I fear
they will not react well to the order. Their hatred of the
Avatars blinds them to more far-sighted objectives."

"You have the names of all the Pajists?"

"All the leaders, lord."

"They will see the destruction of the Avatars, and my
promises kept. Then they must die."

"Indeed they shall, lord."

A cloud obscured the sun. The king shivered. "Let us
go inside. I am hungry."

Questor General Rael was not often surprised. In his
eight hundred years he had experienced all that human
life could offer and, like many of the older Questors,
found himself living in a constant circle of previously
experienced events. He had known friendship and betrayal, love and hate, and all the misty maneuvring that
swam between them. In the course of his eight centuries
friends had become enemies, loved ones had sought to
harm him, and bitter enemies had become brothers of
the blood. There was little new to experience. So when
surprise touched him he treated it like a gift. Even when
it was a gift tarnished by pain.

He stood now on the wall above the eastern gate of
Egaru, staring out over the rich farmlands spreading out
on both sides of the Luan River. Like all Avatars he was
ageless, seemingly no more than thirty, his blue hair
close-cropped, his lean body clad in a white shirt-tunic
of heavy silk, embroidered with gold thread at the high
collar and the cuffs. His long legs were encased in leggings of the finest leather, and he wore knee-length riding boots crafted from crocodile skin. Rael carried no
weapons, and boasted no jewelry. No rings glittered upon
his fingers, no circlet of gold gleamed upon his brow.

The sun was bright and hot in a clear blue sky above

the city and Rael gratefully accepted the cool drink his aide Cation proffered to him. Cation was not yet seventy, one of the few Avatars not to have been born when the world fell. Like all the younger men, he eschewed the full head of blue hair, but followed the fashion set by Viruk of having the temples dyed. Cation was of Rael's line—the great-grandson of Rael's third great-grandson. Rael liked the lad. "What have we discovered about Judon's plans?" he asked.

"The tribal leaders have been called to a gathering to discuss territorial matters," said Cation. "The Mud People refuse to attend, but all others have accepted. It is to be held in five days at Ren-el-gan, which the tribes believe was once the Well of Life. It has always been a meeting place and is considered holy ground."

"What reason did the Erek-jhip-zhonad give for their refusal to attend?"

"The king told them the date was inauspicious, as it coincided with a religious festival."

Rael smiled. "He wasn't asked to joint-lead the Gathering?"

"No, sir. Judon of the Patiakes is acting alone."

"What do we know of Judon?" asked Rael. He already knew the answer, but wished to see how much study the younger man had given to the current crisis.

"He has been Lord of the Patiakes for seventeen years, taking the mantle following the death of his father. He has more than twelve thousand warriors from a tribe numbering almost forty thousand. They are nomadic by nature, and exist in sub-clans. These number almost three hundred."

"The man, Cation. Tell me about the man."

"He is a harsh ruler, and claims to be descended from the prophet who discovered the Well of Life." Cation fell silent for a moment. "I am sorry, sir. I don't know what else to tell you."

"You could tell me that he is fat and weighs more than any three men in your section, which implies he is a greedy man. You could add that he has forty wives and more than fifty concubines, which suggests he lusts after more than he can sustain. This prophet you speak of promised that the tribes would one day own the world. He predicted the coming of a warlord from his line. Judon, in claiming to be his descendant, is trying on the mantle of that warlord. These things alone would suggest he has great ambitions. This Gathering has not been called to discuss minor territorial disagreement between the tribes. It is to declare Judon as the warlord, and will mean an army of close to fifty thousand will attack the five cities before the autumn."

"We will not be able to stop them, sir," said Cation.

"Not once they march," agreed the General. "Now, what progress has been made in tracking down those responsible for the killing of Questor Baliel?"

"We are still gathering information, sir. But there has been much talk in Egaru concerning a group calling themselves Pajists, which in the old Vagar tongue means—"

"I know what it means. Assassins."

"Indeed, sir. We have many informers, and they have all been instructed to gather information about the group. However, though there is much talk, there is little evidence so far."

"I have read the reports," said Rael. "Two of your best informers have died recently. Is that not so?"

"Yes, sir. What is your point? Both were accidents. Several witnesses saw the first leaving a tavern drunk. He fell from the wharf and drowned. The second was a blacksmith. He was kicked in the head by a horse. Witnesses observed the accident."

"Bring in the witnesses and question them under duress," ordered Rael.

"For what purpose, sir?"

"Cation, you are a blood relative, and I love you dearly. But you do not *think*. The drunk would have had to walk two miles to the docks in order to fall into the sea. His home was in the opposite direction. Even assuming he had staggered for two miles do you not think he would have sobered sufficiently to avoid such a fall? And what was he doing at the docks at midnight? The gates are locked. Are you suggesting the drunken man walked two miles out of his way, then climbed a gate, with the express purpose of hurling himself into the sea? As to the blacksmith, the back of his skull was caved in. How many blacksmiths do you know who would approach a horse backwards?"

"I see, sir. I am sorry. I have been remiss."

"Indeed you have. Both men were murdered. First bring in the witnesses to the blacksmith's death. When you have questioned them for several hours, keeping them from sleep, send for me. I will conclude the examinations."

"Yes, sir."

Dismissing Cation he walked back along the wall, down a circular stairwell and out into the compound. Soldiers were training here under the watchful eyes of their Avatar officers. As he passed, the Vagar soldiers saluted.

Questor General Rael entered the officers' section, passed through the empty halls and climbed to his study on the third floor. Once there he sat at his desk, swinging the chair so that he could look out of the window and see the distant mountains.

Today there had been two surprises, one curious, one joyful.

For the moment he concentrated on the joyful. One of Questor Anu's acolytes had brought him news of the success of the southern expedition. They had replenished four chests and were on their way home. They should arrive within two weeks.

Rael had expressed his thanks and his best wishes to Anu. The acolyte bowed.

"You may express your thanks in person, my lord, for Questor Anu asked me to invite you to his home. At noon, if it is convenient."

This was the second surprise. Anu, the Holy One, had withdrawn from public life more than thirty years before. It was, he said, his intention to age and die. He had given his crystals to Rael and retired to his home on the hill above the bay. His decision affected his popularity among the Avatar. He was the Savior, the one Avatar to predict the fall of the world. He had convinced more than 200 people to join him on a trek to the north, leading them over rugged plains and barren mountains, across deserts and valleys, arriving at last at the gates of Pagaru, the first of the five cities. There were only sixty other Avatars this far north, and they greeted the arriving column with cold courtesy.

The following day the earth had tilted and the sun had risen in the west.

Anu's prediction had been correct, and he had become the Holy One. But his decision to age and die was obscene. No Avatar would even consider such a course. The full Council of Questors voted to place him under house arrest in order to prevent Vagars from witnessing the grotesque deterioration of a supreme being. The five cities contained more than 200,000 Vagars. They were controlled by a mere 570 Avatars. The Questors feared that if Anu was seen to age like any mortal the Vagars would cease to hold them in such awe. Avatar soldiers now guarded the exits, and all of Anu's Vagar servants had been taken away.

He was attended now by three Avatar acolytes, and had not been in contact with any on the Council since that day thirty years ago.

Now he requested the presence of Rael.

The Questor General left his office and moved through to his apartments. A Vagar servant bowed as he entered, and informed him that the Lady Mirani was in the roof garden. Rael climbed the circular stair and emerged into the sunshine. The garden had been designed by Viruk twenty years before, and the air was heavy with the scent of roses and honeysuckle. Mirani was sitting in the shade of an arched trellis, that was adorned by a climbing multi-colored rose of yellow, red and white. Rael paused and took in a deep breath. Even after a hundred years he found Mirani's beauty intoxicating. Her long, fair hair, dyed blue at the temples, was tied back now with a white ribbon, and she was leaning forward, paintbrush in hand, adding delicate touches to a newly shaped pottery vase. A touch of blue paint had marked the skin of her cheek. Rael felt the burden of responsibility lift from him. He was a man again. Sensing his presence, she turned and smiled.

"What do you think?" she asked him, pointing to the vase.

"It is beautiful," he said.

"You haven't looked at it." Moving across the garden he knelt by her side. The vase was tall and slim necked, and Mirani had painted exquisite female figures all around it. They were running and laughing. "The Maidens of Contar," she explained. "You remember the myth? They heard the enchanted music of Varabidis, and left their homes to seek him on the mountain."

"As I said, it is beautiful. But where is Varabidis? Should he not be present?"

"They did not want him, they wanted his music." Mirani leaned back. "What brings you home so early?"

He told her about the summons from Anu. "Perhaps the Holy One has repented of his decision to die and wishes to join the Council once more," he concluded.

"I do not think so," said Mirani. "Anu is not a fickle man."

"I do not wish to see him withered and ancient. The thought is obscene."

Mirani shook her head. "You see old people all the time, Rael. If Anu has called for you then the matter is of importance. As I said, he is not fickle, and he certainly is not frivolous. Perhaps he has experienced another vision. You must go to him."

"I know." Taking a cloth he wiped the blue smear from her cheek. "You should return to the Council," he said. "You are ten times wiser than Caprishan."

"I no longer have any interest in politics."

"That is something I have never understood."

She smiled. "The moment you do you will walk away as I did."

"You think what I do has no merit?"

"Not at all. Society will always need to be governed. But here is a question for you, my dear. What does a normal man desire?"

"A family, a home, children. Enough food on the table. Health and a little wealth," he said.

"Exactly. And when a man has these things, but desires to control—as a councillor—the lives of others, that makes him abnormal. A man who seeks to rule *everyone* must necessarily be extremely abnormal. It could be argued that such a desire to rule should disqualify any applicant."

Rael laughed. "In that case you are the perfect councillor, since you have no desire to be one."

Her smile faded. "Perhaps. But I served for sixty years, Rael, and I saw too much. Now go and see Anu. Give him my love."

• • •

On his favorite gray gelding the Questor General rode through the Park of the West, and up over the clifftops. There was a cool breeze coming from the sea, and the smell of salt was strong in the air. He rode down through the small wood and onto the paved road that led down to the docks. Then he cut to the right, guiding the gray up along the unpaved trail until he reached the wrought-iron gates of Anu's home. Two Avatar soldiers saluted as he dismounted. Leaving his horse with them he strolled through the grounds and was met by the same acolyte who had brought the message. This man, his head shaved, but his beard dyed blue, led him through the house and up to a small library on the first floor. Heavy curtains were drawn across the windows, shutting out all natural light, and the room was lit by three glowing lanterns. Anu was sitting in a deep leather chair, an open scroll upon his lap. He was asleep, but woke as the acolyte gently touched his shoulder. "Ah, Rael," said the old man, running his bony fingers through his white, shoulder-length hair. "Welcome to my home."

Rael found Anu's appearance sickening. The old man's skin was dry and flaking, like a lizard left in the sun. His neck scrawny, fleshless and withered. Rael kept his disgust from his face and sat down opposite the frail old man. "Why are you putting yourself through this?" asked Rael.

The ancient face broke into a smile. "Why are you not?" he asked.

Rael shook his head. There was no point in arguing. That had all been done years ago. "Shall I draw back the curtains? It is a glorious day."

"No, Rael. I like the gloom." He settled back and closed his eyes again.

"You wished to see me," said Rael, holding his temper.

Anu's eyes snapped open. "I am sorry. One of the penalties of age, you know. Ah, of course, you *don't* know. Anyway ... You have four full chests, Rael. They will be the last. A volcanic eruption has destroyed the line."

"Four will give us a few years. Much may happen in that time."

"Indeed it certainly will." The old man's eyes closed and, for a moment, Rael thought him to be sleeping. Then he spoke again. "We lose much, Rael, by being ever-young."

"And what is that?"

"Flexibility. Understanding. Perspective. The physical frailties are many, but they are assuaged by a wealth of insights. All living things in nature grow, die and are reborn. Even the earth, as we have so painfully witnessed. Not so the Avatar. We have forgotten how to grow, Rael. To adapt and change. We are what we were a thousand years ago. Perhaps not even that. A thousand years ago the Avatar Prime and I designed the White Pyramid. It was a wonder, a work of genius from among a gifted people. What new inventions can we boast from the last two hundred years? What strides have we made? We are frozen in time, Rael, and we exist as merely echoes of a great song."

"All that you say may be correct, though I doubt it," said Rael, "but do you think that by aging and dying we would improve? And even if that were true, how many would accept it? I, for one, would not. I like being young and strong."

"The crystals were the blessing that became a curse," said Anu sadly. "But I have learned much in these last years." The old man smiled. "Once I stopped using the crystals my visions became sharper. I see much now that was hidden from me."

"Is that why you wished to see me?"

"In part, Rael. Would you fetch me some water?" The Questor General rose and moved to a slender table crafted from bronze in the shape of a bush with golden leaves. Upon the bronze leaves lay a long, rectangular slab of blue-stained glass and upon this a clay pitcher and two golden goblets.

Rael chuckled. "The gold looks incongruous against the clay," he said. "I shall send you a more suitable pitcher."

"It is suitable," said Anu, accepting a goblet of water with a trembling hand. "It reminds me that no matter how great our wealth the source of all life comes from the humble earth."

"Always the teacher," said Rael amiably, seating himself once more opposite the old man.

"It is my nature," agreed Anu.

"And you are a great teacher, my old friend. Without you the empire would have died. We should have listened to your teachings."

"You still should, Rael. But that is a debate for another day. I want you to give me one of the chests."

The request surprised Rael. "For what purpose?"

"I shall build a new pyramid, to almost the same specifications as that of the Avatar Prime."

Rael remained silent. The ramifications of the offer were enormous. Such a pyramid would ensure the rule of the Avatars for the next thousand years. "How can you do this? The Music is gone. How will you fashion twenty-ton blocks and move them? And if you find a way to do that, how will you raise them into place? It is impossible."

"The Music is not lost, Rael," the old man told

him. The words were spoken simply and without arrogance.

"Show me!" whispered the General. From the pocket of his cavernous gown Anu drew forth a small flute. Pushing himself to his feet he stood before Rael. "Drop to your knees and extend your right hand," he told him. Rael did so. Anu lifted the flute to his lips and began to blow a series of notes, soft as an autumn wind through the grass, light as down, sweet as the first bird call of spring. For a moment only, Rael became lost in the music, and then he saw Anu step onto his outstretched hand. He tensed, expecting the old man's foot to stamp on his fingers, driving them into the floor. Instead his hand did not move, and the ancient Questor levered himself up to balance on Rael's palm. The music died away.

"Rise, Rael," said Questor Anu. "Lift me to the ceiling."

Rael rose easily, raising his arm as if it carried no more than a feather. He could feel no weight at all from the old man. "Now bring me down," said Anu. "Lower me to my chair."

Rael lowered his hand, then took hold of Anu's bony arm and watched him float gently into the wide armchair.

"Why did you not tell us?" asked Rael.

"What purpose would it have àchieved? I wanted other Avatars to pursue the ancient knowledge—to master it. To prove to me there was a future for our race. But none have come forward. Save perhaps Ro, and he is too rooted in the past to stretch his hand towards the future."

"But you could have taught us!" said Rael, torn between feelings of awe and exasperation. "These have been difficult years for us. With your powers we could have achieved so much more."

Anu shook his head. "The answers were always there, in the mathematics. But you still do not grasp what I am saying, Rael. My mental powers have *increased* since I stopped using the crystals. It is mortality itself that gives us the desire to learn, to adapt, to forge new paths into the future. Without that we become locked in place, desiring only more of the same. Now, will you grant me a chest?"

"I will. But why have you changed your mind? What vision have you experienced?"

"Ask me again when two moons appear in the night sky."

Rael took that to mean Anu was unwilling to discuss his reasons. He considered the offer, and found that his mouth was dry. What the Holy One was suggesting was almost frightening. For it meant the rebirth of hope, and the consequent fear of despair.

"How long will it take?" he asked, knowing the answer would be in decades, and wondering how they could survive in the meantime.

"Six months."

The answer was a shock. Rael sighed. Was the old man senile after all? "You taught me mathematics, Anu. Now, if I remember correctly there were a million blocks in the White Pyramid . . ."

"One million, one hundred and seventy thousand," the old man corrected him.

"Very well. If I divide that number by the number of days in a year I find you will need to quarry, cut, move and place two thousand nine hundred blocks a day— blocks weighing more than thirty tons."

"Three thousand four hundred and twenty-two," said Anu. "That is why I need the chest."

"With a hundred chests you could not do it!" snapped Rael. "You are limited by the speed of your workmen."

"Not at all," said Anu softly. "I am limited only by time. How long have you been here, Rael?"

"Half an hour, perhaps a few minutes longer. Why?"

"You arrived, as requested, at noon. Now you may draw the curtains."

Rael strode across the room and dragged back the heavy velvet cloth. Beyond the window it was night, the stars bright in the sky. Rael blinked, stared at the pale moon, then swung back to the old man. "An illusion?" he asked.

"No. You have been here for ten hours. Time is also part of the Music, Rael. You are quite correct. Even by dismantling the four failed pyramids, and using some of their blocks it would take six hundred skilled workers more than twenty years to complete. We do not have twenty years. We have—at best—six months. I shall use the Music to make time dance for me. Here in this room I have slowed time. In the Valley of the Stone Lion I shall—with the power of the chest—increase it twentyfold."

"But you have done this here *without* crystals? It is hard to believe."

"The crystals merely enhance our powers. The true strength comes from within. *That* is the knowledge we have lost." He paused, and fixed Rael with a searching gaze. "Now, there is something else you will need to consider, Questor General—and it is a revolutionary thought."

"And that is?"

"My six hundred workers."

"What about them?"

"They will age at twenty times the normal rate. Many of them would not see out the year."

"I will find you more."

Anu shook his head. "You do not understand, Rael. The timing is vital. Six months. Not a day more. I cannot achieve this if my workforce is aging and dying around me. Every day that passes, within the Dance, they will become more skillful, increasing the speed of the project. This too has been used in my calculations. As has the slowing of the Dance every five of *your* days to allow three months' supplies to be brought through to us."

Realization struck Rael. "You think to use crystals on Vagars? By Heavens, man, the Council will never allow it."

"Then don't tell them."

"I have no choice."

"It is a military decision, Rael. And that means it is yours to make alone."

"The pyramid is not a weapon, nor are we under attack."

"I do not lie, Rael. It is a military decision. As to the Vagars, they will not know they are crystal-fed. All they will be told is that we are using great magic. The men I hire will be told a part of the truth—that twenty years will pass in the Valley of the Stone Lion, while only two seasons will touch the world beyond. I will also promise them that, because of the magic, they will not age. And each man will receive a wage totalling thirty years of service. Each of them will be rich when he returns."

"You are asking for a lot of trust," said Rael. "Both from me—and from the men who will toil for twenty years."

"Much could go wrong," admitted the old man. "But I must not fail, my friend. You have no idea how important this is."

"I am sure you will tell me in your own good time, my friend," said Rael, rising to leave. "By the way, Mirani sends her love."

Anu relaxed and smiled. "She is a good woman—too good for you, I fear."

"Who could disagree," replied Rael, returning the smile. "She will not return to the Council. She spends her time now crafting pots and painting them."

"There will still be potters when we are a fading memory," said Anu.

Chapter Nine

And he was called Old One Young, for he was
born ancient and grew younger with the seasons.
His wisdom was very great, for the hand of the All
Father rested upon his shoulder. He knew the num-
bers of the stars, and the circle of the world. No se-
cret could be hidden from Old One Young. Not a
secret of the past, nor a secret of the soon to be.
One day he began to weep, and the tears from his
eyes made a terrible rain that flooded the land. The
other gods came to him and asked him the reason
for his tears. But he would not tell them.

From the *Noon Song of the Anajo*

The following morning Anu, with the aid of his favorite acolyte Shevan, made his slow way up three
flights of stairs to the tower rooms. High arched windows had been set into the four walls, and Anu moved
to the eastern window. Sunlight was glittering on the estuary of the Luan River, and from here, on the opposite
coast, he could see the marble towers of Pagaru.

"Do you regret your decision, sir?" Shevan asked him.

"I regret many things," said Anu, his gaze scanning
the city on the opposite shore. "Built too fast," he said
softly.

"What was too fast, sir?" asked Shevan.

"Pagaru was the foothold city, the fortress. When we first came here six hundred years ago the tribes were all at war and we needed to build fast, before they perceived the threat we posed. The walls were in place within two weeks. Too fast. They are not as strong as they might be, nor as aesthetically pleasing. A hundred years later we built Egaru. Far stronger. The others followed, strung out like pearls along the shoreline. Boria was my favorite city for a long time. Many artists and poets lived there, gentle men. Aye, and philosophers. I spent many a happy evening sitting upon the white beach debating the meaning of life. Have you been to Boria?"

"Of course, sir. I was trained there."

"Ah yes. I had forgotten. Did you know it was the last city built with the Music?"

"Yes, sir. You have told me. Many times."

"I have never visited Pejkan and Caval. I am told they are ugly and squalid."

"They are merchant cities, sir, and few Avatars live there. But, yes, they are not attractive."

Moving to the western window Anu squinted against the setting sun, which turned the sea to blood. "That is where the future lies, Shevan," he said. "The unknown hinterlands of the western continent. We charted the coastlines, but never ventured far inland. It was a mistake, I fear." He sighed. "We have made so many mistakes."

Shevan waited until the old man had moved to the southern window. Here he fell silent, his grey eyes spanning a distance no rule could measure. "It could have been so beautiful. No diseases, no hunger, no death."

"We have conquered these things, sir," Shevan pointed out.

"Yes, we have. We five hundred. Much of the world

shivers under a blanket of ice, thousands starve, millions die prematurely. But we five hundred hold the keys to immortality's gates. And we guard our knowledge so well."

"We have no choice," said Shevan. "The barbarians are not ready for such knowledge."

The old man chuckled and sat down in a wide leather chair. "Not ready? Indeed they are not. But then we make sure they are not. We have made no effort to prepare them for the journey. Quite the reverse. We encourage them to believe in our divine right to eternity."

"Is that not also a truth?" asked Shevan. "Are we not divinely chosen?"

"Perhaps," agreed Anu. "As perhaps the race before us was chosen. I do not know. What is certain is that I am the oldest living man on this world. Next year will be my two thousandth. What do you think of that?"

"I thank the Source for it, sir."

Anu shook his head. "Sometimes I don't know whether to thank the Source or curse it." Leaning forward he laid the crystals on a narrow desk, where they glittered in the fading light. "What do you see?" he asked the slim younger man.

Shevan moved to a chair opposite the desk and sat down, his blue eyes staring hard at the white, blue and green crystals. "I see that the blue is down to less than half-power, but that the white and green are almost fully charged," he said. "What should I be seeing, sir?"

"Lost souls and the mathematics of eternity," said Anu, sadly.

"I do not understand, sir," said Shevan. "What has mathematics to do with souls?"

"The universe is based on mathematics," answered the old man. "Perfection in apparent chaos. But this is no time for lessons, Shevan. Leave me, for I must become young again."

• • •

Viruk had no doubts concerning the holiness of Questor Anu. The One God had spoken to the man, warning him of the terrors to come. He had preached the word at the Temple in Parapolis. The seventeen-year-old Viruk had watched him being jeered and mocked. When Questor Anu concluded his address and walked back down the temple steps Viruk had run to intercept him.

"How did he speak to you?" asked Viruk. Anu had stopped and turned to scrutinize the young man.

"Through mathematics," he said. Viruk had been disappointed, for he too had heard the voice of the Source, and he knew it to be soft and sibilant.

"I don't understand," he said.

"Walk with me," said Anu, and together they had strolled through the deer park. Anu had explained that ancient records spoke of a great disaster, during which the stars would move in the sky and the sun rise in the west. "It is a cycle," said Anu. "And it will happen again very soon. Some time during the summer. The mathematical formula has taken me two centuries, but I now believe I have calculated the time of the event down to within a few weeks."

"If the world is going to topple, then how can you survive?" asked Viruk.

"I believe our colony in the far north will escape the worst of the cataclysm. I hope to lead a thousand of our brethren to the sanctuary of the Luan River."

"God speaks to me also," the young Viruk told him.

"Then ask him what your course should be."

"He doesn't *listen* to me," said Viruk. "He merely *tells* me to do things. I know nothing of the northern colony. What is there?"

"Hostile savages. But think carefully before committing yourself. The way will be hard, young man. And, I fear, violent and full of many dangers. We will face attack from tribes, and peril from ferocious animals."

"I will come," said Viruk instantly.

He had been one of the 200 and, as Anu had predicted, the journey was hazardous. Viruk had enjoyed it immensely. Three times they had been attacked, and on each occasion Viruk had killed many, watching their bodies writhe. He had been disappointed when the attacks ceased. Word moved among the tribes to let the Avatars pass, for they were fearsome warriors and their weapons were terrifying.

They had reached the first of the five cities on the fourteenth day of summer.

Then the world fell, and Questor Anu became the Holy One.

Two prophecies had come true. Questor Anu had predicted the cataclysm, and Viruk learned that the Source was true to his word. For his inner voice had told him that killing would prove the ultimate pleasure. *Kill for me*, it said, *and know joy*.

During the past seventy years Viruk had known enormous joy. He felt bonded to Questor Anu, for they were both committed to the work of the Supreme Being.

Viruk felt at peace as he rode from the village of Pacepta. Ignoring the villagers who bowed low as he passed, he cantered the horse through the gates and headed northeast, towards the border of the Mud People. He hoped to discover more raiders, to deliver more souls into the flaming maw of the Source.

He knew no fear as he rode. He felt immortal. Invincible.

It is good to be holy, he thought.

Sofarita had come to believe herself a good judge of human nature. She had observed the curious posturing of the village men during courtships, and the occasional violent displays that followed heavy drinking in the village hall. She had witnessed outpourings of grief, and moments of great joy. She thought she understood how men's minds worked.

Now she knew differently.

She had run from the house to where her father and mother were waiting in the small home of her Aunt Kiaru. The whole family was sitting in the main dining area as she entered. Kiaru, as always, was beside the hearth, making yet another rug. Her husband, a short, slender man, round-shouldered and worn out by years of work, was standing by the window, leaning on the ledge. Bekar and her mother were sitting at the table. Three small children were playing on the floor.

"He healed me!" said Sofarita, happily. "He said I had a cancer and would die, and he held a crystal to my breast and he healed me. I am going to live." The sheer joy of knowing she would live radiated from her, and in the blindness of its glow she failed to see the stiffness leach into the faces of her family.

No one spoke for a moment. Then Bekar glanced up. "You should be in your home," he said coldly. "Not running through the village trumpeting your shame."

Sofarita stood very still. "Shame?" she enquired. "What shame? I did what you told me."

"A decent woman would have crept away to hide," he said, not looking at her. "Not . . . not danced through the streets like a whore!"

A sense of unreality settled on her, as if she was walking through a dream. She could make no sense of the reaction. Instinctively she ran his words through her mind, seeking understanding. Then she realized. He had called her a whore. A cold anger settled on Sofarita. Bekar had always been a hard man, but until now he had been a fair one. "A whore, am I?" she said, her voice trembling. "You come to my home. You beg me to rut with him. You plead about the safety of the village. And when I reluctantly agree, and do this vile thing, you call me a whore? Well, what does that make you, father? The whoremaster. The pimp! The procurer!"

With a savage roar he surged to his feet. Sofarita stood her ground and his fist cracked into her cheekbone, hurling her back into the wall. She hit hard, and struggled to regain her balance. But dizziness swamped her and she slid to the floor, unconscious.

When she opened her eyes the men had gone. She was lying on Aunt Kiaru's bed. Her head throbbed with pain. "There, there, child," said Kiaru, her fat face, normally so jolly, looking drawn and worried. She was dabbing Sofarita's face with a wet cloth. "There, there!" she cooed.

Sofarita groaned as she sat up. Instantly her mother rose from a nearby chair and moved to her side. "How are you feeling, Tia?" she asked. "Is there much pain?"

Sofarita shook her head. Who could describe the pain she was feeling inside? Bekar was a cold man sometimes, but he had never before struck her, or any of his children. Swinging her legs over the side of the bed Sofarita tried to stand. Giddiness made her stumble, and she sat down swiftly.

"It'll pass," said Kiaru soothingly. "All this anger will pass and then your father will forgive you."

"He will forgive me?" said Sofarita, the tone hard-edged. Kiaru did not seem to notice.

"Of course he will, dear, of course he will. Everything will be all right."

Sofarita turned to her mother. "He made me do it," she said. "How could he insult me so?"

"You weren't expected to enjoy it, Tia. That's what hurt him."

Sofarita looked into her mother's careworn face,

seeking some secret sign that would say: I don't mean it the way it sounded, but I have to say it. There was none.

Sofarita struggled to her feet once more. The giddiness had passed and she moved slowly to the bedside chest, upon which was a small oval mirror. Lifting it she looked at her face. Her right eye was bruised and swollen shut and her cheek showed two purple bruises where Bekar's knuckles had struck her. Replacing the mirror she walked into the main room and then out onto the street, crossing it swiftly to the small home she had made with Veris.

From a chest at the back of the bedroom she took her savings. Twenty-six silver pieces in a canvas pouch. She hung it around her neck, hiding it in the folds of her white dress. From a cupboard she took a small shoulder sack and stuffed her second dress into it. Veris had owned a black pony and it was stabled behind the house. Sofarita filled a sack with what food she had to hand: a fresh-baked loaf, a chunk of honey-roasted ham and a wedge of cheese wrapped in muslin. Then she walked to the stable and saddled the pony. It took her some time to ease the bridle bit into place, but at last she managed it.

It was a 30-mile ride to the city of Egaru. She would not make it before dark.

Moving back to the kitchen she found Veris' hunting knife, a long curved blade set in a hilt of deer horn. Belting the sheath at her waist she threw a black hooded cloak around her shoulders and returned to the pony.

Veris had taught her to ride and she mounted smoothly. Then she rode along the side of the house and out into the main street, heading for the gate.

Bekar came running from his new house, shouting for her to wait. Sofarita swung the pony.

"Where do you think you are going?" he thundered. A crowd began to gather.

"I am going where no decent woman is ever forced to rut with strangers," she said, her voice loud, almost strident. "I am going to a place where fathers do not give their daughters to every swordsman who happens by."

His fat face reddened. "Get off that pony now," he ordered her, "or I will drag you from it."

Without haste she drew the hunting knife from its sheath. "Come near me again and I will kill you," she told him. He stood, blinking in the fading light, the eyes of the villagers upon him. She felt no pity for him.

He stood very still, his huge arms falling to his side. All the strength seemed to flow from him. "I am sorry, Tia," he said at last, his voice breaking.

"So am I," she told him.

"Stay with us. I will make it up to you. We will be friends again."

"We will never be friends," she said coldly. "For I never intend to see you again."

With that she rode the pony out through the gate, heading west toward the setting sun.

Viruk followed the line of the Luan River for several hours, hoping for sign of more raiders. But there was none, and he was growing bored. Across the wide river he could see Mud People settlements, huts of mud-caked wattle, and poorly constructed paddocks. The tribes bred like lice and if Viruk had his way he would bring an army down on them, wiping them from the face of the earth. There were just too many people now in this land and a cull was needed.

The Questors spoke of the migration of the tribes, caused by the ice and floods that now covered more than half the planet. To survive, the northern tribes moved south to this fertile land, while the tribes far to the south were pushing north.

Soon there would not be enough corn to feed them all.

Viruk's pony was tiring as dusk approached and he stumbled as Viruk forced him up the last hill before the old stone bridge. The river narrowed here. Viruk dismounted and gazed down at the crossing. This had been his last hope of making a good kill. But there were no soldiers to be seen.

An old man came into sight, leading two oxen pulling a heavily laden wagon. A small golden-haired child sat upon the wagon. Viruk heard the rumbling of the wheels on the stone of the bridge. There would be little satisfaction in killing the man, he knew, but then a little satisfaction was better than nothing. Mounting his weary pony Viruk rode down the hillside.

The old man did not see him at first, and when he did he waved and gave a cheerful smile.

"Good evening, lord," he said.

"Good evening to you," said Viruk. The old man was dressed in a long robe of dark blue velvet, and his white hair was drawn back from his brow by a circlet of gold studded with amber. "Be so kind as to tell me," said Viruk pleasantly, "why you are encroaching upon Avatar land."

"Not encroaching, lord, trading," said the man. "I have ten barrels of fine wine for the Questor General, and a note, with his personal seal, giving me authority to bring them to his home. I must say I am pleased to see you for I feared making this journey. These are troubled times."

Viruk dismounted. "Show me this paper," he said. The man drew a parchment from within his robe. Viruk scanned it. It was irritatingly correct in every detail.

"Your pony is very tired, lord," pointed out the old

man. "Perhaps you would like to travel for a while upon the wagon? The seats are not uncomfortable, and I have a flagon of wine beneath it. I am sure you will find it to your taste."

Viruk gazed at the man and pictured his smile freezing as a dagger opened his scrawny throat. He toyed with the idea of butchering the trader, but held back. If he killed him then he would be forced to drive the wagon all the way to the city, sitting behind the large arses of two oxen. Even as the thought occurred to him one of the beasts defecated. The stench was appalling.

"Move on," said Viruk. Taking the reins the old man led the team along the road. Viruk tied his pony's reins to the rear of the wagon and climbed aboard. The golden-haired child, a girl of around seven, smiled at him as he sat alongside her.

"Your hair is turning blue," she said.

"Annoy me, child, and I shall tear off your leg and beat you to death with the wet end."

She laughed happily. "That's a terrible thing to say," she chided him. Viruk leaned down and found the flagon of wine.

"There are some copper goblets in the box beside the seat," the old man called back.

Viruk found one, broke the wax seal on the clay flagon and poured the wine. He was expecting little, and was pleasantly surprised to find the taste rich and mellow. His mood lightened.

"Why is your hair blue?" asked the child.

"Because I am a god," he said.

"Are you? Truly?"

"Truly."

"Can you do miracles? Can you make a blind man see? Can you bring the dead to life? Do you know why the ox doesn't need to clean its bottom?"

Viruk drained his wine and refilled the goblet. The

old man scrambled up to the driving seat beside the child. "Have to lead them over the bridge, lord," he said. "They don't like the sound of the water."

"He says he's a god, father," said the child. "But he doesn't know about oxes' bottoms."

"Hush, child, the lord does not need to hear you prattling."

"I give up," said Viruk. "Why does an ox not need to clean its bottom?"

"It has two bowels," said the girl. "One inner, one outer. The inner one pushes out and . . . and . . ."

"Deposits," said the old man.

"Yes, that's it. Deposits the droppings. Then it draws back inside. So there is no mess."

"A fact I shall carry with me to eternity," said Viruk.

"So," continued the child, "can you bring the dead to life?"

"My talent is rather the reverse," he said, sipping the wine, and enjoying the taste upon his tongue.

"What is reverse, father?" she asked.

"The lord is a warrior, Shori. He protects us from bad people," said the old man. "And it is best you stay quiet now. Climb into the back of the wagon and play with your toys." The child scrambled over the back of the seat.

"Aren't you a little old to be siring children?" Viruk asked the old man.

"It would certainly appear so, lord," replied the man.

"Where have you travelled from?" asked Viruk.

"Ren-el-gan, lord. My vineyards are close by."

"I have heard of the place. Which tribe are you?"

"Banis-baya, lord. There are not many of us left now. Perhaps fifty. But we are no longer persecuted. The Avatar Lords have forgiven us, I think."

Tribal history had never been of interest to Viruk. The sub-humans were always warring on one another.

And the wine was making him drowsy. Climbing to the rear of the wagon he pushed aside the child's dolls and lay down.

The sun was setting and, as he fell asleep, he felt the girl's warm body snuggle down alongside him.

Children liked him. They always had. Which was strange, considering he loathed them.

Chapter Ten

With the sun setting, Boru angled the wagon down a shallow slope and hauled the team to a halt beside a narrow stream which flowed into the Luan River. Kicking the brake into position he climbed into the back of the wagon and gazed down on the sleeping Avatar.

How easy it would be to cut your throat, he thought.

His daughter Shori was cuddled in close to the Avatar and she was sleeping deeply, her right thumb in her mouth. Had the Avatar been alone Boru would have killed him, but he was frightened that Shori would wake, and then the blood nightmares would begin again. Taking a blanket he covered Shori. This meant covering also the hated man who slept beside her. Boru swallowed back his hatred and moved past the sleepers, gathering two feed sacks of grain. These he took to the oxen and fed them.

Then he built a small fire within a group of boulders and sat watching the sunset.

"Aren't you a little old to be siring children?"

Boru stroked his white beard, and felt the gnawing ache of arthritis in his bones. Shori was seven. He would not live to see her grow into a young woman, would not be there as she tossed the grain and swung the veil. Bitterness touched him then, but he pushed it aside.

He had been twenty-three years of age when the Avatars captured him, following the revolt. He and 200 others had been taken in chains to Pagaru, the second city. There they were put on trial. Boru had never been inside a city, and the scale of the buildings had, for a brief moment, swamped his fears for his life. There were wide paved streets and columned temples. There was a marketplace, with shops and taverns, and at the center an intricately fashioned fountain, with a jet of water rising thirty feet. Boru was from the desert where water was revered, and he gazed from the prison cart with reverence at the gushing fountain.

The courtroom was also impressive, and two Avatar magistrates sat high upon a carved dais looking down at the prisoners, who were brought in ten at a time. Boru found himself standing next to Fyal the Baker's son. The two had been friends since childhood and they exchanged glances. Boru whispered, "What will they do?" Fyal shrugged.

One of the magistrates, a slender man with shoulder-length blue hair, leaned forward. He was wearing a gown of shimmering crimson and upon his head was a skull-cap of silver inset with runes.

"You men," he said, his voice somber, "have been accused of crimes against the empire, to wit"—he glanced down at a scroll on the desk before him—"taking part in an unlawful gathering, being in possession of swords and other weapons, and of making an assault on a government building in the village of Asep." His pale eyes fastened on the men in chains. "One of you will speak in answer to these charges. You!" His skinny finger pointed at Boru. "You will speak for yourself and your comrades."

"What would you have me say?" asked Boru. "We do not accept your laws. You sent armed men into our ancestral lands and declared them under your control. We resisted. We continue to resist. We will always resist. How could we be men otherwise?"

"This then is your defense?" asked the second magistrate, a bald man with a forked blue beard. "You claim your rights are superior to those of the Avatar? We have brought you learning and law. We have supplied the means by which you can avoid starvation. And you repay these gifts with acts of savagery and attempted murder."

"Your gifts were unwanted," said Boru. "You imposed them upon us. And we slew no one. Nor was that ever our intention. The Avatar in our village was captured and held—despite him killing three of our comrades. The Banis-baya have always been a people of the land. We have never been warriors or killers. We are free men."

"You are not *free*, little man," said the second magistrate. "You are servants of the Avatar. And you are disobedient servants. I found your defense lacking and non-persuasive. Your friends will lose their lives. You, as is our custom, as the speaker for the condemned, will not die. The sentence upon you is thirty years. Take them away."

The men were led from the courtroom and into a long corridor. An Avatar guard took Boru by the arm and led him through a side door into a long narrow room with bench seats. "Sit down," said the guard. "You will wait here until your name is called. Then I will come for you."

Stunned by the sentence, Boru had not resisted. As the day wore on another ten men were brought in to sit with him. Boru knew each of them well, but no one spoke. The scale of the calamity which had befallen the Banis-baya was too great for conversation.

By mid-afternoon three of the men had been led away. As dusk settled they came for Boru.

He followed the two guards to a circular room. There were three Avatars there, each wearing blue silk robes. At the center of the room was a stone sarcophagus filled with green crystals which shimmered in the lantern light.

"Remove his chains," ordered one of the blue-clad lords.

As they fell away Boru straightened. He was young, and tall and strong, his hair the color of ripening corn. "Climb into the sarcophagus," ordered an Avatar.

"What is happening here?" he asked them.

"Do as you are told. This will not last long and you will be free to go within the hour."

"Free? But I was sentenced to thirty years."

Two of the guards took him by the arms and led him towards the glittering crystals. Shrugging them off, he climbed the sarcophagus and sat upon it. "Lie down upon the crystals," came the order. Boru did so. The men moved back. He could feel the gems digging into his skin. "Close your eyes," they ordered him. This order he also accepted. Bright lights played painfully upon his eyelids and he felt sickness rise in his belly. Then he passed out.

Some time later—it could have been an hour or a day—he awoke. The two Avatar guards hauled him from the sarcophagus and led him, without chains, back into the corridor, along past the courtroom and out into the light of day. "Go back to your home," they told him.

Confused, he had wandered down the courtroom steps into the fountain square. By the time he reached it he was tired, which was surprising, since it was only a short walk. He sat down on the marble wall of the fountain and felt the cool spray from the column of water. As he sat he leaned forward, his elbows resting on his knees.

Then the shock hit him. His arms were skinny, the flesh gone, the skin wrinkled and dry.

A young woman approached him. "Are you all right, old one?" she asked, laying a hand on his bony shoulder.

"I am a young man," he said, his voice grating.

She glanced nervously back at the court building. "I am sorry," she said. Then she hurried away.

Thirty years they had taken.

The twenty-five-year-old Boru sat by the stream, holding out his skinny fingers to the blaze, and thought of the Avatar sleeping in his wagon.

"I will see you fall," he promised himself. "All of you."

Viruk awoke with a start. He had not intended to sleep so deeply. He rolled to his side. Someone had covered him with a blanket, which was thoughtful, for the night air was chill. Then he remembered the old man. It was so good to find sub-humans who understood respect. Viruk sat up. As he did the golden-haired child stirred beside him. But she did not wake. Viruk climbed over the side of the wagon and saw the old man sitting by a small fire.

The stars were bright in the sky and the moon shone full. "I trust you slept well, lord," said the man.

"I did indeed. Where are we?"

"I should reach Egaru around noon tomorrow, lord. But if you ride early you will be there soon after sun-up. I have fed the pony with grain, but it is still tired. It will not, I fear, carry you fast."

"What is your name, tribesman?"

"Boru, lord."

"You have been kind to me. I appreciate such courtesies."

"It was nothing, lord. It was a pleasure to have been of service."

"I am sure that it was," agreed Viruk. He clapped the old man on the shoulder. "I like you, Boru. I shall give you a gift." Viruk drew his green crystal from its pouch and touched it to Boru's chest. The old man stiffened in fear. "There is no harm being done to you," said Viruk. Boru felt the arthritic ache in his back and arms subside. "There," said Viruk, at last. "You are ten years younger. Use the years wisely," he said, with a smile.

Boru stood and bowed. "My thanks to you, lord," he said.

"It was nothing." He stared closely into Boru's face. "There is some yellow in your beard now. And your hair is thicker. Perhaps you gained a little more than ten years. I am not greatly adept at using these crystals on sub-humans. Still . . . enjoy!"

"I will, lord. I cannot thank you enough."

"That's true," said Viruk, with a broad smile. "And now I must be on my way."

Moving to the pony Viruk vaulted into the saddle. Without a backward glance he rode towards the west.

It was pleasant to be a god.

Boru had been quite right. The pony was still tired. Anxious to be back in Egaru Viruk used crystal energy upon it. The little horse was immediately invigorated and Viruk kicked it into a gallop. The beast died within half a mile of the city gates. As it collapsed under him Viruk jumped clear, landing lightly on his feet. It was an oddity of the crystals that they could not bring genuine strength to four-footed animals. They acted upon them like short-lived stimulants. Viruk was annoyed that the pony had not lasted a little longer.

Once back at his home one of his servants informed him that the Questor General was eager to see him.

Viruk bathed and changed his clothes, then rode to Rael's palace.

The Questor General was in the high study, poring over maps and scrolls when Viruk entered. Rael wasted no time in pleasantries. "Judon of the Patiakes has called a gathering at Ren-el-gan," he said. "He seeks to bind the tribes under his leadership and storm the cities. Change his mind."

"My pleasure, sir," said Viruk.

Rael pushed back the maps and stood. "I understand you found the raiders and dispatched them. That was good. What was not good was sending that message to Ammon. One can only hope the messenger was sensible enough to disobey you."

Viruk shrugged. "What does it matter? We'll have to fight them eventually."

"Ideally it will be when Talaban returns with the recharged chests."

"Questor Ro succeeded? There's a surprise. A nice one, admittedly."

"It is double-edged," said Rael. "They have four chests charged, one lost and one still empty. Worse news is that a volcanic upheaval destroyed the site, and unless we find another we will be powerless within a few more years."

"Much can happen in a few years," said Viruk. "But tell me, sir, how you wish Judon's mind changed?"

"In whatever way suits you," snapped the General.

"Consider it done."

"I do," said Rael. "You will need a fast horse and there is none faster than my own Pakal. Treat him well. I want him back."

"Yes, sir."

"Good. Now make your report about the raiders— and leave nothing out."

Viruk did so, down to ordering the death of the headman. When he had concluded, Rael walked around the desk and sat back upon it, directly in front of the officer.

"I have had a complaint that you raped a village woman."

"I'd hardly call it rape. I was tired and somewhat tense so I sent for one of the village whores. The new headman, Bekar, had her brought to me."

"The race laws are specific, Viruk," said Rael. "There is to be no cohabiting with lesser orders. You know this perfectly well."

"I *know* she was soft and sweet and yielding. But it is not as if I *married* her. I merely rode her for a while."

"The Council will call for your censure and—if she falls pregnant—her death."

"I have been censured before. It is not a problem."

Rael took a deep breath. "It is not a problem because I protect you. But does it not concern you that every time you yield to your desires a Vagar woman risks death for them?"

"Why should it concern me? Vagars die all the time."

Rael shook his head. "There is no point to this discussion. Go and deal with Judon. And make sure there are live witnesses."

Touchstone's recovery was not swift. Talaban's crystal had healed his broken ribs, and he had offered to do the same for the wounds caused by the talons of the kral, but Touchstone refused. The scars were those of battle, and thus to be treasured, as indeed was the pain of the wounds, for this pain showed that his enemy had been powerful, and he had stood against it. Admittedly he had not killed the beast, but he had faced it. Suryet would be proud of him.

"How are you feeling?" Talaban asked him on the morning of the fourth day.

"Good. Strong," lied Touchstone. He had a rising fever and one of the scars was weeping pus.

"Show me the wounds."

"They heal quick."

"Show me anyway." With a grunt of pain Touchstone lifted his shirt. "I shall remove the infection," said Talaban. "But do not be concerned. The scars will remain." Lightly he touched the crystal to the angry wound. Touchstone felt the inflammation die away.

"Strong magic," said Touchstone.

"Not magic at all, my friend. A long time ago we discovered a link between such crystals and health. We merely refined it and found a way to increase the power through the strength of our minds."

"Long ago," said Touchstone. "Always long ago."

Tucking his shirt into his leggings he moved across the small cabin and poured himself a cup of water. "The meaning of your words is lost on me," said Talaban.

"Everything long ago. Magic tower. Long ago. Ships of wonder. Long ago. What you achieve *now*?"

Talaban looked thoughtful and did not speak for a moment. "Now we survive," he said finally. "The last of our great men of learning chose to age and die. There is no one now who understands the mysteries of the past. I don't know why."

"You not survive, captain. Your day almost gone. Sunset. You come with me. West. Find new home. Teach my people magic stones."

Talaban rose. "You rest today," he said. Then he left.

After he had gone Touchstone ate a little dried meat then left the cabin and climbed to the middle deck. Here he leaned upon the rail, watching the dolphins racing alongside the ship. He had always enjoyed the antics of the Osnu, the people of the sea. Sometimes back home when he had swum out into the warm waters of the bay they had surfaced alongside him, leaping and diving, always friendly.

"Strange creatures," said the Vagar sergeant Methras, moving alongside him. Touchstone glanced up at the tall balding soldier. He liked Methras, sensing in the man a striking loneliness that matched his own.

"Not strange," he said. "Magic are the Osnu. Great healers."

"A fish that heals? Hard to believe."

"These eyes see it," said Touchstone. "Child born, grow, no talk. Sit. Stare. Shaman he call the Osnu. They came."

"Wait a moment, Touchstone," said Methras with a smile. "I understood the part about the child. But how did the Shaman call the dolphins?"

"He stood on clifftop. Make chant. Light singing smoke fire. Dusk they came. Twenty Osnu. All the way to shallow water. Shaman he carry child out to them. Then Osnu spoke. High sing-song. No words. Shaman take child. Put him in water, hands clasped on Osnu fin. Osnu swim around bay, pull laughing child with him. That day child spoke. Osnu magic."

"And this you saw? Truly?"

"These eyes saw. Osnu magic."

"Good magic," agreed Methras, and together they leaned on the rail and watched the dolphins in silence. After a while Methras straightened. "One day I would like to swim with them," he said sadly.

"They heal you too," Touchstone told him.

"I don't need healing."

Touchstone shook his head. Reaching out he placed his hand on the soldier's chest. "Empty place here. Need filling," said Touchstone.

"You see too much, my friend," said Methras. Then he turned and was gone.

A great black and white shape crested the waves. The dolphins scattered. The killer whale dived after them.

"You catch nothing today," whispered Touchstone.

The sun dipped low on the western horizon, sinking fast into a blood-red sea. As darkness fell the ship's lights came on. Touchstone cursed. The globes were unnatural. They disturbed his spirit.

Closing his eyes against the brightness he sang the song of the Osnu, his voice rich and deep.

Chapter Eleven

There was little about Ren-el-gan to suggest its importance to the tribes. A flat area of sandy desert overshadowed by high mountains, its only man-made structure was a well wall constructed of sandstone blocks. A bucket stood on the wall, a slender rope tied to its handle and fastened to the lych pole above the well. There were no statues, no monuments, no inscriptions carved into the rock faces close by.

Yet it was here that the tribes came for the Gathering. Here, to the Well of Life, from which the Source of All Creation had produced the water that softened the clay, and molded the body of the first man.

Ren-el-gan was a holy place. Blood was not spilt here.

To the east lay the Dream Desert, vast and largely uninhabitable. In the heat of summer the desert floor would leach all moisture from a man in less than a day, and kill a horse within two. And every year it grew. To the south lay the once-verdant river valleys of the Pati-akes, the Goat People. To the north, across the mountains, the lands of the Erek-jhip-zhonad and a score of lesser tribes stretched for almost 700 miles.

But it was to the west that the eyes of the tribes were turned. The rich cities of the seashore filled their minds, liberating their imaginations. As the desert slowly sucked the life out of their lands the tribes looked to the rich grasslands around the cities as the answer to their growing problems. If the cities were under their sway all the riches of the Avatars would be theirs. No longer would they worry about the spring rain and the vanishing grass. Instead they would own fine houses and perhaps, like the Avatars, learn the secret of perpetual youth.

A half-mile from the Well of Life, under a silken canopy, Judon of the Patiakes sat on a huge, ornate throne, his vast bulk filling the seat, his fat silk-clad body squeezing the softness from the cushions beneath and behind him. On either side of the throne stood his two bodyguards, large men with cold eyes. Before him, on rugs set upon the ground, sat the leaders of eighteen major tribes.

"Why should we pay taxes to the Avatar?" Judon asked them. "Who granted them ownership of our lands? Why do we allow them to dominate us, to keep us impoverished while they grow rich upon our sweated labors? The time has come, my friends—my brothers!— to rid ourselves of these leeches."

"And how do we accomplish this?" asked an elderly leader. "Their weapons would tear an army asunder. I myself took part in last year's revolt. Eight thousand died upon that battlefield."

"They did not die in vain," said Judon. "The weapons you speak of are almost exhausted. I know that there are less than fifty zhi-bows left among the Avatars."

He had their full attention now. "The tribes represented here can muster forty thousand warriors within the month. The cities could be ours before the first cool wind of autumn. Think of that, my brothers."

"Aye, we can think of it," said another leader. "But I have two questions: firstly, how do you know the strength of their weapons, and secondly where are the Erek-jhip-zhonad? They should be here."

Judon smiled. "I know because I know. I have friends in the five cities. Good friends who are tired of Avatar tyranny. As for the Mud People . . ." he spread his fat arms wide. "Perhaps they remain in fear of the Blue-hair. I do not speak for them. When we have taken the cities they can come to us on bended knee and beg for scraps from our table."

"They have twenty thousand warriors," said the first speaker. "I do not think they will need to beg. And I, for one, will not commit my soldiers to battle the Avatars without the People of the Stars."

Judon masked his irritation. The speaker was Rzak Xhen, leader of the Hantu tribe, whose lands bordered those of the Erek-jhip-zhonad. If he were won over he would bring more than 5,000 fighting men with him.

"My dear Rzak, your caution is commendable. I would also prefer the Mud People to ride with us. But, when we conquer, there will be greater riches without them. Now let us break off and eat. The sun is high and hot, and we can meet again this evening."

Judon's huge arms pressed down on the side supports of the black throne. With a monumental effort he heaved his bulk upright and moved back into his tent. Here he lay down on padded cushions.

A slender figure stepped forward from the rear of the tent. His face was youthful, his head covered with the white linen burnous of the Hizhak tribe. He sat down beside Judon. "Rzak Xhen is a mouthpiece for the Mud People," he said. "But I think I know how to sway him."

"We should cut his treacherous throat," advised Judon.

The young man smiled. "Invite him here this evening, before the meeting. I will bring him to our cause."

"How will you achieve this miracle?" asked Judon.

"As I did with you, my lord."

"That is too much!" objected the king.

"How badly do you want his help?"

Judon filled a goblet with wine and drained it. "Do it, then—but once we have won I'll want his head."

Rzak Xhen was a serious man. Left to his own devices he would have worked tirelessly for his Hantu people, increasing their wealth and their prestige, quietly building their strength. Not a man of war, yet he was a fine soldier and strategist, and he was held in great respect by the leaders of minor tribes surrounding Hantu lands. His warriors did not encroach on their territories, and where lesser leaders used sword and spear to dominate their neighbors Rzak Xhen used trade. He had little regard for Judon of the Patiakes. His line was predatory, and inclined to war.

Rzak sat in his tent awaiting the invitation he was sure would come. His eldest son, Hua, sat beside him.

"He will offer us riches," said Hua Xhen. Rzak shook his head.

"Land. He will promise to increase Hantu lands."

Hua smiled. "Better than gold, father. We could ask for the Griam Valley. That would give us a route to the sea, and better trade."

Again Rzak shook his head. "He will not offer what he himself possesses. He is too greedy to part with anything he already owns. No, he will offer us Avatar land—perhaps one of the five cities."

"What will you do?"

"I will offer to think on it. Then we will go home and prepare our soldiers. When we refuse him he will attack us first."

"Why refuse him, father?"

"Because he is a pig, with a pig's appetite. He will—ultimately—share nothing."

"And you believe Ammon will?"

The older man looked into his son's eyes. He smiled. "That is better," he said, a touch of pride in his voice. "Now you are *thinking*. Of course Ammon will not share. He will expect us to be his vassals. And we will be. Loyal and true. That way the Hantu will continue to grow strong. There is a significant difference between Ammon and Judon. Can you tell me what it is?"

"Both are kings, both seek glory," answered Hua. "I do not detect any great dissimilarity."

"Think on it, my son. The answer will come to you."

Rzak fell silent. Hua was a sensible lad. Not a great intellect, but he was, at least, capable of learning and, given time, he would make a capable leader of the Hantu. The difference between the two kings was obvious to Rzak. Both kings sought glory, but Judon wanted it for himself, whereas Ammon of the Erek-jhip-zhonad desired it for his people. Such men build civilizations. Warlords like Judon destroy them.

The invitation came at dusk, and Rzak struggled to his feet, his arthritic knees paining him. Slowly he walked across the desert floor to the silken tent of Judon. The Patiakes guards offered him no salute, but they stepped aside for him, opening the tent flap. Rzak stepped inside.

The fat king was lounging on padded cushions, a golden goblet full of wine in his chubby hand. A younger man was sitting cross-legged beside him. He was wearing a white burnous, and a white cotton robe. Judon gestured Rzak to join him. The elderly leader suppressed a groan as he sat.

"Welcome, my brother," said Judon. "You honor me with your presence."

The words were oily, as was the smile that accompanied them. "How can I be of service?" asked Rzak.

"You could offer me five thousand warriors," Judon told him. "The Avatars are finished. One great attack would bring them down. Think of the riches that would accrue to the conquerors."

"I have riches," said Rzak. "More than I could spend in what remains of my lifetime."

"Then think of the new lands which will be open to you. I am willing to open a tract of the Griam Valley, allowing you a route to the sea. Added to which you will control Pagaru, the first of the five."

Rzak sat back against the silk cushions and looked into Judon's deep-set eyes. For him to have offered the Griam Valley so easily made Rzak suspicious. He flicked a glance to the young man in the white burnous. He was annoyed, but was trying to mask his irritation. This confirmed Rzak's suspicions. The offer was too high, too soon. And that made it worthless. When at last Rzak spoke his voice was even and he managed a small smile. "You are very generous, Judon. I will think on what you have said."

"My offer is not yet done," said the king. "What is it that the Avatar possess which fills your heart with yearning?"

"Immortality," said Rzak at once.

"This I can also give you."

Rzak Xhen gave a cold smile. "It would be best not to mock me, Judon. I make a very good enemy."

"There is no mockery," said the king. Turning to the young man he spoke. "Show him!"

The youth rose smoothly and stepped across to where Rzak sat. Reaching into the pouch at his side he produced a cheap green crystal. As he leaned over the Hantu leader Rzak reached into his sleeve and drew a short dagger which he held to the young man's belly. "I do not like tricks," he said.

"No more do I," agreed the young man. Touching the crystal to Rzak's chest, he closed his eyes. Heat permeated Rzak's skin and the throbbing pain from his joints ceased. The young man stepped back.

"Your arthritis is gone," he said. "I have given you a taste of what is to come."

Rzak stretched out his arms. It was true. There was no pain, no stiffness.

"I told you I had many powerful friends," said Judon smugly.

Rzak Xhen seemed to ponder this. Then he spoke. "Why would an Avatar wish to see the fall of his own cities?" he asked.

"I am not an Avatar," said the young man, calmly.

"And yet you have mastered their magic?"

"I have. And it is not magic."

Rzak leaned forward and picked up the king's empty goblet, then he drained his own. In one sudden move he tossed both goblets towards the young man. Instinctively his hands swept out and he caught both goblets cleanly.

"You are an Avatar," said Rzak Xhen. "Why deny it?"

"You are wrong. My father was an Avatar. My mother was Vagar. They tried to run away together. But they were caught. My mother was returned to her home that day as an old woman, bent and crippled. My father was crystal-drawn—murdered."

"Not an unusual tale," said Rzak. "Save that you survived. I thought all offspring of such unions were dispatched."

"My brother was . . . as you say . . . dispatched. But we were twins. My mother told me that I had a fever the day before the soldiers came. I was in the house of a medicine woman. When the soldiers took her they took my brother with them. I survived. My mother raised me for four years—then old age and decrepitude took her. She was twenty-one."

"And because of three deaths you are willing to sacrifice five cities?"

"Yes," said the young man. "To see an end to tyranny."

Rzak masked the smile he felt. How short-sighted were the young. Did this hate-filled Vagar truly believe that by helping Judon to absolute power he would see an end to tyranny? What did it matter whose boot was upon your neck, Avatar or Patiakes? It was still a boot. "Show me the magic gem," he said, holding out his hand. The young man dropped it into his outstretched palm. Curling his hand into a fist he felt the sharpness of the crystal against his skin. But nothing else. "Where is the magic?" he asked.

"In here," said the young man, tapping his own temple. "Such crystals can be purchased in any marketplace. Once fed with power only those with Avatar blood can use them."

Judon struggled to his feet. From behind the cushions he lifted a silver mirror, which he tossed to Rzak. Rzak looked at his reflection. There were dark streaks in his beard. He chuckled. "Take another ten years away and you shall have my five thousand," he said.

Viruk sat by the roadside and examined the petals of a small white flower edged with blue. He didn't recognize it, but found its beauty exquisite. There were clusters of the plant on both sides of the road, and a heady scent filled the air. The gray horse tethered by the trees let out a whinny and stamped his foot. Viruk rose and stretched, then strolled across to the stallion. "Impatience is not to be encouraged," he said. "Not in men or horses. I don't much like sitting here either, but this is the road back to Patiakes land and some time or other the fat king will travel along it. Now let us have no more shows of petulance, or I shall prick out one of your eyes and tell the General you caught it on a thorn."

The horse tilted its head and stared at the smiling man. Then, stretching its neck, it nuzzled against his chest. "Stupid beast," said Viruk, reaching up and scratching its ears. "Is it possible that you like a man who threatens to mutilate you? I thought animals had a sixth sense for danger." The stallion's ears came up and he swung away, looking back towards the east. Viruk untied the tether and stepped into the saddle. "There now, the wait is nearly over," he said. "Then we can ride back and enjoy a fine rest."

Touching his heels to the white flanks he rode out through the flowers and sat waiting in the center of the road.

The chariot appeared over the crest of a hill, two riders flanking it, a third bringing up the rear. The fat king was sitting on a velvet-covered seat, his driver urging the two black horses on. They were breathing heavily. "See how lucky you are," Viruk told the stallion. "But for an accident of birth you too might have been pulling that mammoth around the desert. There's a fine prospect, eh?"

The horse flicked its ears back as the man spoke, but made no other movement. "I like you," said Viruk. "You're not much of a conversationalist, but you are a fine listener."

The two riders galloped their horses forward, dragging them to a stop just in front of Viruk. The Avatar lifted his leg over the pommel of his saddle and leaned his elbow on his knee. "Good afternoon, peasants," he said.

The lead rider, a wide-shouldered swordsman wearing a burnished helm of bronze, reddened, and laid his hand on his sword hilt. Viruk smiled at him, a bright engaging smile. "Much as I would like to shed some of your neanderthal blood I have been told to ensure there are witnesses to my conversation with your king. So you would be best advised to leave that pig-sticker in its scabbard."

"What do you want here, Avatar?" said the man, his voice deep, his eyes angry.

"From you, turd-breath? Nothing at all. I need to speak to the waddling pig you serve."

The bronze sword hissed from its sheath as the rider spurred his horse forward. Viruk's arm lifted, then snapped forward. A small throwing knife flashed through the air, slamming into the rider's throat and pitching him from the saddle. He hit the ground hard, struggled to rise, then slumped back. Viruk glanced at the second rider and smiled. "I don't know what the world is coming to," he said, his voice light and tinged with regret. "You try to be pleasant. You make it as clear as rainwater what your intentions are. And what do you find? Violence and unpleasantness. I do hope we do not find ourselves in a similar misunderstanding." The man glanced nervously back towards the chariot, awaiting orders. Judon of the Patiakes heaved himself to his feet. "How dare you accost me in this manner?" he bellowed.

Viruk steered the stallion forward until he was alongside the king. "The Questor General bade me come to you and convince you of the error of your ways. War is such an unpleasant business. You sub-humans dress up in your battle finery and we Avatars shoot you down like dogs. There is no sport in it. You understand? It is all so boring."

"I have no intention of declaring war," said Judon. "There has been a grave misunderstanding. The Avatars are my friends."

Viruk raised his hand, his expression one of mild distaste. "Please do not use the word friends. It suggests an equality that does not exist. You are servants. Your ingratitude is baffling." He shook his head. "What were you before we came among you? Little more than animals, grubbing around in the Luan mud. We taught you to build, to irrigate your lands. To store your surplus. We have given you laws. We have raised you like children and you repay us with petty wars and raids. It really is galling."

"As I said, there is no war," Judon told him. "What is your name?"

"I am Viruk."

"Well, Viruk, rest assured I shall be reporting this incident to the Questor General. I am not accustomed to watching my men murdered."

"Oh, I shall report it myself upon my return. The only question is, what course of action to take."

"Action?" queried Judon.

"You see, here is my problem: the Questor General says you are planning a war. You say you are not. Do I ride back to him and tell him he has made a mistake? I think not. Difficult, isn't it?"

"All men make mistakes," said Judon, forcing a smile. "I'm sure the General understands that. You can assure him of my goodwill towards your people."

Viruk was about to reply when he saw the king's glance flick to his left. Instinctively Viruk swayed in the saddle. The knife hurled by the rider behind him sliced the air and flew on to clatter to the ground. "Now that wasn't friendly," said Viruk, drawing his sword. The third rider drew his own blade and heeled his horse forward. Viruk ducked under a sweeping cut and slashed the flat of his blade to the man's temple, dislodging his bronze helm and hurling him from the saddle. The knife-thrower charged him, this time a sword in his hand. Viruk parried a thrust, leaned across his saddle, grabbing the man by his cloak and dragging him from his horse. The rider landed heavily but struggled to his feet. The flat of Viruk's saber sent him sprawling.

The fat king stood open-mouthed as his men fell. Viruk turned to him. "Do you believe in the Great God?" Viruk asked him conversationally.

Judon nodded.

"As do I," said the Avatar. "Give him my best regards when you meet him."

With that Viruk rode away. Judon stood watching him. At one hundred paces the Avatar turned. In his hand was a zhi-bow. Judon blinked, then jumped from the chariot and began to run.

The bolt struck him between the shoulderblades, lifting him from his feet. He landed face-first on the road, his clothes aflame around a huge hole in his back. Viruk rode back to where the warriors had regained their feet.

"You really are the clumsiest opponents," he said. Turning to the charioteer, a small man with thinning black hair, he spoke again. "I think the horses may enjoy the return journey now. I have rarely seen a man so fat."

"Yes, lord," said the charioteer nervously.

"Don't worry, little man. I was told to leave witnesses. You are quite safe."

"Thank you . . . lord."

Viruk swung the gray and rode several paces. Then he turned in the saddle and asked one of the soldiers: "What are those little white and blue flowers called?" The man glanced down at the blooms.

"Sky stars," answered the soldier.

"An odd name. I must look into it. Thank you."

Heeling the gray into a run, he headed west toward Egaru.

Chapter Twelve

As the sun set, and the ship's lights flickered into life, Methras began his rounds, moving first to the crew's quarters on the lower deck. The high spirits that had accompanied the *Serpent*'s rebirth had faded now, as the sailors began to reconsider their careers. None of them were needed now that the masts had been cut away and hurled overboard. Talaban controlled the *Serpent* from the high cabin, and the mood of the sailors was low.

Methras entered the long room and found several of the men playing dice bones. "Soon be home," he said.

"And then what?" asked the first mate, a surly mariner who had sailed with the *Serpent* for the past seven years.

"There will be roles for you all," said Methras. "This ship is equipped to carry four hundred people. Now that it is fully charged there will be many expeditions and good sailors like yourselves will always be needed."

"Easy for you to say, sergeant," said another man. "Always a need for soldiers."

"Would anyone like to make a wager?" asked Methras. "I'll bet a gold piece to a silver that all of you will be hired for the next voyage." The men looked at one another, but no one took him up on his offer. "There," he said, "you are not as pessimistic as you pretend."

"Not at all," said the second speaker, a young Vagar on his first voyage. "We just know what a bad gambler you are and we all like you too much to take your money."

Methras chuckled and moved through to the makeshift galley, checking the stoves and the pans and tasting the broth being prepared. It was good, but a little too thin for his taste.

"We are short on meat supplies, sir," said the cook. "But there's plenty of dried fruit left."

Methras continued on through the galley and up to the central inner deck. Other sailors were already asleep here and he did not disturb them. He paused at the locked doors beneath the prow section and wondered once more just what was behind them. In six years they had never been opened.

Climbing the circular stairwell he emerged on the center deck and saw the native, Touchstone, leaning on the guard rail. He liked the savage. The man had a wry sense of humor and a seeing eye.

"Good evening," he said. Touchstone glanced up.

"Not good," said Touchstone. "Bad visions."

"Are we in danger?" asked Methras, well aware of the tribesman's uncanny talents.

"Not know. But dream was bad. Two moons in sky. Fire from mountains. Big seas."

"There is only one moon, Touchstone. There can only be one moon."

The tribesman nodded. "This I know. But two moons will come. This I also know."

Methras was well versed in the skills needed to converse with Touchstone. "Let me understand you," he said. "What you saw was two objects in the sky that were *like* moons?"

"No. One moon. Same moon. Twice. Same time. One rise one fall."

"Perhaps it was not a vision. Perhaps it was just a dream," ventured Methras.

Touchstone considered this, then shook his head. "Vision it was. Two moons coming."

"Was that the whole vision? You mentioned big seas?"

Touchstone nodded. "First one moon in sky. Then same moon appear in different place. Two moons. Sea rise up. Big wave. Big as mountain. Land cracks and fire-blood flows from wound. This I see."

Methras fell silent. The moon, he knew, exerted an enormous gravitational pull on the seas. If a second moon were to appear then tidal waves were likely, as indeed would be volcanic eruptions. However, the idea of a second, identical, moon was preposterous. "Have your visions ever been wrong?" he asked the savage.

Touchstone nodded. "When young. Before medicine bag was full. Not since."

"I think you are wrong now."

"Hope so," said Touchstone. "How soon we home?"

"Late tomorrow. After sunset. Are you anxious to see the city?"

Touchstone shrugged. "Hate city," he said. "Land I love. Under feet. Firm. Solid."

Methras leaned on the rail and watched the last of the sunset and the birthing of the stars. They were so bright out here, so clean and sharp. Suddenly he laughed. "There are your two moons," he said, pointing at the horizon. One moon hung in the sky, the second was its reflection on the surface of the sea.

"Could be," said Touchstone. He seemed relieved.

"The dolphins have gone," added Methras.

"They take message to Suryet. Tell her I come home soon."

"Is that another vision, my friend?"

"No. That is hope," said Touchstone sadly.

• • •

Methras completed his rounds and returned to his small cabin. He found Talaban waiting for him there. The tall warrior was seated on the cot bed, staring through the narrow window and out across the western sea.

"Good evening, sir," said Methras, surprised.

"And to you, sergeant. How is the mood of the men?"

"They are worried, sir. They wonder about the security of their roles aboard the *Serpent*. Especially the rig-climbers and the sail-men."

"Did you reassure them?"

"As best I could."

"Good." Talaban rose. "Follow me," he said. Together the two men made their way up to the high deck and the circular control cabin. Here Talaban showed the Vagar the correct way to open the triangular gold plate on the door, and the correct code for the seven symbols beneath it. The door opened. Both men stepped inside. Methras found his mind racing. No Vagar was allowed within this place. Talaban seemed unconcerned. "There are few men left alive who know how to handle ships like the *Serpent*," he said. "So watch me closely, and if you have questions, ask them."

"I have one question immediately, sir," said Methras. "Why are you showing me this? This is Avatar knowledge, and merely being in possession of it could cost me my life."

"Times are changing, Methras," Talaban told him. "Now watch and learn." Talaban moved to the controls, a series of handles and levers, wheels and studs. "As you can see," he continued, "the controls were designed for the ambidextrous. Come stand beside me. This lever controls forward motion . . ." One by one he explained all the principles by which the *Serpent* was powered. Methras absorbed the information easily. Finally Talaban stepped back. "Take the ship through three hundred and sixty degrees," he said. Methras took a deep breath then placed his hands on the two most prominent levers, black metal with molded hand grips. The *Serpent* swung. "Not too sharply!" warned Talaban. "Feel the craft as if it is your own body. You are the *Serpent*'s heart." The ship slowly made a long circle. "Now bring her back on course, in line with the Fangs of the Hound. Methras glanced up through the glass window, and located the Hound star. Smoothly he swung the *Serpent* back towards the north.

Despite his fear at this forbidden knowledge Methras found his excitement growing. He felt energized and curiously powerful. Turning, he grinned at Talaban. Then his eyes scanned the panels before him. "What does this one do?" he asked, pointing at a closed black section with golden hinges.

"One task at a time," said Talaban. "Bring her to a gentle stop." Methras did so, and immediately the ship began to pitch in the swell. "With no forward motion you must compensate for pitch and roll with this," said Talaban, leaning forward and gently adjusting a golden wheel set at the center of the panel. Immediately the ship ceased pitching.

For an hour Talaban instructed the Vagar sergeant in the intricacies of the *Serpent*. Then, locking the door behind him, he took Methras back to his own cabin and filled two goblets with fine wine.

"You did well," he said.

"Thank you, sir. But I still don't understand why you shared this knowledge with me."

"It is a question of trust, Methras. Simply that."

"I will not betray that trust," Methras assured him.

"I know. For all my faults I am a good judge of men. Now go and get some rest. Tomorrow I will teach the crew some of the finer points of seamanship aboard a fighting *Serpent*."

Methras saluted and left the cabin. He still had no idea why Talaban had honored him so, but he felt good for it, and he lay upon his cot bed recalling the heady sensations of riding the *Serpent*.

Three cabins away Touchstone found sleep hard to come by. Every time he drifted towards slumber he would see again the two moons in the sky. Rising from the floor he took his medicine bag in his hands and tried to concentrate on Suryet. It was useless. Her serene face would form in his mind, then fade into a vision of a ghostly moon.

Troubled, the tribesman left the cabin and climbed to the outer deck, tasting the salt upon the air, and watching the bright stars in the dome of the night sky. The moon was low on the horizon.

Three dolphins surfaced close by. One leapt high into the air, its sleek silver form spinning before it dived down into the water. Touchstone felt his spirits lift. Big seas would not trouble the Osnu. They would continue, no matter what disasters befell the human race. Transferring his gaze to the stars once more, Touchstone sought inspiration. He knew what needed to be done and yet feared the result. If he failed he could die, or worse, could become like poor Eagle-With-No-Feathers, slack jawed and imbecilic. Dream walking was a perilous enterprise at best, and then few walkers would consider the journey without the aid of a shaman.

Touchstone had walked twice in his life, both times with the aid of One-Eyed-Fox. He was the greatest of shamen. All the tribes understood this. On the second walk Touchstone had become lost in the stars of the Great Sky River. One-Eyed-Fox had brought him back.

The tribesman would not have considered the dangers of a walk, had it not been for the persistence of the two moon vision, and the fact that it seemed linked to the fate of Suryet. Every time he tried to picture her the vision roared into his mind.

Touchstone sighed, then made his way to Talaban's cabin.

The captain was making more marks on white paper as Touchstone entered, little symbols carefully constructed in lines. He had explained that other men could read these symbols, and they were of value. Touchstone liked and admired the man, so he did not laugh.

"You look troubled," said Talaban, putting aside his pen.

"Big troubled. Need help." Talaban offered him a seat, then sat back. "Bad vision. Need dream walk to find answer. Fly high. Walk among stars. See future."

"You have spoken of dream walking before. You said it had many dangers, Touchstone."

"Yes. Many dangers. But must answer riddle."

"I thought you needed a shaman for the journey. To help you home."

"You must bring me home."

"I don't know how, my friend."

Touchstone shook his head. "You share walk. You see what I see. But you hold to ship. To . . ." he struggled for the right words, "to life," he said, at last. "One hand to ship. One hand to me. You draw Touchstone back."

"And this vision is important enough to risk your life?"

"And yours," said Touchstone.

Talaban grinned. "Well, dream walking is something I have never done. So how do we begin?"

"We sit. On floor. Find trance. Then we fly."

"Let's do it," said Talaban.

Talaban locked the door then knelt on the rug facing Touchstone. The tribesman put his hands on Talaban's shoulders. Talaban copied the move. Then Touchstone leaned forward, lowering his head until their skulls touched.

"Hold to ship," warned Touchstone. "Or both be lost."

Talaban did not reply. Relaxing his mind he sought the trance state: focus without concentration, physical tension allied to mental relaxation, the melding of opposites, the closing of the circle. He felt himself moving, spinning, as if he and Touchstone were involved in a bizarre dance. He knew it was not so and that they still knelt together on the rug of his cabin, and yet he allowed the feeling to grow. Colors danced in his mind, swirling rainbows passing over, around and through him. And then he heard music, soaring and primal, the drumbeat of the universe, the eerie singing of cosmic winds, the sighing of unborn stars.

He was floating now in darkness and scenes from his past flowed before his mind's eye; his first voyage to the Hidden Islands and the school there where he studied Anu's star maps, his courtship of Suryet, as they ran together in the high hills above the tepees of the Anajo, his capture of Touchstone, his capture by Talaban. With a jolt he struggled to free himself from the complete union of minds. Drawing back, he held to his own identity, and became aware that Touchstone was going through a similar struggle. The colors flared into life once more and, momentarily, he felt the rug beneath his knees and the movement of the ship.

Separated but still together the two men relaxed once

more, their minds soaring back towards the music. Sights of infinite beauty filled Talaban's mind, planets and stars, moons and comets, all moving and spinning in the great dance that was eternity.

Excitement swept through him, followed by ecstasy. All the secrets of the universe were flowing through him, too fast to make sense of, but slow enough to see that there was a unity and a sense of underlying purpose to all the scenes. Lost in the wonder of it he floated among the stars of the Great Milk River of the Sky.

He had forgotten Touchstone, forgotten the ship, lost touch with his own small, meaningless life. Here were the answers to every question, every mystery. And he was free—free of care and trouble, free of strife and discord. Here was harmony. Here was a joy undreamed of.

Time was meaningless here and he floated on, watching, learning, observing, filled with a sense of increasing wonder. He watched the birth of stars and the death of planets, growing ever more part of the dance.

Two moons.

It was as if a voice had spoken to him, yet without sound. What did it mean? And then he remembered the mystery. So tiny it seemed now, so inconsequential. But even the thought of the riddle gave him a desire to find the answer.

Colors swirled around him once more and he found himself gazing down on a blue planet. Then he was hurtling towards it, passing through clouds, and hovering over vast mountains. Down and down he flew until he recognized Parapolis and the White Pyramid at its center. People were moving through the marketplace and the temple grounds.

And there, moving across the great courtyard, he saw himself being approached by a Vagar mystic, a ragged man in ragged furs.

The scene shimmered.

He was still above Parapolis—but there was no white pyramid. This time it was a golden ziggurat, stepped and flat-topped. The ragged mystic was there again, but this time he was being held by guards. One of them drew a golden knife with a serrated edge and dragged it across the little man's throat.

Again the scene shimmered and changed. Talaban floated higher.

It was night, and a great wind was blowing over the continent. Talaban swung and looked to the north.

The tidal wave was bearing down upon the city.

In that moment a second moon appeared in the night sky, bright and gleaming. And the city disappeared— just as the tidal wave swept over it.

The euphoria Talaban had experienced moments before was gone now. He had witnessed the impossible and it brought his consciousness surging back to life. No longer passively observing, he was thinking again, remembering the ship, his life and . . .

Touchstone!

Where was Touchstone?

He could not feel him, nor sense his presence.

With an effort of will he concentrated on the ship, the rug, the cabin, his hands on Touchstone's shoulders. The universe span and Talaban was hurled back into his body. Touchstone still knelt before him. Talaban shook him and called his name. There was no response and his body fell to the floor.

Struggling for calm, Talaban once more entered the trance state, seeking a route back to the stars. For an hour or more he sought it but to no avail.

For the first time in decades he felt the beginnings of panic. Rising from the rug he poured himself a goblet of water and drank it swiftly, seeking calm. He stared down at the prone figure of the tribesman.

He trusted you!

The panic flared again. Talaban swore, allowing anger to wash over him, swamping the negative forces seeking to unman him.

Touchstone's right hand lay flat against the rug, the medicine pouch having fallen from it. Talaban returned to his position and took up the pouch. Everything of value in the tribesman's life was represented by the contents of the pouch. Touchstone believed in its magic. Talaban needed it now.

He had once heard Touchstone chanting in his cabin. Talaban's Avatar training allowed him to recall every note, every nuance. Holding the pouch to his chest he began the chant. Colors flared in his mind, the bright blue of a summer sky, the deep multi-shaded greens of the forest trees. Sounds whispered to him: distant bird song, the faint call of the Osnu. Then something terribly cold slammed into his brain, the pain exquisitely focused.

"You are moments from death," came a voice colder than the pain.

"I must find Touchstone. He is lost," said Talaban.

"Open your mind to me," came the command. Talaban felt as if talons were ripping at his skull, tearing it open. *"Do not resist!"*

Forcing himself to relax, the Avatar gave in to the pain. The cold was replaced by a searing heat that made him cry out. Red-hot wires seemed to be penetrating his brain, worming their way through the soft wet tissue. Bile rose in his throat and he vomited on the rug.

Then the pain eased and the voice came again. *"You must find him."*

"I do not know how."

"You have the pouch. Use it. I can lead you back to the Milk River. But only the holder of the pouch can find him."

"What must I do?"

"Hang the pouch around your neck. Then hold to his body with your left hand. Reach out with your right. Once among the stars when you feel something solid it will be Touchstone. He will not want to come back. He will fight you. He will claw and bite and rend and tear. He will take many shapes and forms. They will all be illusions. Hold to him. No matter what. You understand?"

"Yes."

"Do not let go. There will be no second attempt."

"I understand."

"Be strong. If you are not he will kill you."

"How can an illusion kill me?"

"The pain will be real enough. If you believe in it you will die."

Talaban looped the pouch over his head. "I am ready," he said. "Who are you?"

"I am the One-Eyed-Fox. Take hold of my grandson." Talaban did so. "Now close your eyes and reach out with your right hand."

Colors blazed against his eyes, bright, burning and painful. He felt himself floating in a sea of agony and he tried to cry out, but had no voice. Then he was falling, drifting through fire. He heard a voice—many voices, all screaming at him. Phrases burst through the cacophony . . .

"Loathsome child. Can you not master simple tasks?" *My father hated me. He knew the truth.*

"There is nothing you cannot do, my son." *My mother adored me. She was the truth.*

"He is useless. Good for nothing. It is hard to believe that I sired him."

"A talent for fighting is not what made the Avatar great, boy. The mind. Use the mind." *Endar-sen, my teacher. Without him I would have been lost.*

The sounds grew, voices screaming, shouting, whispering, singing. Talaban fought for sanity amid the noise. Where were the bright stars and the music of the universe?

"They will come," came the voice of the One-Eyed-Fox. *"First you must fall inward and then we will fly outward. Listen to the voices. Know who you are."*

"I know who I am."

"No. Find what was lost."

"Touchstone. He is lost."

"Find first the lost man within yourself, Talaban. Then seek Touchstone."

"I don't understand!" But he did understand—and tumbled into an ocean of voices.

"A man must have a dream, Talaban," said Endarsen. "Without it we are merely animate. We eat and drink, but we gain no sustenance. We listen and talk but we learn nothing of value. We breathe, but we do not live. What is your dream?"

"There is nothing you cannot do, my son. You are special."

"I have no dream! There is no dream for me. All dreams died beneath the ice. All hope was buried there."

"Loathsome child. Can you not master even simple tasks?"

"Come to me, Talaban. I will be yours and yours alone." *Chryssa was the best of them. She loved me. With her I could have built dreams.* The sounds faded and he saw again the last meeting, her fragile beauty almost gone, her skin like glass. No one understood the nature of the disease. It afflicted perhaps one in ten thousand Avatars. They called it *Crystal-wed*. Use of crystals somehow changed the body chemistry. Soft tissue hardened, the body taking on the properties of the crystals themselves. Once it had begun there was no reversing it. Sometimes the process would be slow and ag-

onizing, at others swift and terrifying. Chryssa had
thankfully fallen into the latter group. Talaban had sat
beside her bed. He could not hold her hand, for fear of
breaking her fingers. She had lost the power of speech,
and only her eyes—sweet, blue eyes—remained soft and
moist. He told her he loved her, would love her for all
time. A tear appeared on her crystal cheek, then her
eyes hardened, and she was gone.

The world ended then for him, and the fall of the
world the following year was an anti-climax.

The pain of the memory was intense. It burned him
and chilled him.

That was the day I lost everything, he thought.

"No. That was the day you surrendered everything,"
said the One-Eyed-Fox. *"Today is the day you reclaim
it."*

The voices were gone now and Talaban floated free,
high and fast, spinning and turning.

Below him the blue planet shone like a midnight
lantern. His speed increased, the planet shrinking to a
tiny pebble. Two comets flashed across his path, drawn
towards a colossal planet, and plunging deep into the
huge storm clouds that swirled around it. Great plumes
of fire billowed out.

Talaban flew on.

Now he could hear the music, the heartbeat of the
cosmos. He yearned to be a part of it, to let himself go
and live among the rhythms of eternity. *"Hold fast!"*
ordered the One-Eyed Fox. *"That is the route Touchstone chose."*

Talaban dragged his mind from the music and
reached out. There was nothing.

*"Close your eyes and picture the medicine pouch.
Touchstone will be drawn to you."*

He was no longer spinning. He was floating, suspended amid the stars. Closing his eyes he followed the

advice of the shaman. He could feel the medicine bag in his left hand. Something whispered against his fingers. He grabbed at it and missed. It came again—and this time his fingers hooked to the surface. A sharp pain lanced into his arm. Opening his eyes he saw a huge mottled snake, its fangs embedded in his arm. His fingers jerked open, but he overcame his fear and gripped the round body once more. The snake's fangs flashed for his face, sinking deep, and he could feel the poison seeping into his flesh.

Illusion. It is all illusion, he told himself. The wounds disappeared instantly.

He was holding a rock. Worms were sliding from holes in its surface, eating into his palm, their tiny teeth ripping away his flesh.

Concentrating on the medicine pouch he pictured the ship, seeking a way back. The worms ate their way into his wrist. They were laying eggs in the arteries. He felt them swimming through his veins. The eggs hatched, and more worms began to grow inside his chest and belly, his neck and his loins, bursting through the skin.

He was being eaten alive.

"Help me, shaman!" he said. But there was no answering voice.

What if this was all a trick? What if there was no Touchstone here? Had he been lured into a trap?

A worm burst out through his cheek and flopped down his face.

The rainbows were spiralling about him now, and he clung to the rock.

Almost home, he thought. Almost safe.

"You are hurting me," came the voice of Chryssa. Talaban's eyes snapped open. He saw her fragile body, the splintering cracks running up her crystal arm under the pressure of his hand. "Why do you want to hurt me?"

"I don't want to hurt you," he told her.

"I was safe among the stars. If you take me back I will turn to glass and dust."

Squeezing shut his eyes he ignored her and sped on. A great roaring filled his ears. Massive talons ripped into his face, tearing out his left eye and slamming down into his chest. The lion pressed against him, its fangs ripping into his shoulder, snapping the bones.

Still he clung to its black mane.

I am dying, he thought. I cannot survive these wounds.

The blue planet roared up towards him and he felt his head strike the rug on the floor of his cabin.

Beside him Touchstone groaned. Forcing himself to his knees, he shook the tribesman.

Touchstone's green eyes opened. "I sleep now," he said, and fell forward.

Talaban dropped the medicine bag alongside the unconscious man, then rose and walked back to his desk. There were no marks upon his body, no wounds, no jagged tears. But his mind still reeled from the remembered pain.

That was a foolish thing to do, he told himself.

Chryssa came to his mind. Instinctively he sought to suppress the image, but then realized he no longer felt tormented by the loss of her. Tentatively he summoned the memories of her, their walks together in the high hills, with the spring flowers carpeting the hillsides, and her reluctance to tread on the blooms. She had picked her way carefully among them, her movements delicate and graceful. The memory was warm and very fine. At that moment Talaban finally understood what a fool he had been. By ruthlessly suppressing all thoughts of Chryssa he had buried the joy as well as the despair. You are an idiot, he told himself.

Opening the rear door he stepped out onto his private deck. The stars were bright in the night sky. Suddenly a light appeared to the east. Talaban glanced up . . .

. . . to see a second moon shining in the sky.

The sea beneath the ship began to churn and rise. Talaban was hurled to the left. Someone on the decks above him screamed.

Then the second moon vanished and the seas grew calmer. He stood for a moment, transfixed. Then a second surprise shook him.

Floating in the doorway of his cabin was a shimmering translucent figure, an old man wearing a buckskin shirt decorated with fingers of bone. His hair was white and braided with beads and his eyes were deep and knowing. "The evil is upon us, Talaban," he said.

Then he vanished.

Chapter Thirteen

The king of the gods, Ra-Hel, was troubled by the changing sky. He sought out Old One Young and asked him for a prophecy. The Day of Endings has begun, said Old One Young. And war will rage among the gods. The mighty will fall, the heavens weep, and evil will stalk the land. But he did not speak of the goddess to come, nor the Queen of Death. For the time was not yet upon them.

From the *Noon Song of the Anajo*

There was excitement in the cities when the two moons appeared, but panic followed when earth tremors cracked the east wall of Egaru and brought down two of the older buildings in Pagaru. The other three cities escaped serious damage, but twenty-six people were killed in Egaru when the buildings fell, with more than seventy others injured.

The Questor General ordered the troops out of their barracks to patrol the streets, and the Vagar authorities mobilized volunteers to dig through the debris seeking other survivors. One old woman and two small children were found alive.

Across the River Luan the main city of the Mud People had been badly struck. Their homes of mud-bricks had collapsed, as had part of the palace. The Luan had burst its banks, bringing floods and a river of silt and mud that swept through the darkness dragging hundreds to their deaths.

In the Valley of the Stone Lion Questor Anu had ordered his 600 workers to move to the high ground one hour before the phenomenon. Not one man was injured when the earth split across the valley, briefly opening an abyss that belched smoke and dust into the night sky.

At the quarry three miles away a section of sandstone weighing more than twenty tons sheared away from the face crushing six workers and two whores. The men had remained behind against the orders of Questor Anu, having previously arranged a rendezvous with the women.

By dawn the land was again quiet, but an emergency meeting of the High Council was called to discuss the astronomical phenomenon and its meaning.

The Questor General did not head the gathering, but rode instead to the valley, seeking out Anu.

The newly young Questor was walking down the mountain, leading his workers in a long column, as Rael rode up.

"We need to talk, my friend," said Rael, turning his horse and riding out across the grass. Anu walked over as the General dismounted.

"I sense you are annoyed with me," he said.

"You could have been more forthright. You knew the event was to take place. Was it some kind of illusion?"

"No."

Trailing the reins of his mount Rael walked to a rocky outcrop and sat down. Anu joined him. "Would you care to tell me why you kept this from me?"

"You would not have believed me, Rael. You would have thought me demented."

"It would have been pleasant had you allowed me the right to make my own judgment. However, be that as it may, the event has now happened. What does it mean?"

"It will not be easy to explain," said Anu, rubbing his slender hand through his close-cropped blue hair.

"I have time."

Anu smiled. "We may have less time than you think. I want you to open your mind, Rael, and listen to what I have to say without any questions. Agreed?"

"Agreed."

"Our myths tell us that there were once gods who could journey through time, opening gateways to distant lands. You remember the Tale of the Twins? Bezak god of thunder and the twin brother he never knew he had?" Rael nodded. "That myth always baffled me," continued Anu, "for you would have thought that Bezak's mother would have known whether she had twins or not."

"Spare me the myths, Anu."

"Patience, Questor General. First you must peel back the skin before you find the fruit. The point I am making is that there are other realities, living alongside our own. As we faced the prospect of the Great Fall so did others on their own worlds. But at least one group accepted the conclusions of their wise men, and took action to save themselves. They used the entire power of their civilization in a bid to stave off the tidal wave. It worked—but not in the manner they intended. What they did was open a massive gateway between realities. They moved their capital city, and all the surrounding lands—shifted it to this reality. That is why, for a few heartbeats only, two moons hung in the sky. They are here now. Far across the western sea.

"Know this also, Rael. Thousands of people from our world died as the moons appeared—buried as the city and its hills and mountains appeared, stamping down like a colossal hammer upon the wide plains."

"You were quite right," said Rael. "Had you told me this before I saw the two moons I would have thought you demented. Even now I can scarce believe it."

"I saw the vision," Anu told him. "I knew what was to come—and what is to come. Within two months a golden ship will sail into the port of Egaru. It will bring messengers from the west."

"And these people are Avatars like us?"

"Not like us, Rael. Their power is no longer derived from the sun. It comes from ritual slaughter. They are a malevolent people."

"How many of them survived?"

"Thousands."

"And they have zhi-bows?"

"No, but they have developed other weapons equally deadly."

Rael swore softly, then rose and walked towards his horse. Swiftly he mounted. "We few Avatars are clinging to life by our fingertips," he said. "We are surrounded by enemies who wait like wolves for the kill." Guiding his horse back to where Anu sat, he leaned on the pommel of his saddle. "I hope you have some good advice for me, Holy One," he said.

"They must not be allowed to win," said Anu. "They will plunge the world into darkness and evil."

"Then find a way for me to defeat them," said Rael.

"I will—once my pyramid is completed. Until then, Rael, you must use your wits."

The first few days in Egaru had been difficult for Sofarita. She had visited the city four times with her parents and once with her husband. But each time they had stayed only one night, at a tavern called the Peace

Raven. To Sofarita's dismay the tavern had been closed that spring and she knew nowhere else to stay.

It was close to dusk when she arrived and gave her name to the guards on the eastern gate. Had she known then that the tavern was closed she could have asked them for directions. Instead she found herself sitting upon her pony outside a once-familiar building, made cold and hostile by the boarded-up windows and the plank hammered across the main doors.

Heading deeper into the city she scanned the buildings for sign of a tavern, but saw none.

The streets grew more crowded and the little pony became anxious. Sofarita tried to soothe him, but he was unused to such noise and bustle. A dog darted under his legs and the pony reared. Sofarita clung to the saddle. A burly woman in flowing gowns of gaudy red, yellow and gold moved from the crowd, grabbing the pony's bridle and stroking its long neck. "Steady now," she said. "Steady." Sofarita thanked her. "You can't ride much further, child," said the garishly clad woman. "No Vagar riders allowed in the city center. Where are you going?"

"I wish I knew. I'm looking for a place to stay."

"Do you have coin?"

"Yes. A little."

"Come then," said the woman. Leading the pony by the bridle she turned into a narrow side street and through a stable yard into a lantern-lit square. Tables had been set out and candles flickered upon them. Some twenty people were already eating, and serving maids were carrying food and drink on wooden trays to other waiting customers. "Climb down, girl," said the fat woman.

Sofarita slid from the saddle. Her back ached from the ride and the inside of her thighs felt stretched and painful. "My nephew owns this place," said the woman. "He's a good lad, and you'll not be troubled here. Where are you from?"

"Pacepta." The woman looked blank. "It is a farming village close to the lands of the Erek-jhip-zhonad."

"And you are seeking work in the city?"

"Yes."

"Well first you will need a permit. Without one you will get no employment. But—and here's the stupidity of it—if you have no employment you will be refused a permit."

"I don't understand."

"No more do I. Avatar rules, child. They are not meant to be understood, merely followed." A thickset young man appeared in the doorway. The woman called out a name and he strolled over.

"Take this pony to the stable," she ordered him, "and then bring this young woman's belongings inside."

Leading Sofarita by the arm she made her way through the tables and into the main building. Here too there were diners, and the rich smell of roasting meats came wafting from the kitchens.

A tall young man spotted the pair, gave a wide grin, and came to meet them. He was wearing a white apron the front of which was stained by gravy. "Good evening, aunt," he said. "Come to check on your investment?"

"You are too thin, Baj," she scolded him. "Cooks should be sturdy men. It shows that their food is well worth the eating." He chuckled and looked at Sofarita, his gaze frank and appraising. She felt momentarily discomfited.

"And who is your new girl, aunt?" he asked.

"She is not one of my girls. I found her riding the Avenue in search of lodging. She's a country lass and quite unspoilt, as far as one can tell. So you treat her with respect, young Baj, or I'll want to know why. You can also sell her pony for her. She'll have no use for it in Egaru and I should think the money will be useful." She turned to Sofarita. "Do not accept less than ten silver pennies for it. You might get as much as fifteen." She looked hard into the younger woman's face. "How old are you? Sixteen?"

"Twenty-two," said Sofarita.

"You look younger. But I guess you'll have learned a little wisdom, and that's always a help for a city woman. You look after her, Baj. I will be back to check on her."

The fat woman patted Sofarita's shoulder, then swung away and strode out of the tavern. Sofarita felt light-headed, as if a small storm had passed. "Is she always like that?" she asked Baj.

The young man gave a wide, good-natured grin. "Always," he said. "Come, I will find you a room." She followed him through a dimly lit corridor and on up a flight of rickety stairs lit by a single lantern on the first landing. Baj removed the lantern and held it ahead of him as he climbed into the gloom. "It will be brighter later," he called back to her. "I'll have more lanterns lit."

The stairs ended at a gallery which circled the eating area below. Baj moved to a sturdy door, pressed the latch and opened it. Within was a small bedroom boasting a stone fireplace and a tiny window. Baj hung the lantern on a hook above the fireplace. "It is a little musty," he said, "but you'll not find better for a silver penny."

"A month?" she asked him. His laughter was unforced.

"A day, pretty one. This is the city."

"Every day?" Sofarita was appalled.

"Every single day. But you get three meals, and you'll

be safe here. Believe me, that is a special rate. This room would normally earn me ten silvers a week."

"I'll take it," she said.

"Wait here and make yourself comfortable. I'll bring you some food." After he had gone Sofarita sat down on the bed. The mattress was thin, but the blankets were thick and warm. For the first time the enormity of her action overwhelmed her. She had left a secure life in the village for the utter uncertainty of life in an environment she knew nothing about. Rising, she moved to the window and stared down on the diners below. Their clothes seemed rich and wonderful, far more graceful than the homespun garments she wore. And the colors of the dyes: rich greens, bright golds, reds and blues. One of the women below wore a dress of heavy silk, embroidered with white beads. And her hair was braided with bright wire that glinted in the lantern light.

Lisha!

The name flickered into Sofarita's mind, and with it came a sudden vision of the woman below. She was not dining nor dressed in fine clothes. She was sitting on a threadbare rug, holding a dead baby and weeping. A feeling of sorrow washed over Sofarita. Not her own, but that of the woman below. For a moment only, she saw what the woman was seeing, a chubby older man, spooning food into his mouth. He smiled at her. A piece of dark meat was lodged between his teeth.

Sofarita squeezed shut her eyes, moved back from the window and almost sagged to the bed. The vision had been startling, and her hands were trembling. Baj returned carrying a heavy tray. He lowered it to a small table, which he then lifted and set down before her. Upon the tray was a plate of roast meat, covered with thick gravy, some heavy dark bread, a large pat of butter and a chunk of fresh cheese. "Eat," he said. "You look very pale." From the pocket of his apron he produced three candle stubs, which he lit from the lantern and placed in small pottery dishes around the room.

Sofarita cut a piece of meat and tasted it. It was roast beef, and delicious beyond words. Slowly and steadily she finished the meal, mopping the last of the gravy with the bread. She looked up. He was squatting down some five feet away, his elbow resting on his knees, his chin in his hand. "I do take great pleasure from watching people enjoy my cooking," he said.

"It was a fine meal. But I am too full to eat the cheese. May I keep it for later?"

"Of course. What kind of employment are you looking for? Or do you intend to work for my aunt?"

"I don't know. What does your aunt do?"

"Do? You don't know?" He looked closely at her, then smiled. "Of course you don't. How stupid of me. Well, what can you do?"

"Anything I set my mind to," she told him. "I have planted crops, nursed them and gathered them. I can sew, spin, embroider. I can shear sheep, and know the medicines to ward off the blow-fly. I know the herbs that can help heal wounds and others to cure headaches and ease the pain of rheumatism. And I am strong now. I can work hard. Harder than any city woman."

"You are also trim and beautiful," he said. "My aunt will point out that there is great money to be made by using those gifts."

"How?"

"My aunt . . . entertains the wealthy and the powerful. She has a large house and many young women— and young men—are in her employ."

Another vision struck her. A large bedroom, with a circular bed covered with sheets of satin. Two women and a man cavorted upon it. What was happening to her? Sofarita struggled to appear calm. "Your aunt operates a whorehouse?"

"Indeed she does, but her employees prefer to be called entertainers. They can earn more in one night than I make in a week. And much more than you will earn in a full season as a serving maid or a household servant."

"How much do they earn?"

"My aunt tells me it depends on the requirements for the role, and the wealth and generosity of the recipient. In other words, if you find a rich man who likes you then you could earn a hundred silvers a night. More likely though, it will be twenty or thirty."

"So much?"

"Are you tempted?"

"Should I not be? Is there something you are not telling me?"

"Nothing," he said. "It is just that *entertaining* is not considered an honorable profession in Egaru. In some of the cities of the Mud People—so I'm told—whores are considered almost holy. Among the Patiakes they are highly regarded. But in Vagar settlements they are generally looked down upon."

"Could I work here? For you?"

"You could, but on the wages I pay you would not be able to afford this room for long."

"I will think on it," she said.

Crowds gathered on Egaru's docks to watch the *Serpent* as she sailed majestically into harbor. Some of the older Avatars were misty-eyed, the younger filled with a sense of wonder. Gone were the clumsy sails, the pitch and the roll of a crippled ship. Instead she sailed serenely into port. Most of the crowd were Vagars who had never seen a fully powered *Serpent*. They were even more astounded by the vessel.

Talaban brought her close to the dock, where sailors threw out ropes to the waiting dockers. Once the ropes were fastened Talaban eased down the power. The ship settled in the water.

Within the hour Questor Ro had organized the wrapping and removal of the four remaining chests, three full, one empty. He had argued with Talaban about leaving the *Serpent*'s chest in place. Talaban had overruled him. "If the Questor General requires the ship to be disabled once more then I will have the chest removed," he said. "Until that time she remains empowered."

The chests were carefully carried to a waiting wagon. Ro ordered the driver to proceed to the palace. The little Questor climbed to sit alongside the Vagar. He did not look back or wave as the wagon trundled out of sight.

Talaban assembled the crew, paid them, and ordered those taking shore leave to watch for the assembly lists pinned to the dock gates. "We may be leaving soon," he said. "It is vital you are ready."

Leaving a skeleton crew, commanded by Methras, to protect the ship Talaban and Touchstone strode down the gangplank and onto the wharf. Moving through to the dock gates Talaban hired an open carriage to carry them to his home on Five Tree Hill. The house was situated close to an orchard of cherry trees. It was not an imposing dwelling, boasting only nine rooms. Its walls were bare of ornament and stained white, its long sloping roof of red terracotta tiles. Slatted wooden shutters covered the windows, shielding the rooms from the worst of the sun.

Talaban climbed down from the carriage and paid

the driver. The front door was open as he and Touchstone approached the building, and a middle-aged woman stepped from the doorway. She bowed to Talaban. "Everything is ready, lord," she said. "My husband saw the ship. He has aired your bedroom and prepared your bed. The water is heating for your bath, and there is food set in the couch room."

"Thank you," said Talaban, moving past her.

"And a messenger arrived from the palace, lord. There is a meeting of the Council at dusk. You are required to attend. A carriage will call here." Talaban nodded and moved through to the couch room. It was on the western side of the building and a high white archway linked it to the gardens and the orchard beyond. The room, with its three large windows, was filled with light, the air perfumed by the scent of blooms from the garden, jasmine and rose, sweet-dew and honeysuckle.

Talaban pulled off his boots and sat down on a long couch. A man entered and bowed deeply. Setting down a pitcher of watered wine and two goblets on a nearby table he bowed again and left the room. Touchstone poured wine for his captain, but took none himself. Instead he moved to the long table and helped himself to the sweetmeats there. Fresh fruit, cold salted meats—ham, beef and pigeon—a variety of cheeses and a loaf of fresh-baked bread. "Good, this," said Touchstone.

The man and woman returned. Both bowed. "Your bath is ready, lord," she said. "Will you be requiring us further?"

"No. My thanks to you," he said. Rising, he gave each of them two silver coins. They bowed again and left the house.

"You don't like see them die," said Touchstone.

"What?"

"Servants. You watch grow old. You sad then. I see your life. When we flew."

Talaban nodded. It was true. His first servants in Egaru—a man and his wife—had been with him for twenty-five years. He had grown fond of them. When the wife became ill Talaban had healed her. Word got out and he was summoned to the Council. It was against the law for Avatars to use crystal magic on inferior races. Talaban had been ordered to dismiss them. Either that or watch the woman die. Since then he had hired temporary servants.

Touchstone was busily munching his way through the food. Talaban rose and stretched. "I am going to bathe," he said.

As he lay in the scented water he thought again of Chryssa, of her joy and how everything she saw seemed to fill her with wonder: sunshine on spring flowers, a white dove at dusk, the moon dancing fragmented on the night-dark sea.

The memory of the two moons flashed into his mind, and with it the shimmering figure of One-Eyed-Fox. He had not spoken to Touchstone about the apparition. Not yet. He needed time to think it through.

Climbing from the bath he towelled himself dry, then knelt on a rug and slowly took his mind through the Six Rituals.

An hour later he was dressed in a tunic of dark blue silk, edged with silver, his long, dark hair held in place by a silver circlet inset with a white moonstone. Around his waist was a jewelled belt hanging from which was a hunting knife, its black hilt embellished with silver wire. His leggings were white wool, his knee-length boots of silvered lizard skin.

Touchstone grinned at him, and he could see the light of mockery in the tribesman's eyes.

"It is palace garb," said Talaban, somewhat defensively.

Touchstone nodded. "Very pretty," he said.

"I seem to recall you dressed in a cloak of eagle feathers, wearing a beaded cap, for your marriage to Suryet. You were also wearing a codpiece made of shells and your lips were painted white. I too shared your memories."

"Different," said Touchstone. "Eagle feathers bring great magic. Shells bring virility."

"It is all a question of style," said Talaban, smoothing down his tunic.

"Very pretty," repeated Touchstone, with a booming laugh.

Talaban grinned and shook his head. It was impossible to argue with Touchstone. "We need to talk when I get back."

"About going home?"

"About the One-Eyed-Fox."

"You wake me. We talk."

The carriage arrived on time and Talaban sat in the back, gazing over the city. It had grown in the last fifty years, almost doubling in size. Many of the older buildings, on the five hills of the original city, were finely constructed, but most of the new were built from fired mud-bricks. In narrow streets and packed centers they housed the worker population—potters, bakers, stonemasons, clothes makers, carpenters, house servants, and many more. The Vagars now outnumbered their Avatar overlords by a hundred to one. And the ratio would continue to increase.

Talaban's mood was somber as the carriage continued, crossing the old stone bridge in the Avatar center of the city.

Here the buildings showed a sharp rise in quality, huge houses fronted by expertly worked marble, flanked by beautiful statues. Here there were fountains and man-made lakes, parks with elaborate walkways. The carriage moved out onto the wide avenue and past the Library and the Museum of Antiquities. Both these structures had been designed when the old empire was at its height, the massive 80-ton blocks lifted into place by a handful of workers using the legendary music of the Avatar Prime. Talaban had seen just such an exercise when he was a child back in Parapolis. First a Questor would play a simple tune on a long flute. Then the trumpets would sound. Avatar stonemasons would step forward, their movements in perfect rhythm to the music. Huge blocks would be lifted as easily as sacks of grain. People would gather alongside the construction sites to marvel at the magic and listen to the music.

The Library was huge, the great lintel stone above the doorway held on the shoulders of two 30-foot-tall statues. Seated on a massive throne set upon the lintel was a statue of the last Avatar Prime, his hands outstretched towards his people. The original idea had been to symbolize that, although he was raised above other men, it was only by the will of the people. Hence the two Vagars holding him. Now, to Talaban, it merely highlighted that the weight of Avatar rule fell squarely on the shoulders of the Vagars.

The carriage moved on. Hundreds of people strolled along the perfectly laid stone footpaths, stopping to peer in at items on display in the many shops. The people here were better dressed. Most were Vagars, the families of rich merchants.

Many Avatars saw the Vagar merchant class as their greatest allies among the sub-species. Talaban was not fooled. The merchants were the most eager to see an end to Avatar rule. Their profit margins would increase dramatically if they had full control of the city's commerce.

The carriage trundled on. Talaban could see the palace outlined against the night sky. Bright lights shone from its windows, and he knew that one of the chests had been installed there. The palace had been built 200 years before, designed by Avatar architects, and built when the empire still possessed the power and the energy for such projects. It was probably the finest building left above the ice. The roof was covered with gold sheeting, the walls decorated with a multitude of statues and scenes from Avatar history.

The huge bronze gates were open, and two Avatar guards waved the carriage through.

Talaban stepped down as the carriage drew to a halt. Then he climbed the steps to the massive double doors. There were sixty-four steps. They were divided by symbols into groups of eight, and represented the journey of life. Conception, birth, puberty, adulthood, maturity, wisdom, spirituality, and death.

On either side of the steps statues had been placed, their regal faces frozen in time, their blank eyes staring impassively at the mortal men who climbed by them. Heroes and teachers, mystics and poets. Their names and their deeds were recorded on the marble beside them.

Talaban paused at the statue of Varabidis, the poet mystic, the creator of the Six Rituals. The statue depicted a young man holding a dove aloft, its wings spreading for flight. Below the statue was the inscription: *The bird does not seek the past, it flies ever hopeful into the future.*

Not any more, thought Talaban.

Once inside the palace a Vagar servant led him through to the wide waiting area outside the council chambers. Couches and deep chairs had been set against the walls, and food and wine placed on three long tables. Most of the councillors were present. Fat Caprishan, dressed in a billowing silver robe, sat by the western window deep in conversation with his aides.

Niclin, the richest and therefore most powerful of the councillors, stood beneath the high gallery chatting amiably to several of his colleagues.

Talaban scanned the room. There was no sign of Questor Ro.

A tall lean figure moved into Talaban's line of sight. "Good evening, cousin. I hear you had an eventful trip."

Viruk was dressed in a tunic of heavy black silk edged with silver thread. His hair and beard were freshly washed and oiled, and he sported no weapons. "Good evening, Viruk," said Talaban. "I am sure that life here, for you at least, has not been boring."

"Indeed not. But let us not dwell on my humble activities. You are the hero of the moment. Thanks to you, Avatar supremacy is assured for a few seasons." Talaban looked into the man's pale gray eyes.

"It would be good to think so," he said.

"Always the diplomat, Talaban. I hear you had an encounter with krals. Are they as ferocious as described?"

"They are fast, and very deadly."

"I would like to kill one. Perhaps I could accompany you on your next voyage."

"Your skills would be very useful, but that is a question for the Questor General to answer."

The doors to the council chamber swung open. At exactly that moment Questor Ro appeared and, without a word to anyone, strode through to take his seat.

"I suppose we will all have to sit through a pompous speech from the little man," said Viruk.

"He has earned the right to bore us rigid," put in Talaban. Viruk chuckled, and placed his hand on Talaban's shoulder.

"I like you. I really do." He paused, and his smile

faded. "My astrologer tells me that one day you and I will fight to the death."

Talaban smiled. "Let us hope he is a poor astrologer. But if he is not, rest assured I will see you buried with full honors."

Viruk's laughter rang out. "I really do like you, Talaban," he said.

Chapter Fourteen

Viruk appeared to be listening intently as Questor Caprishan addressed the Council. In fact he was comparing Caprishan to the dead king of the Patiakes. Both were fat to the point of obscenity and both oozed sincerity like leaking oil. Viruk pictured Caprishan's bloated body under the impact of a zhi-bolt. The thought of it made him smile. Caprishan saw the smile and faltered in his speech.

"Something I have said amuses you, cousin?" enquired the councillor.

"My apologies, cousin. I was merely enjoying your rhetoric." Viruk gave him a dazzling smile.

Caprishan returned it, then concentrated once more upon his speech. There were thirty councillors present around the table and two Avatar scribes taking notes. Viruk scanned the faces as they listened to Caprishan. The fat man was very rich and this had earned him many friends. At least eight of the listening dignitaries would vote for anything Caprishan proposed. Viruk flicked his gaze to his right where the slender Niclin sat, his chin resting on his steepled hands, his receding hair brushed fiercely back and bound by silver wire into a ponytail. He was also a man of power, with perhaps ten councillors upon whose votes he could rely. Three seats down from him sat Questor Ro. Almost as rich as

Caprishan, and as cunning as Niclin, he should have enjoyed wide support. This was not forthcoming, for few Avatars liked his pomposity. Ro was a brilliant but cold man, with little understanding of human nature. Viruk liked him. Transferring his attention to Caprishan he listened to the conclusion of his speech.

"The point I would make, most strongly, is that if Anu is correct that these newcomers are Avatars then we should welcome them warmly. Together we can ensure Avatar rule for centuries to come. Through our shared knowledge we might even advance our civilization."

The Questor General rose. "That would depend, cousin, on whether they perceive themselves as our equals or our betters."

"We have no betters, Questor General," put in Niclin.

"That may well also be their view," replied Rael. "However, we cannot adequately prepare a plan of action before we know whether or not the new arrivals are hostile. In the meantime I have ordered the recharging of every zhi-bow and an increase in recruitment for the Vagar army. But now let us move on to happier tidings, the triumphant return of our cousin Ro. As you will all have heard, he succeeded in recharging four chests. Hence the bright lights which surround us, and the replenishing of our weaponry." Turning to Ro he gave a slight bow. "Perhaps you would like to tell us of the expedition."

To Viruk's surprise Ro's speech was not pompous. It was short and succinct. The expedition had succeeded—just—but no further voyages would yield results. There were two reasons for this: one, the volcanic eruption had destroyed the Line, and two, far more importantly, the White Pyramid was all but exhausted. Ro did not mention the fight with the krals, nor point out to the councillors that many of them had doubted his ability to achieve Communion. It was a strangely muted speech, and took them all by surprise.

When he sat down there was, at first, silence. Rael gave him a curious glance, then rose to applaud him. The other councillors followed suit. Ro sat impassively throughout. As the applause died down Rael motioned Talaban to give his report. The officer spoke from his seat: "I cannot add much to the statement offered by the esteemed Questor. There was loss of life among the Vagar team, following an attack by creatures known as krals. These were beaten back by the efforts of Questor Ro, my scout Touchstone, and myself. The voyage home was largely without incident, save for the phenomenon of the two moons. I concur with Questor Ro that future voyages to the south would not be advisable. The eruption was colossal and the chance of finding another Line there are remote indeed.

"However, thanks to his persistence and vision we now have a *Serpent* under full power. I would suggest her power chest be left in place. We know that the new Avatars will be crossing the ocean. We can only assume that their ships will be powered in a similar fashion to our own. I believe it would be a mistake to have no means of fighting them at sea."

"I disagree," said Niclin. "We have a mere four chests. One, I understand, has been offered to Anu for purposes the Questor General has not made clear. Another is being used to power the city's weapons. Now you want a third left in the bowels of a ship, which could be sunk in battle. No! I say the chests should be brought into the city where they can be guarded. They are too valuable to risk."

"With respect, councillor," said Talaban, with a friendly smile, "I think you are forgetting the importance of a show of power. If these newcomers are anything like us they will be arrogant and convinced of their superiority and divine right to rule. Think of what might have happened had we somehow escaped the fall of the world, our empire almost intact, our capital city undamaged. We would have sailed our *Serpents* across the new oceans, seeking other races, and subduing them, as we have always done. And let us imagine we found a race similar to our own, save that they had no sources of power left to them, and boasted no ships, no armies, no real means of defense. Would we have welcomed them like brothers? I think not. The newcomers will not know, at first, that we have only one *Serpent*. They should see her in her battle glory. Then perhaps they will think of us as equals."

"I agree with Talaban," said Questor Ro. "His analogy is a good one. We are arrogant—as indeed we have every right to be. But we are facing unknown dangers here. The *Serpent* should be battle ready—though we can pray she is not needed."

"Perhaps we should vote on the question," said Niclin.

"No vote is required," put in Rael. "This is a military decision, and that makes it mine alone. The chest will remain—for the time being—in the *Serpent*."

Niclin raised his hand. "As you will, Rael, but before we move on, may I ask a question, captain . . . is it true that you struck Questor Ro while upon the ice? Struck him in full view of watching Vagars?"

Viruk had heard no such rumor and was fascinated. He glanced at Talaban and saw his expression harden. "The Questor and I fought the krals," said Talaban, "and then there followed the eruption. I ran to help the Questor and he stumbled as the earth cracked open. I caught him. I fail to see how that constitutes a blow, but then perhaps it looked like one from afar."

"You are saying then that you did not strike him?"

Viruk noted the captain's hesitation as the question was put. "Surely," said Talaban, "that would be better asked of the Questor himself. But I would be interested to know the origin of this . . . bizarre tale."

"A seaman from your vessel told it to his friends in an ale house," said Niclin. "Happily he was speaking loud enough to be heard by an officer of the Watch. He was arrested, questioned and crystal-drawn at dusk. Other members of the crew are now under interrogation. If necessary they will all be crystal-drawn."

"I think I prefer the word *murdered*," said Talaban, coldly. "And that is not going to happen. They will be released instantly."

"That is not your decision," said Niclin. The councillor's face was reddening. Viruk smiled. The man was struggling to hold his temper.

"No, the decision is mine," said Rael firmly. "Does anyone else have anything to add?"

"Surely, Questor General," said fat Caprishan, "we should ask Questor Ro to confirm or deny the veracity of the tale. If it is true then all the Vagar crew should be crystal-drawn forthwith."

"The point is well made, cousin, and I thank you for it," said Rael. He turned towards Ro, gesturing for him to speak.

Questor Ro was silent for a moment, then he glanced at Talaban. "The captain saved my life upon the ice. Without him I would have been dead. That, I think you will find, is what it says in my report. I have nothing to add."

"Let the sailors be freed," said Rael. "Now, let us move on. Most of you will know by now of the timely demise of Judon of the Patiakes. I believe his death has averted any immediate threat of revolt. But we are facing other problems from within. There is a group within the five cities calling themselves Pajists. They were responsible for the death of Questor Baliel and are also believed to be behind the attacks on prominent Vagar citizens who show great loyalty to our rule. We are currently hunting down the leaders, but be advised, my friends, we are in great danger. I want no councillor to travel the city without guards, and a greater security must be maintained in our homes and our places of work. I myself questioned three men. Even under torture they would not divulge the names of their leaders. But we did learn that the attacks would escalate."

"How is this group financed?" asked Caprishan. "Do we know?"

"Not yet," said Rael, "but it is safe to assume they are receiving aid from the Erek-jhip-zhonad."

"You want me to kill their king?" asked Viruk.

"Not yet, cousin. We have enough enemies for now. At this stage we must be careful. Attacks upon Avatars must not succeed. We rule a hostile population. Once they begin to perceive us not as lords but as targets . . ." He did not finish the sentence.

"These people must be found—and quickly," said Niclin.

"They will be," Rael promised. "We are currently hunting a tribesman we believe is a courier. He is a very old white-haired man, and he travels with a young golden-haired child. Our information is that he brings instructions to the group, as well as gold to finance them. He poses as a merchant and our agents are scouring the city for him. When we find him we will find the leaders."

"What kind of merchant?" asked Viruk, his good humor evaporating. He knew the answer before Rael spoke.

"He peddles wine, I understand," said the Questor General.

First instincts, thought Viruk, are always the best. I should have cut the old man's throat. He sighed. The day was blighted now and nothing would rescue it. He leaned back in his chair, trying to look interested as the talk turned to tax revenue and collection. He glanced across at Talaban. Was he enjoying the meeting, he wondered? Or was he as bored as Viruk himself?

There was no way to tell. Talaban's dark features were impassive, his concentration fixed on the speaker. Viruk's gaze drifted to Caprishan, who was explaining the problems of gathering tribal duties. His many chins wobbled as he spoke, and sweat was trickling down his face. Viruk watched a rivulet reach the chins then flow along one of the creases. He stifled a yawn.

By the time the meeting ended he would cheerfully have strangled everyone present. Rael offered them all refreshments, but Viruk declined and left the palace, setting off on foot for his home. It was more than a mile, but the night was pleasantly fresh, the air cool on his face. Unlike the others, he hoped the new Avatars would prove hostile. Perhaps then he would find enemies worthy of his talents.

He had enjoyed killing the fat king, watching the zhi-bolt explode into his back, spraying blood and bone across the pretty flowers. Ah yes, he thought, the flowers. What did they say the name was . . . ? Star petals? Star blooms? No. Sky stars. That was it. Delightful plants. He could still remember the scent, delicate and light. Tomorrow he would tell Kale about them and have them planted close to his bedroom window.

Viruk strolled on along the wide avenue then cut to the right along the narrow Street of Sawyers. No one was working at this hour, but he could still make out the musty smell of the fresh cut timbers. The street was dark and Viruk's foot squelched down on a pile of horse dung. A foul stench filled the air. Viruk was about to scrape the sole of his boot when he heard a whisper of movement from behind. He spun on his heel. Moonlight glinted on a knife blade. Blocking the blow with his forearm he slammed his fist into his attacker's jaw. The knifeman stumbled and fell. Viruk leapt to his right as a second attacker materialized from a nearby alley. This one held a sword. Viruk backed away. "Have you mistaken me for someone else?" he asked, his voice, as always, amiable.

"We know who you are," said the swordsman, advancing slowly. He was dressed in dark clothing and a scarf was drawn about the lower half of his face. The knifeman was on his feet now, moving crab-like to Viruk's right. "You are Viruk the Killer," continued the swordsman. "Viruk the Insane."

"Insane? That is very rude," Viruk told him. "I think I shall kill you with your own sword."

The knifeman hurled himself forward. Viruk stepped in to meet him, swaying aside from a clumsy lunge and hammering his elbow into the man's face. With a strangled cry the man staggered back. The swordsman sent a vicious cut toward Viruk's head. The Avatar ducked under it, then launched himself in a flying dive, his shoulder thudding into the man's belly and pitching him from his feet. They hit the ground hard. Viruk reared up and struck the swordsman three times in the face, then grabbed his hair and slammed his head against the road twice. The swordsman groaned. Viruk pushed himself to his feet, and wrenched the sword from the man's hand. "Pitiful," said Viruk. "Truly pitiful."

Spinning he sent the blade slashing through the air— and into the neck of the knifeman, who was creeping up behind him. The blade sliced through skin and tendon, smashing the vertebrae and slicing through both jugular veins. The man's head flopped to the right and his legs buckled.

The swordsman had struggled to his knees. "No!" he cried, as his friend died.

"No?" queried Viruk. "The time for saying no was before you attempted this ridiculous assault. I wouldn't mind—save for the fact that you knew who I was. You have no idea how insulting that is. I mean, two of you!" Crouching down before the kneeling man he reached out and dragged the scarf clear. The face he saw was young, barely out of his teens. "I take it you are Pajists," said Viruk.

The youngster nodded, then a gleam came into his eyes. "Yes. And proud to die for the cause. I may not have been good enough to kill you—but one day someone will. Kill you and all your foul kind."

"Perhaps," agreed Viruk. "Now why don't you tell me the names of those who sent you?"

"Never!"

"That's what I thought," Viruk told him with a wide smile. "It does make matters so much more simple." With one sudden move he swept the sword up and plunged it into the young man's belly with such force that the blade penetrated his back. "Hurts, doesn't it?" said Viruk. The swordsman screamed and sagged forward into the arms of his killer. Viruk kissed his cheek and pushed him away.

Rising, he remembered his soiled boot. Wiping it clean on the clothing of the dying man he made his way back to the palace to report the attack.

The Questor General sent a squad of soldiers to the spot, but by the time they arrived the bodies had been spirited away.

"What do you remember about them?" Rael asked Viruk, who was sponging blood from his black silk shirt.

"They were young and not very skillful," said Viruk. "But they were waiting for me. One of them said as much. Called me Viruk the Killer. I can't believe they sent only two. Do you think they were trying to annoy me?"

"They didn't send only two," said Talaban, moving forward. "Someone else was close by. Otherwise they would have had no time to remove the bodies."

"Ah," said Viruk. "That's more like it. They sent three—but one of them was a coward. Even so, three is still somewhat of an insult."

"You were *unarmed*, Viruk," Rael pointed out. "They probably thought three would be enough."

"I expect you are right," said Viruk. "Can you still see blood on the shirt?"

"I think it is gone," Rael told him. "Now, can you think of anything else? Anything at all?"

Viruk thought about the question, picturing the events once more. "No," he said at last. "They came at me from the darkness. It was all over very quickly."

"Then get home and rest, cousin," said Rael. "And this time take a sword."

"He is a fool," said Talaban, after Viruk had gone. "Had he kept the swordsman alive we could have questioned him."

"As he said, they came from the darkness," Rael pointed out.

Talaban shook his head. "He was unarmed. He took the swordsman's blade and killed the knifeman. That left the swordsman unarmed. He could have captured him."

"I know that!" snapped Rael. "But Viruk is not a thinker. He likes to kill. That is his talent, and his obsession. But if we are speaking of fools, Talaban, let us review your report to the meeting. Was it your intention to create enemies here? You spoke of arrogance, and your summation of Avatar characteristics was offensive. How did you put it? *If these newcomers are anything like us they will be arrogant and convinced of their superiority and divine right to rule.* Because of that you angered Niclin and he sought to have your crew put to death. Had Questor Ro not supported you it would have happened."

"I merely spoke the truth," said Talaban.

"Pah! The truth. Why is it that men always believe the truth is like a single crystal, hard and unchanging? What you perceive as arrogance, others see as pride. You want the truth? You cannot have it, for it is based on perception, like a beautiful woman. Where one man sees a whore, another sees an angel. When you spoke of our arrogance the Council looked at you, and what did *they* see? A man who despises his own people, perhaps."

"That is not true!" stormed Talaban.

"There you go with the truth again. What is it you mean? That Niclin does not see it as true, or that you do not see it as true?" He held up his hand as Talaban tried to answer. "It does not matter. What they observe is a man who eschews the *look* of an Avatar. Where is the blue in his hair? Why does he not want to look like one of us? Is he ashamed? Or is it that he knows he is a Vagar? Are the stories about his mother true? And here we come to the word 'truth' again. Well let me tell you, I am sick of other men's truth!

"Do not misunderstand me, Talaban. I value you highly, which is why I support you, but you must realize that we are a race under siege. We live with the constant threat of extinction. Such a situation breeds paranoia."

"You are right," said Talaban softly. "I do despise what we have become. Once we ruled the world. Now we are parasites, sucking the blood from the Vagars. We contribute little."

Rael laughed aloud. "I might argue that we contribute greatly to the stability of the region. We are the enemy. We give them reason to unite. Without us there would be constant tribal wars and great devastation. All the while they look to us with hatred the general peace is maintained."

Talaban smiled. "You say you *might* argue that. I take it you do not believe it."

"I tell no one what I believe," said Rael. "I am the Questor General. Do you know why Ro supported you?"

"No. It was a surprise."

"It should not have been. He supported you because Niclin called for the deaths of your crew. Ro hates Niclin. It is that simple. I know you struck Ro, because he came to me, calling for your crew to be crystal-drawn. I asked him to wait until the meeting to raise it, and then made sure that Niclin was apprised of the incident. Had Ro called for your crew to be killed, Niclin would have opposed it."

"I thank you," said Talaban. "Once more I am in your debt."

"You are an intelligent man, Talaban, but you are cursed—or perhaps blessed—with a romantic turn of mind. You see absolutes where there is only shifting sand. In many ways you are like the Pajists. They see us as tyrants and believe that the world would be better, and more just, if we were overthrown. What they do not realize is that the world is created for tyrants. It always has been. You were a student of history. Can you tell me of a time where there were no rulers? No law-makers?" Rael moved to the far table and poured himself a goblet of watered wine. "Society," he said, "is like a pyramid. The poor make up the base, and slowly the whole building narrows until a single stone is placed at the top. The king, the emperor, the god. It can be no other way."

"I am not convinced of that," said Talaban.

Rael chuckled. "Of course you are not. You are a romantic. Well, let us deal with history again. Three thousand years ago, when the empire was very young and a rigid class system was in place there were several revolutions. The most interesting—for the sake of this argument—was the third, when the people killed the king. An assembly of senators was created with no overall leader."

"It could have been a golden age," said Talaban. "Fairer laws were passed. Universities were created."

"Indeed they were. But within ten years there was a king again."

"Not so, surely. Perjak took the title First Senator," objected Talaban.

"Who cares what he called himself? He might have taken the title Fourth-sheep-from-the left. The title was immaterial. He had absolute power and he ruled like a king. His enemies were put to death. The poor remained poor, the rich got richer. What I am saying is that Man requires leadership. We are like the wolves, the elk, the deer, the tuskers. Always there is a leader of the herd. At this time in history the leader is the Avatar race. One day it will be another race. It may be unjust, but it is natural." Rael poured Talaban a goblet of wine and handed it to him. "But these political matters are not what concerns me most about you, Talaban.

"In all my life I have only truly loved two people—loved them with all my heart. My wife, Mirani, and my daughter Chryssa. When Chryssa became crystal-wed I wanted to die. If it were possible to give my life for hers I would have offered it gladly. But when she died I accepted it. I buried her. And I moved on, Talaban. I chose to live, as fully as I could. It is time for you to do the same."

Talaban nodded. "I know that now. I learned it on the voyage home. What is it you would have me do, Rael?"

"First put some blue in your hair," said Rael, with a weary smile. "Then take a few days' rest. After that gather your crew. None of them has ever fought on a fully charged *Serpent*. Take them out to sea. Train them. I shall also give you thirty Avatar soldiers."

"All the ship's weapons need to be recharged," said Talaban. "That will require more than a hundred crystals."

"I will send them to the ship."

"You think the newcomers will seek a war?"

"It is inevitable." Rael gave a weary smile. "For they will be arrogant, just like us, and believe in their superiority and divine right to rule."

The tavern was deserted, the diners departed, the tables empty. Yet still Sofarita did not sleep. She sat on the windowsill, tense and fearful, gazing down at the silent square. She could not relax for if she did, images would flow past her mind's eye, people she did not know, places she had not seen, words and conversations she had never heard.

Each time the visions came she felt as if she were flowing with them, drowning in a sea of lives. She feared the flow. Once, as a small child, she had fallen into the Luan, tumbling down the mud bank to disappear beneath the fast-flowing water. A farmer had plunged in to rescue her, dragging her clear. But there was no farmer now to pull her back from this river of other people's dreams.

Sofarita could not understand why this mystical phenomenon should be happening to her. She had never before experienced visions. She wondered if it could be a sign of approaching madness. Perhaps the visions were not real, but just her imaginings. Perhaps she had a fever. She lifted a hand to her brow. It was not hot. Rising from the sill she walked back into the room and drank a cup of water. Weariness dogged her, and she longed for the bliss of sleep.

But what if she never woke? What if the river of dreams carried her away?

She knew no one in the city to whom she could turn for help. You are alone, she told herself. You must help yourself. This thought was curiously helpful. True, she could rely on no one and yet, conversely, no one relied upon her. She was truly free for the first time in her life. Not subject to the whims of a father who believed women were of little worth, nor of a husband she had liked and respected—but never truly loved. No longer chained within a close-minded village society.

The river of dreams at least offered excitement.

Sofarita lay down upon the bed, her head upon the pillow. Drawing the blankets over her shoulders she closed her eyes. There were no visions, no haunting scenes.

She was in the cellar of the tavern. Baj was sitting at a narrow table, his head in his hands. He was weeping. A man was sitting close by. He was middle-aged, with silver-streaked yellow hair and beard. There was a golden-haired child asleep on a cot bed by the wall. Sofarita watched the scene, dispassionately at first, but then Baj's distress touched her. She moved forward to comfort him—and realized she was floating above the scene. The men could not see her.

"Stop your crying, man, and tell me what happened," said the older man.

"He killed them. It was horrible." Baj looked up, his face a mask of anguish. "I did nothing, Boru. I stood frozen in the shadows."

"He would have killed you too," said Boru. *"To attack Viruk was stupidity beyond belief."*

"Forjal saw him walking to the meeting. He was unarmed. If I had acted . . ."

"But you did not," said Boru harshly. *"Did Forjal talk before he died?"*

"Yes, but he only told Viruk that someone would kill him. He refused to say who sent him. But what if they find the bodies? Forjal worked for me. I could be implicated."

"Stop your whining, man! They will find the bodies, but not the heads. They are in a weighted sack, which I hurled from the dock. But understand this, Baj, there must be no further acts of individual violence. Everything must be planned. You and Forjal risked everything by one act of indescribable stupidity. Now he and the other fool are dead. And, were it left to me, I would cut your throat now. But you are to be given another chance. From now on you will follow orders. You will take no precipitate action. Do you understand this?"

Baj nodded. *"I am sorry."*

"Apologize to the spirits of Forjal and his friend."

Sofarita opened her eyes. The bedroom was dark, lit only by a shaft of moonlight coming through the small window. She felt incredibly rested, though she could not have been asleep for more than an hour. She had blown out the lanterns before climbing into bed, and she had no means now of lighting them.

Even as the thought occurred to her, one of the lanterns flickered into life and a gentle glow filled the room. Sofarita sat up. Looking across at the second lantern she pictured it alight.

The wick flamed instantly. Sofarita leaned back on the pillow. There was no panic now.

For this had to be a dream. Settling down and pulling the blankets around her she slept again.

Chapter Fifteen

The home of Methras was on the eastern outskirts of the city, close to the lumber yards, and closer still to a slaughterhouse, built two years ago on the old meadow. A hundred years ago the area had been highly popular with well-to-do Vagars, men who were not yet rich but who were climbing through the ranks of the merchant classes. Now it was run-down and shabby, though some of the older homes were well built, and occasionally fronted with marble.

Methras had walked the four miles from the wharf and, as he opened the small gate that led to the rear garden, he saw two horses tethered in the shade behind the house. He was tired and in no mood for company as he strolled along the garden path. A figure in a dress of sky-blue satin stepped into the garden. She saw him and ran to meet him. In her late forties, his mother was still a handsome woman, though her once-trim figure had thickened a little and there was now grey in her golden hair. She kissed his cheek. "Welcome home, my son," she said, taking his arm and leading him inside.

"Who is here?" he asked her.

"An old friend of yours, come to greet you upon your return," she told him. "And his uncle from beyond the Luan."

Pausing in the kitchen he poured a long, cool drink of

water from a pottery jug and drained it. Then he turned
to his mother and smiled. "It is good to see you. You
are looking well. Is that a new dress?" With a wide
smile she stepped back from him, and twirled. The
heavy satin of the dress lifted briefly as she spun.

"Do you like it?"

"It is very becoming. Does this mean you are in love
again?"

"Don't be sarcastic," she scolded him gently. "You
think I am too old for love?"

"You don't look a day over twenty-five," he assured
her. "Who is this lucky man?"

"He is a merchant, recently arrived from Pagaru. He
is a fine man. Very witty and entertaining."

"How old?"

"Fifty—or so he says. I think he's closer to sixty. But
he's a fine figure of a man."

"He would have to be," said Methras. "Now tell me
who is here?"

"Don't you want to be surprised?"

"I don't like surprises."

"You used to," she said. "I remember when you were
very young . . ."

"Not now, mother," he said, gently. "Who is here?"

"It is Pendar." She leaned in close. "And he is rich
now," she whispered. "You should have accepted his
offer and joined him in partnership. Perhaps he still
wants you."

"I am sure that he does," said Methras with a wide
smile.

His mother reddened. "Oh you know I didn't mean
that," she said. "I know Pendar—" she struggled for
words "—prefers the company of young men. But I
know he values your judgement."

Methras kissed her cheek. "Of course. He loves me
for my mind," he said.

"What he needs—" she began.

Methras held up his hand. "If the phrase *the love of a good woman* is hovering on your lips, do not say it. You are far too intelligent to be caught in that cliché."

"What I was going to say is that he needs the guidance of someone he can trust. He has a way with money, but he is like a straw in the wind. You could help him, Methras, and become rich yourself."

"I have no interest in wealth or power," he said. "I am a soldier. It suits me well."

"You are very much like your father," she told him.

"Too much—and not enough," he said sadly.

Moving through the house, he entered the wide living area. Two men were seated in the archway leading to the front garden. Pendar, as always, was immaculately and expensively dressed. His pearl-grey tunic and leggings were woven from heavy silk, his shoes crafted from lizard-skin. He was tall, very slim and still boyish, his hair dyed with streaks of gold. The man beside him was more strongly built, with wide shoulders and powerful hands. His beard was silver and yellow.

"My dear friend," said Pendar, as Methras entered. Moving smoothly across the room he embraced the soldier and kissed his cheek. "It is so good to see you. How are you?"

"Fit and well, Pendar. Who is your friend?"

"Not a friend, exactly," said Pendar. "More a business acquaintance. He is a fine man. Trustworthy. His name is Boru. He is of the Banis-baya, a tribe who dwell close to the Well of Life."

Boru rose and moved forward, his hand outstretched. Methras shook it briefly.

"Good as it is to see you, my friend," said Methras, turning once more to Pendar, "I must tell you that I am very weary, and was looking forward to some sleep this afternoon."

"We won't keep you long," said Boru. "I understand you have just returned from a long voyage."

"Yes, to the southern ice. It was successful."

"By which you mean . . . ?" asked Boru.

"We found what we were looking for," he answered. "That would seem to me to constitute a successful trip."

"As I understand it, Vagars died upon the ice," said Boru, "and what was found made the Avatars more powerful than they were before. Some might argue that as a great failure."

"A soldier of the empire would not argue so," Methras pointed out.

"He might," said Boru. "These are changing times. The hourglass of history is about to be spun. Some men believe that within a few years these cities will once again be controlled by Vagars. What then will befall those loyal to the old empire?"

Methras did not reply. Ignoring Boru, he turned to Pendar. The golden-haired man was about to speak, but Methras lifted his hand and shook his head. "Say not a word, my friend. It is best you leave, and when you return come alone. What I have not heard I cannot report."

"He is right," said Boru. "We are wasting our time here."

"No, it is *my* time you are wasting," snapped Methras. "Leave now."

Boru swung on his heel and stalked from the room. Pendar stood still for a moment, confused. Methras put his hand on his friend's slender shoulder. "Walk with care, Pendar, for the road you travel is very dangerous."

"Boru is right," said Pendar softly. "The days of the Avatar are coming to an end. Once they are overthrown all their friends and allies will be killed. I do not want to see you hurt."

"How can you believe the Vagars will be allowed to rule their own cities? If the Avatars fall then the Erek-jhip-zhonad or the Patiakes will conquer them, and they will have merely exchanged masters. Stay out of politics, Pendar. It will destroy you."

"*Their* own cities?" countered Pendar. "Do you not mean *our* own cities? Or is your Avatar blood taking hold? You are like me, a half-breed, caught between two races. If the truth was discovered even now we would both be crystal-drawn. The Avatars will never accept us. I will not give my loyalty and my life to people who would wish me dead if they knew of my blood. They are the enemy, Methras. One day you will see it too."

"They are not all enemies. There is Talaban."

"Ah yes," said Pendar, with a mischievous smile, "the beautiful Talaban. Do not be deceived, my dear. He is still a member of the god-race, and his long life is maintained by the deaths of Vagars, crystal-drawn against their will."

"You must go now," said Methras.

Pendar nodded, and gathered up his heavy black cloak. "I think of you often," he said. Methras walked past him and out into the late afternoon sunshine.

He stood there for some time, until he heard the two horsemen ride away. His mother joined him, linking her arm through his.

"Did he want you to work with him?" she asked.

"Yes."

"Will you?"

"I don't believe that I will."

"You could be making a mistake," she said.

"One of us is," he agreed.

The problems facing Anu were many. His 600 workers had begun work on the pyramid in good spirits, making jokes about the seemingly perpetual sunshine. After ten *days*, with the sun having inched its way to its first noon, the mood among the Vagars had changed. Anu felt the tension. It was bizarre to work for hours with the sun almost frozen in the sky, to sleep for five hours, and to awake with the sun still high. It jangled the nerves. Many men reported sick, others found difficulty in sleeping. Tempers flared, and on the fourth day one man slammed a hammer into the skull of a co-worker. One of the Avatar guards slew the murderer. Separated from the holding magic of the chest the two bodies rotted instantly, becoming covered in maggots. A hundred workers saw the scene, and it frightened them. Accelerating time, as Anu was discovering, produced a host of allied problems.

Bread became stale within minutes, fruit rotted even before it could be removed from the barrels. Grass grew at twenty times the speed. A man could sit and watch it grow. Anu eventually solved the food problem by adjusting the power of the chest to encompass the supplies. The same method was used on the plants and grasses that grew in the valley. But even so the mood among the hired men was deteriorating. Thirty had so far asked to be relieved, and this request was granted. They trooped home on the next occasion that Anu slowed the Dance to allow supplies into the valley.

At Shevan's suggestion he sent a request for fifty whores to be brought in, and built a series of huts for them on the edge of the valley. The service provided by the whores was free. The men were given special coins of baked clay, which the women collected against payment from the Treasury at the end of their allotted service. This mollified the workforce for a while. Then came the interminable twenty-day *night*. Now the men grew more fractious, and several fights broke out. One of the workers committed suicide during this first period of night. This puzzled Anu for a while, until he concluded that sunlight was somehow important to the brain, and without it men became depressed. Along with the services of the women he now allowed strong drink and opiates to be offered to his workers, and organized dances, competitions and other forms of entertainment for those who had finished their labors.

By the thirtieth *day* the foundations of the pyramid— a deep and perfect square of limestone blocks, stretching for 750 feet on each side—were finally laid in place. Anu arranged an impromptu party, allowing the men to vote for a Foundations King. The winner—a foreman named Yasha—was crowned with laurel leaves and carried around the foundations, which were then inscribed with his name. Anu liked Yasha, a big man, wide-shouldered and tall, with a booming laugh and a powerful way with other men. He was an imposing figure and his crew of thirty were the best by far.

Shevan watched the procession and smiled. "They seem happier now, sir," he said.

Anu nodded. The work was still slower than he had expected and he decided to make changes to the rotas. From now on the crews would work in three shorter shifts instead of two long ones, and there would be rewards for those who matched the work targets set them. "What is the hourly rate for placing the blocks?" he asked Shevan.

"A week ago it was six, but now we are closer to nine. It is getting better, sir."

"It needs to be higher than twelve. What is the situation at the quarry?"

Shevan looked troubled. "The tools are wearing out much faster than anticipated, sir. And there is a problem with the pegs. It appears—"

"That the wood is not absorbing water."

"Yes, sir. You anticipated this?"

"I wish that I had," replied Anu wearily.

Stonemasons drilled holes in the sandstone then drove dry wooden pegs into the holes. When water was added the pegs expanded, splitting the stone neatly. This is how the blocks were created. But, somehow, the acceleration of time was affecting the absorption rate.

Anu strolled across to the Gepha pyramid. It had been the first attempt, seventy years ago, to build a power source. It had failed. As Anu had known it would, for it was built without the Music. Now it served as a base for his own work, and laborers were busy chiselling out the blocks, harnessing them and, by careful use of massive hides full of water, were counterbalancing their weight and lowering them to the ground. The work was slow and dangerous. Had he possessed two chests Anu would have used the enhanced power of the Music to lessen the weight of the blocks, but with only one he needed to conserve the energy for the courses of his own pyramid.

A commotion began some way to his left. It was close to the mist barrier he had summoned around the valley. He and Shevan hurried across to where a crowd of workers had gathered.

An incredibly old man lay on the ground. His limbs were twitching, and, as the men watched, the flesh fell away from him, the skin drying, becoming leather, then peeling away from his bones like worn papyrus.

"It was Jadas," whispered one man. "He crossed the mist last night to meet his wife."

Anu stepped forward. "Be calm!" he said. "You have all been warned about the magic used here. I told you all that it would be death to cross the mist."

"We are prisoners here!" shouted another man.

"That is not true," said Anu. "I explained the dangers when you agreed to the work. But any who wish to leave can do so when the supplies are due, and the mist is lifted. I am Anu. I do not lie. This man was a fool. There are many fools in the world. He was told of the dangers and chose to disbelieve them."

"What happens if the magic goes wrong?" shouted the first man. "We could all end up like Jadas."

"Come now, lads," said Yasha, the Foundations King, striding forward to stand among them. "You've all heard of the Holy One. He's not a liar. And I, for one, am looking forward to going home with eight thousand silver pieces. I'm going to *build* this wonder for Anu, and then I'm going to *buy* a home. Not build it. *Buy* it! I'm going to sit in the shade and drink fine wine. And upon my knee will sit the prettiest whore in Egaru."

"We could all die here, Yasha!" objected the first man.

"You die if you want to, Podri. I'm going to live to be rich. Now let us bury this bag of bones and get on with the Wonder."

"You honestly believe we're safe?" asked another man.

"Safe?" replied Yasha with a chuckle. "Safe? When has a laborer ever been safe? But for eight thousand silvers I'll risk a little danger." He swung to Anu. "Am I safe from your magic, Holy One?" he asked.

"You are. I promise you," Anu told him.

"Good enough for me," said Yasha. "Now I'm off to find the least ugly whore."

With that he strode away, his laurel crown still in place. The crowd broke up. The bones of Jadas crumbled to dust and blew away on the breeze.

"He is a good man," said Shevan.

"Yes," answered Anu absently. He was already planning for an increase in the absorption rate of wooden pegs.

● ● ●

The gardener was kneeling on an old cushion in the sunshine, carefully weeding the rockery. A straw hat, wide-brimmed and frayed, protected his neck from the harsh noon sun. Brightly colored flowers were growing all around the rockery, pale pink rock jasmine, golden bloomed alyssum, white and yellow bellflowers, with their delicate, drooping blooms. The gardener's fingers gently tugged at the weed stems while he probed the roots with his copper fork. Placing the weeds in a canvas basket by his side he climbed over the higher rocks to continue his work among the scented thyme that grew against the garden's rear wall. He worked with the endless patience of a man in tune with the earth, never tearing at the weeds, never disturbing the roots of the plants he sought to protect. There was no tension in him, and his mind was perfectly at peace.

An older man moved along the paved path beneath the rockery. He was a big man, heavy-boned and broad in the shoulder. His close-cropped hair was peppered with silver, and his skin was deeply tanned and leathered by a lifetime of work in the open. The gardener saw him, smiled and climbed back down to the path.

"It is looking fine, Kale," he said. "You have done well. But I am concerned with the violets."

Together the two men strolled across the rock garden to a deep pocket of royal blue speedwell growing alongside a crimson wild thyme. At the border of the rocks was a stand of yellow wood violet. The leaves were dull and speckled.

"The soil is not holding enough moisture, lord," said Kale, kneeling down and pushing his fingers into the earth. "It could do with some peat or rotted straw. I will fetch some this afternoon." He glanced over his shoulder at the rising sun. "And they are getting too much sun."

The gardener nodded. "It had enough shade until the

juniper died. We need to build a screen to the west, with a fast-climbing flower, to give time for the weeping birch to take hold. A jasmine, do you think?"

"A screen is a good idea, lord. Though I prefer the yellow clematis as a climber. But I think you put too much faith in the birch. Such trees do not like this soil. It is too thin."

"A garden needs trees. They lift the eye, and the spirit, and they add depth and shadow. Anyway the cypresses are doing well here."

"Indeed they are, lord, but you spent a fortune for the irrigation work. Without it they would die within a month."

The gardener laughed. "What else is money for? It is there to be spent. A garden is a thing of beauty, and pleasing to the Source."

"Speaking of money, lord, the marsh marigolds will be here tomorrow. It appears that most survived the journey."

"Excellent. That is what the far pond needs, Kale. A touch of gold. Now remember they should be planted just above the water's edge, the soil kept continually moist."

"I have never seen a marsh marigold, lord," said Kale. "I will not know how to nurture it."

The gardener smiled and clapped the man on the shoulder. "You will learn, Kale. And if they die I'll buy more. Eventually we will get it right."

A newcomer moved along the path. Kale bowed and backed away as the Avatar approached. "Your gardens are a constant delight, Viruk," said the Questor General. "So many colors and scents."

Tension returned and the gardener faded back. Viruk the warrior brushed the dry dirt from his hands and led the General to a rest area where comfortable chairs had been set under a canopy of vine leaves. It was cool in the shade. "To what do I owe the pleasure of your visit, cousin?" he asked, removing his straw hat and dropping it to the ground.

"Ammon is training a regular army. My spies tell me that they are well disciplined and hardy."

"How many men in this army?"

"Five thousand, split into fifty groups of one hundred each. Every man has a bronze breastplate and helm, and a bronze-reinforced shield of hard wood. Most are armed with short swords, though the front rankers use twelve-foot spears."

"An interesting development," said Viruk. "You want me to kill Ammon?"

"No. We may need this army."

Viruk laughed. "You think the Mud People will fight alongside us?"

"If they don't they will be either assimilated or annihilated by the newcomers."

"You fear they will be that strong?"

Rael leaned back in his chair and rubbed his tired eyes. "We have maintained control with a mere five hundred. The newcomers—and their major cities—have survived. There will be thousands of them, Viruk. The Source alone knows what kind of weaponry they possess."

"What would you have me do?"

"Go to Ammon. Tell him what has happened. Assure him that if the Erek-jhip-zhonad are attacked we will support him in any way we can. But do not ask for his help. There must be no show of weakness. If he offers it, accept graciously."

"Would this . . . embassy . . . not be better undertaken by a Questor, cousin? I am no diplomat. I would as soon cut the savage's throat as dine with him."

"That is why you are the best man for the role, Viruk. Ammon knows of you and your skills. He will be wary, but he will listen. I have watched him closely since he became king. He is a stronger man than his father, and wiser than any chieftain we have dealt with so far. He could be a strong ally."

"Or a deadly enemy."

"Indeed so. Remain in his capital as my ambassador. I have sent him a message that you are coming."

"I would prefer to be here when the newcomers arrive," objected Viruk.

"I am sure that you would."

"This means you have turned down my request to join Talaban on the *Serpent*?"

"There will be battles enough, I fear. When they come I want you to support Ammon."

Viruk rose and filled a goblet with cool water from a stone jug. "The five cities could soon be under attack, cousin. You have no one who fights as well as I. It is folly to send me away at such a time."

"You may be right, Viruk. But what if their ships sail past us and into the mouth of the Luan? What if their first assault is into the lands of the Mud People? Then they would be both before and behind us. If I were attacking this coast that is what I would do. The five cities are strong, the Mud People less so. It would be hard for us to fight on two fronts, Viruk. And since this is my *greatest* fear I am sending my *greatest* warrior. Take ten Avatars with you. The very best."

Viruk chuckled. "You seek to win me over by flattery. And damn my soul if it hasn't succeeded. Very well, cousin, I will do this for you."

Rael nodded and rose. "If they come, Viruk, defend Ammon as if he was your own blood. If they attack they will seek to kill the king. They must not succeed. And if they break through get him here, with as many of his men as you can."

Viruk laughed. "Only a few days ago I sent him a

promise to rip out his entrails. Now I am to defend him? Life is never dull with you, Rael. Now, if you will excuse me, I have work to do in my garden."

Rael smiled. "I notice your gardener is looking well. I could have sworn the last time I saw him he looked older."

"Working with me obviously agrees with him," said Viruk.

Rael shook his head. "You break too many rules, cousin. Be careful."

"Kale is very valuable to me. He saved my *pulsatillas* by improving the drainage and cutting back surrounding growth to allow them more light. They would have died without him. And what would a garden be without *pulsatillas*?"

"I have changed my mind," said Rael, with a broad smile. "Do not think of Ammon as one of your blood, but as one of your flowers."

"Well, it's true I'd like to see him planted in the earth," replied Viruk.

Questor Ro had been sitting in judgment for two hours and he was growing bored. In the main the cases brought before him were petty, and only two defendants had been sentenced to be crystal-drawn—and these would lose only five years each. He gazed down at the two lists before him. One detailed the cases, the other the needs of the Crystal Treasury. According to the latter they needed today twenty-two full sentences of death in order to meet the treasury requirements. Ro fully understood the need to maintain power, and he had little regard for Vagars. Yet the law was the law, and no amount of pressure would make Ro yield on any point of it. If a man stole bread—without use of violence—to feed his family it was a misdemeanor, punishable by a maximum of five years. Ro had rounded on the prosecutor who tried to claim that when the victim gave chase to the thief he fell and sprained his wrist, making this a crime of violence.

Questor Ro was not in a good mood. He did not like courtroom three in the eastern district. It was small and cramped, the magistrate's dais raised only two feet from the floor, the magistrate being forced to enter from a side room, walking past and beneath the public seating. This alone left Vagars looking down on Ro, which he felt was not becoming. The magistrate should enter from behind the dais, as in all other courtrooms.

Ro tugged at his forked blue beard and fixed his gaze on the public gallery. There were no Avatars present, and the benches were only half full. Ro adjusted his royal blue robes, sipped water from a crystal cup and nodded to the guards to bring in the next defendant.

The case was one of rape. The victim, a rich fat Vagar woman of middle years, claimed her gardener had climbed into her room and subjected her to a horrifying ordeal—an ordeal that was only ended when her husband burst in. The prosecution called for the death sentence.

"Were any weapons found on the scene?" Ro asked the prosecutor.

"No, Lord Questor. The man used his physical power to overwhelm the lady."

Ro idly examined the evidence sheet, then looked up at the short skinny defendant. The man was blinking nervously and sweat was dripping into his eyes. "I see his clothes were found downstairs, along with the lady's gown. How, pray, did he convince her to go upstairs with him?" asked Ro.

The prosecutor—already aware of Ro's growing irritation—visibly paled. "He threatened her life, Lord Questor."

Ro read the evidence sheet once more. "According to

this he has been employed by the lady and her husband for four years and lives, with four other workmen, in a small house on the estate. Is it your intention to try to convince this court that a man would risk his life and his livelihood, in the sure and certain knowledge of being caught, in order to bed his employer's wife against her will? I do hope not, prosecutor. According to the evidence there was no bruising upon the alleged victim, nor any tearing of her clothes. Her gown, I understand, was neatly folded over a couch. Added to which two goblets of wine were found in the bedroom. Come forward."

The man approached the dais. He was a young Avatar, the son of a minor Questor serving the eastern district. Ro leaned across the desk. "You are not—one supposes—a foolish man. So why has this ridiculous case been brought before me? It is obvious she was seducing her employee when her husband caught her. She has invented this tale. And a poor invention it is."

"Her husband is one of our staunchest supporters, Lord Questor. He is a man of some standing among the Vagars."

Ro waved him back. "The charges against this man are dismissed," he said. "Bring in the next defendant."

The guards brought in a tall young woman with long dark hair. She was dressed in a simple gown of green homespun wool, poorly dyed. She was charged with three offenses: magicking—contravening an ancient law first brought in by the Vagars long before the Avatar conquest; taking employment within the city limits without a permit; and having upon her person less than five silver pieces, thus falling foul of the law governing vagrancy. The vagrancy charge could cost her two crystal years, the lack of a permit another five. But the ancient law could invoke the death sentence.

Ro read the evidence sheet carefully and slowly. The

woman was a newcomer to the city, and had—apparently—healed a baby sick with fever. A crowd had gathered, calling out for healing of boils, headaches and various other minor disorders. She had laid her hands on them all. Before long the crowd was so large it was blocking the thoroughfare and two Avatar soldiers had pushed their way through and arrested the woman.

"Your name?" asked Questor Ro.

For a moment the woman looked distracted, gazing up towards the fluted ceiling. She was exquisitely beautiful. Ro pushed such thoughts from his mind, and asked the question once more. Her deep blue eyes focused on him. "I am Sofarita, lord," she said, her voice husky.

"Your place of birth?"

"The village of Pacepta, lord."

"Occupation?"

"I have none, lord, for I am recently arrived and not yet in possession of a permit."

"Is this why you sought to earn coin with magicking tricks?"

She seemed to be struggling with her concentration, as if she had been taking opiates. Perhaps she has, thought Ro. Or perhaps she is merely mentally afflicted. Yet when she spoke her voice was firm again. "I took no coin, sir. The silver pieces the officers removed were mine. I came to the city three days ago with twenty-six coins, but I have had to take lodgings, for which they charge me a half-silver a day. Added to this I have bought items of clothing. But the remaining money is mine."

"So you did this magicking for no reward?"

"Yes, lord."

"But you do maintain it was magicking?"

"I suppose that it was. I have never experienced such powers before coming to the city. Something has happened to me, but I don't know what it could be. But now I can make lanterns light without flame, and heal disease. And I can see things . . . terrible things." Her voice trailed away, and the faraway look returned to her eyes.

"What is it that you see?" asked Ro.

"Golden ships, men with weapons of fire coming across the sea. Children buried alive on mountaintops, women, with their hands bound being carried to an altar and . . . and . . . murdered." She began to tremble. "I went for a walk this morning, to clear my mind. I hoped the noise and the bustle would help me to put aside the images. There was a woman with a sick child. I knew it was about to die, so I went to her and removed its fever. I don't know how. I just laid my hand upon it, and the heat moved up my arm and into my own head. Then it dispersed. The mother began to cry out that it was a miracle, and others gathered. I committed no crime, lord."

"On the contrary, Sofarita," said Questor Ro, "you committed a great crime. Magicking is punishable by death. However, the law is an ancient one, and I need to review it before passing sentence. Take her away," he commanded the guards. "But keep her close. I will want to question her privately."

Chapter Sixteen

The All Father watched with great sadness as the evil came to his children. In the beginning they had begged him to allow them freedom to live their own destinies. The All Father had promised them he would not interfere. Yet now they faced their doom. With a whisper he could have saved them, but his promise was iron, and it weighed upon his soul. So, in the quiet of the night, he reached out and scooped a handful of earth. This he fashioned into the shape of a woman. Plucking a star from the sky he bathed her in its light, then set the star into her brow. And this was the birth of Star Woman.

From the *Sunset Song of the Anajo*

By the end of the day Ro had sentenced six men and one woman to be fully crystal-drawn, and three others to lose five years. Back in his chambers he removed the magisterial robes and ate a light meal. There was no need to study the ancient law concerning magicking. The woman should have been crystal-drawn. But she had mentioned golden ships and men coming across the sea, and this more than intrigued Ro.

He ordered her brought to his chambers. The room

was small, furnished with a narrow table and two chairs, and when the guards brought her in Ro became even more aware of her beauty. Her hair was dark and lustrous, her lips full and inviting. And, in the close proximity of the small room, he could smell the cheap lemon-scented soap she had used in bathing that morning. He felt suddenly hot and uncomfortable. Bidding her to take a seat he moved away, putting the desk between them.

"Tell me about yourself," he said. She glanced up at him.

"You want to know about the golden ships," she told him. "They frighten you." She hesitated. "I frighten you."

"I do not fear you, woman," he said, sharply.

"Yes, you do. For I remind you of . . . a day in a great park. Children are playing. You are holding the hand of a beautiful woman, yet you are thinking of . . . numbers . . . calculations. She was your wife."

"Tell me of the golden ships," he said, his mouth dry.

"Why is this happening to me? I want it to stop."

"I will help you. But tell me of the ships."

"They are coming across the sea now. Evil men are coming. One with a face like glass. It is not real glass. He has decorated his eyebrows and his chin to make it appear like crystal. He is an awful man. His thoughts are all of blood and death."

"Where are the people from?"

"I don't want to do this," said Sofarita. "I don't want to see them anymore."

"I need to know," said Ro. "It is important. Do they come for war?"

"I cannot see the future, lord. Only what is, and what has been. They are a terrible race. They kill and they maim. They take children and bury them alive to feed . . ." The faraway look returned.

"Look at me! What do they feed?"

"There is a building, four-sided, narrowing to a point. It glitters in the sunlight."

"A pyramid, yes. They feed a pyramid?"

"Yes, they kill people at its peak. The blood runs into channels, and then down into the building. And the pyramid feeds . . . No! Not the pyramid itself, but something inside. Something buried. Something . . . alive!"

Ro licked his lips. His mouth felt suddenly dry. "Can you see inside this pyramid?"

"No. But something lives there."

"And it is fed by blood?"

Sofarita blinked. "And crystals. People sacrificed in other cities have their blood poured over crystals. These are then carried to the pyramid. There are openings and the crystals are poured into them. They clatter and fall." She fell silent.

Ro waited a moment. "How many ships are coming?" he asked. She did not respond. He asked her again, his voice a little louder. She jerked.

"Would you like to see them?" she asked him, suddenly. "The ships?"

"What do you mean?"

She rose from her chair and moved around the desk. Then she extended her hand to him. "I will show you the ships," she said. Now the scent of her was close. He could smell the fragrance of her hair. Reaching out he took her hand.

And was lost in an explosion of color that sent him spiralling out of control. Panic engulfed him, but he heard her voice soft and warm inside his mind, calming him. *"Open your eyes, and see the sky."*

Ro did so, and found himself floating among the clouds above a shimmering sea. He could feel no heat or cold, nor see his own body, but her closeness brought with it a warmth that bathed his soul.

"Down there!" she whispered. *"Can you see them?"*

Thirty golden ships were sailing across the open sea. They had no sails, yet they cruised swiftly through the waves. Ro found himself diving towards them. All fear was gone now, as he floated above the lead ship. It was vast, twice the size of *Serpent Seven*, multi-decked and yet still sleek in the water. Up close he could see that the hull was cunningly crafted from timbers that had been covered with beaten gold. The ship was close to 300 feet long, and 40 feet high. Judging by the opaque blue glass windows there were four decks above the water-line.

Upon the upper deck, above and behind the prow, he saw three large metal structures, adorned with a series of wheels and balances, and protruding like a spear from each machine was a long metal tube some two feet in diameter. Ro had no idea as to their purpose. Beyond the machines a group of men were studying charts. The men were tall, their skins the color of copper. They wore clothes of gold and elaborate headdresses sporting metal feathers stained red and green and blue.

"How soon will they reach Egaru?" he asked Sofarita.

"I don't know. But there are other ships to the south."

"Show me."

In an instant Ro found himself hovering above the familiar ice caps and glaciers where only recently he had found Communion. Five ships were anchored here. Sofarita led him inland to where a camp had been established. The newcomers had created a structure of golden poles laid flat in the shape of an octagon. At its center lay three men—nomads by their appearance. They were dead, their chests open, their hearts ripped out. Blood-covered crystals filled the open cavities.

There were some thirty newcomers in the camp. Despite the intense cold none of them wore furs or any warm clothing. Most were dressed in thin tunics of cotton and seemed oblivious to the glacial temperature around them. Two men caught Ro's spirit eye. One was wearing armor of gold and a tall feathered headdress. The man beside him was shorter, and hunchbacked. Together they were scanning a map painted on hide.

"What are they looking for?" asked Ro.

"I do not know. They came here two days ago and killed a group of nomads."

"Take me closer. I want to see their map."

Ro was now floating directly behind the tall man. The map was covered with symbols Ro could not read, which was galling for an Avatar versed in all the languages known to man.

"Why can we not hear them?" he asked Sofarita.

"These powers are new to me. I cannot read their minds either."

A troop of soldiers came marching from the north. Ro glanced at them. These were wearing furs, and they were big men. As they came closer Ro saw that they were not men at all. They were krals, huge and lumbering. Crossed belts of black leather adorned their chests and they carried clubs of iron. Ro saw that two of them were carrying a long pole, from which hung a nomad, tied by his hands and feet. The krals halted before the tall leader and bowed.

He stepped forward and drew a golden knife with which he cut the ropes holding the prisoner. The man fell to the ground. The leader placed his hand on the man's brow.

Noise burst into Ro's brain like sudden thunder. *"Can you hear them now?"* asked Sofarita.

"Yes. A little warning would have been helpful. I almost died of fright."

The leader was speaking to the prisoner. "Now do

you understand me? Am I speaking your tongue?" he asked.

"I hear you," responded the prisoner sullenly. He was young, and a gash to his face was leaking blood.

"My men have seen a palace built near a lake of ice. Does it belong to your people?"

"No. It was built by the Avatars. Long ago."

"The Avatars? A race of gods? Immortal? Undying?"

"Yes."

"And where are they now?"

"North. The gods toppled them. The sea destroyed them. It is said they hold sway over northern lands. I do not know. I have never been there."

"Have you seen them, these Avatars?"

"Yes. A ship came and they walked this ice. My chieftain saw them. Sold them tusker horns. Then they fight krals with magic bows."

The leader rose and turned to the hunchback. "Draw out his knowledge." The hunchback knelt by the prisoner, clasping both hands on the man's head. He held this pose for more than a minute, then stood.

"It is done, lord," he said.

The leader swung to the krals. "Now you may have him," he told them. Two of the great beasts dropped down. Talons flashed, severing the prisoner's jugular and snapping through his ribs. He did not have time to scream.

"Take me back," ordered Questor Ro.

He opened his eyes back in his chambers. "Your powers are a gift from the Source," he told Sofarita, then realized he was still holding her hand. Swiftly he let go—and instantly regretted it. It had been a long time since he had allowed himself such contact.

"You are a lonely man," she said.

"You must call me lord," he said gently. "We will be

meeting others, and if it is seen you are disrespectful there may be trouble for you."

"You said you would help rid me of this curse."

"First we must understand the power. And, indeed, use it. We are all in danger from these newcomers. Your new talents will be a great help to us."

"If I help you, will you help me?"

"I will do all that I can." Ro was surprised to find that he meant it.

Talaban worked the crew hard for two days, running the *Serpent* at full speed through rough water, simulating combat conditions by sharp changes of direction, swinging the ship to port, into the onrushing waves, then hurling her to starboard. Although all the ship's movements were guided from the upper cabin, there were many duties for the crew. On each side of the vessel there were hidden boxes, containing powered controls. Some of these activated devices for preventing the *Serpent* being boarded. Others lifted curved shields into place to protect archers.

On the morning of the third day Talaban took Methras to the locked doors behind the prow. These too had a golden triangle, which when removed displayed a set of symbols. Talaban showed them to Methras and the two men entered.

Talaban activated a glow globe and Methras found himself staring at a large metal tube as thick as a man's thigh. It was clamped to the ship's timbers. At the base there was a large chest. Talaban slid back a panel upon it and showed his sergeant a series of wheels and dials.

"The chest contains white crystals and three large rubies," said Talaban. "When activated it builds up a charge of power which can be released by pulling this lever. Watch closely!" Talaban slowly turned a dial. Two sections of the wall slid back. The tube slid forward, clearing the first opening. "At long range great judgment is called for," said Talaban. "But I do not believe we will be fighting at long range. The second window is used to sight the weapon. It is like a giant zhi-bow and releases a bolt a hundred times as powerful. It could pierce a city wall twenty feet thick."

"That is indeed powerful, sir," said Methras. "It must take enormous energy."

"It does. Three bolts and then the weapon needs to be recharged. We do not have the power to recharge it. Three hits and it is gone—perhaps forever. Therefore we have no opportunity for practice, and no margin for error. This will be your place, Methras."

"I will not fail you, captain," said the sergeant. Talaban looked at him closely.

"Is something wrong?"

"Not at all, sir."

"I have noticed that you and the crew seem . . . more distant. Is it because of the new duties, or fear of battle? What? Speak freely."

"I would, sir, but I am not aware of any change. We are your Vagar crew. We live to obey your commands. What more do you ask of us?"

"A little honesty would not go amiss," said Talaban. "But let us put that aside and return our attention to the weapon here. When these ships were first commissioned there were telepaths among the crew. It is a skill we have lost. One would stand with the captain, another wait below with the weapon handler. That way the captain could issue an order to loose the fire. We do not have telepaths and therefore need another signal. What I intend is to flicker the glow globe above you. The next ship you see through the aiming window will be the target."

"I understand, sir."

Talaban ran his hand through his long dark hair and sat back upon the tube. "We do not know how many ships the newcomers will have, nor what weapons they carry. In order to loose the lightning I will be forced to drop our defenses for a few heartbeats. Therefore the moment of our greatest strength is also the moment of our greatest weakness."

"As I said, sir, you can rely on me."

Talaban nodded, then talked Methras through the controls twice more. When he was convinced that his sergeant understood fully the workings of the weapon he ordered him to draw it back and close the openings.

Then the two men left the room and locked the door.

Talaban returned to his cabin. He was perplexed at the new coldness in Methras and the crew. They had served with him for years, and he felt a certain rapport had been established. Apparently he had been wrong. They obeyed his orders swiftly and without question, but gone were the easy smiles. Conversations died away as he approached.

Opening the rear doors Talaban stepped out onto the small, private deck and breathed deeply. The wind was fresh and southerly and he could taste salt upon the air. Seagulls were circling overhead and Talaban could see storm clouds on the horizon.

"You want food?" asked Touchstone. Talaban spun. The tribesman had appeared from nowhere.

"How do you move so silently?" he asked. "My hearing is good, but every time you approach you surprise me." Touchstone grinned.

"Big secret. Much work. Anyways you lost at thinking."

"The phrase is lost in thought. And, yes, I'd like some food."

"On table," said Touchstone. Talaban walked back

into his cabin. A tray had been set on the table, bearing a jug of fruit juices, a small loaf, a plate of dried meats, and another of cheese. A crystal goblet was also standing close by. Talaban gave a wry grin and shook his head. The tribesman had entered the cabin carrying a tray laden with crockery and had set it down silently.

"Compared to you a cat would sound like a tusker," said Talaban.

Touchstone grinned again and walked out onto the rear deck. Talaban ate. The bread was a little stale, but the dried smoked meats were tasty and filling. When he had finished Touchstone returned. "Storm comes," he said.

"The wind is pushing it away from us."

"Wind will change," said the tribesman.

The *Serpent* could ride out any storm, but it would waste power. "I'll find a bay," said Talaban. Touchstone leaned across the table, picking up a piece of meat and stuffing it into his mouth. It was a gesture of easy familiarity and Talaban welcomed it.

"What is wrong with the crew?" he asked.

"Wrong? They sick?"

"No, not sick. Have you not noticed? They have changed. They are like strangers to me now."

"They not change. You change."

"Me? I am the same."

"No," said Touchstone. "Hair at temples blue. Big change." Lifting the tray, the tribesman left the cabin.

Talaban was shocked, but he knew Touchstone was right. Talaban had performed many times for Rael as a scout, moving far into the tribal territories. Blue hair would have been inappropriate on such missions, putting him in danger. But his crew had seen it as a statement, an indication that he was not so different from them. They had looked at him and seen a man. Now they saw an Avatar, one of the ruling gods.

Of course a gulf had been created, and Talaban felt foolish that he had not anticipated such a reaction. His men came from a slave race, and they dreamed of a day when they would be free. And for Methras it would have been a double blow for he was of Avatar blood. The cabin door swung back on its hinges and slammed against the frame. Talaban moved to the rear deck. The wind had changed and, as Touchstone had predicted, the storm was moving in.

Climbing to the upper deck he activated the ship's power and headed the *Serpent* for the coast.

Yasha lay back on the bed, the whore's head resting on his shoulder, her thigh across his legs. The hut was warm, and lit by a single flickering lantern. It was pleasant here, and he felt at peace.

From beyond the huts he could hear the faint music created by the flute of Questor Anu, the Holy One. It was lilting and strangely beautiful, bringing to all who heard it a sense of peace and calm.

According to Yasha's calculations they were almost halfway through the twenty-day *night*. He had worked twelve shifts in the constant darkness and eaten twelve meals. He smiled. And he had rutted with eight whores.

"Why do you smile, my big man?" she asked him. "Did I please you?"

"You always please me," he said, twisting his head to kiss her brow.

"You are the only one who kisses me," she told him. The music of the flute drifted into the distance. He has moved behind the structure, thought Yasha. So far the work was still behind schedule, but they had raised six courses of stone in a series of gradually decreasing squares. What was baffling to Yasha was why the interior had so many channels and tunnels built into the design. It was not as if anyone was going to live inside the pyramid. As if reading his thoughts the woman raised herself up on her elbow.

"What is it for?" she asked him.

"What is what for?"

"This . . . big building?"

"It is for the Avatars," he said. "Every thirty years or so they seem to want to create some lasting monument. My father worked on the pyramid we are tearing down. There's no sense to it. Some of the lads were excited about the prospect of seeing what was inside it. There wasn't anything. No gold, no treasure, no bodies. Nothing. Just empty. Crazy, isn't it?"

He sat up and swung his long legs over the side of the bed. Reaching for the wine jug he lifted it to his lips, drank deeply, then wiped the moisture from his thick, dark beard. The flute sounded closer again.

"It must be *for* something," said the woman. "Why else would the Holy One himself be here?"

This was a question that haunted Yasha. He did not object to the vanities of the Avatar, nor even care much that they ruled the five cities. Someone had to rule, and as long as Yasha had employment and wages enough to buy food and whores he was content. But his curiosity was aroused by the Holy One and his magic. When he played the flute heavy rocks became light, perhaps a twentieth of their weight, and four men could maneuver huge blocks into place. For the first few *days* this had caused much excitement and unease in the workers. Now they were used to it. Yasha heaved himself upright and pulled on his leggings and shirt.

"What was it like being a king?" she asked him. He laughed aloud.

"I wasn't a king," he said. "It was merely an amusing interlude to mark the first course being completed."

"But you were carried on the shoulders of the men and you wore a laurel crown. And even the Holy One bowed as you passed him. Did it feel very fine?" Yasha thought about the question as he pulled on his heavy shoes.

"It felt good," he admitted. "But not half as good as a roll with you."

"Do you mean that? Do you really?"

"Of course."

"Will you come back after your next shift?"

"How could any man stay away from you . . . dear-heart?" he concluded, having forgotten her name.

Leaning over, he kissed her once more then, leaving the clay payment tablet on the small table beside the bed, he stepped out into the night and strolled across to the infant pyramid. Questor Anu was striding along the top of the sixth course still playing his flute. Yasha watched him for a while and, when the Holy One had ceased playing, he waved to him. Anu waved back, then climbed down to stand alongside the huge foreman.

"We are doing well," said Anu. "But we need to work faster yet."

"It will come, Questor. Already the skills of the workers are increasing."

Anu smiled and turned away.

"Tell me, Lord, why do you play music for the blocks when they are already in place?" he asked. Anu paused, then swung back to face the Vagar. In the bright constant moonlight his blue hair shone like polished silver.

"The stone remembers my tunes," he said seriously. Then he laughed at the look of confusion on Yasha's face. "Each block is created by the bonding of millions of fragments, and each fragment also contains millions of particles. Possibly each particle is also a composite of many smaller pieces. The Music goes into the stone, absorbed into each fragment, each particle. And the song goes on—perhaps forever—within the structure."

"I can't hear it," said Yasha.

"And yet the Music is all around us. The universe is a song, Yasha. We are part of it. Have you ever wondered why Man is so drawn to music? Why we gather wherever it is played. Why we dance to it, adjusting our bodies to the rhythms?"

"Because it feels good," said the Vagar.

"Yes, it feels good. It feels *natural*, for that is what it is. Those moments when music touches our souls remind us that we are part of the Great Song. All of us—Avatar, Vagar, tribesman, nomad. And every tree and plant, and bird and animal. We are all essential to the harmony of the Music."

"Maybe so, Holy One, but it seems to me that the Avatars have been granted all the best tunes." He regretted his words instantly, for they came dangerously close to dissension. But Anu merely nodded.

"You are quite right, Yasha. But nothing is forever, whatever my brothers prefer to believe. This structure we are creating together is not for the Avatar alone. It is for the world. For you, and your children, and the children of your children."

"I do not have any children, Holy One."

Anu laid his slender hand on Yasha's shoulder. "You have seventeen children," he said. "And you sired another this evening. You really should make an effort to keep in touch with your women."

Yasha chuckled. "The women I sleep with have many partners, Holy One. Hard to say who fathered which child. And I like it that way. Have you ever been married?"

"No, I cannot say the idea ever appealed to me."

"Me neither. Maybe when I get old and I want a little more warmth in my bed."

"I have been old," said Anu. "There is some joy, but no warmth to be found."

With that he bade his foreman good night and walked slowly away to his tent.

Chapter Seventeen

Sofarita sat quietly in an anteroom outside the Council Chamber, her eyes closed, her face serene. Two Avatar guards stood close by. One was thinking of the new horse he had acquired, and whether it would be as fast as its sire. He was also considering whether or not to have it gelded. The other guard was thinking of Sofarita, and how good it would be to bed her. Their thoughts were intrusive and Sofarita tried to push them away.

The simplest method was to float free of her body and close her spirit ears to their considerations. This she did, and was immediately rewarded with a sense of peace. Now they were merely anonymous soldiers.

It had been a long and interesting day. First Questor Ro had taken her to his house. Sofarita had never been inside so spectacular a home, with its bright rooms, exquisite furniture, its wonderfully woven rugs, and its garden filled with flowering trees and shrubs. Here she had eaten a mouth-watering meal and had been waited upon by servants. The plate upon which her meal was served was blue and white, glazed to a brilliant shine, and her wine was deep and red and rich beyond anything she had tasted before. During the afternoon Questor Ro sent for a gown-maker. He had arrived with a score of dresses and ankle-length gowns in mate-

rials so soft and intoxicating that the woman Sofarita
had once been could easily have believed she had died
and been brought home to live with the gods. But she
was not that woman any longer, and the luxury and
splendor of Avatar life seemed now to be ephemeral
and insubstantial. Water drunk from a golden goblet
was still water, and the same, free, sunlight glittered
from glass and diamond alike. Wealth merely symbol-
ized might, and Sofarita needed no symbols. Day by
day her intellect was growing. And with it her power.

Dressed, as now, in a flowing gown of shimmering
white satin, she had met with the Questor General. He
was, it seemed to Sofarita, an intelligent man, cultured
and sensitive.

She had taken him on the same *flight* as Questor Ro.
He had observed the thirty golden ships and had estimated their arrival at Egaru within twenty-four hours.

He had questioned her at length about her powers,
and asked her if she had ever come into contact with a
healing crystal. Sofarita was not skilled at lying, but
equally she knew that Viruk had broken the law by
healing her cancer. "Yes," she said, finally. "I was dying
and an Avatar healed me. I will say no more."

Rael nodded, as if understanding her reticence. His
thoughts were easy to read, but of little interest to Sofarita. He was still thinking strongly of the golden ships
and how to deal with them. But one striking thought
came through, tinged with dread.

Crystal-joined.

Sofarita picked up an image of a young girl, slowly
turning to glass, dying in cold and brittle agony. She felt
Rael's pain and drew back from him, allowing him privacy in his remembered grief.

Coming back to the present she wondered how the
debate was proceeding within the chamber, and drifted
through the wall to hover above the long table. The

Questor General was sitting at the head of the table, a slim man with close-cropped blue hair and keen, discerning eyes. He and the other twenty people present were listening to a hugely fat man. He was adorned with gold, rings on every chubby finger and a massive gold torque upon his swollen neck. Sofarita scanned the councillors. Questor Ro looked angry, his face pale. Beside him sat a slim hawk-faced man fighting to keep a smile from his features. As the fat man continued to speak Ro suddenly stormed to his feet, pointing and shouting. Sofarita, her spirit ears closed, wondered what the row was about.

Tentatively she allowed sound to penetrate. ". . . insane! Have you completely lost your wits, Caprishan?"

"Not I, but you," replied the fat man. "Whatever were you thinking of, Ro? The Vagars exist as our servants. That is what the Source intended. To allow one to live who has demonstrated such power is to undermine everything we stand for. It sends a message to all Vagars that they can aspire to be our equals. And that, my friends," he said, turning his gaze from Ro, "would be the beginning of the end for us. I recommend that the woman be put to death forthwith!"

As he sat down the Questor General signalled for Ro to speak. The little man tugged on his blue forked beard. "These are desperate times, my friends," he began, still struggling to control his temper. "I have seen the enemy and he is powerful. Very powerful. Thirty ships are on their way here and others have already landed in the far south. Through Sofarita's power we can observe them, listen to their plans perhaps, and outwit them. Without her we are blind to their ambitions. To talk of continuing Vagar subjugation at such a time is to miss the point entirely. When an avalanche threatens a house one does not wonder whether people will be available to clean the windows."

The hawk-faced man raised his hand. "We recognize our cousin Niclin," said the Questor General. Ro sat down.

"There is a major flaw in Questor Ro's reasoning," he said. "We do not know whether the newcomers represent an avalanche or a blessing. They are Avatars, like us. We could be at the dawn of a new age of greatness. Until they arrive, and state their intentions, we cannot judge them. What we do know is that they possessed a power source that enabled them to escape the cataclysm in their own world. Together our combined knowledge could create awesome possibilities for the future. But that is surely a secondary question.

"Here and now we are discussing the implications for our culture of a young Vagar woman possessed of powers we ourselves no longer enjoy. Caprishan is quite correct to point out the psychological effect that such a woman would have on the Vagars we rule.

"What future would we have if this woman did—in the unlikely event of a war against the newcomers—help us to victory? The Avatars would have been rescued by a member of an inferior species. Why then should they accept our domination? I agree with Caprishan. The woman should be crystal-drawn."

Once more Ro leapt to his feet. "Questor General, I appeal to you! You have seen her power and the might of the enemy. This is a military matter and should not be decided by vote."

Rael sat back and was silent for a moment. Then he too rose. "We rule," he said, "through a mixture of fear and awe and selfishness. The Vagars know that we have mighty weapons and are almost immortal. They know also that to live in the five cities, under our control, means good food, high wages, and a standard of life unknown in the outer lands. Each of these three—fear, awe and self-interest—is vital to the other. But by far the most important are the first two. The moment the Vagars cease to fear the Avatar they will rise against us and we will be swamped. If they see that one of their own has power in excess of ours they will no longer hold us in such awe. Then they will question why they should fear us.

"I accept what Questor Ro puts forward. The woman would be a powerful weapon for us. But I must agree with Councillors Caprishan and Niclin that, in our own best interests, she should be crystal-drawn forthwith."

A cold anger settled on Sofarita. Returning to her body she opened her eyes. Her hands were trembling with suppressed fury. She felt the eyes of the guards upon her. Sofarita looked up. "I am leaving," she said.

Rising smoothly she walked towards the door. One of the guards stepped into her path. It was the man who had pictured her naked and dreamed of bedding her. His hand closed on her arm. He screamed as his fingers wrenched back and snapped. Falling back from her he scrabbled for the knife in the bronze sheath at his side. Both his legs gave way, the bones of his thighs cracking and splitting. Sofarita walked on. The second guard ran at her. She swung and raised her hand. He stopped two feet short, as if slamming into a wall. "Not one of you Blue-hairs will ever touch me again," she told him. He struggled to move forward.

At that moment the Council Chamber doors swung open and the Questor General ran out, closely followed by Ro and several other councillors. Sofarita stood her ground.

"You are fools," she said. "I offered you my aid, and you sought to kill me. As Ro said you now face the greatest danger of your lives. The newcomers—the Almecs—will behave just as you do. Think of it, you stupid men! One came to you who had power. Did you greet me with open arms and ask for friendship? No. You decided to destroy me. The Almecs will be exactly the same. You will say to them, 'But we have power just like you.' And they will see that it is true. And they will set out to destroy you. They will say, 'Yes, they have power, but they are not Almecs.' " Sofarita looked into the eyes of the Questor General. "You know that I speak the truth. I read it in your thoughts. And you!" she said, stabbing a finger towards Niclin. "You sought to have me killed merely to annoy Questor Ro. You are doubly an idiot. Know this, I could kill you all. But I shall not. The Almecs will do that." She swung again to Rael. "You spoke of awe and fear. I do not hold you in awe, and you should learn to *fear* me!"

The guard with the broken bones cried out. His legs were twisted grotesquely and one thigh bone had pierced the flesh. Blood had stained his leggings and was flowing to the lush green rug beneath him. Sofarita turned her back upon the silent councillors and strode out of the hall.

Rael was the first to react. Crossing the anteroom floor he ran up a flight of stairs and along a wide gallery. At the far end he threw open the door and emerged onto the parapet above the roof. An Avatar archer stood guard there. "Give me your bow!" ordered Rael, snatching the weapon from the surprised man.

Focusing his concentration, Rael linked to the weapon. Strings of flickering light appeared and he moved to the edge of the parapet. The woman in the white gown emerged onto the wide avenue below, a slender tiny figure. Extending the bow arm, he took aim.

"Don't do it, Rael!" shouted Questor Ro, emerging on the rooftop.

Momentarily Rael froze, but then took aim again. At

that moment the woman slipped into the crowd beyond and was lost to his sight.

The Questor General swung towards Ro. "Do you have any understanding of what she represents?" he said, fighting to keep the anger from his voice.

"A chance of survival," snapped Ro. "She is right, and you know it. The Almecs will not want peace. They are coming for conquest. You don't send thirty warships in order to establish ambassadors."

"I am not talking about the Almecs, Ro. Can you not see what she is? What she is becoming?"

"I don't know what you are talking about."

"She is crystal-joined, Ro."

The words hung in the air. Ro blinked. "That is not possible. The odds—"

"One in a hundred million," interrupted Rael. "I know the odds. Her power will grow daily, because she is drawing it from every crystal in the city. Now do you understand?"

"You could be wrong, Rael," said Ro.

"I pray that I am."

Agents were sent throughout the city seeking sign of Sofarita, and well-known informers were told that a huge reward was on offer to anyone who could discover her whereabouts. The councillors, together with armed guards to prevent attacks by Pajists, returned to their fortified homes. Rael and Ro stayed at the council building.

A fierce storm lashed at the city throughout most of the night, lightning blazing above the Luan estuary. The shutters rattled against the window frames in the high room above the Council Chamber as Rael paced back and forth. Ro had never seen the Questor General this unsettled.

"I made a mistake," said Rael at last. "I hope it will

not prove fatal." Ro said nothing. He was thinking of the dark-haired Vagar woman, and struggling to understand his volatile emotions. He did not disagree with Rael concerning the need for fear among the subject races—indeed he had spent the greater part of his life extolling the virtues of such a policy. But this time . . . All he could see was the way she tilted her head when she spoke, and how the tawny flecks of her eyes caught the light.

"We should concentrate on the newcomers—the Almecs," he said.

"She was right," said Rael. "They will not come in peace, and they will certainly not treat us as brothers. How did we become so arrogant, Ro?"

"It is the nature of rulers," said the little man. "We flick our fingers and lesser men come running. They bow and scrape, and thus reinforce our belief in our superiority. It is a game we all play, Avatar and Vagar."

"Are you well, my friend?" asked Rael, moving to sit opposite the Questor. "This does not sound like you."

Ro sighed. "I have learned so much today. It makes the last hundred years seem a waste of life. I cannot believe the events of this evening. A young woman with amazing talents was prepared to help us and we condemned her to death for it. What is worse, had Niclin brought her to the Council I too would have called for her life. What petty men we have become."

"I regret it also, Ro," said Rael. "But we must put it aside. The golden ships will be here with the dawn. And we must make plans, and issue orders."

The two men talked through most of the night, then Rael sent for his most trusted officers and dispatched them to gather their troops.

By the dawn the storm had swept inland and the sea was calm, the horizon clear, the sky a glorious blue.

Rael, Ro and all the other senior councillors gathered at the harbor to await the arrival of the Almecs. Avatar soldiers closed off the area, and the wharf was silent as the city leaders stood waiting.

The first of the golden ships hove into view minutes after the sun had cleared the eastern mountains. Even at this distance they could see the awesome size of the vessel. Rael and Ro had already seen it, thanks to the newborn talents of Sofarita. But those who had not felt the beginnings of fear. Niclin's cold eyes narrowed. Fat Caprishan began to sweat. The huge ship gleamed in the morning light as it clove the water. Other vessels followed, spread in a long fighting line. Rael counted them. Twenty-four. As they neared the coast the fleet separated, eight ships moving slowly down the estuary between the two cities of Egaru and Pagaru. Eight more sailed to the south. The last eight came to a serene halt just outside the harbor and the lead ship smoothly approached the waiting men, swinging at the last moment, then nestling alongside the stone wharf. The ship was colossal, rearing high above the wharf. A ten-foot section of the upper hull detached itself, dropping slowly to the stone, forming a wide curved gangplank.

A tall man, red-skinned and wearing a breastplate created from bands of gold, strode into view. Upon his head was an ornate helm adorned with golden feathers, and gold circlets graced his wrists, biceps and neck. He wore a kilt of gold-embossed red leather and a wide belt, the buckle of which was fashioned around a huge triangular emerald.

But it was his face that caught the attention of the waiting group. Not just for the skin color of burnished copper, but for his features which shone strangely in the bright sunlight. It was as if his face was coated with grease. The man walked slowly down the gangplank, pausing to stare around him. He carried no weapon and seemed at ease. Halfway down he raised his arm. Instantly twenty other gangplanks dropped to the stone. Warriors clad in black armor and helms began to march down them. They were carrying what appeared to be thick black clubs around three feet long.

At that moment fifty Avatar soldiers, armed with zhibows, stepped into sight from the buildings and alleyways close by, their iron breastplates shining like silver, their white cloaks flickering in the breeze. Once more the leader raised his hand. His warriors halted, and stood silently on the gangplanks.

The leader strode down to where Rael waited. His face shocked the Avatars. His eyebrows, cheekbones and chin appeared to be made of glass, giving an inhuman cast to his features. "Welcome to Egaru," said the Questor General smoothly. "We have awaited your arrival with great interest. Will you join us for breakfast?"

"With my men?" replied the leader, his voice cold.

"I think not," Rael told him with a smile. "The people we rule are very fearful. It would be better if they saw you and I walking together back to the council building in friendship. The sight of so many soldiers might unnerve them."

"As you wish. I shall bring only my aides."

"They will be welcome," said Rael.

With an imperious flick of his hand the leader signalled the ship. The Almec soldiers swung and climbed back inside the golden vessel. All but one of the gangplanks were raised. Three officers strode down the last, then this too closed.

The officers were also copper-skinned, but their features were human, their eyes dark brown, their faces sharp. There was a coldness about them, an arrogance in their movements.

Rael led them to a waiting carriage which took them

through the city to the council building. Rael rode with them, but there was no conversation, nor did the newcomers appear interested in their surroundings. They sat very quietly, their faces impassive.

Once inside the Council Chamber Rael bade them sit down. They refused offers of food or drink and sat waiting for Rael to speak. The other councillors had filed in and taken their places. Rael rose. "First let me introduce myself," he said. "I am Rael, Questor General of the Avatar Empire. These men seated here are the senior councillors. May I welcome you to our lands and congratulate you on the manner in which the Almecs escaped the cataclysm in your own world."

The Almec leader spoke from his seat. "I am Cas-Coatl, Lord of the Third Sector. I appreciate the warm words with which you greet us. It is my hope that unity can be established without destruction and bloodshed, and the transition of power completed without discord."

His words were met by a stunned silence. Rael struggled for inner calm. "And what do you offer the Avatars?" he asked.

Cas-Coatl's expression did not change. "Life," he said, simply.

"Life we already have," Rael pointed out.

"There is little point in discussion," said Cas-Coatl. "You were preeminent. Now you are not. You were powerful. Now you are weak. The Almecs are strong. The strong rule. Do you see a flaw in the logic?"

"Perhaps you underestimate us, Cas-Coatl," said Rael, softly.

"Your cities have few defenses, your army is less than seventeen hundred men—fifteen hundred formed from an inferior slave race. We shall leave now and give you two hours to make your decision." He held out his hand. The first officer to his left handed him a folded cloth of bright green. This he laid upon the table. "If you decide wisely have this flag flown from the highest building at the wharf. I shall bring in my ships and we will discuss further the transition. You may then retire to your homes and live out your lives as you wish. If not . . . We will land anyway and march our soldiers through the rubble that remains."

Cas-Coatl rose, his officers with him.

"You can, of course, hold us hostage, or even kill us. It will make no difference. Another Lord of the Third Sector will be appointed immediately and you will have lost your two hours."

"You are free to go, Cas-Coatl," said Rael.

The Almec and his officers strode from the chamber. Rael sent two officers to arrange a carriage for them back to the ship.

As the door closed behind them Rael gazed around the faces of the councillors. All were in shock.

"At least we know where we stand," said Rael.

"On the brink of an abyss," observed Questor Ro.

"The man was crystal-wed," said Niclin. "How is it that he could still move?"

"From what I saw of their ships they have advanced along different lines of learning," said Ro. "The vessels are mechanically, rather than crystal, powered. Obviously this new line of knowledge allowed them to master the problem. But that is rather irrelevant now. It seems, my friends, that we are facing our doom."

Chapter Eighteen

Immediately a clamor began in the Council Chamber. Rael leapt to his feet, his arms in the air. "Enough, my friends," he shouted. "We have two hours. Surrender is unthinkable, and therefore we must use the time we have to marshal our defenses. All of you—bar Questors Caprishan, Niclin and Ro—should return to your duties. The enemy will certainly have weapons of long-range destruction upon their warships. Go to your districts and organize an evacuation of non-combatants to the eastern sections of the city. Vagar captains have already been told to hold their men in readiness for just such an event, and also to prepare units for recovery and burial. Liaise with the captains in your districts. And keep runners with you, ensuring at all times there is a line of communication between the War Council and yourselves. Go now, my friends. Time is short."

The councillors filed out, and, as the last left the room, Caprishan spoke. "This is a war we cannot win, cousin," he said.

"I know that," snapped Rael, "but this is not the time to discuss it. As we all saw, eight ships have sailed down the estuary towards the lands of the Erek-jhip-zhonad. I would estimate there to be perhaps three hundred fighting men per ship. That means around two

thousand five hundred warriors will be landing somewhere to our rear. An equal number have sailed south.
Were I in command of their battle fleet I would land my
forces on the marshes three miles south of Pejkan. This
is the weakest of the five cities. It will fall within a day.
Boria and Caval will follow. There is only a token force
of Avatar soldiers in each of the three cities, and they
have orders to march to Egaru as soon as the enemy is
sighted. The city councils have been ordered to surrender if approached. Most Avatar families have already
left, and all crystals and power sources have been removed or dismantled."

"We are giving them up without a fight?" said Niclin.
"I don't like the sound of that."

"You think I do?" snapped Rael. "As Cas-Coatl so
rightly pointed out we have fewer than two hundred
Avatar soldiers, and only fifteen hundred trained Vagars. You may recall that the Council has always believed in—how did you put it, Caprishan?—the folly of
having too large a Vagar force within the cities. Now
we pay the price."

"I was not alone in my fears," said Caprishan.

"No, you were not." Rael sighed. "And in many
ways I agreed with you. But none of us could have fore-
seen the arrival of such an enemy. In the past our zhi-
bows have more than compensated for lack of numbers.
Not this time, I fear. All our efforts must be concentrated on Egaru and Pagaru," insisted Rael. "The walls
of both are high and strong, and the power chests are
here. In the short term we have two elements in our favor. *Serpent Seven*, under the command of Talaban, and
one land-based Sunfire which, on my orders, Questor
Ro has hidden, fully charged, in the Harbor Tower."

Niclin interrupted him. "The Sunfire has not been
charged or used in . . . what? . . . two hundred years.

Even if it does not explode on first use, the enemy will see where the blast comes from and concentrate their attack upon the Harbor Tower. It will be a death-trap."

"In which case, cousin, you will finally be rid of me," said Ro, "for I shall be manning the weapon."

"I do not wish to see you die, Ro," said Niclin, softly. "We are rivals, and political enemies. But it would grieve me to see harm befall you." He turned to Rael. "What is it you wish me to do, cousin?"

"Get to Pagaru before the enemy closes the estuary to us. Hold it to the last. Make them suffer for every inch of ground they take. You will have only sixty Avatar soldiers, but more than two hundred zhi-bows. Ensure a supply is always fully charged. Caprishan, you will go with Niclin. Your role is to ensure supplies continue to get through to the two cities, and also to Questor Anu. This will not be easy once the enemy has landed. The mist is due to be dropped tomorrow. Make sure a message gets to Anu about the situation here."

Caprishan nodded. "Anu and his workforce are twenty miles inland. We cannot protect him."

"He will need no protection," said Rael. "Any of the enemy who cross the mist will rot and die within a few heartbeats. The danger will come when he drops the mist to allow supplies through. You must see if there is any way he can create a secret channel through it."

"I will, cousin, but surely if he can wield such power in the valley he could wield it here? Could he not lay a line of mist before the cities, destroying our enemies as they land?"

Rael shook his head. "He would not contemplate it," he said. "Anu is not a killer. And there is no way I can force him into such an act. Believe me, I have tried. Now are there any further questions?" The Questors remained silent. "Good. Let us be about our business, my friends, and may the Source bless our endeavors."

• • •

Within the hour the evacuation had begun. Vagar troops moved through the streets, ushering bewildered city dwellers from their homes. There were some arguments, but the presence of blue-haired Avatar councillors quelled the crowds. No one wanted to be arrested for civil disobedience and subsequently crystal-drawn. Assurances were made that Vagar troops would patrol the deserted areas, protecting homes and possessions from looters.

But it was a slow business, and as the two-hour deadline approached more than a thousand homes had yet to be cleared. Refugees choked the roads and avenues, and more than once fights broke out, once as a wheel fell from a heavily laden wagon, causing the line to stall, and again when a Vagar merchant tried to spur his horse through the throng. A woman was hurled to the ground and her husband dragged the merchant from his mount and began to beat upon him with his fists. Vagar troops moved in on both occasions.

Questor Ro crouched inside the Harbor Tower and applied a little oil to the gears and wheels of the Sunfire. Three Avatar soldiers waited with him, and further back ten Vagar laborers awaited orders to remove the machine once it was discharged. The tower was constructed of heavy stone blocks and seemed safe enough, especially here on the ground floor. But Ro had no idea what weaponry would be brought to bear on it. With a soft cloth he wiped excess oil from the gears and idly polished the long bronze tube. The weapon had been aligned with the small window, but there was only a narrow field of fire. Ro moved to the window and stared out across the bay. From here he could see all eight golden ships. But they were at least a half-mile from him. Could they loose their weapons from that distance? Ro did not know.

The Sunfire had been kept in the Museum for almost ninety years. Ro had been present when such a weapon had last been used, against the warships of the Khasli. They had been destroyed utterly. As indeed had the Khasli themselves during the Fourteen Year War. We are the Khasli now, he thought. Ro struggled to remember the delay between shots, as the crystals repowered. But he could not. All he knew was that once fired the weapon needed some minutes to recharge.

Calling the soldiers forward Ro re-sighted the tube, covering the mouth of the bay. With a long rule he checked its positioning, needing it to be parallel to the floor. It was out by a hair's breadth. Mentally he calculated the effect this might have over a range of 400 yards. Sweat trickled from his temples. Ro was not a warrior and had little experience with the weapon. But then, apart from Rael, neither did any other Avatar in Egaru. The Sunfires had not been needed in almost 200 years. Zhi-bows had been more than adequate against the tribes. Moving to the rear of the weapon he raised the sight, a thin arm of bronze to which was attached a circle of gold. This he lined up with the short spike at the far end of the tube.

His mouth was dry and he requested a cup of water. One of the soldiers filled a cup from a pottery jug. Ro sipped the liquid and flicked his gaze to the hourglass. The colored sand was trickling slowly through. Not long now, he thought.

Three of the golden ships began to move, heading across the bay toward Pagaru. Four others began to glide toward the harbor. There was something about their movements which filled Ro with fear. Serene and assured, they radiated strength of purpose and enormous confidence. This is what it was like for the Khasli who faced us centuries ago, thought Ro. He shuddered inwardly. And activated the Sunfire. As the charge built up the machine began to hum. Ro could feel its vibration. This small movement in the weapon made the coming battle suddenly real. Ro felt panic welling within him.

You are an Avatar, he told himself sternly. Sweat dripped into his eyes. He wiped it clear with the oily cloth.

"You want us on the roof, Questor?" asked one of the soldiers.

"No. Remain here. If we can, we must carry the Sunfire clear. It is too valuable to be lost in only one action."

Ro crouched down behind the sights. Once we were truly gods, he thought. We strode the earth like giants. We brought law and knowledge to primitive peoples. We taught them the secrets of agriculture and building.

And we made them slaves . . .

The first of the golden ships was slowly moving into his line of fire.

Slaves. In doing so we made slaves of ourselves, he thought. Slaves to tradition, slaves to our past.

Ro pulled the firing lever.

Nothing happened. He swore softly, his fingers flicking open the control chest. One of the crystals had slipped from its niche. He pushed it back and closed the lid. The first ship had moved on, but a second was closing. A series of dull thumping sounds came from outside, followed by a whooshing of disturbed air. Then three powerful explosions rocked the foundations of the building.

"There are fires on the dockside!" shouted one of the soldiers. "They have machines upon the decks sending balls of fire over the city."

Ro ignored him as the second ship came into his sights. He pulled the lever. Blue fire crackled from the mouth of the tube, then a brilliant white light exploded

in front of Ro's eyes. Blinded, he fell back from the machine—and did not see the lightning spear slam into the
warship. The gold-covered timbers were torn apart as
the bolt smashed through them, expanding upon impact
with terrible heat. The explosion that followed ripped
the ship into three parts. Bodies were hurled through the
air. A wave of heat struck the Harbor Tower. Ro, on his
knees, his hands over his eyes, felt the heat wash over
him.

He opened his eyes, blinking back the tears. His vision was returning slowly. Moving to the window he
gazed out over the scene of destruction. Floating debris
was all that was left of the golden ship. Ro felt a savage
sense of elation.

Moving to the rear of the Sunfire he placed his hands
over the tube, feeling the vibration of the recharge.

We have a chance, he thought. They are not as powerful as they think.

Outside, in the bay, the first of the golden ships
swung back. A ball of fire whooshed up and sailed over
the water, landing some 40 feet from the Harbor Tower.
The explosion was awesome. Rocks and stones split under the impact and the nearest Avatar soldier was lifted
from his feet and hurled back against the Harbor Tower
wall, his spine smashed to shards by the impact.

The two remaining soldiers aimed their zhi-bows at
the vessel, sending bolt after bolt towards the upper
decks, where they exploded against the timbers, causing
little damage.

A second ball of fire soared from the ship. The Avatar
soldiers began to run. They had made no more than 30
yards when the ball struck the wharf causeway. The
blast lifted the fleeing men, hurling them high over the
water, their lifeless bodies disappearing below the surface.

Inside the Harbor Tower Ro was covered in dust and

broken stones. A third ship was sailing towards him. Ro knelt behind the Sunfire. It was still vibrating towards full charge.

The wall to his left buckled under another explosion. Part of the ceiling collapsed. A massive support timber fell, coming to a wedged halt on the top of the door frame. Ro lined up the sight and peered through the choking dust. The vibration died away. Shutting tight his eyes, he pulled the lever.

The third ship took the impact of the bolt high behind the stern. Ro opened his eyes to see the explosion that followed. The rear half of the ship disappeared in a mighty blast. The prow and the mid-section broke away. Slowly the ship toppled and slid below the waves. Some survivors leapt clear and began to swim for the shore.

A ball of flame struck the roof of the Harbor Tower. The sound of thunder followed. The roof was ripped away, and the ceilings of the four upper storeys were punched downwards, smashing through the body of the building and burying the Sunfire and Questor Ro beneath tons of rubble.

Hidden in a narrow alleyway beside the docks the Questor General watched the destruction. Behind him buildings were ablaze and he could hear the sounds of screaming coming from trapped men. But his gaze was fixed on the first golden ship as it swung again towards the wharf.

Fifty Avatars waited with him; another 200 Vagar soldiers were hidden close by. Smoke billowed around them and several men began to cough. Rael tied a scarf over the lower half of his face. His aide Cation moved back out of sight and reappeared moments later with a bucket of water. Some men soaked their red cloaks and held these over their faces. Cation offered the water to

Rael. Dipping the scarf into it he retied it. Breathing was easier now.

The golden ship closed in, nestling against the stone wall of the wharf. For a moment there was no movement. Then a score of gangplanks dropped and soldiers armed with the black clubs began to run down them. They were lightly armored with breastplates of stiffened leather and helms of copper. They carried no shields.

As the first of them reached the dock Rael led his fifty Avatars from hiding. Swiftly they formed a fighting line and zhi-bolts slammed into the gathering enemy soldiers. Scores died, but the survivors, with great discipline, did not panic. Instead they raised their black clubs to their shoulders. The sound of thunder followed. More than half Rael's men were punched from their feet. From further along the dock the 200 Vagars emerged and charged the attackers. It seemed to Rael that their fire-clubs were suddenly useless, and only sporadic shots followed. Vagar swordsmen hacked and cut their way through the enemy ranks. Rael yelled to his remaining archers: "The openings! Aim for the openings!" Lifting his zhi-bow he sent a flashing bolt through the first of the gangplank doors. It exploded within, creating a burst of bright light and flame. Bolt after bolt followed. Fire sprang up within the ship.

On the dockside the Vagars in their armor of iron continued their advance. The golden ship drew back. Soldiers still on the gangplanks toppled into the bay. The fighting on the dockside was fierce now. More than a hundred of the copper-skinned warriors had made it to the shore, but they were heavily outnumbered and fighting for their lives. Casting aside their fire-clubs they drew daggers or short swords. But they were no match for the heavily armored Vagars.

As the ship pulled away a ball of fire whooshed from it. Rael saw it. "Get back!" he shouted to his Vagars.

No one heard him above the battle clamor. The fireball exploded in the midst of the fighting men. Scores on both sides died instantly, their clothing aflame, their limbs torn from their bodies. Others began to writhe in agony on the dockside, hair and skin on fire.

Panic-stricken, the surviving Vagars ran back. Almec soldiers leapt into the sea and tried to swim towards the ship.

Rael pulled his Avatars back to the alley. Flames were flickering inside the golden ship, but these were soon snuffed out.

Turning to his men he took ten of them and smashed the door to the warehouse that backed onto the alley. Once inside he ran to the stairs, climbing up to the roof and emerging high above the dock. The golden ship was approaching again. A fireball sailed over the dock. The roof of the next building exploded. Rael began to count, slowly and evenly. As he reached fifteen a second ball hissed overhead, falling behind the building.

"On my mark shoot at the mouth of the fire weapon!" he ordered his men.

Running to the edge of the roof they aimed their bows. Rael counted slowly to ten then loosed a bolt which struck the long bronze tube jutting from the forward deck. Light blazed, but there was no damage to the weapon. Other bolts struck home—to no effect. Rael fired again. This time the bolt flashed into the mouth of the weapon just as the fireball was emerging. It exploded in the tube. The weapon was ripped away in the explosion, sections of bronze soaring into the sky. Fierce, raging flames engulfed the ship's prow.

Listing to port, the golden vessel backed away. Another ship entered the harbor. Rael swore softly.

Questor Ro tried to open his eyes. His body was a sea of pain, his left eye swollen shut, his left arm pinned beneath a mound of rubble. He tried to move his right hand—and realized that three fingers were broken. His chest felt cramped, his breathing restricted. Opening his right eye he saw that one of the roof beams had fallen across him. His right hand was wedged against the Sunfire. It was no longer vibrating. Broken stone blocks had half-covered the weapon and the roof beam was resting on its barrel. That was why Ro had not been crushed. As the ceiling fell the beam had struck him but then been stopped by the Sunfire.

Am I dying? he wondered. The pain was excruciating. His legs ached and he tried to move his toes. It seemed to him that he could, but then he remembered an amputee once telling him that he could still feel the fingers of the hand that had been lost. Ro dragged back his broken right hand and tried to reach the pocket of his torn tunic. The fractured fingers flared with fresh pain as he reached inside and he was unable to draw out the crystal. Instead he laid his hand gently upon it and began to speak the first of the Six Rituals. The pain subsided and he felt the bones begin to knit. As his strength returned he pushed away the rocks covering his belly and legs and wriggled free. As he did so he saw one of the golden ships, its prow aflame, backing out of the harbor. A second ship was moving alongside.

Ro scrambled to the rear of the Sunfire, pushing aside the rubble. The firing handle had snapped off halfway down and the rear sight was gone. Even so he could see that the weapon was pointing directly at the two ships.

He paused momentarily. Even if the weapon fired he could only take out one of the vessels. The other would certainly destroy him.

Death. That long descent into darkness. It was an appalling thought for a man who could live forever.

What is life without honor? he asked himself. Grabbing the broken handle he wrenched it down. For a moment nothing happened. Then a blue flash erupted from a fracture in the barrel—and the last bolt it would ever fire tore itself clear of the Sunfire. The weapon had been tilted by the roof fall and the massive bolt of energy almost missed the second ship. The charge struck high on the upper deck, ripping the control cabin clear. Deflected, the bolt shot high into the sky where it burst with the sound of a hundred thunders.

The stricken golden ship increased its speed and clove through the water towards the docks. It loosed no fireballs, nor slowed as it approached the wharf. Its prow struck the stone. The timbers shivered and gave. And the ship ploughed on, smashing its hull, then listing heavily. Men scrambled to the decks and jumped over the side.

Ro eased himself clear of the ruined Harbor Tower and sat down on the rubble. He was tired and still in great pain, but he watched with dispassionate interest as Rael and his archers killed the survivors.

The golden ship tilted once more, then rolled and sank.

Outside the harbor the lead ship drew back. Across the bay four more of the golden vessels were sending fireballs into the helpless city of Pagaru.

Crouched on the western battlements of Pagaru, Niclin and four senior officers waited for the invasion. Behind them a score of buildings were ablaze. Bodies littered the streets. A section of the wall to Niclin's right was torn away. Three Avatar soldiers were carried to their deaths.

Keeping low, Niclin edged along the battlements and peered through the hole in the wall. The first of the golden ships was gliding towards the dockside. Openings appeared in the ship's hull and Niclin could see warriors gathering there.

Suddenly a huge explosion lit up the sky. Niclin blinked, and transferred his gaze out to sea. One of the golden ships was listing badly, smoke pouring from her midsection. As Niclin watched she toppled and sank swiftly below the waves. Below, in the harbor, the openings in the golden ship's hull were swiftly being closed as the vessel drew back. His view restricted, Niclin pushed himself to his feet—and saw salvation!

Like a black shadow of death *Serpent Seven* hove into sight, her dark prow cutting through the waves at full speed. A blast of light flashed from her, striking a second golden ship, ripping away the stern. The two remaining Almec vessels sped out to sea, and the *Serpent* swung back into the harbor.

Avatar soldiers moved from their hiding places at the dockside and began cheering. Niclin himself felt a wave of exultation, but he quelled it and marched back along the battlements to where his officers waited. Keeping his voice calm he told them to organize fire crews and rescue workers. Then he strode down to the dockside.

As the gangplank was lowered Niclin boarded the ship. A young Vagar sailor led him to Talaban's cabin. Niclin entered. The tribesman Touchstone was seated on the rug. Talaban rose from behind his desk, bowed and offered the Questor a goblet of wine.

"Your arrival was timely, captain," said Niclin, accepting the drink. "Though it would have been more pleasant to see you an hour ago."

"The fault was entirely mine, Questor. We took shelter from the storm last night. It delayed our arrival."

"A shame it did not do the same for the Almecs."

"They are under no power restraints," said Talaban. "Are your casualties high?"

Niclin sipped his wine. He did not like Talaban, but he knew he was being surly toward a man who had proved the savior of the city. He sighed, and when he spoke his voice softened. "Rescue work is just beginning, but I would think several hundred lost their lives. You used the Sunfire well, Talaban. If we had five more like it we could even win this war."

"It is not lost yet, Questor," Talaban pointed out.

"No, not yet. Eight of the golden ships sailed up the Luan. They will have landed an army to our rear. An equal number moved south. The Questor General has sent orders to Pejkan, Boria and Caval to surrender without a fight. He believes such a move will prevent excess casualties, and destruction to property. I disagree. If he had commanded the Vagars to fight they would have killed at least some of the enemy."

"And been wiped out in the process," Talaban pointed out. "And that would have affected the morale within the twin cities."

"Those are all we control now," said Niclin, sourly. "Five golden ships have been destroyed. Nineteen remain. And, within days, there will be two—perhaps three—land-based armies to oppose us."

"One problem at a time, Questor," said Talaban. "Today we have a victory. Let that suffice for now."

Niclin nodded, and when he spoke again there was sadness in his voice. "I saw three Avatars killed today. In an instant. Men I have known for more than two hundred years." He flicked his fingers. "Like that they were gone. This morning they were immortal. They were gods. Now they are twisted dead flesh. If I were a religious man I would suspect that the Source has deserted us."

Talaban poured a goblet of wine and handed it to Niclin. "It seems to me," he said, "that victory always goes to the strong. The Source—if such a creature there be—has little to do with it."

Touchstone chuckled and shook his head.

"You have something to say, savage?" said Niclin.

Touchstone moved smoothly to his feet. "You dream small dreams," he said. Then he left the room.

Thirty-five Avatars had lost their lives on this, the first day of battle. Thirty-five immortals. Men whose lives had spanned the centuries. Rael sat in the Council Chamber, his heart heavy. With him were Questors Niclin and Caprishan and strewn on the table before them were several of the black fire-clubs. Lifting one, Rael examined it. There was a long hollow metal barrel, encased in polished wood, and a number of sprung levers. "It is not a weapon of magic," said Niclin. "It is not linked to the mind of the user." Opening a pouch found on the body of a dead Almec he tipped the contents to the table. It was filled with a gritty black powder. A second pouch contained small round balls of heavy metal. "In some way," continued Niclin, "these balls are propelled with great force along the barrel."

"Find out how," said Rael.

"We captured fifty Almecs," said Caprishan. "They are being questioned now. But they are hardy men and are saying little."

Rael glanced up. His eyes were cold. "Take ten of them to the Crystal Chamber. Draw the life from one of them while the others watch. Then see how swiftly they want to speak."

"The weapons are not as effective as zhi-bows, Rael," said Niclin.

"I want to know everything about them. Their range, the speed of use. On the dock they were used once only. I saw men struggling to recharge them. How long does such a recharge take?"

"We will discover these things," said Niclin. "The question is, what action do we take now?"

"There is nothing we can do," said Rael. "They act, we react. We do not have the men to carry the battle to them. Not yet. But Viruk has gone to aid Ammon. With his army, and the tribes who owe him allegiance, we can yet destroy the invaders."

"You really believe we can achieve a victory?" asked Caprishan.

"I have to believe it," said Rael.

It was midnight before the carriage came to a halt outside his home and Questor Ro climbed down wearily, neglecting to thank the driver. Ro's broken hand was extremely painful, and his ribs and left leg were aching. He had used the ritual to begin the healing process, but broken bones needed at least four sessions, and no more than two in any single day. Otherwise the point of the break remained brittle and liable to snap easily.

He limped towards his front door. A servant saw him coming and, bowing low, stepped out to greet him. Ro paused at the steps and stared back over the city. From the high ground where his imposing home was situated Ro could look down on the harbor and the estuary beyond. Some buildings were still burning, and a red glow hung over the docks. He sighed, and felt the pain of his wounds.

"May the Source be praised that you are alive, lord," said Sempes, bowing again. Ro looked closely at the old man and wondered if he meant it. It was not a thought that would have occurred to him before today.

"How long have you been with me, old one?" he asked.

"Thirty-three years, lord."

"Are you married?"

"I was, lord. My wife died last year."

"I am sorry for your loss." The old man looked at him quizzically.

"Are you ill, lord?"

"I think that I have been. Would you be so kind as to prepare me a bath?"

"I shall arrange it immediately, lord. The water is already being heated."

Ro stepped into the hallway and gazed around at the lantern-lit walls. They were covered with beautiful paintings, landscapes of Parapolis and the surrounding countryside. "Let me remove your boots, lord," said Sempes, kneeling beside a gold-embossed chair. Ro sat down and extended his right leg. Sempes pulled the boot clear. Ro winced as the old man tugged at his left boot. "Your leg is hurt, lord. I am sorry."

"It will heal. Do not concern yourself."

Sempes moved away and returned with soft velvet slippers, which he eased into place. Ro felt indescribably weary and was about to tell the old man to forget the bath when Sempes spoke again.

"Your guest is in the garden room, lord. I lit a fire for her."

"My guest?"

"The raven-haired lady you brought home earlier. She has been here since late last night. I hope I did right in allowing her to stay."

"Yes, you did." Ro pushed himself to his feet and made his way across the hall, through the narrow library and on into the garden room. Pausing in the doorway to allow his eyes to become accustomed to the dim light from the dying fire, he scanned the room. There were four couches and two deep, hide-covered chairs. Sofarita was asleep in the chair by the fire.

As he entered, the four unlit lanterns in the room

flickered into bright life, sharp shadows forming in the three arches that led to his garden. Sofarita sat up.

"Do they still seek to kill me?" she asked him.

"They have other problems on their minds," he told her.

"Come to me," she commanded him. And, to his surprise, he obeyed her. Sofarita rose and took his injured hand in her own. All pain vanished. Lifting his hand he curled his fingers into a fist. The bones were completely healed. "You were very brave, Questor Ro," she said, softly. "When you loosed the third bolt you thought the weapon would explode in your face. You thought you were going to die."

"Yes, I did."

"And yet you fought on. That was noble."

The little man reddened. "Why did you come here?"

"You will still need my help, Avatar. Tell me, how is the soldier whose legs I broke?"

"Resting. It will take time for such breaks to heal."

"I hurt him badly," she said. "I allowed my anger to overwhelm me. It will not happen again. Tomorrow I will heal him also."

Ro sat down in a chair opposite hers. "How soon will they return, do you think?" he asked her.

Sofarita shrugged. "I do not believe they will attack the cities by sea again. But they have landed an army to the south. Three thousand men, and beasts. Another army is sailing down the Luan. There will be great slaughter and destruction."

"What can we do?"

"What else can you do but follow your natures?" she told him. "You are what you are."

"Do you hate the Avatar so much?" he asked, hearing the contempt in her voice.

She gave a wistful smile. "You misunderstand me,

Questor Ro. I was not talking of the Avatar. I was speaking of Man. So much is clear to me now and every day it grows clearer still. We do what we are born to do. My Aunt Lalia has a cat. It is well fed, and wants for nothing. Yet it will—with its belly full—creep into the meadow and kill a bird. It does not eat the bird. Why then does it kill? One might as well ask why a flower grows or the rain falls. It kills because it is designed to kill. That is its purpose. It has fangs and claws and great speed. It is a hunter. If then it does not hunt what purpose does it serve?" Sofarita fell silent for a moment. Then she spoke again. "A few weeks ago I was a widow living in a small village. I knew my role, and I played it well. I was demure in the company of men, and I worked in the fields with the other women. When my period of mourning was done I would have accepted my father's choice of a new husband and I would have borne him children. I am no longer that village girl. I see the world with larger eyes. And I can fly on the winds of time. Today I journeyed far, I saw Man. I watched him as he crept from the deep jungles, his body covered in thick fur. I saw his intelligence develop and his skills increase. Those skills were always allied to death. Do you know the greatest discovery made by man six hundred thousand years ago?" Ro shook his head. She laughed, but there was little humor in the sound. "He learned that a javelin's weight must be heaviest a third of the way from the point. It ensures good flight and maximum killing. He had a language based on grunts and gestures, but he learned to make a javelin. I have seen many things, Questor Ro. Events to break the strongest heart. Man is like the cat. No matter what wealth he possesses, no matter how contented his life, no matter how advanced his learning, he will yearn to fight, to defeat and kill a perceived enemy."

"Not all men behave in this way," said Ro.

"That is true," she conceded. "And what is their fate? I have watched them also, the poets, the spiritual leaders, the dreamers of harmony. Can you name more than a handful who were not murdered?"

"I cannot. What you say is true, but what choice do we have *now*? The Almecs are evil and seek to destroy us. What else can we do but resist them?"

"*You* can do nothing else. For you are a man. But beware when you speak of their evil. They are merely a distorted reflection of the Avatar. They live on the blood of others, ritually sacrificing thousands, tearing out their hearts. You Avatars are little different, save that your crystals draw life without the accompanying gore. If the Almecs are evil—then so are you. And they *are* evil, Questor Ro."

Ro settled back in his chair and closed his eyes. He was weary now, and the truth of her words hung on him like the weight of death. "Why is it that I could not see this before?" he asked her. "Why is it so clear to me now?"

"I had not touched you then. The power is new to me, and I have not yet learned how to control it. I inadvertently opened a window in your soul that had long been closed. I could close it again for you, should you desire it."

Ro shook his head. "I do not want to lose it again. I feel whole now. Like when I was a child, and the world was full of wonder. What happened to me? How did I lose that youthful passion, that belief in humanity?"

"Speck by speck," she told him, "so that you did not know what you were losing. It is the nature of men to build walls around themselves. They think it will protect them from hurt. It does the opposite. The hurt still gets in, but now it rattles around the walls, unable to get out. So you build more walls. You are now seeing the world without walls. You are free, Ro. Free to hurt and free to heal."

"What would you have me do?"

She smiled then, a radiant smile, and, leaning forward, took his hand. "Go and take your bath. Then rest. Tomorrow I shall speak with the Questor General. You will bring him here."

"You are still willing to help us?"

"I will aid you in your battle with the Almecs."

Chapter Nineteen

As Ro left the room the lanterns died down once more. Sofarita closed her eyes and freed her spirit, flying high over the ocean. Such was the speed of her flight that she chased down the setting sun, watching it appear to rise majestically from the west. As a simple villager she had assumed the earth to be a vast flat plate, the sun slowly revolving around it. She had been surprised and delighted to discover its true shape and its place in the heavens. Now she experienced another delight. The western continent was bathed in sunshine while the eastern lands were covered by a cloak of darkness. She had moved from midnight to mid-afternoon in the space of a few heartbeats.

The land below her was rugged and mountainous, the valleys lush and green, the rivers huge and sparkling. To the north she could see yet more mountains, snow-covered and ancient. South she flew, over mountains and hills and vast plains. Far below her she saw what appeared to be a colossal brown snake gliding slowly over the grassland. Dropping lower she realized she was gazing at a massive herd of shaggy brown animals moving along the line of a river. There were too many to count, and the herd stretched back for miles.

On she flew, soaring above forests of tall trees, and

glittering lakes fed by rushing water from the melting snows of the mountains.

The first people she saw were living by a lake, their few dwellings created from hides stretched over poles. Several children were playing by the water's edge, while four women were stretching out hides and scraping the grease from them with sharp stones. There were no men to be seen, and Sofarita decided they must be hunting.

As she flew further south she came across larger camps. As she hovered over one that stretched on both sides of a wide river she felt a prickling sensation, as if someone had reached out and touched her.

Surprised—and a little fearful—she sped away.

Sixty miles farther on she saw vultures below her, feeding. Others circled in the sky. She dropped toward the earth and saw hundreds of human bodies sprawled in death. The vultures had torn at them, but she saw several that the birds had not yet violated. Each had its ribs splayed open, the hearts torn from the chests.

Anger touched her then, and she rose into the air. To the south she saw another Almec army, camped beyond a small wood. There were some 500 warriors, each armed with fire-clubs and short swords. And away to the left were a score of krals, sitting in a circle around a fire. A hundred prisoners, roped and tied, sat forlornly in the open.

On she flew until she reached a towering escarpment, like a wall stretching across the land. Two hundred feet high and sheer, it seemed eerily out of place. At its base a forest grew. Sofarita glanced down and saw that hundreds of trees had been crushed there, as if the whole escarpment had dropped down onto the forest like a hammer from Heaven.

This was the land of the Almecs.

Higher now she flew, over cities of alien stone, built

with craft and cunning, with canals and wide avenues, teeming with people. There was evidence of earthquake damage in all of the cities. Many buildings showed jagged cracks, others had crumbled. One canal was completely dry, its walls collapsed. The farther west she flew, the greater the damage. At the farthest western edge of this new land she came upon the remains of a city. It had been spectacularly ruined, the earth rising sharply, the buildings that remained jutting from the earth at an incredible angle. Most had been torn away, the ruins scattering the slope below. Sofarita scanned the area. It was as if a giant hand had grabbed this 100-mile section and wrenched it upward. Moving west again she saw the reason.

The transported lands of the Almecs had appeared mostly above a vast, flat plain. The impact had caused the earthquake damage she had seen to the east. But here there was no escarpment. This small section of land had descended upon a range of mountains, which had thrust up through the invading earth like spear points. The death toll among the Almecs must have been enormous.

Sofarita flew back toward the east. The Almec capital loomed in the distance, and in the light of the setting sun she could see the gleaming golden ziggurat that housed the Crystal Queen.

The Crystal Queen!

The title surprised her. From where had it come? She had told Questor Ro that the golden ziggurat was somehow alive, but now she knew instinctively that it contained the . . . soul? . . . of a woman. Once again she felt the sensation of someone reaching out to her but, unlike the almost gentle whisper of movement she had felt above the tribal encampment, this was harsh and chillingly malevolent.

"*Who are you?*" The voice was sweet and compelling, but beneath its tone Sofarita felt raw and terrible power.

She fled instantly, flying faster than ever before, hurtling toward the night-dark lands of the east.

Back in her body she gestured towards the fireplace. Two chunks of wood rose from the log pile and settled in place upon the dying fire. As the flames sprang up Sofarita gazed down at her trembling hands. They were shining as if oiled. Lightly she stroked the skin of her knuckles. It was as smooth now as glazed pottery. She flexed her fingers. They felt stiff and sore.

"*That is just the beginning,*" came the voice in her mind. It was the same woman's voice, the tone cold and infinitely cruel. Sofarita shivered.

A vision danced into her mind. A young woman, white-haired and sleek, with large eyes of shimmering green. The face floated closer. Sofarita saw that the eyes were crystals, multi-faceted and gleaming. "*I am Almeia,*" she said.

"You rule the Almecs. You are the Crystal Queen."

"*That is what they call me.*"

"What do you want from me?"

"*I want for nothing, child. I am eternal and complete. I had also thought myself unique. Imagine my surprise when I sensed you above my home, my resting place, my tomb. How does it feel, Sofarita, to possess such power, to roam the skies, and read the hearts of men?*"

"Frightening," said Sofarita.

"*Frightening? Yes, I remember that feeling. But it passes. Everything passes. Except knowledge. It grows and it grows. Of course there is a price to pay—as you will see. Some might call it a terrible price. I used to think so.*"

"What price?"

"Once I was like you, a creature of soft flesh and transient desires. And I recall how fine that felt, the grass beneath the feet, the scent of summer blooms in the air, the taste of wine upon the tongue. Most of all the feel of a man's warm body pressing upon the skin. All these things are lost to me now. As they will soon be lost to you."

"What are you saying?" asked Sofarita, the beginnings of an awful fear rising in her belly.

"I think you already sense the answer, Sofarita. There are certain humans who should never be touched by the healing crystals. Some—perhaps lucky, perhaps unlucky—become crystal-wed. They swiftly turn to glass, and they shatter and die. More rare are those who become crystal-joined. All the powers of the crystals are unleashed in them. And why? Because they are destined to become the ultimate crystal. Oh yes it is slow. And yes it is infinitely painful. First you notice—as you have already—a sheen to the skin, brows and cheekbones, knuckles and chin. That is only the beginning. Within a year you will scarce be able to move. Within two you will be paralyzed, locked like a statue. Within five your body will no longer be discernible. It will twist and change. Slowly, so slowly. By the twentieth year there will be little hint of humanity. After fifty years you will be merely a block of beautiful crystal. Within it you will survive for a little longer. Another hundred years perhaps. Unless fed, of course. Unless life washes over you in the richness of blood. As long as this is done you will remain, powerful and eternal. Is this what you desire?"

"No. I will not allow it. I will die first."

Sofarita's mind was filled with pealing laughter, a sound metallic and artificial. "I do believe I said the same thing," Almeia told her. "But I can help you, my dear."

"Why would you do this?"

"*Is the answer not obvious? What would be the advantage of having two crystal queens? Would you like my help?*"

"You are evil," said Sofarita. "This I know. And evil is not to be trusted."

"*Such silly words are for smaller minds, Sofarita. Is the sun evil? Or the sea? Each kills, each gives life. That does not make them evil. Everything I do is for self-preservation. All creatures of flesh and blood understand this. I kill to live. As do you. Each mouthful of meat you devour comes from a living creature who would not have chosen to die for you. Are you evil, Sofarita?*"

"I do not have children buried alive to feed me, nor do I tear the hearts from prisoners taken in war."

"*Ah, we are talking merely of scale, then. One lamb is food, ten lambs is a feast, a thousand lambs is gluttony. What then creates evil, the deaths of a million lambs? And what is the difference between a man and a lamb? Everything dies. Most men die uselessly. Those whose lives feed mine at least serve a purpose. In return I give my people prosperity, freedom from want and disease. My trusted councillors also gain eternal lives. They might argue that everything I do is for the general good.*

"*However, let us talk about what would be good for you. I can take away your powers, draw them into myself. It will not harm me. And you would become a farm girl again, soft of flesh.*"

Sofarita's spirit eyes looked deep into Almeia's green crystal orbs. "How would you do this?" she asked.

"*All you need to do is relax. You will be free to live your life as you choose.*"

She lies, came another voice. *She means for you to die!*

Sofarita lay back in the chair, her mind sleepy, her limbs relaxed.

She is already doing it! Push her out, woman. Your life is at risk!

Sofarita blinked and tried to sit up. She felt weak and nauseous. The floating face before her was all eyes now, huge, and green and luminous. Anger flared within her, roaring up like a tidal wave. The image of Almeia flickered—and was gone.

Sofarita shivered. *You must beware*, said the voice. *She will attack again. You are her mortal enemy. She will not rest until you are slain.*

"Who are you?"

Another face flickered into her mind. A middle-aged man with leathery skin and deep-set dark eyes. He wore a beaded headband over his black and grey braided hair. Two eagle's feathers were embedded in the band.

"*I am the One-Eyed-Fox,*" he said, "*shaman to the Anajo, the First People. I tried to reach you when you flew over my village.*"

"I remember. Did you hear all that she said to me?"

"*Most of her words.*"

"Was it true? Am I doomed to become like her, a block of crystal?"

When he spoke there was sadness in his voice. "*I am not strong enough to fight her, only to hide from her. Yet I sense the truth in those words. What she spoke of did indeed happen to her hundreds of years ago. I have walked the Gray Road and have seen this. Once she was gentle and caring, and used her power to heal. Now she demands thousands of sacrifices. Her need for blood and death is insatiable.*"

"Then I shall destroy her before I die."

"*Someone must destroy her before we all die,*" he said. "*Where is Talaban?*"

"I do not know the name. Is he an Avatar?"

"He is the captain of the black ship. He will know where the last battle must be fought."

"And where is that?" asked Sofarita.

"I do not know yet. But Talaban will when the time comes. He and Touch-the-Moon will stand upon the mountain, like lanterns against the dark."

His voice faded away—and Sofarita was alone.

Alone and dying! There had been so many small plans in her young life. To find love and to raise a family. To build a home in the mountains, near a waterfall, and to have a flower garden. Tiny dreams that had comforted her in the first year of widowhood. She had, after a fashion, loved her husband. Veris was a good man, but twenty years older than Sofarita. Her father had made the match because Veris owned land abutting his. The bridal price was two meadows. Sofarita had made no objection. She had known Veris all her life. He was a kind man, given to laughter. His lovemaking had been gentle and Sofarita knew she could be content with this man. On the last morning of his life, eleven weeks after the wedding, he had kissed her cheek and left for the fields. As he reached the doorway he paused, then turned back and hugged her.

"You have made me happy for the first time in my life," he said.

They were the last words he ever spoke to her.

A month after he died she developed a chill, which deepened into a painful hacking cough. The weight dropped from her and her strength was failing. She was, at that time, almost resigned to death.

Not so now.

The Avatar's magic stone had rekindled all her hopes and dreams, and it felt so cruel to have them dashed in this terrible way. Village life was generally too pragmatic for the subtleties of irony. But she understood it now. Possessed of remarkable powers, and an ability to heal any wound or disease, she could not save her own life. Viruk, it seemed, had not saved her at all, merely set her on another road to extinction.

She had told the shaman she would help destroy Almeia before death could snatch her soul. But the words had been spoken in sudden anger and now she felt the weight of despair descend upon her.

I have done nothing with my life, she thought. Nothing worthwhile.

Then do it now, she told herself. Help to defeat the Almecs.

Talaban!

Who was he? The thought cut through her despair.

Closing her eyes she let her spirit soar over the city. Fires were still burning down by the docks and across the estuary in Pagaru. Sofarita flew on to the harbor and saw the black ship nestling against the wharf. Dropping down she sank beneath the decks, searching for the captain's quarters. She entered many cabins, but they all seemed small and cramped. At last she moved toward the stern and entered a larger room. A man was seated at a desk. Like all Avatars he looked young, his face square-cut and handsome, his hair almost black, but dyed blue at the shorn temples. There was a hardness to his features, but no sign of cruelty. He was talking to a Vagar—no, she realized, not a Vagar. The man was a tribesman of some kind. His dark hair was braided and he wore a black vest adorned with white bone.

She opened the ears of her spirit. The tribesman was speaking.

"Bad visions I have. Suryet needs me. The People suffer."

"I want to help you, Touchstone. You know I speak the truth. But my people are also suffering, and until the

Questor General gives us permission I cannot sail the *Serpent* to the west."

"This I know," said the tribesman sadly. He was about to speak again when suddenly he turned and looked straight at Sofarita. "Who you be?" he asked her.

At first she was too shocked to reply. Talaban cut in. "Who are you talking to?"

"Beautiful woman. Spirit."

"*I am Sofarita,*" she said. "*And you are Touch-the-Moon.*"

"That is name I won. Not to be spoken by strangers. You may call me Touchstone."

"*Then I shall. How is it that you can see me?*"

"I see many things. Are you dead?"

"*Not yet.*" She glanced at Talaban, who was sitting quietly, watching the tribesman intently. "*He will think you have lost your senses.*"

"You wait for me," he said. "Not easy speak in this tongue."

As she watched him he closed his eyes. A glow began around his head and chest, flickering from red to purple. Then he rose from his body. "*Now we can speak freely, you and I, in the language of spirit,*" he said. "*Where are you from, Beautiful One?*"

"*I live in the city,*" she told him. "*The One-Eyed-Fox spoke to me. He told me to find Talaban, and that he alone will know where the last battle is to be fought.*"

"*He doesn't know yet.*" He gazed back at the silent captain. "*He is a good man, that one. The best of them.*"

"*There is a sadness about him.*"

"*He lost his love, and the flames of his heart burn low. Are you wed?*"

"*No.*"

"*You could blow upon the flames.*"

"You seek to match me to a man I have not met. You are very forward, Touchstone."

He smiled. *"You tell me where to find you and I shall bring him to you—even if I have to club him over the head and carry him."*

"I am at the house of Questor Ro. Bring him tomorrow. At dusk."

She watched as the tribesman's spirit settled back into his body. His eyes opened.

"And where is the beautiful woman now?" asked Talaban, with a smile.

"She wait. We see her tomorrow. You like her, maybe."

The smile suddenly left Talaban's face. "She is the woman the Council sentenced to death. The Vagar with magical powers."

"Maybe," agreed Touchstone.

"Is she still here?"

Touchstone turned and gazed at Sofarita. "No, captain. She gone now."

"What did you make of her? And I'm not interested in beauty. Is she a danger to my people?"

"How I know this?" responded Touchstone. "But she speak with One-Eyed-Fox. He say she fight Almecs. You think it right to kill her?"

"No I do not. But it puts me in a difficult position. I am a servant of the Council, and it would be my duty to report a meeting with anyone declared as an enemy of the Avatar."

"Talk first. Report later," said Touchstone.

Talaban sighed. "Do you trust her?"

"Good woman," said Touchstone.

"Then I shall trust you. We will speak with her."

"Wear pretty clothes," advised Touchstone. Talaban laughed, the sound rich and almost musical. Sofarita was amazed at the change the laughter wrought in him.

Gone was the hardness, replaced by a boyish warmth which radiated harmony.

And yet somehow it filled her with the knowledge of her own impending doom. Rising through the decks she flew back to her body.

As was usual following *flight* she awoke refreshed, her body rested. She stretched and rose from the chair. A shadow crossed the doorway opposite and she thought Questor Ro must be awake. Then a second shadow flitted across the opening. Sofarita felt a charge in the air, a prickling sensation that made her fearful. Moving swiftly and silently across the room she stepped out into the darkened hallway just in time to see a figure move from the top of the stairs and into the corridor beyond. Reaching out she felt the emotions of the man above. He was thinking of knives, and blood and death. The death of a hated Avatar.

Questor Ro!

Sofarita ran up the stairs. The door to Questor Ro's room was open. She moved inside. Two men were there. Both wore black scarves about their faces and both carried knives. One was approaching the bed in which the little man was asleep. The knife came up—and slashed down. Sofarita made a sudden gesture with her right hand. The blade stopped inches short of the sleeping man—to the obvious astonishment of the attacker. The second man saw her and swung towards her. His knife dropped from his fingers, clattering on the stone-tiled floor. Questor Ro awoke with a start. The first knifeman tried to stab him again. This time the knife flew from his fingers to the ceiling, where it lay flat, as if upon the floor.

"What is happening?" shouted Ro. "How dare you . . . ?"

"All is well, Questor," said Sofarita. "These men are

Pajists. But they will not harm you." Ro glanced up at the knife hovering on the ceiling.

"They came to kill me," he said. "I shall summon the Watch."

"No," said Sofarita. "They will return to the man who sent them. He will convey a message to the leader of the Pajists. I shall visit with that leader tomorrow at noon. You," she said, pointing to the man by the bed, "hold out your hand." Slowly he did so. The knife floated slowly down from the ceiling, settling gently into his palm. "Leave now, and deliver my message. Say also that there are to be no more attacks."

The second man scooped up his knife and both assassins edged around Sofarita and out of the room. She heard them run down the stairs.

"You know the leader of the Pajists?" asked Ro.

"I do now," she said.

"Why did you let them go? We could have arrested them all."

"To what purpose, Questor? This is not a time for revenge, but for reconciliation. The Pajists have contacts among the tribes. Most notably with the Erek-jhip-zhonad. You will need all their support to prevent the Almecs from domination."

Ro shivered. "Suddenly I am no longer tired," he said. "I thank the Source you were here."

The house was an old one, built a century ago for an Avatar family. It was three-storeyed, and dressed with blue-veined white marble. Landscaped gardens flowed around the old house and a stream had been diverted to ripple over terraces adorned with blocks of white stone and multi-colored pebbles. Flowering trees grew everywhere and the air was heavy with the scent of jasmine.

Mejana sat on a wooden bench, her large frame wrapped in a pale blue shawl over an elegant, though voluminous, white gown. Gold bands glittered on her wrists, gold rings shone on every finger, and she wore a gold torque upon her neck. Beside her sat Boru, the agent of Ammon.

"You cannot stay here, Mejana. She will bring Avatar soldiers."

"Where would I go?" replied the middle-aged woman. "And, besides, had she wished me to be captured she would have held my men captive. No. I will see her."

"I cannot be here when she comes," said Boru, glancing up at the sky. The sun was nearing noon. The burly man rose and leaned in to kiss the fat woman's cheek. As he did so he produced a dagger from behind his back and plunged it into her chest. She gasped and fell back. "I am sorry, lady," he told her. "But I cannot risk your capture." Dragging his knife clear and wiping it clean on the dying woman's shawl, he strode from the garden.

Mejana slid sideways, then fell from the bench. She was lying on her back now and looking up at the clear blue sky. Three gulls flew high overhead, and she watched them bank and head back over the sea. There was little pain from the wound, but she felt her mind swimming, losing focus.

She had always known that once she took on the might of the Avatar her life would be at risk. But she had never dreamed the death blow would come from an ally. In that moment she knew with certainty that the Erek-jhip-zhonad were never truly allies. I have been used, she thought, sadly. Images crowded her mind, vying for attention. Her grandson Pendar, her nephew Baj, her daughter Lari. So beautiful. Lari had been crystal-drawn twenty-two years ago for the crime of loving an Avatar. One of her twins had also been killed. Pendar had escaped that fate, for he had been ill and was in the house of a neighbor. The Avatars had not killed Lari, but they had robbed her of youth and middle age, releasing her the same day as a withered crone. That had been hard. So hard. So savagely against what nature intended. Mejana had been in her late thirties, still attractive and supple. Now she nursed her aged, almost senile, daughter. Mejana had used her considerable wealth to try to buy back those lost years. She had bribed officials, sent gifts, petitioned the Questor General. She had begged and pleaded for Lari to be given a second chance at life. Then Lari died.

Mejana groaned. Now there was pain. The wound in her chest was hot and prickly and deep inside Mejana could feel blood filling her lungs. Breathing was becoming increasingly difficult. Lying very still she thought again of Lari. After the funeral Mejana had been inconsolable. For days she sat in her house, organizing no parties for rich Vagars, arranging no orgies. Her girls had come to her, beseeching her to allow them to work.

Slowly her grief turned to anger, then to hot rage, and finally to a cold impenetrable fury. The Avatars were the enemy, and Mejana knew she would devote the rest of her life to bringing them down. Once arrived, the thought stayed with her. She brought in builders to work on the house. The twenty rooms used by her entertainers were made a little smaller, creating narrow gaps between the walls, and spy holes were set along them. Now when the rich men and women arrived for their pleasure they could be observed and heard. Her entertainers, both male and female, were urged to get their clients to talk about themselves. "It will make them relax," she said. "Everyone loves talking about themselves and what they do. They will enjoy your company all the more, and will pay you even more handsomely."

Once the house had reopened Mejana took to creeping down the hidden gaps, listening and noting. Day by day, week by week, Mejana gathered information. Infinitely patient she wrote everything in a huge ledger. For two years she did nothing more than gather information. Then she contacted the ambassador to the Erek-jhip-zhonad. His name was Anwar, and he was a trusted adviser to the old king. She gave him information concerning troop movements near the borders and kept him apprised of regiment strengths. Closing her house she wintered in Morak, the Erek-jhip-zhonad capital. Anwar taught her many things—ciphers and codes—and schooled her in the arts of information retrieval.

"It is unlikely, in the immediate future," said Anwar one day, "that the Avatar will be overthrown by an outside force. The seeds of destruction must be sown from within. There are hundreds of thousands of Vagars. If they should rise, not all the power of the Avatar can stop them."

Mejana returned to Egaru with a new brief: to recruit and train an army of freedom fighters from within the cities. A secret army that would, one day, take control. Slowly, over the next ten years, she built such a force. And now the Pajists had sympathizers in every aspect of government, including the Vagar army.

Mejana's work was perilous. Mostly she stayed in the background, using others to relay information or to seek sympathizers. But on three occasions in the last four years agents of the Erek-jhip-zhonad had been arrested and crystal-drawn. Each of them could have betrayed her. None did.

When the old king died and his son Ammon succeeded him Mejana had wondered what level of support she would continue to receive. Anwar, old now but still possessed of great cunning, was promoted to First

Councillor, and with increased funding the Pajists grew in strength.

Earlier this year Mejana had authorized a daring plan. Attacks were made on prominent Vagars who supported the Avatar regime. Three were killed, one paralyzed when he tried to flee and fell from his balcony. Now the work of the Pajists became an open secret. Wherever people gathered they would talk about the attacks and what they meant. Through this Mejana's agents were able to gather more information and recruit still more fighters to the cause.

But the most important breakthrough came when Mejana ordered the kidnapping of Questor Baliel. The youngest of the Avatar High Council, Baliel was considered by Mejana to be less than courageous. He had attended private orgies at her home and she had observed him closely. He was filled with petty ambitions and believed his lack of political success could be laid at the door of those envious of his wit and intelligence. Like most stupid people he regarded himself highly, and when faced with superior men branded them "intellectual" or "lacking in common sense."

Four Pajists had grabbed him as he left the house. Throwing a grain sack over his head they had beaten him unconscious and carried him to a warehouse close to the dock. Here Mejana had visited him. The Avatar was locked in a dark and windowless cellar. When Mejana entered he had thrown himself at her feet, begging her to help him.

"I am surprised and saddened to find you like this, lord," she said. "The evil men who have captured you have asked me—as a friend of yours—to tell you their demands."

"Demands?" he said, from his knees. "I will pay them anything. Anything!"

"They do not require money, lord. They require information."

"What information?"

"They told me to tell you that you must teach the Six Rituals to a young man. They want a Vagar to learn to use the crystals."

"Sweet Heaven! I can't do that. No Vagar could master the art. Please help me, Mejana."

"I can do nothing, lord. They have me locked in a cell close by. They say they will kill me if you do not obey them. And they will certainly kill you."

"Kill me? I cannot die. Oh Mejana, what must I do?"

Crouching down beside the whimpering man she stroked his long blue hair. "If, as you say, no Vagar can learn the rituals, then what harm is there in teaching them? It will keep you alive. And they have promised to move you to a better room, with lanterns and good food. Also," she said, dropping her voice to a whisper, "they have promised that I can go free. Once I am clear of them I can alert the Watch and you will be rescued."

"Yes. Yes, that is the answer. I will teach them. You must get a message to Rael. He will know what to do."

"It will be as you say, lord," she told him.

For three weeks Baliel taught Pendar the Rituals. At first the young man made little progress, but on the twenty-seventh day he managed to revive a dying flower, bringing it back to full bloom. After this, progress was swift.

Outside, in the city, the Avatars were searching for the missing Questor.

One morning Viruk arrived at the house. Mejana had heard of him. And what she had heard was not encouraging. He was ruthless and cruel, his malice disguised by a great physical charm and charisma.

As he was ushered into the room by a frightened serving girl Mejana rose. "You do my house great honor, lord," she said. "However, I cannot accommodate you for, as you know, the race laws are very harsh."

He smiled. "My dear lady, let us not play games. The services of your entertainers are offered to any with the gold to purchase them. And that includes some of my Avatar colleagues. So let us not flirt with one another. Tell me the last time you saw Questor Baliel."

"My clients always respect the fact that I keep their confidences, lord," she said. "My house would not be filled were it known that I was loose-tongued."

"Oh very well," he said, sorrowfully. Drawing his dagger he moved towards her. "I shall cut the left breast from your body, you fat cow, and then we shall speak without games."

"Three weeks ago," she said. "He came three weeks ago."

Viruk did not sheath his dagger. "What time did he leave?"

"With your permission, lord, I would have to ask the . . . entertainer who kept him company. I do not always see my friends leave."

"Then do so."

Mejana walked to the door and called out a young man's name. Within moments he entered the room, and, seeing Viruk, bowed deeply. Mejana asked him about Baliel, and the time of his departure. The young man replied that it was just after midnight.

"Did you walk with him to the door?" asked Viruk.

"No, lord. I fell asleep."

Viruk asked the man's name and his address and then allowed him to leave. "I trust," said Mejana, "you will not tell the noble Questor that we spoke of him. He is a very good client, and honors us with his presence."

"I doubt he will be honoring you again," said Viruk. "Who would know of his trysts here?"

"He visits on the same two days every week, lord. I

know this, as do all my entertainers. He has a carriage waiting for him at the end of the Avenue, a walk of perhaps a half-mile. His driver would know, as would any who saw him leave. Has something happened to him?"

"I expect so," said Viruk cheerfully. "He was a windbag and a blowhard. He will not be missed. Even so, the man was an Avatar, and therefore the investigation will continue. By the way, how much did he pay for his pleasures?"

"Five gold pieces, lord."

"You must miss him greatly."

"I do not like to lose customers. I thought he had moved to one of the other cities. I know he has a house in Boria. Perhaps he has gone there."

"No one has seen him since he came to your brothel. Did you speak to him on that last night?"

"Yes, lord."

"How did he seem?"

"He was always happy here, lord. I sincerely hope he will be again."

Viruk stared at her for a moment. She felt the intensity of his pale gaze and found that her heart was beating in panic. "I shall question the boy he slept with tomorrow. Send him to the Officers' Building on Military Square. Have him ask for me."

"I will, lord. But I promise you he is a good lad and would not wish any harm on the Questor. He is very fond of him."

"Then he has nothing to fear."

The following day the boy was crystal-drawn to death.

Mejana groaned as the pain flared once more. She could not move now and her eyelids were growing heavy. Death was whispering to her like a trusted lover.

On the news that the boy was dead she had walked to the warehouse and, with the aid of two strong men, had up-ended Baliel into a barrel of salt water. She had stood and watched as his legs thrashed around, the bubbles rising from his tortured lungs. The body was later thrown from the wharf.

She heard movement in the garden. A hand touched her. Heat roared through her chest and she cried out.

"Be still, Mejana, and let me heal you."

She opened her eyes and saw the village girl she had taken to the inn. "I am beyond healing," she said.

The girl smiled. "I do not think so."

Chapter Twenty

In her private apartments Mejana stripped off her blood-soaked clothing and stood naked before a full-length mirror. There was no sign of a wound upon her pale flesh. Not even a mark to show where the knife blade had punctured the skin. Tidy, as always, Mejana carried the stained clothes to a laundry basket and dropped them inside. Then she dressed in another voluminous gown, this one of pale green linen. Returning to her outer rooms she saw the girl sitting by the window, looking out over the bay.

Mejana paused and stared at her. Outwardly she looked no different to the naive villager she had found wandering the city, the shy girl she had taken to Baj. But something about her had changed. There was a radiance to her features and a new confidence in her movements.

"How are you feeling?" asked Sofarita.

"Better than I expected. How did you master the Avatar crystals?"

"I have no crystals, Mejana. The power is mine alone."

"I had no sense of it when I last met you," said the older woman, moving to a large chair and sitting opposite the girl.

"It had not manifested itself at that time. Now it has. And all is changed."

"And now you serve the Avatar?"

"No. I *serve* no one."

"Yet you dwell with Questor Ro and you saved his life."

"Indeed I did—and would do so again. Just as I saved yours."

"Mine is worth saving," said Mejana. "I have a mission and a purpose. To free my people from Avatar tyranny."

Sofarita shook her head. "No, you desire only revenge for the death of your daughter. But your motives are not important now."

"What is important, then?" asked Mejana.

"The defeat of the Almecs. They are a cruel and malevolent people, ruled by a goddess of crystal. She is fed by blood, by ritual sacrifice. If they succeed here then the Vagars and all the people under their dominion will be merely food for the goddess."

"My daughter was food for the Avatar. She fed their crystals with her life."

"I am not defending the Avatar, Mejana. Their day is almost gone. However, I want you to trust me. I want you to understand how terrible is this new enemy."

"What are you asking of me?" snapped Mejana.

"The Almecs have landed armies upon the coast and they are sailing to attack the Mud People at Morak. More ships are arriving daily along the coastlines. Soon there will be thousands of Almec warriors. It is vital that we coordinate our efforts. You have contacts with Ammon and the tribes. Your grandson Pendar is close to the Patiakes. He made a friend of their king."

"Until Viruk slew him," Mejana pointed out.

"That is past. Viruk slew Judon, you killed Baliel,

and ordered the deaths of others. You did not listen as Baliel cried for mercy. You held his legs as he thrashed around in the barrel."

"How do you know these things?" whispered Mejana.

"There are no secrets I cannot find," Sofarita told her. "But, as I said, this is all in the past. In two hours I shall meet with Questor General Rael. You will be there. Together you will plan the campaign against the Almecs."

Mejana laughed. "Rael will have me arrested and crystal-drawn."

"He may," agreed Sofarita. "But that is a risk you will take."

"Why should I?"

"Because if the Almecs are comprehensively defeated you will be closer to your goal. Freedom for the Vagars. The coming battles will exhaust the Avatar. At that point change will be inevitable."

"You ask a lot of me. So tell me, what do you gain from all of this?"

"I will merely die," said Sofarita. "Now take my hand, and I shall show you the nature of the enemy."

Rael had never been more angry. He struggled to speak through his rage. "How dare you!" he stormed. "How dare you bring this murderess into my company?"

Mejana sat silently, watching the Questor General. Niclin stood back, his eyes hooded, his emotions masked. Questor Ro stood in the archway to the garden, his eyes on the calm, tranquil figure of Sofarita, seated on a low couch. Rael loomed above her, his face ashen. "I would sooner die than deal with such . . . such scum!"

"Sit down, Rael," said Sofarita, softly. "Try to put aside your rage and listen to your intellect."

"I will not sit. I will not remain in this house. My guards are outside and I will have them take this murderess to her death."

"As you took her daughter and countless thousand others," said Sofarita, her voice even. "As you took her grandchild and drew its tiny life into your crystals. How can you talk of murder when you live only by sucking the life from others? By all that is holy, Rael, you should be long dead. You breathe only because you have stolen life from others."

"I do not need to listen to this," stormed Rael. "And I do not need some Vagar whore to tell me what is right. If her daughter was sentenced it was according to the law."

"Now there is an interesting concept," said Sofarita. "If a few Avatars decide that planting a flower in the earth is wrong, then that becomes the law. And Vagars will die for it. You speak of the law as if it flows from the Source. What right have you to make the laws?"

"The right of conquest!" he replied, instantly.

"Exactly. And now Mejana and her people are ready to conquer you. This will give her the right to make the laws. Perhaps she will decide that having blue hair is a capital crime. Then all Avatars will be law-breakers. Enough of this, Rael, it is beneath you. Rage is no basis on which to build cooperation."

Rael took a deep breath. "What is it you are proposing?" he asked.

"A chance for survival. The tribes will not gather under Avatar leadership. They will fight singly, and they will be overwhelmed. You must give way. The Avatars will be the spear point, but others will have their hands upon the haft."

"These are our cities, our lands," he said, his voice calmer. "What is it that you are suggesting?"

"They are no longer your cities. You will surrender power now to Mejana and myself. You will remain the Questor General until the war is concluded."

"Are you listening to this?" sneered Rael, turning to Niclin and Ro. "Can you believe what you are hearing?" He swung back towards Sofarita. "We are gods, woman. We do not give way to lesser beings."

"You are not gods, Rael. You are men with power. But let us assume for a moment you are right and that your powers do make you a god. In that case I am a goddess, and infinitely more powerful than you."

"A dying goddess," snapped Rael. "You think I do not understand what it means to be crystal-joined? It has happened before. Twice. You have a few years of power, then you will become nothing more than a block of crystal."

"This time you are absolutely correct," she said without hint of anger. "And I hope that saying it gave you pleasure."

The anger drained from Rael. "Yes, it did," he admitted. "And it shames me."

"The truth is sometimes painful, Rael," she said. "But know this: I could choose otherwise for myself, like Almeia, the goddess of the Almecs. She is fed with blood daily. She survives, and her power is very great indeed. I do not, however, wish to live upon the blood of others. But that is not the real issue here today. What I am suggesting for the Avatar will happen regardless of any path you choose now. You are the last remnants of a dead race. Your domination rests only on the power chests charged by Questor Ro. You are pitifully few in number and the people you rule outnumber you by thousands to one. Even without the Almecs, power would have changed hands within a few years. It is inevitable. What I am saying is, that if it can be today, then you have a chance to defeat the Almecs." She spread her hands. "Or you can choose to drag the tribes and the Vagars down to death with you and leave the survivors in the hands of a terrible enemy."

Rael glanced at Questor Niclin. "Do you have anything to add, cousin?" he asked.

Niclin shook his head. Rael swung toward Ro. "What about you, Questor?"

The little man tugged his forked blue beard. "What she says is true. Our day is almost done. We cannot survive alone against the Almecs and, in truth, we could no longer quell an uprising among the Vagars. The only question that really remains is how this exchange of power will be organized."

Mejana rose. "May I speak?" she asked Sofarita.

Sofarita nodded, and Mejana turned to Rael. "Earlier today I was stabbed and lay dying," she said. "By an agent of Ammon who did not want me to meet Sofarita. Happily she arrived at my home and restored me to health. Being so close to death made me see many things differently. I was, it is true, consumed by hatred for the Avatar—and I still despise you. The only way you could justify your vampire lives was to think of us as sub-humans. I understand that. I loathe it, but I understand it. But it ends here. From this day no human being of any race will be crystal-drawn. All Vagars currently awaiting trial on race laws will be released forthwith. The race laws will be rescinded from today. A new High Council will be elected from among the Vagar and the Avatar. Since there is little time for elections to be made by the people I shall nominate the Vagars to sit upon the first council. You, Questor General, will nominate the Avatar councillors. The balance will be even, sixteen from each group. You, as the Questor General, will have the deciding vote on all matters military and civil."

Rael stood silently for a moment, then he nodded. "As you say, so let it be. We will meet, with you and your representatives, at the Council Chamber this evening." He turned to Sofarita. "And now perhaps you will tell me what you have seen of the enemy?"

"Even as we speak," said Sofarita, "they are attacking Ammon's capital. It will fall within hours. Another force has landed farther east, and marches inland. Two other armies have beached their ships to the south."

"How many men?"

"Altogether the eastern armies number three thousand, the southern force double that. And more ships are coming every day."

"I have sent Viruk to fetch Ammon," said Rael. "Is there anything you can do to help him?"

"I will try," said Sofarita.

Rael looked at Mejana. "I will see you and your people this evening," he said. Gesturing to Niclin he walked toward the door.

"Wait, Questor General," said Sofarita. He paused and glanced back at her. "I want your promise that neither you nor any other under your command will seek to harm Mejana or any of her people."

"What oath would you have me give?" he asked.

"Swear it—on the soul of your daughter, Chryssa."

Rael blanched. "I so swear," he said, then stalked from the room.

"Did he mean it?" asked Mejana.

"Yes, though he will seek to find a way around it before the end."

"As I suspected."

"Now you will give me the same oath," said Sofarita. "There must be no more attacks on Avatars. Your time has come, Mejana. Accept victory with magnanimity. No more thoughts of revenge."

"I so swear," said the fat woman. "And now I must go."

As she left the room Questor Ro approached Sofarita. "I fear I am no longer in favor with my colleagues," he said. "Rael did not ask me to accompany him, and I do not think I will be invited to sit on the new council." He saw that she was pensive. "What is wrong?"

"Rael believes he is making a short-lived alliance. He is putting his faith in Anu's new pyramid. When that is complete he plans to seize back power. As for Mejana, she dreams of a day when all Avatars can be dragged from their homes and put under the knife. Their hatred, their prejudices are deeper than oceans."

"Why did you not change them, as you changed me?"

"If I had done so they would have become alienated from the people who serve them. As it is, both groups follow leaders whose views reflect their own. Come, let us walk in the garden and breathe in the scent of blooms."

Talaban had been superbly trained. He could read maps, lead men, sail the oceans, and construct battle strategies at a moment's notice. But nothing in his 200 years of life had prepared him for the moment he saw Sofarita. It was as if he had been struck dumb.

He had been fine as he approached Ro's house with Touchstone. They had climbed down from the carriage in time to see Rael and Niclin leaving. The Questor General pulled him aside. "Be careful what you say and think, Talaban. She is powerful and can—I believe—read a man's thoughts."

"Is she still under sentence of death?"

"No. There is a new council being elected. Be at the

chamber tonight, at the nineteenth hour. You will replace Questor Ro."

"What has happened to him?"

"She has bewitched him, Talaban. Beware that the same does not happen to you."

With that the Questor General moved away to his carriage.

Talaban and Touchstone entered the house. Ro himself greeted them. His manner seemed friendly and he was relaxed in a way Talaban had never seen before. "You are welcome, my friends," said Ro. "Come, the lady waits."

They followed Ro into the garden room. The woman was sitting on a low couch. She glanced up as the men entered. Talaban looked at her, and his pace faltered. Her eyes were tawny brown, with flecks of gold, her hair dark and long, her skin tanned gold. She was exquisite, and he found himself staring at her beauty, unable to think clearly.

"Welcome, Talaban," she said.

Struggling to clear his mind he found himself saying "I am Talaban," which was ridiculous, considering she had just greeted him by name. He took a step forward and his foot caught on the rug, almost making him stumble.

"And it is good to see you again, Touchstone," she added, smiling at the tribesman. Touchstone bowed, but said nothing.

The smile tore into Talaban like a lance. She is bewitching you, he thought. Just as Rael prophesied. Be careful!

"What . . . did you wish to . . . why did you call for us?" said Talaban, clumsily. Anger at his own stupidity raged through him. He had never before been so inarticulate. He felt foolish and awkward.

"I am Sofarita," she said, "and we needed to meet.

We have both talked with One-Eyed-Fox, and we both know that this terrible enemy must be defeated." She told him of Almeia, the living crystal, the heart of the Almec people. Talaban listened as she described the horror that awaited the peoples of the world should the Almecs conquer. She also outlined the discussions with Rael and Mejana. The warrior tried to concentrate, but his thoughts kept straying. The line of her neck was beautiful, her shoulders perfect. He looked at her lips as she spoke, trying to focus on her words. Soft lips, full, glistening . . .

"Are you well, captain?" she asked him suddenly.

"Well? Yes, I am well. Are you bewitching me, lady?"

"Not by intent, sir," she told him, coolly. Touchstone chuckled beside him, the sound washing over Talaban like spring water, easing his tension.

"I am not usually this foolish," he said. "I apologize, lady."

"You have nothing to apologize for, Talaban. But, tell me, are you not surprised by the turn of events? How do you feel about this new alliance with the Vagars?"

"I cannot say," he replied, truthfully. "It has all happened so suddenly." He looked into her eyes, and was delighted to discover that he could do so and still think clearly. "Once the seas covered Parapolis we were finished. It was only a question of time. That time—it appears—is now upon us."

"Does it sadden you?"

"No," he told her. And was surprised to find that he meant it.

"Good. I fear most Avatars will not agree with you. With no one being crystal-drawn your dreams of immortality will cease. You will grow old as other men."

"Not if Anu completes his pyramid," he said. "It will draw power from the sun and feed the crystals without need of human sacrifice."

"Questor Anu is a great man," she said. "But he will not finish his pyramid in time to save the cities of the east. That will be left to men like Rael and yourself."

Talaban nodded. "I accept that, lady."

"But something troubles you."

"Yes. You talk of helping us, but, from what you describe, this Almeia is more powerful than you. Her armies are stronger than any force we can muster. I do not see how we can win."

"In truth I do not know if we can," she said. "But when faced with evil it is vital to oppose it, whether victory is achievable or not. And, for a while at least, my powers will continue to grow. Who knows what we might achieve? And now you must go and prepare for your meeting with the new council. Would you object if Touchstone remained here? He and I have much to talk about."

Talaban felt a twinge of jealousy. But he bowed and forced a smile.

Ro walked him to the door. "She is an amazing woman," said the little Questor.

"Indeed she is."

As he left the house Ro took hold of his arm. "Do not let Rael deceive you, Talaban. There is no evil in her."

"Are you in love with her, Ro?"

"With every fiber of my being."

Boru sat in the prison cell, his golden-haired daughter cuddled in close to him. "I don't like it here. I want to go," she said. He stroked her hair. So soft and fine, he thought, threads of lovingly woven sunlight.

"We have to stay for a little while," he said. "The door is locked."

"Why are we locked in?" she asked him.

"Just rest, little one."

"I don't want to rest. I want to go outside."

"Sometimes we can't do what we want to do."

Boru cursed himself for a selfish fool. He had always known there was a chance he could be caught, but as each mission passed without incident he had become careless. For years now he had travelled between the cities, gathering information, passing messages between the Pajists and Anwar. And, in his arrogance, he had even started taking Shori on his trips. When the guards at the eastern gate had detained him he had still not realized it was over. But when they brought him here he knew the truth. The two of them were to die. And he was to blame. She stood up in his lap and tugged at his yellow and silver beard. "Don't be sad," she said.

"I love you, little one, and I am sorry."

"Why are you sorry? Have you done something wrong?"

"Yes. I should have left you with your aunt."

"But I like coming with you," she said. "I like crossing rivers."

The door opened. Boru took a deep breath and, gathering Shori in his arms, he rose.

Mejana stood there, two Avatar soldiers beside her. Boru blinked in surprise.

"Bring him," she said. Then she walked down the corridor and out of his sight. The guards stepped aside. Boru carried Shori out and along the corridor, then up a flight of stairs. Mejana walked ahead of him and did not say a word. Finally they came to a long room with a high, vaulted ceiling. Some thirty people were seated around a huge table. At least half were Avatars, but the rest were Vagars, many of whom Boru knew. They were Pajists. He stood transfixed, his brain numb. What was happening here?

At the head of the table was a slim Avatar with piercing eyes and short-cropped blue hair. He rose and gestured Boru forward. A guard poked Boru in the back and he stumbled toward the table.

"You are Boru, agent of Ammon?" asked the Avatar.

"I am."

"You know some of the people here."

"No."

"It was not a question, Boru. It was a statement of fact. You are not being tricked, and the Vagars you see here are not prisoners. They are new members of the High Council. I am Rael, the Questor General."

"What do you want with me?" said Boru, his tone openly hostile.

"Personally I would like to see you crystal-drawn, but that is no longer an option."

"It's been done already, Avatar," snapped Boru. "Thirty years you took."

Rael gave a humorless smile. "Do as you are bid and you could get them back."

"I will rot in seven hells before I serve you." The angry words frightened Shori, and she began to cry.

"I want to go! I want to go!" Boru hugged her and kissed her head.

"It is all right. It is only a little argument," said Boru. "It is not important." Her crying subsided and Boru returned his attention to the Avatar. "I'm listening," he said.

"Ammon's capital is under siege. A war has begun that could see us all enslaved. I have sent messengers to Ammon, offering him assistance. I want you to go to him and convince him to bring his warriors to Egaru. It is the natural center for defense."

"And for this you will return my youth?"

"Yes."

Boru turned to Mejana, who was now sitting beside a Vagar merchant. "How is it that you live, woman?" he asked. "I know the blow was well struck."

"I was healed, you treacherous cur," she told him icily. "Now, will you do as the Questor General requests, or will you have your head cut from your shoulders?"

Boru grinned. "You may not believe it, Mejana, but I am glad you are alive. And it is fascinating seeing you all sitting down with the enemy. I suppose, ultimately, all life is compromise." He swung toward Rael. "Very well, I will try to find Ammon. But know this: I am your enemy, and as long as blood flows in my veins I will remain so."

"A threat to bring me many sleepless nights," said Rael, turning away. "Your wagon will be brought here presently. You may leave your daughter with the Lady Mejana."

"What? No! She comes with me."

Rael moved in close. "She will be safer here than on a battlefield, Boru. But if you would prefer I can have you both killed now, and find another messenger. Make your choice swiftly."

Boru was beaten and he knew it. He carried the child to where Mejana sat. "She is all that I love in this world," he said.

Mejana's face softened. "No harm will befall her—whatever happens. This is my promise."

Chapter Twenty-one

Anwar watched as the fireballs rained down on the capital then turned to the young king. "We must leave, highness. The royal guards will not be able to stop them."

Resplendent in a gown of brilliant blue satin edged with gold, the king swung towards him. "Where is my new army, Anwar? Where are my soldiers?"

"They are training, my lord, in the hills to the north. But I fear even they would prove ineffectual against these . . . savages."

A fireball struck the side of the palace. A large section of painted plaster fell from the ceiling of the king's bed-chamber. Dust filled the air. "I rather think now is the time, highness."

Ammon moved to the window and stared malevolently across at the golden ships. Three of them had come close to the shore. Copper-skinned warriors in golden armor were streaming down lowered gang-planks. Fifty of the king's guards rushed at them. The enemy soldiers were carrying what looked like short black clubs. They held them to their shoulders. Fire spewed from them. The first line of guards were hurled from their feet. The remainder broke and ran.

Hundreds of enemy warriors were ashore now. Ammon swung from the window.

"Where would you have me go, my friend?"

"I would suggest the opposite direction to that of the enemy, highness. And let us move *now*!"

Anwar led the king through to the rear of the apartments, down the narrow stairwell, and out to the servants' entrance. A young slave was cowering below a kitchen window. Anwar called to him. "Come here, boy! Do it now!" The slave blinked nervously, then crept forward. "Remove your tunic. At once." The boy lifted the drab grey cloth over his head and stood naked. Taking the tunic, Anwar gave it to the king. "Be so good as to put this on, highness," he said.

"You want me to dress in a rag?"

"I want you to be alive at the day's end, highness."

Ammon pulled the satin gown from his shoulders, letting it drop to the floor. Then he donned the grey tunic. Anwar opened the side door and looked out. Refugees were streaming away from the city center. A fireball landed in their midst. Three men and a woman were lifted high into the air and dashed against the wall of the palace. Anwar moved out into the throng, closely followed by the young king. They flowed into the crowd, which surged towards the southern quarter of the city. Anwar linked his arm with the king. The old man was breathless now, his lungs burning, his legs weary. Ammon threw his arm around him and half-carried him. Terrified screams broke out from the refugees ahead of the fleeing column. Huge beasts wearing black leather cross belts on their fur-covered chests had appeared from an alleyway. They were tearing into the refugees with fang and talon. The crowd panicked and began to run faster.

Anwar saw an opening to an alleyway on the left and pulled Ammon into it. He no longer knew where he was, but he stumbled on. Ammon took him by the arm, pulling him to a halt. "Rest for a moment," said the king. "You are exhausted."

Anwar shook his head and struggled to move on. The king held him. "You are too valuable to me, Anwar. If you keep this up you will have a seizure. Now let us walk."

"They were krals!" said Anwar. "I saw one once, while journeying south. It was dead. But it was huge and terrifying nonetheless."

Ammon gazed about him. The street was very narrow and human excrement had stained the road below the small windows. A rat moved out from a doorway and scuttled across Anwar's foot. The old man jumped back. "You take me to the most interesting places," remarked Ammon.

More screams sounded from a parallel street. The king now led his councillor, moving swiftly to another alley, then cutting right into a deserted market square. A small child, little more than a year old, was sitting on the steps of a building. It was wailing loudly. Ammon swept it into his arms. "What are you doing?" cried Anwar.

"Seems a shame to leave the mite," said Ammon. "And he's not heavy."

Anwar was lost for words. Had the king lost his senses? Had the attack on the capital unmanned him? "Let us move on, highness," he said.

At the next corner they rejoined the line of surviving refugees who were heading towards the southern gates. The king came to a halt. "What is it?" asked Anwar. They were on high ground now, and Ammon pointed to the land beyond the city walls. Enemy soldiers had fanned out across the gateways. The toddler, exhausted by his wailing, was now asleep on the king's shoulder.

"That's what we should do," said Ammon. "Find a place to sleep."

"They will search the city for you."

"Thirty-six thousand dwellings. That will take time."

Ammon swung left again and, holding the toddler close, moved back into the narrow lanes and alleys of the poorer quarter. Here there were people who had not run. Their clothes were rags, their faces filthy, their eyes devoid of emotion. Scabrous figures sat in open door-ways and everywhere there was the stench of poverty. A stick-thin woman emerged to stand in front of Anwar. "You wants to pass through here, rich man? Well you can pay the toll." She held out a filthy hand.

"I am carrying no coin," said Anwar.

"Oh give her your ring, Anwar. I'll buy you another."

"You listen to your pretty boy, old man," said the woman, producing a small knife and holding it to An-war's throat.

Holding the toddler in his left arm Ammon's right hand flashed out, his slender fingers snapping around the woman's wrist and twisting it. The knife clattered to the stone. Ammon picked it up and tossed it to the woman. "You do not seem too frightened by the inva-sion," he said, conversationally.

She rubbed her wrist. "What difference will it make to the likes of us? They won't kill us. We're nothing to them. Just as we're nothing to the likes of you. Life will go on. Or it won't." She shrugged. "Now give me the ring!"

"First you will take us to the village of potters."

The woman grinned, showing brown and broken teeth. "You want to have a vase made?"

"And several goblets. Do this for me and I will pay you handsomely." She gazed at his rough grey tunic.

"I don't see no money pouch."

"She has a point, Anwar. Are you carrying coin?"

"I . . . I don't think this is the time or place to discuss it . . ."

"Give it to me."

Anwar reached inside his purple gown and produced a small, but heavy, pouch. "Lead on, lady," said Ammon.

"You are a strange one and no mistake," she said. With a wink to a man standing in the shadows she moved off. Ammon passed the sleeping toddler to Anwar and followed her. He seemed uninterested in the slim man who followed them. Anwar cast nervous glances in the man's direction and kept close to the king.

They walked for almost half an hour, passing through foul-smelling alleys and several derelict areas. In the distance they could still hear explosions and faint screams. Finally the woman pointed down towards a winding stream. Small houses were built on both sides of it, the village being joined by a small stone bridge. "That's the village of potters," she said. "Now pay me handsomely!"

Ammon opened the pouch. The coins inside were all gold. He removed two and handed them to the woman. The slim man moved forward. "I think we'll take it all," he said, drawing a long thin dagger.

"Greed is so unbecoming," said Ammon. "You have more gold than you have seen in a long time. There is no more to be had. Now, I have other matters to attend to. And I do not wish to kill you. So be content."

"Should we be content, my dove?" the man asked the woman.

"Nah!" she said. "Gut him, Beli."

The knife flashed forward. Ammon parried it with his right forearm then slammed the heel of his palm into the man's filthy face. The point of contact was just below the nostrils. Without a sound the robber fell forward to the ground. The woman stood and stared at the fallen man. Then she dropped to her knees alongside him. She started to shake him. "There is no point," said Ammon. "He is dead."

"You killed him, you bastard!" she screamed. Ammon spun on his heel, the edge of his left hand thundering against her neck. There was a sickening crack and she fell across the body of her lover. Kneeling beside the corpses Ammon retrieved the golden coins.

The toddler awoke and started to cry. Ammon took him from Anwar and rubbed his back. "There, there, little one. Be still. We'll find you food in the village."

"You amaze me, highness. You are very skilled at fighting."

"Skill is relative to the quality of the opponent. They were hardly expert."

"Even so. Where did you learn to make those moves?"

"You remember the charming boy who visited us from the north. The tall one with yellow hair?"

"Yes."

"He taught me to. The secret, apparently, is in the lack of speed with which the move is begun. It is rather effective."

"You mastered the art very well, highness. But there is a great difference between practice with a friend and combat."

"Indeed there is. Combat is far more exhilarating." Ammon moved out down the slope towards the village.

"What made you ask for this place, highness?" asked Anwar.

"I have a friend here."

"You have a friend who is a potter?"

"Not a friend exactly," admitted Ammon with a smile. "But he does owe me his life."

Sadau the potter had been frightened now for most of the morning. The explosions in the north of the city, the fleeing refugees and the news of the invasion had turned his bowels to water. All that kept him from fleeing himself was the thought that, whoever the enemy, they would need pots. He was not an important man—had never wanted to be. And now his very anonymity would protect him.

He hoped.

Which caused the sight of the disguised king standing at his door to unnerve him utterly. Sadau stood, open-mouthed and wordless as he recognized his monarch.

"I think you should invite us in," said Ammon, pushing past the potter. An old man followed him. He was carrying a small sleeping child.

"Wh . . . what do you want . . . sire?" asked Sadau. The king moved into the dingy room and sat down on a wicker chair.

"Somewhere to rest for the night. A little food for myself and my friend. Oh . . . and some milk for the babe."

Sadau stood stock-still, his mind in a whir. The enemy—whoever they were—would be hunting for the king. They would search all the houses. And probably kill whoever they found hiding him. It was like a nightmare. "How . . . how did you find me?" he asked.

"I knocked at the door of one of your neighbors."

"My *neighbors* know you are here?"

"I rather think they did not recognize me. The poor rarely have the opportunity to observe me closely. Now, come along man, play the host. Fetch us some food."

"You can't stay here, highness. They will be searching for you."

"Exactly so. But I really don't think they will expect to find me in a hovel." Ammon rose from his chair and approached the potter, laying his slender hands on the man's shoulders. "You are a very lucky man, Sadau. You tossed my brother's head into the Luan and you did not die for it. Now you have an opportunity to earn the king's gratitude. Once I have escaped and gathered my army, I shall smite these invaders and retake my kingdom. Then you will be well rewarded."

"I don't want to be rewarded. I want to be *alive*!"

"A noble aim, potter. But let us concentrate on one thing at a time. And the first priority is food. Fetch some."

Sadau stumbled into his small kitchen, returning with a fresh-baked loaf and a plate of raisins. "I have no milk for the child," he said.

"Borrow some from your neighbors. But be quick, for there are beasts abroad."

Sadau was in a daze as he unlocked the door and stepped out into the sunset. All was quiet now and he felt like running away, sprinting to some darkened place where he could lie down, close his eyes, and pray that he would wake and find this was all merely some fevered dream. Suddenly he heard screams in the distance and a terrible howling. The little man ran to the home of his cousin, Oris. The small house was dark, the shutters closed. Sadau tapped on the door. "It is me, Sadau," he called.

Inside there were no lanterns lit. Oris was not at home and his wife Rula was sitting in the dark, her two small children beside her, her babe in her lap. "Are we all going to die?" she asked, her voice breaking. She was a mousy woman, round-shouldered and perpetually weary. As indeed anyone would be who had to live with Oris. The big riverman was a noisy, boisterous man, who treated his friends like loved ones, and his loved ones like servants. Rula had been worn down by his infidelities and his endless lies.

"No, we are not going to die," said Sadau. "Where is Oris?"

"He did not come home. He left this morning to

work at the river. What am I going to do, Sadau? What will happen to my babes if he's dead?"

Her distress touched him, cutting through both his fear and his dislike of her. "Come to my home," he said. "We will wait for Oris there. I am sure he is not dead." Probably hiding in the home of some whore, he thought. Carrying one of the children and leading the other by the hand he led them back to his home. Rula seemed less frightened now, but the children were unusually quiet.

As they entered the house Rula stiffened. "You have friends here," she said. "Perhaps I should wait at home."

"It is all right," Sadau assured her. "They are customers of mine." Locking the door he put down the child he was carrying. She sat upon the floor and began to cry. Ammon approached her, kneeling down beside her.

"Don't cry, little one," he said. "It is just a game. Tell me your name."

"Saris," said the child. "My daddy owns the river."

"What a coincidence," said Ammon. "My daddy owned the river too." The small room was crowded now. The toddler carried by Anwar began to wail.

"He's hungry," said Ammon, glancing up at Rula. "Do you think you could feed him?"

She nodded and, passing her own sleeping babe to Sadau, moved to the toddler, lifting him to her lap and opening her dress to expose a large breast. Instantly the toddler began to suckle greedily.

A silent hour passed. Then there came a knock at the door. Sadau almost fainted with the shock. "Who is it?" he called.

"Oris. Is Rula with you?"

Sadau opened the door and a heavy-set young man

entered. Rula ran to him, hugging him close. "I was so worried," she said.

"You and me both," he confided. "It's terrible out there. Corpses everywhere. It's quiet now. They say the king is dead, and all the nobles either fled or slain. When the attack started I thought they were Avatars. But they're not. They're red-skinned. The palace is a ruin."

Ammon stepped forward. "You say they killed the king?"

Oris stared at him, suspiciously. "Customers," said Sadau, lamely.

"Yes. They dragged his body out to the main square and hung it from a rope."

"How did they know it was the king?" asked Anwar.

"How would I know? He was dressed in a long blue robe. They found him in the palace, I guess."

"How sad," said Ammon. "I always liked him."

"We better be getting home," said Oris. "The gods alone know what tomorrow will bring."

As they were leaving, Ammon asked Rula if she would take charge of the abandoned toddler. She said that she would and he gave her a gold coin which she instantly handed to Oris. The big riverman looked closely at Ammon. "Have I seen you somewhere before?" he asked him.

"Quite possibly. I travel the Luan regularly."

"Right. Well, may the gods protect you. May they protect us all."

Sadau closed the door behind them. Then he turned to the king. "They think you are dead," he said happily.

"Not for long. Someone will see the body and know it is not me. But for now we appear to be safe. Tomorrow you will help me find a way to leave the city."

"Please, lord," begged Sadau, "I am not a brave man!

I learned that when I watched the Avatar, Viruk, kill all my comrades."

Ammon smiled. "You underestimate yourself, potter. You mistake natural fear for base cowardice. You are not a coward. Had I been in your place I too would have thrown the head into the Luan. That is one of the reasons why I did not have you killed. Look at me. Look me in the eye." Sadau did so. "Do I look to you like a foolish man?"

"No, lord."

"Then trust what I say. You have more courage than you know. And tomorrow we will leave this city and you will be safe. Is that right?"

"Yes, lord," said Sadau, glumly.

Rael was in a cold and bitter mood. The council meeting had been awkward in the extreme, the Vagars saying little, leaving Mejana to voice their concerns. Well might they be silent, he thought. Traitors all. What especially galled him was that most of the Vagars present were men known to him, men who had prospered under Avatar rule, merchants and artists, many of whom had been entertained by Rael at official functions. Now he knew they had plotted to kill men like Baliel and Ro. Perhaps even himself. He wanted to strike out at them, send soldiers to their homes and drag them from their beds.

Forcing such sweet thoughts from his mind he turned his attention to Talaban, who was sitting quietly on a couch staring into a goblet of wine.

"You are very quiet," he said. "Did she bewitch you?"

"I rather think she did," said Talaban with a rueful smile. "I made a fool of myself. I couldn't take my eyes off her. My tongue seemed twice its size and I spoke like a dolt."

"Do not be deceived, Talaban. She is the greatest enemy we could imagine."

"Hard to believe, sir."

"Trust me. You don't know what she is—what she will become."

"I know she is helping us and she is ready to take the battle to the enemy."

"That is *now*," said Rael. "Every day she will grow in strength and knowledge. She will change, Talaban."

"How can you be so sure?"

"She is crystal-joined."

Talaban reacted as if struck. "No! That cannot be!"

Rael misread the cause of his concern. "It can—and is. Viruk found her in a local village. He bedded her and realized she had a cancer in her lungs. Typically he broke the rules and used his crystal to heal her. No real problem there. Except that she happened to be that one in a score of millions. The crystal changed her, became part of her. The process is continuing. Today she can read minds, heal wounds, and her soul can fly to the farthest corners of the earth. But tomorrow, or next month, or next year, she will be like the Crystal Queen, her powers vast. Do you believe that such a being will willingly die?"

"She will become crystal," whispered Talaban, "like Chryssa."

"Not like Chryssa," snapped Rael. "Like the Crystal Queen, or the third Avatar Prime. How many thousands died in the Crystal Wars? How many gave their blood to keep him alive? According to contemporary accounts more than a hundred thousand died to feed him."

"How long does she have in human form?" asked Talaban.

"I don't know. Two years. Five. Who cares? The question is, what can we do to regain the initiative?"

Talaban felt a sickness in the pit of his stomach at the thought of Sofarita dying. His mind reeled at the thought. Pushing the dread back he looked up at Rael. The Questor General was tired, his eyes dark-rimmed. "How long since you slept, sir?" he asked.

"Three days. I will sleep soon. So, tell me what you think."

"I think it is pointless to try to plan against either Sofarita or the Vagars. The Almecs are the immediate enemy. They must be defeated. In truth we have little chance, but none at all if we are divided. The council meeting did not bode well. The Vagars were tense and uneasy. No real effort was made to draw them into the discussions. But I like the woman Mejana. Her words are careful and well thought out. She is no fool."

"She ordered the murder of Baliel."

Talaban rose from his chair. "May I speak frankly, cousin?"

"Always."

"Put your hatred aside. It will affect your judgment. One enemy at a time. Mejana is, for the moment, an ally. She needs to be wooed like any tribal chieftain. The Almecs require all your thinking, all your enormous gifts of strategy. When they are dealt with, then you can worry about other enemies."

Rael sighed. "I know what you say is true, but it is hard, Talaban." He filled a wine goblet and drank deeply. "You say you want to command a land force. Why?"

"You are short of commanders, cousin. Viruk is a fine fighter, but he is no leader. You need someone who can carry your strategies through on the battlefield. I do not wish to sound immodest, but I am the best you have."

"I cannot afford to lose the *Serpent*, Talaban."

"You will not lose it. I have another captain in mind. He is bright, courageous and skilled."

"I know of no one with the training to take command."

"He is my sergeant, Methras."

Rael hurled the empty goblet across the room. "A Vagar! You would put our most powerful battle weapons in the hands of a Vagar? Are you insane?"

"He has Avatar blood, Rael," said Talaban softly. "There is no question of that. And he is loyal."

"Loyal? Yesterday I would have considered the Vagars at the meeting loyal. I would have considered you *loyal*. Now it seems you have been training Vagars behind my back, breaking the law. My law."

"Yes, I broke the law," admitted Talaban. "And I am sorry that has caused you pain. As you know I have tried in the past to teach other Avatars the secrets of handling the *Serpent*. None proved adept at it. None showed any aptitude. When I knew we were facing ships of battle I had to find someone who could take my place if I was injured. Equally I needed someone who could loose the Sunfire. When we sailed into Pagaru's harbor it was Methras who sank the enemy ships."

Rael fought for calm. "It is done now, but what is done can be undone."

"Think for a moment, sir," urged Talaban. "You will want, at least in the short term, to win over the Vagars on the Council, to convince them that they genuinely have a voice in matters of state. What better way than to announce a Vagar as captain of the *Serpent*—how did you put it?—our most powerful battle weapon? We both know it is only of real use against other ships. Admittedly the Sunfire could be used against land targets, but it only has three charges. Added to which there will be Avatars aboard, all armed with zhi-bows. Methras could hardly overpower them all."

Rael sank into his chair. "There is truth in what you say," he admitted. "It would help win over the Vagars. But let us be honest with one another, my friend. We need a miracle. I pray that Viruk has reached Ammon. That would be a start."

Chapter Twenty-two

Though Virkokka was deadly, and loved by none, yet did he keep the world alive. His greatest enemies were the Frost Giants. Every year they would attack the fertile lands, covering them with ice and snow. Mortals would shiver, and crops would die. Then they would beg Virkokka to save them. And every year he came, as still he comes, with sword of fire, and lance of sun flame, to drive the Frost Giants from the land. And from his hands would spill fresh seeds from every tree and flower. Maize would spring up where he walked, and grass grow where he rested his head. And though no mortal ever loved him, the trees would whisper his name, the grass sigh with it, and the flowers make their scent for him alone.

From the *Evening Song of the Anajo*

Viruk was not in the best of spirits as he led his ten Avatars towards the last ridge before the lands of the Erek-jhip-zhonad. He still believed Rael was wrong to send him away from the front line and he had no wish to spend any time at all with foreign sub-humans. It was bad enough being surrounded by Vagars back home.

Rael had told him to choose ten of the best soldiers. Viruk had commandeered the first ten men he had come across at the barracks. He knew them all by name, though none were close to him. Few people were, and he had no friends.

He rode now, slightly ahead of the group, lost in thought, his zhi-bow resting on his saddle. His horse suddenly stumbled. Viruk almost fell across its neck. The zhi-bow tumbled to the ground. Annoyed, Viruk hauled on the reins and dismounted.

At that moment thunder broke all around the riders, a ferocious wall of sound that stunned Viruk. Five riders were smashed from their saddles, four horses went down screaming in agony. Viruk swept up his zhi-bow. The strings danced into light. On the ridge above them he saw a score of copper-skinned warriors carrying ornate black clubs. One of them pointed a club at Viruk. Smoke and flame belched from the weapon. Viruk felt a whoosh of air pass his face. His zhi-bow came up. The warrior's chest exploded and he was hurled back into his comrades.

Three of the Avatars began to loose bolts into the enemy, who dropped their fire-clubs, drew serrated swords and charged down the slope. Viruk killed five of them before they had covered half of the distance. The charge faltered. On the slope above more Almec soldiers appeared. The fire-clubs boomed again. Two of the remaining Avatars fell. Viruk transferred his aim to this new force, killing three before they dropped from sight. The first attacking group of Almecs had almost reached the last surviving Avatars.

Viruk shot two as they closed upon him, and then a third as the man screamed a war cry and raced towards him, sword raised. Viruk's bolt took him full in the face. His head disappeared. The last Avatar soldier killed two more, but a third stabbed him in the belly, and a fourth thrust his sword through the Avatar's throat. Dropping his zhi-bow Viruk drew sword and dagger and leapt at the three Almecs. The first died, his throat ripped open, the second staggered back and fell with Viruk's dagger in his heart. The last man turned and sprinted for the slope. Sheathing his sword Viruk knelt by the dead Avatar, lifting his zhi-bow. It took several seconds to attune his mind to the warrior's weapon, then he sent a bolt into the fleeing man's back. There was a burst of flame from the Almec's dark armor and he pitched forward and lay still.

From the slope the fire-clubs blasted once more. Two of the surviving horses were punched from their feet. Viruk ran back to where his own zhi-bow lay, swept it up and grabbed the reins of his horse. The animal was bleeding from a hole in its flank. Vaulting into the saddle Viruk kicked the beast into a run.

Shots came from behind him, but nothing struck. The horse galloped on for almost half a mile then collapsed. Viruk leapt clear. Ahead was a grove of trees. Carrying the two zhi-bows he ran for them. Glancing back he saw more than thirty Almec soldiers moving into the open. They had spread out in a fighting line and were advancing warily.

Viruk ran on. The area was not thickly wooded and he could see no natural defensive point. He tried to picture exactly where he was in terms of the Luan and the many settlements along the border. He decided he was at least 10 miles from the nearest Vagar village and almost double that to Ammon's capital. The ground was rising and Viruk pushed on. He could just see the soldiers entering the trees some 400 yards back. Reaching the top of the rise he came to a sudden stop. The ground dropped away sharply and he found himself standing on the brink of a cliff overlooking the Luan River 200 feet below. "Oh this is pleasant," he said, sourly. A series of shots sounded from behind him. Instinctively he ducked down, listening again for the whooshing of wind close to him. There was nothing, save that dirt spurted up from the ground some 20 feet behind him. Viruk grinned. Hefting the soldier's zhi-bow he sent three bolts flashing through the trees. The first struck a branch, which exploded in a shower of sparks. The second took a man in the shoulder, ripping his arm from his body and puncturing his lung. The third thundered against a tree trunk. Fire spurted from the bark and black smoke began to billow from the hole.

The Almecs took cover behind the trees, occasionally darting forward to another hiding place closer to the fleeing man.

Viruk was not a man given to great angers, but he felt an exception was called for here. Ten Avatars were dead, he had no horse, and he was facing almost thirty warriors. Behind him was a murderous drop to a stony riverbed. Two shots whizzed by him. With a soft curse he rose and began to run along the cliff edge, looking for a way to climb down. A wicked blow took him high in the shoulder, ripping the skin. Dropping the soldier's bow Viruk stumbled a few feet farther. The Almecs ran from their hiding places, fire-clubs raised.

Viruk jumped from the cliff edge.

The Almecs swept forward, running to the edge and looking down. There was no sign of the man they were pursuing. They milled at the lip for some moments then, gathering up the zhi-bow, walked back into the woods.

Ten feet down, his body hugging the cliff wall beneath a narrow overhang, Viruk heard them move away.

"This has not been a good day," he said. "Not good at all." His arm was aching abominably. Swinging his legs he sat upon the ledge, removed his green crystal from his pouch and held it to the wound. The flesh began to knit almost immediately, but the bone beneath was badly bruised. The collar of his black leather jerkin was ripped. Viruk lifted his hand to it—and felt something small and round lodged there. Pulling it clear he saw it was a blood-smeared ball of lead.

"Foul weapons," he said. "No beauty in them at all." Viruk sat for some time, his long legs dangling over the ledge. From here he could see the red and gold cliffs opposite, rearing up against a blue sky. He scanned the landscape. It was rugged and deeply beautiful. Few flowers grew, but the pale green of the trees by the river's edge and the different shades of gold in the cliffs was greatly pleasing to the eye.

Rolling to his knees he edged along the cliff, seeking hand and footholds to climb back to the top. It would not be possible to make the climb carrying his zhi-bow, but he was loath to leave it behind. From where he stood it was around 12 feet to the lip. Leaning out from the ledge he threw the zhi-bow high into the air. It sailed up and over the clifftop. Slowly and carefully he climbed the face. His shoulder throbbed with pain, but there was no lack of strength to trouble him. Heaving himself over the top he picked up his bow and walked back into the trees.

He knew the mission was over and that it would be foolish to go on. Ammon was either dead or in hiding. Either way there was little likelihood of finding him.

And yet his orders were clear. Find Ammon and protect him.

Ten Avatars were dead and Viruk was wounded. The enemy had already landed and their troops were patrolling the riverbanks. What chance for a single Bluehair to avoid them and find a man he had never seen? Viruk thought about it. The odds appealed to him.

Added to which there was the certainty that he would kill more enemy soldiers.

With that thought in mind he set off with a light heart.

Sofarita, Questor Ro and Touchstone were sitting cross-legged on a rug in one of the garden archways. Their eyes were closed. Questor Ro's oldest servant Sempes entered the room and stared at the trio. Their faces were calm and relaxed. Confused, the old man cleared away the used goblets and plates and quietly left them.

Ro was in a kind of heaven. Golden light shone around him and he could both hear and *feel* a surging music circling him. It was curiously discordant and yet enchanting. And it did not intrude on his communication with Sofarita and Touchstone. In fact it was almost the reverse, as if the music was the channel through which they spoke. In moments, or so it seemed, he had learned the language of the Anajo from Touchstone, their minds joined together by the power of Sofarita. Language skills had always come easily to Ro, but this method of learning was wondrous beyond description. Images and words formed in his mind, rolling together with utter clarity. It was a vivid language, full of direct imagery. In an instant he absorbed all the myths of the Anajo, tribal histories and heroes and, more importantly, their enormous love of the land.

Sofarita brought them back, and as Ro opened his eyes he felt a powerful sense of loss.

"Welcome to my home," he said, in perfect Anajo, as Touchstone woke. The tribesman grinned.

"Your pronunciation is perfect," he replied. "It is good to hear the language of my people spoken again."

Ro stretched and rose. Sofarita remained for a mo-

ment with her eyes closed. Then she sighed and smiled
at the two men.

Old Sempes entered the room. He bowed to Ro. "E
caida manake, Pasar?" he said. The words meant nothing to Ro. He wondered for a moment if the old man
was making fun of him. Then he realized with a shock
that his mind was locked into the language structure of
the Anajo. Sempes was speaking the common tongue.
And Ro had forgotten it!

"What is he saying?" Ro asked Touchstone. The
tribesman looked surprised.

"He wants to know if we are hungry."

Sofarita reached out and laid her slender hand on
Ro's arm. He felt heat flow through him, and his mind
relaxed. "Are you ill, lord?" he heard Sempes ask.

"No I am fine. You have worked hard today, Sempes.
Enjoy the rest of the day. Go for a walk. Whatever you
wish. I will attend to the needs of my guests."

"Yes, lord. Thank you, lord."

As the old man departed Sofarita spoke. "How interesting," she said. "Somehow the speed of learning
Anajo affected your ability to return to your own
tongue. It was as if the new language replaced the old
completely." Ro nodded. He was already finding his understanding of Anajo becoming more hazy.

"Some skills need time to acquire—even with the aid
of magic," he said. "Somehow that is comforting.
When do you meet with Rael and Mejana?"

"Soon," said Sofarita. "I said I would go to the
Council Chamber."

"I shall harness the horses," said Ro. He paused.
"Actually I don't know how to harness horses. Still, it
cannot be too difficult—not for a man who can learn a
foreign language in a few heartbeats. Will you give me a
hand, Touchstone?"

Together they left the room. Sofarita moved to a couch and lay down. Rael would need information on the Almecs. She closed her eyes once more—and rose through the building to float above the roof.

First she flew south over the three cities of Boria, Pejkan and Caval. The last was a smouldering ruin. Sofarita could hardly believe what she was seeing. The houses had been systematically destroyed and there were bodies everywhere. She moved closer. The dead numbered in their thousands. Down by the harbor two golden ships were being loaded with scores of chests. On the open decks more were being stacked and tied. Sofarita pushed her face against the dark wood, passing through it. Within the chests were blood-smeared crystals, thousands of them. She recoiled from them and flew high above the harbor.

The people of Caval had been slaughtered for the Crystal Queen. The chests would be carried back over the ocean, the crystals poured into one of the many openings in the golden pyramid. Then Almeia would feed.

Swiftly she flew on to Pejkan. Here there was less destruction, but outside the city several hundred people had been herded into a meadow, where they were being guarded by the giant krals. The Vagars sat huddled together, silent and fearful.

On she travelled to Boria. Fifteen golden ships were docked there and two more were sailing in. The streets were largely deserted, but she saw Almec soldiers marching down the wide avenue, heading for a camp they had set up in the Great Park. The camp was neat and well-ordered, huge tents set in tight lines. She estimated the numbers of men there at more than 3,000.

Then she sped east, to Ammon's capital. Hundreds of bodies littered the streets here, and she saw soldiers marching through the poorer quarter, rounding up people and herding them towards a makeshift encampment by a narrow stream. Along the banks of the stream were fifty open chests, filled with glittering crystals.

Standing in front of the chests was the tall officer she had first seen, his face shining like glass. He was wearing a breastplate of gold and a tall golden helm with three feathers set into the visor. Beside him stood a hunchback dressed in a green tunic. The latter was holding a rod with a golden circle at the tip.

The Mud People were forced to move out onto open ground and stand in a ragged line. A column of Almec soldiers moved into sight, filing out to stand before the prisoners. The officer gave a command. The black fire-clubs came up—and thundered! The prisoners were hurled backwards. Some still lived, and struggled to rise. Soldiers ran forward, stabbing them. When all were dead the soldiers slit open their chests, tore out their hearts, then filled the open cavities with crystals.

Sofarita had seen enough. Rising high she flew over the city, making a count of the enemy soldiers. At least another 3,000 were here, and more than a hundred krals.

Rael had told her that Viruk was somewhere close by, seeking the king. She concentrated on him, picturing his cruel handsome face. Then she relaxed and flew with her spirit eyes closed, holding his image in her mind.

At last she slowed and opened her eyes. Some ten miles from the city a man was sitting by the riverbed, rubbing red clay into his hair. He was whistling a tune as he did so. Some distance away she saw movement in the trees. Two huge beasts, covered in white fur and wearing black cross belts, were moving toward the man. He had not seen them.

"Viruk!" she called. He did not hear her.

There had to be some way to communicate with him. But she did not know how. Floating closer she pushed her spirit hand against him. He did not flinch and she felt no contact. The krals were close now. She could see the blood lust in their strange round eyes. Saliva was dripping over their fangs.

Suddenly they charged.

Viruk swept up his zhi-bow and spun. A bolt of light tore into the chest of the first beast, exploding with a brilliant flash. Blood and shards of bone sprayed into the air. The second beast was almost upon the man. Viruk stood there calmly. As the kral lunged he ducked suddenly and threw himself to the right, rolling to his feet as he landed. The kral blundered on for several paces and swung again. Viruk laughed and sent a zhi-bolt into his face. The head disappeared. "Clumsy, clumsy," said Viruk. He scanned the tree line for more enemies. Satisfied he was alone he returned to the riverbed and continued to rub red clay into his hair. Then he dragged the sorry mess back and tied it in a ponytail. Leaning over the water he glanced down.

"Do you look the part, my dear?" he asked himself. "I am afraid the answer has to be no. One cannot make silk look like sackcloth. But it will have to do."

There had to be a way to communicate with him, thought Sofarita.

She was crystal-joined and powerful. It was inconceivable that she could not touch this man. Joined to crystal! That could be it, she thought. He was wearing a belt pouch. Sofarita reached inside it. There were two crystals there. She concentrated on them. They began to vibrate. Viruk felt the movement and, puzzled, drew them out. Sofarita's spirit hand rested on the first of the green crystals.

"Can you hear me, Viruk?" she said. He swung round. "Speak to me," she urged him.

"I can't see you. Are you a voice of the Source?"

"Yes," she said, thinking that he would react better to that thought than if she announced herself as the village girl he had bedded.

"I usually hear a man's voice," he said. "Still, who do you want me to kill?"

"You must find Ammon. Rael needs him."

"I already know that," he said. "I am heading for the city now. Of course the task is a little difficult since I don't know what he looks like and if he escaped he's probably in disguise. Are you an angel of death?"

"No, I have been assigned to protect you," she said.

"Oh, that's nice. Protect me from what, exactly? I didn't notice you warn me when the krals were close by."

"You needed no help there. Wait here. I shall return soon."

Detaching herself from him she sped back to Egaru. Ro and Touchstone were waiting quietly in the garden room. She opened her eyes. "Have you ever seen Ammon?" she asked Ro.

"Yes. Tall man, womanly. Beautiful face." Rising from the couch Sofarita crossed the room and took his hand.

"Show me! Think of him!"

Ro did so. Without another word she returned to the couch and freed her spirit. Using the same technique as she had in finding Viruk she flew east, coming at last to a series of cliffs. In a cave on the eastern slope she found three men: one old, one frightened, and one standing guard in the cave mouth. He was tall and, as Ro had described, had a face of exquisite beauty, with deep violet eyes. Rising into the air she returned to where Viruk sat by the river's edge. He was hurling flat pebbles out over the water, watching them skim.

"Ammon is some twelve miles southeast of here. He

is travelling with a bearded old man and one other. Close your eyes." Viruk did so. Sofarita filled his mind with a picture of the three. He cried out and clapped his hands.

"The little potter," he said. "Well, well! I almost killed him, you know. Of course you know. You were there. Are you sure there's nobody you want killed?"

"No one," she said.

"How strange. Usually when the Source speaks to me he asks for deaths."

"Not this time. Go and find Ammon."

"Can you take human form?"

"No," she said.

"That's a shame. I could really use a woman. I get very edgy after a battle. Do I have time to find one?"

"No! Now go and do your duty."

She pulled back from him and returned to Egaru.

She opened her eyes and breathed out a long sigh. "Viruk is completely insane," she said.

"Yes," agreed Ro. "All Avatars know that."

"How has he survived so long?"

"He's rather good at what he does," said Ro.

Ammon stood in the mouth of the cave, staring out over the golden cliffs and the distant, shimmering Luan. That morning the three of them had crept along a dry watercourse to the southern wall. They were moving slowly and with great care when they heard the sound of marching feet. Crouching down against the crumbling dirt they had listened as prisoners were brought out onto the flat ground above them. Sadau's bladder had released and the little man pushed his face into the dirt in embarrassment. Shots rang out. People screamed in agony. For an hour or more the killing continued. Ammon could not see the horror but the sound would haunt him for the rest of his life. He heard children wailing and begging, women pleading for the lives of their young. None were spared. Eventually the soldiers marched away. Ammon pushed himself to his feet and peered over the lip of the watercourse. Bodies lay everywhere, dead eyes staring up at the sun. His gaze flickered over them. And stopped. Some 20 feet away was the woman who had come to Sadau's home the night before. Her children lay close by, as did the toddler Ammon had rescued. All the victims had their chests ripped open.

Ammon forced himself to look at all the faces, determined that he would never forget any part of this dreadful slaughter.

Then he dropped down to where the others waited. "I should have stayed at home," whimpered Sadau.

"I do not think so," said Ammon. "Come, let us move on."

The watercourse had once flowed under the southern wall, joining a tributary to the Luan. The three men moved out into the shadow of the outer wall. The land here was open, with little cover. If there were sentries upon the parapets the fleeing men would be seen as soon as they moved out. Remaining where they were throughout the day they crept away under cover of darkness.

Now, as he stood in the cave mouth, Ammon was still fighting for calm. His immediate desire was to find his army and march back to the city, bringing bloody retribution to the killers. But he knew that his men, though well trained, could not stand against the fireclubs of the enemy. The need for revenge was immense and he struggled with it. Now was a time for cool thinking, he knew.

Anwar approached him. "You are very quiet, my king."

"I was thinking. They killed my people like cattle. I must find a way to make them pay."

The old man looked close to exhaustion. His face was grey with fatigue. "Marshal your thoughts, sire, and remember my teachings. What is the first rule?"

"Establish priorities," answered Ammon, with a smile.

"Good. What is the first priority?"

"Escape."

"And the next."

"Become strong. Find the army. Then establish a new chain of command. Summon the tribal chieftains, and create a force to win back my kingdom."

"Each in its turn, my lord. Concentrate on one problem at a time. Give it your full attention. There is a time for emotion, a time for action. But always there must be *thought*. What have we learned about the enemy?"

"They are deadly, and they are evil," said Ammon, instantly.

"More than that."

Ammon considered the question, but could find no answer. "You must tell me, councillor."

"They have not come for conquest, lord, but for slaughter. Had they wished to subdue the city they would have established curfews, brought in city leaders and put in place new laws. Instead they are simply murdering the inhabitants. For what reason I do not know. But death is their prime consideration. The question is, have they only attacked us? Or have other peoples suffered? Have they, for example, attacked the Avatars? Are their cities conquered? Before we can make any plan of action we need to know the scale of the invasion."

Ammon nodded. "You are right, but these are questions for another day. You talk of establishing priorities,

Anwar. The first priority for you is rest. Eat some of that bread, then sleep."

"We must get farther away, lord," objected the old man.

"And we will. But only after you have slept."

Anwar sighed, then smiled. "I must confess that I am weary," he said. He shuffled to the back of the cave and lay down.

Ammon glanced up at the sky. "I have never been entirely convinced of the existence of a supreme being," he whispered. "But now would be a good time to convince me."

"Would you like some bread, lord?" asked the little potter, moving alongside the king.

Ammon tore off a chunk and sat down, indicating that Sadau should sit beside him. The potter did so. "The woman you brought to your home, what was her name?"

"Rula, lord."

"Do you believe in the Great God?"

"Of course."

"Then say a prayer for her. She and her children were among those murdered as we hid."

Sadau's face crumpled, and tears fell from his eyes. "I am sorry, little man," said Ammon. "But it does seem I have saved your life again. Had you remained in your home you would have died with them."

"Why would anyone want to kill children?" asked Sadau. "What did they gain from such a . . . such a crime?"

"I cannot answer that. But I will do all that I can to avenge them."

"It won't bring them back, will it?" said Sadau, moving away to the rear of the cave.

"No, it won't," said Ammon, softly.

• • •

Ammon was asleep, his dreams dark and bitter. He awoke with a start and sat up. The cave was dark now, but some noise had stirred him. Anwar was still sleeping, as was the potter. The king turned toward the cave mouth—and froze. Silhouetted in the entrance stood a monstrous shape. Almost eight feet tall and covered with pale grey fur, which shone like silver in the moonlight, was one of the beasts he had seen back in the city. Ammon slowly pushed himself to his feet. The creature's face was hairless and pink, its eyes round and vaguely human. The mouth was open, showing huge fangs. It made no move to approach. It was wearing cross belts of black leather, from which hung two clubs of pitted iron. Ammon did not move. On the beast's shoulder, tucked under the cross belt, was a golden scarf. Ammon recognized it. It was one he himself had worn only two days before.

The king had heard of dogs belonging to men in the northern tribes who could track down fugitives by scenting a cloth worn by them. But this was no dog.

The creature stood still, its round eyes glittering. But it made no hostile move. Ammon nudged the sleeping Anwar with the toe of his boot. The old man grunted and woke. He saw the beast and lay very still. Soldiers would be following the creature, Ammon knew, and the knowledge filled him with a sick sense of despair. Anwar had been right. They should have pushed on. Now, perhaps, there would be no opportunity for revenge against these wanton killers. The potter awoke—and screamed. The sound was shrill within the cave and Ammon jumped. The beast still did not move.

"It is well trained, at least," said the king, fighting to keep his voice calm. Sadau threw himself on his face, covering his head with his arms. Anwar sighed and climbed to his feet.

"This does not bode well, sire," he said, unsuccessfully trying to sound as calm as the king.

From beyond the kral came the sound of men climbing the rock path. The beast faded back into the night and four men entered the cave. The first was dressed in a gold breastplate, a feather-decorated helm upon his head. The others were merely common soldiers carrying fire-clubs.

"You would be Ammon," said the officer, approaching the king.

"Indeed so."

"They said you looked like a woman. They were right."

The officer lifted a small sack from his shoulder and laid it on the cave floor. As he did so the drawstrings came partly undone and half a dozen green crystals tumbled to the ground. Turning to the soldiers, the officer said, "Well, what are you waiting for? Kill them!"

"A moment of your time," said Ammon conversationally.

The man glanced at him, surprised by the apparent lack of concern in the victim.

"Make it quick," he said. "I am cold and looking forward to a hot meal."

"Before I die I would be interested to know your purpose in my lands. As I escaped the city this morning I could not help but observe the mass executions taking place. Is it merely that you love slaughter, or is there a reason for your actions?"

"The finest reason in the world," said the officer. "We feed the goddess. When you are dead I will open your chest and pour in these crystals. They will absorb what remains of your life force. The goddess will draw it into herself—and you with it. Then you will know glory and everlasting life. You will become a part of the greatness of the Almec people."

"I see," said the king. "So it is your intention then to kill everyone in my lands?"

"The goddess is very hungry," said the officer. "In saving our race she exhausted herself. Now do you have other questions, or may we proceed?"

"I have one," said Ammon. "Do you have other armies here?"

"Many armies," said the officer.

"Have you attacked the Avatars?"

"The Blue-haired ones? Yes. Their cities will fall, as did yours. No one can withstand the armies of the goddess."

"Well," said Ammon, with a smile, "they are the only questions I have. So, let us get on with it." While speaking he moved in closer to the officer. Before the man realized he was in danger Ammon sprang forward, wrenched the officer's golden dagger from his belt, curled an arm around the man's neck and pressed the point of the blade under his chin. "Now," said the king, "I think we should renegotiate our position."

"You don't understand," said the officer, as if speaking to a child. "This will avail you nothing. My men will simply shoot me, and take my life force for the queen. Then my life eternal will begin earlier than I had thought."

Ignoring him, but keeping the knife in place, Ammon looked at the soldiers. The three men had aimed their fire-clubs at the officer. "Put down the weapons, or he dies," Ammon told them. Before they could answer, the officer thrust his neck down onto the dagger. The blade pierced his jugular. Bright blood spouted over Ammon's hand. The officer spasmed. Ammon pulled the dagger clear and held the man's body as a shield.

At that moment there was a great roar from outside the cave—then a blinding burst of light. Blood, fur and bone sprayed across the entrance. Startled, the soldiers swung away. A dark-clad figure leapt into view and dived into the cave. The fire-clubs exploded. The dark figure lifted a zhi-bow. Two bolts flew from it. Two soldiers died horribly. The third threw down his fire-club, drew a sword and ran at the archer. Dropping his bow the warrior leapt to meet him, drawing a thin-bladed dagger from its sheath. The sword slashed down. The warrior swayed aside and rammed his dagger into the Almec's right eye. As the body fell the warrior dragged his knife clear and wiped the blade on the Almec's tunic. "I am Viruk," he said with a wide smile.

"What in Heaven's name have you done to your hair?" asked the king, staring at the red mud which caked Viruk's head.

"It's a disguise," said Viruk. "I was trying to look like one of your people. It didn't work too well, did it?"

"We don't actually use river mud, Viruk. The clay is mixed with various colors, perfumed, and then applied by a skilled barber." He stepped in close and peered at the matted mess. "And we usually remove the ants . . . and the cattle droppings."

"Perhaps I'll start a new fashion," said Viruk cheerfully. "Who is this?" he asked, nodding towards Anwar.

"My First Councillor, Anwar. The other man is—"

"I know who he is," said Viruk with a chuckle. "How are you, potter? How come you're still alive?"

"I don't know, lord," wailed Sadau. "It is a mystery to me."

"Probably born under a lucky star like me. Well, come on, man, get on your feet. We've a long way to go."

"And where, pray, do you think we are going?" asked Ammon.

"Back to Egaru. The Questor General ordered me to

bring you there safely. He also told me that the Avatars are to offer you every assistance against the newcomers."

"I will march with my own army," said Ammon.

"Wait, sire," said Anwar. "It might be best to change our plans. I can go to the army, and bring them to Egaru. It would be a great weight taken from me if I knew you were already safe there."

"Safe with the Avatars? Now there is a novel thought."

"You know the old saying, sire? The enemy of my enemy must therefore be my friend? It could not be more true. The Avatar have many weapons and their cities are strong. Once your people know that you still live they will flock to your battle standard—wherever it is raised."

"Very well," said Ammon. "I accept your offer, Viruk. I take it you have horses close by?"

"No."

"It will be a long walk."

"Ah, but it will be made in the very best of company," said Viruk, hauling the little potter upright and clapping him on the shoulder. "Isn't that right, Sadau?"

"Anything you say, lord."

Viruk moved to the dead Almecs and hefted one of the fire-clubs. He spent several minutes trying to understand its mechanisms, then hurled it to one side. "Ugly weapons," he said. "Noisy—and the smoke smells worse than a pig fart."

"We obviously move in different circles," said Ammon. "I cannot say I have ever seen a pig's backside. However, I will take your word for it."

Viruk laughed aloud, with genuine good humor. "Can it be," he asked, "that you dislike me? Surely not."

"You are no more than an assassin, Viruk. A man in love with death, I think."

"Your point being?"

"Putting it simply? I despise you and all you fail to stand for. Is that clear enough?"

"You'll change your mind when you get to know me better. Now let us be moving. My zhi-bow has no more bolts. I do not relish the thought of tackling a kral with only a dagger."

Chapter Twenty-three

As they reached the mist barrier Talaban bade farewell to Caprishan and the supply column and led his fifty riders farther northeast. He glanced at the young man riding alongside him. The rider was clad in expensive riding clothes, his tan jerkin crafted from the finest of skins and decorated along the shoulder seams with black pearls. His knee-length riding boots were also of fine leather, each adorned with a silver band at the ankle. He had spoken little since they had left Egaru and then only to answer direct questions.

Up ahead Touchstone was riding scout, and the column moved slowly, seeking to raise as little dust as possible.

The Questor General's orders had been specific. "Harass the enemy. It is time they learned the cost of invasion. Hit them hard, then move. Do not engage in any pitched battles. Strike like the hawk, then ride." Talaban had passed the captaincy of the *Serpent* to Methras, the exchange of power witnessed by Mejana and Rael. The young sergeant had accepted his new role with quiet dignity and Talaban had felt a surge of pride.

He was not as happy with his own appointment. He would have preferred to have chosen his own men, but with power being shared now he had also been forced to accept a compromise. Twenty Avatar archers and thirty Vagar warriors, led by the inexperienced young man who rode now beside him.

Talaban knew little about him—save that he was a merchant, the grandson of Mejana, and he was said to know well the lands into which they rode.

"How far is the first settlement?" asked Talaban.

"Around four miles," the young man answered. He seemed nervous and on edge.

"Touchstone is a fine scout. There will be no ambush, Pendar."

"I am not afraid," said Pendar, his tone defensive. That the Vagar disliked him was obvious, and, Talaban realized, wholly natural. But the Avatar hoped that when they came into contact with the enemy Pendar would have the intelligence to put his hatred aside. Until then there was little point in trying to make a friend of the man.

Urging his horse into a run Talaban moved ahead of the column. The land was becoming more ridged. Towering cliffs of red stone reared to their left and they were approaching the wide Gen-el Pass. Touchstone had reined in his pony and was staring ahead. He glanced back as Talaban rode alongside.

"What have you seen?" asked the Avatar.

"Nothing. But enemy there."

"How can you be sure?"

"Someone watches. I know this. I feel his eyes."

Talaban scanned the pass. The sun was high and there was no movement to be seen. Not a bird flew, and even the breeze had dropped.

Talaban swung his mount and rode back to his Avatars, calling the sergeant aside. Goray was a large man, his short-cropped hair dark, his trimmed trident beard dyed blue. He was a veteran of many tribal wars and was one of the older Avatars, well over three hundred. For sixty years he had been an officer of high rank, but had retired from the army twelve years before to spend more time studying the stars. He had not been best pleased when the Questor General summoned him and other retired Avatars to return to the army. "The enemy is in the pass," Talaban told him.

"I would expect so, captain. What is your plan?"

"Have you ridden this pass?"

"Not in seventy years."

"What do you make of the Vagar?"

"He is untried and his men are wary of him. There is too much of the woman showing in him."

"His sexuality is immaterial to me."

"And to me," said Goray equably. "But that is not what I meant. I am talking about perceptions. Not what it is—but what *shows*. His men are afraid. In war soldiers look to their leaders as wells of courage or inspiration. They drink from those wells. I fear that, for many of his soldiers, he is a figure of fun, someone to mock. This worries me."

"I accept that," said Talaban. "But I asked what *you* made of him."

"He needs a victory, something to give him confidence in himself—and to inspire his men."

Talaban rode back to the column where he called Pendar aside. "Touchstone believes there is a force waiting for us in the pass. Is there another way forward?"

Pendar was silent for a moment. "We could swing north, but that would bring us in close to Morak, Ammon's capital. It would also add three days to our journey both ways. And, since we are carrying supplies for only ten days, it would limit our opportunities to harass the Almecs. Can we not fight them here?"

Talaban ignored the question and stepped down from the saddle, gesturing Pendar to follow him. Moving to an area of bare, dry earth he knelt down. "Sketch me the pass," he said. He watched as Pendar drew his dagger and began to cut a series of lines.

"Once into the mouth of the pass it bends to the right and then undulates. The walls are sheer for the first four hundred yards. After that the pass narrows for a way—perhaps another five hundred yards. There have been many rock falls, and there are hundreds of hiding places among the boulders. After that it becomes sheer again."

"So the main site for an ambush would be around a quarter of a mile into the pass?"

"I would say so, but I am no soldier."

"You are now. Get used to it." Pendar reddened, but before he could answer Talaban spoke again. "Touchstone believes we are being observed. At what point does the pass bend to the right?"

Pendar pressed his dagger into the earth. "Here. Is it significant?"

"If we are being watched it is from high on the cliff. Have you ever been up there?"

"On the left side only. You can walk to the top. There is a narrow series of paths and ledges. The right is sheer."

"Then the watcher is on the left. He will lose sight of us as we enter the pass." Talaban took a deep breath. "Let's move!"

Stepping into the saddle he raised his arm and the column moved forward, across the open empty land. Touchstone rode back. "I see him. He crouches behind big stone. High on left."

"How high?"

"Three hundred feet."

The walls of the pass reared up before them, pale red sandstone sculpted by thousands of years of wind and rain and running water. Deep vertical lines were scored into the towering walls as if chiselled there by a master hand. Talaban halted the column. Dismounting he gazed at the rock wall to his left. It was sheer, but there were no overhangs and he could see a shelf of rock some 60 feet above him. Calling his Avatars to him he outlined a plan and asked for ten volunteers. Every man raised his hand. Talaban chose the slimmest and smallest of the men, then summoned Pendar.

"We are going to climb the cliffs and move out above and behind the enemy. If there are a hundred or less we will shoot down into them. Once we begin shooting it is vital you lead a charge into the pass immediately. For there will be no cover for us, and their fire-clubs will cut us to pieces. You understand?"

Pendar nodded. "But surely any one of the Almecs could look up and see you?"

"Touchstone will ride out and appear to be scouting the pass. Their eyes will be upon him."

"They could just kill him."

"Pendar, they are seeking to ambush our whole force, not one scout. However, you might be right. But then that is soldiering. Nothing is without risk."

Talaban moved to the rock face. Loosening his belt he strapped his zhi-bow to his back then began to climb. Hand and footholds were numerous, but the rock was dry and apt to crumble. Testing each hold carefully he inched his way up the face. At 45 feet the handholds disappeared. To his right a narrow vertical crack in the rock snaked up towards the shelf above it. The crack was no more than two inches deep. Talaban edged his way to it, then thrust his right hand up and inside it. There were tiny holds here, but the crack was not deep enough for him to be able to insert the toe of his boot for a foothold. He glanced up. The crack opened wider some eight feet above him. He could hear the men climbing below him. Looking down he saw that the first soldier had almost reached him.

"Steady yourself," he told the man. "I need your

shoulder." The soldier grinned. Moving up close to Talaban he settled himself against the face.

"Ready, sir."

Wedging his hand into the crack Talaban hauled himself high then, placing his foot on the soldier's shoulder, he levered himself up to where the crack was wider. Using another wedge hold he climbed on, pushing his foot into the crack, and up over the lip of the shelf.

Below him the other ten soldiers were following his lead but this left them one man short, for there was no one to help the last climber. Talaban signalled him to return to the ground, then led his nine men carefully along the shelf.

Seated on his pony Touchstone waited for Talaban's signal. When it came the tribesman swung the reins and walked his mount out into the pass.

It was eerily quiet here and Touchstone could feel sweat trickling down his spine. The ambushers should not react to seeing the scout. They would be anxious to kill as many of the invading force as possible. But there might just be one nervous Almec. Touchstone rode on. Ahead and to the left he saw the signs of many rock falls. A shadow moved behind a boulder, but Touchstone did not react. He looked both left and right as if scanning the pass. He allowed himself one glance up and to his left and saw Talaban and his nine soldiers moving warily along a narrow ledge.

Touchstone drew rein, lifted his water canteen from the pommel of his saddle and took a sip. It was hot here in the pass, the air heavy. Another movement caught his eye, the merest flicker of shadow behind a huge boulder. They are not so skilled, he thought. And they are too anxious for the kill. Swinging his pony he rode slowly back towards the mouth of the pass.

"What did you see?" asked Pendar. The man was sweating profusely, and fear shone in his eyes.

"Hundred I reckon," said Touchstone.

"Then we will fight them?" The thought obviously dismayed the young man.

"You ride hard when battle starts," Touchstone warned him. "Talaban in open. No cover. Get ready. Killing time soon."

Pendar drew his sword. His hand was trembling. Ignoring him, Touchstone cast his eyes over the waiting Vagar warriors. They too were on edge. He grinned at them and lifted his axe from his belt. They did not respond. Fighting men, he knew, took their inspiration from their leader. This Pendar was untried. He was frightened and that fear was contagious.

Touchstone moved his pony alongside Pendar's mount.

And the wait began.

Sweat dripped into Talaban's eyes as he inched his way along the narrow ledge. From here he could see the hidden warriors below. All but the two officers were dressed identically, sleeveless black shirts and dark leggings, no adornments on their arms, no bangles or bracelets of copper or gold. Nothing to glint or shine. Each man wore a small pack strapped to his upper back. The officers also eschewed colorful garb. Their breastplates were of blackened metal, as were their round helms. Talaban estimated that around 130 men were crouched behind boulders, their fire-clubs held ready. They were still and poised, which spoke of good discipline, and Talaban did not believe they would break and run at the first attack. His mouth was dry as he considered his plan. It was fraught with danger. Not one of the Almecs had yet looked up. But they would when the battle started. Exposed as they were here the Avatars would certainly take losses. Indeed, thought Talaban, it was not beyond the bounds of possibility that all of them could be killed in the first volley. He glanced back at his men. The same thought had occurred to them.

The ledge was less than two feet wide—just enough to allow the Avatars to crouch down, creating smaller targets. Talaban signalled them to spread out. They did so, and unstrapped their zhi-bows. "Make your shots fast," he told them. "And let us pray the Vagar comes to our aid with all speed." So saying he raised his bow, honed his mind to the weapon, and aimed at the back of a kneeling warrior.

Ten zhi-bolts flashed down, then another ten. Below—for a moment only—all was pandemonium. The dead did not have time to scream. Their bodies lay, tunics ablaze, black smoke rising from the terrible wounds in their backs. An Almec officer shouted a command and discipline was instantly restored. Fire-clubs were raised and a volley of shots rang out. Lead shot smashed into the rock face. A stone splinter raked Talaban's cheek and he felt blood trickle from the wound. He remained where he was, coolly sending bolt after bolt into the startled Almecs. The man beside him was slammed back into the rock. Then he pitched forward, and fell soundlessly, his body striking the ground head first.

Talaban killed one Almec officer and two other men. Then he heard the sound of galloping hooves. He did not risk a glance but continued to shoot. Another Avatar fell from the ledge, then a third. Below his position Talaban saw Touchstone gallop his pony into the fray. The tribesman threw himself from his mount, the blade of his hand-axe slamming into the head of the last Almec officer. The trilling war cry of the Anajo echoed in the pass.

The Almecs began to fall back, moving from boulder to boulder, seeking cover. No one was now firing at the men on the ledge. Yet there was still no panic among the fleeing men and they retreated at first in good order. The ten mounted Avatars galloped their horses down the pass, shooting from the saddle. The Vagars had dismounted and were fighting hand to hand with a group of Almecs who had taken up a defensive position directly below Talaban and his men. The fighting was fierce. Talaban saw the young Pendar defending himself against an Almec swordsman. The Vagar was ludicrously lacking in skill, his flailing blade causing little concern to his attacker. All that was keeping Pendar alive was the fact that he was backing away furiously.

The Almec suddenly charged forward. Pendar tripped and fell back. The Almec loomed above him. Talaban's zhi-bolt took him in the side of the neck. The head was torn clear and the body fell across Pendar, blood bubbling from the severed jugular. The Vagar dropped his sword and scrambled back.

The surviving Almecs had retreated deeper into the pass, but they were being harried by the Avatars. Down below, the fighting had ended. Talaban rose to his feet. Only five of his men remained alive on the ledge and two of these were wounded, one in the shoulder, the other shot through the elbow. The drop from the ledge was not quite sheer, but it would still make a difficult climb. Sending the three fit men first Talaban edged along to the wounded.

"I can make it, sir," said the man with the shoulder wound. He was sitting holding his crystal over the blood-drenched hole in his leather breastplate. "No bones broken."

"Are you sure?" The man nodded. Then, with a grin, he pocketed his crystal and swung his legs over the ledge. Talaban heard him grunt with pain as he took the weight on his injured shoulder, but slowly the soldier made his way down to the ground.

The other soldier sat with his back to the rock, his face grey with pain and shock. As Talaban moved alongside him he saw that the man had two wounds, the smashed elbow and another hole just below his belt.

"I don't believe I'll be making that climb," he told Talaban, trying to force a grin. Using his dagger Talaban cut away the man's leggings and examined the wound. The ball had struck the hip, tearing the flesh and, apparently, bouncing from the pelvic bone. The gash was bleeding profusely.

"Where is your crystal?"

The soldier pointed to the pouch at his side. Talaban opened it. Placing the green gem into the man's left hand he told him to work on the pain from the elbow. Then he took his own healing stone and used its power to stop the bleeding from the hip wound. After some minutes the man's color began to improve.

"You hurt, captain?" he heard Touchstone call.

"No. Catch my bow!" He dropped the weapon over the ledge. It spiralled down. Touchstone caught it expertly. Returning his attention to the wounded man he gently unbuckled the soldier's belt and then his own. Buckling them together he helped the man to stand. "I'll take you down on my back," he told the soldier.

"You won't make it. Leave me here. I'll make a try later."

Talaban shook his head. "It is not possible with one arm. Now do as you're told." Pushing one end of the belt into the soldier's good hand he slipped it around the soldier's body, then tightened it around his own waist. "Put your arm around my neck and hold on. Not too tight, I'll need to breathe."

"This is not wise," said the soldier.

"We'll talk about wisdom when we get to the ground," said Talaban. "Move slowly with me." Strapped together the two men crouched down over the ledge. "Lean your weight forward onto my shoulders," said Talaban. Bracing himself he lay down on his stomach, then swung his legs over the edge. The soldier's dead weight dragged him back, and for one terrifying moment Talaban thought he was being torn from the ledge. Then his foot struck a jutting rock. Taking a deep calming breath, Talaban began to move down the face. The soldier was heavier than he had appeared and Talaban felt the muscles of his shoulders being stretched to tearing point.

From below men shouted encouragement, telling Talaban where the footholds were. "A little to your left and down. That's it, captain. There's another just below that!"

Talaban's breath was coming in ragged gasps now and sweat was blinding him. His right hand began to tremble with fatigue. Two of the Avatars climbed alongside him, leaning in to help him with the weight of the soldier. Slowly they made their way down. Eager hands grabbed at Talaban as he reached the foot of the face. A soldier unbuckled the doubled belt and helped the wounded man to a boulder where he slumped down and closed his eyes in a prayer of thanks.

Regaining his breath, Talaban summoned Goray to his side. "Report," he said.

"Six Avatar dead, three wounded. Two Vagars dead, nine wounded. None badly."

"The enemy?"

"I've counted seventy-two bodies," said Goray. "The survivors fled to the east. No more than a dozen escaped."

"Gather the fire-clubs, the black powder bags and the ammunition. Give the weapons to the Vagars and explain how they operate."

"Yes, sir." Goray had been one of thirty Avatars to

have experimented with the captured weapons back in Egaru. He had shown great aptitude with them.

Talaban strolled across to where Pendar was seated on a boulder. His sword was still on the ground near the headless Almec some 20 paces away.

"Are you feeling sick?" asked Talaban.

"Not any more. I've emptied what feels like the contents of three stomachs already. Now I just feel weak and faint. I see you are wounded," said Pendar, pointing to the cut on Talaban's cheek. It was still leaking blood which had stained the right side of his face.

"I think it must look worse than it is. A fragment of stone pierced the skin." Removing his crystal, Talaban held it to the cut, which sealed instantly.

"That was a fine climb," said Pendar. "The men will love you for it."

Talaban ignored the compliment. "You have never had training with the sword, have you?"

"No. Was it you who saved me?"

"Yes. I shot fast and high. I am sorry. It must have been a shock when the bolt struck."

"*Shock* does not truly describe it. One moment he was leering at me—the next he had no face to leer with. I would have known then—if I had not known already—that I am really not suited to this kind of work." He smiled and looked away.

"Do not underestimate yourself, Pendar. Soldiering is about acquired skills. You have a keen mind and you will learn. Stick close to me. Observe the routines. It will come to you. You have already made a beginning. You led that charge well. My thanks for that. It was bravely done."

Pendar smiled. "A timely compliment, Talaban." The Vagar relaxed, and scanned the battle site. "So this is what it is like to be a warrior," he said. "I cannot say it has much to recommend it. There is a stench to the air that is gathering flies."

"When men die in combat their bowels open," said Talaban. "There are so many songs about battles and heroes and not one mentions the stench. I think few of the song writers ever fought in one." He sat down beside the Vagar. "Are you feeling better?"

"Yes. What now?"

"We send the badly wounded back to Egaru and we push on to kill as many Almecs as we can. Would you prefer to go back? There is no disgrace in it. I will commend you in my report."

"I don't think my grandmother would appreciate that," said Pendar. "She is grooming me for political office. She thinks that a hero will be well received by the people."

"She is not wrong."

"She rarely is. She's a tough woman, and single-minded."

Touchstone strolled to where the two men were sitting. "I go to clifftop," he said. "Kill watcher. Meet later, yes?"

"Be careful," warned Talaban. "We leave in one hour." Touchstone smiled and loped away.

"I watched him kill four men with that small axe," said Pendar. "It was terrifying."

"He is from a warrior people. They believe that battle is the only route to greatness."

"And *this* is greatness?" said Pendar, gesturing towards the dead.

"No," said Talaban. "This is savagery, and the antithesis of everything civilization stands for. But in some respects Touchstone's people do understand truths we have long forgotten. Only in strife do we grow. What you have learned today, in a few brief moments, no book or song or teacher could ever have imparted to you. You sat upon your horse in the mouth of the pass and you faced death. Then you overcame your fear and you charged. Have you ever felt so alive?"

"No, never," admitted the Vagar. "And yet it was still appalling."

"Yes, it is. All these dead men—Almec, Avatar and Vagar—could have led useful productive lives. Now they are meat for scavenging birds. If your grandmother is right, and you move into political life, you can take what you have learned here and use it to benefit your people. In my long life I have grown to realize that all men sway between being base and noble. They make decisions daily that draw them one way, then the other. Leaders should inspire nobility of spirit. Today you have seen much that is base and more that was noble. You will either be a better or a worse man for it. I think you will be a better man. Now pick up your sword. I think it is time for a few basic lessons."

It had been a long day and Sofarita was bone-weary as she returned to the house. Questor Ro was sleeping; all but one of his servants had retired to their beds. Old Sempes was waiting for her as she arrived.

"Would you like some food, lady?" he asked. "Or perhaps I could prepare you a bath?"

"No, thank you. I think I will just sleep," she said. She slowly climbed the stairs. Her knees and hip joints ached as she did so, yet another indication of the advancing crystallization of her limbs. She paused at the top of the stairs, then pushed on to her room. It was a small, westerly-facing bedroom with a wide arched window and a small balcony beyond. Through it she could see the stars shining above the glittering ocean.

Too tired to disrobe she kicked off her shoes, pulled back the blankets and lay down. The pillow was soft and inviting, but she did not drift away into sleep.

It was eight days since Talaban had ridden from the city with his men. She had observed his first encounter with the Almecs and found herself terrified that he might be killed. He was occupying a great deal of her thoughts now. There was something about him that reached out to her. She could not identify it. He had fought four skirmishes since then, lightning raids on Almec columns, and was now heading for his rendezvous with the *Serpent*, which Methras had sailed up the Luan estuary.

Elsewhere the news had all been dark. The Almecs had slaughtered most of the residents of Boria, Pejkan and Caval, and 3,000 soldiers were now marching slowly up the coast towards Egaru. They would be in sight of the capital in eight days. Another army of similar size was preparing to move from Ammon's capital.

Methras had sunk two golden ships, but more and more were sailing up the river, bringing soldiers and weapons of war.

Viruk, with Sofarita's aid, had linked with the agent Boru and together they were bringing Ammon to Egaru. She had last seen the wagon earlier that day, trundling over the farmlands near her own village of Pacepta. The settlement was deserted, the farmers having taken to the hills in search of safety.

The Almecs had landed armies all over the continent. To the far south they had crushed the nomads, killing hundreds. To the east they had fought a pitched battle with the Hantu tribe. The Almecs had suffered heavy losses, but at the day's end more than 2,000 Hantu lay dead upon the field, among them the leader Rzak Xhen.

Twenty miles from Egaru another Almec army was camped close to the mist barrier around the Valley of the Stone Lion. They had assembled a structure of metal poles, boxes and wires and were studying the mist. Twenty of their men had tried to march through.

One made it back. He died within moments, his body aged beyond belief.

Sofarita had flown through the mist, to find that Anu's pyramid had reached the thirty-first course, and was now almost 200 feet high. She had entered Anu's tent. He was asleep on his cot bed. His hair was sparse and cloud white, deeply etched lines scored his face, and his limbs were stick thin. Anu awoke and gazed up at her. "I was wondering when you would visit," he said, aloud. "Or am I dreaming?"

"It is no dream, Holy One."

Anu closed his eyes and lay back. A faint blue aura glimmered around his body, and then his spirit rose clear. "It is good to see you, child," he said. "How are you faring?"

"The power is growing all the time," she told him, "sometimes slowly, sometimes with surges that over-whelm me. It is not constant. It frightens me."

His spirit hand took hers. "You are a brave woman, Sofarita. The Source chose well. But then he always does."

"I did not ask to be chosen," she said. "Nor did I want to be."

"I think you are wrong. If you had known the terrible evil that was to come, and had been offered the power to oppose it, I believe you would have made this choice. You are strong, and good, and fair hearted."

"And I am to die."

"We are all going to die, child. Everything does." He released her hand. "Tell Rael I need another chest. I must speed the Dance."

"I will tell him. Why is it that you are allowing your-self to age?"

"I have no wish for immortality, Sofarita. It is a heavy burden, with few genuine pleasures."

"When you are gone the Music will die with you."

He smiled and shook his head. "The Music cannot die. All that will fail will be men's understanding of it. Perhaps that is good. Time will tell. But I feel there is enough evil in the world already, without magic adding to it."

"The Almecs are trying to break through your barrier of mist. Can you hold them back?"

"I could, but I will not," said Anu. He paused. "Can you sense the presence of Almeia when she is close?"

"Yes."

"Do you sense her now?"

"No."

"Good, then let us talk. I am not a man given to lies, but I have left Rael and the others with the belief that my pyramid will save them, that it will be a new power source to recharge the chests. This is exactly the opposite of the truth. When the Music flows from it all crystal power will be drained. The chests will empty, the zhi-bows fail. Immortality for the Avatars will cease. Equally, when the Music reaches the west, the Crystal Queen will die. But first I must finish the pyramid. At this moment Almeia believes the pyramid will be a power source for her. While she believes this no attempt will be made to stop me. It is vital that she does not learn the truth. You must keep her focused upon you, Sofarita. In any way you can."

Sofarita remained with him for another hour, discussing strategies. Then feeling the approach of Almeia, she bade him farewell and returned to her body.

Now, as she lay in her bed, she thought again of Talaban.

His bravery had not surprised her, but she had been pleased with his sensitivity in dealing with Pendar. She wondered what it would be like to touch Talaban's skin, to stroke her fingers across his cheek. For a moment only she was a farm girl again, remembering her first time with Veris. Only it wasn't Veris in her imagination. It was the lean, powerful figure of Talaban the Avatar.

Cold reality struck her.

You are not a farm girl any longer. You are a goddess. A dying goddess.

Questor Ro was not asleep. The day had been a long one, supervising the training of new recruits at the three barracks. The task was not easy. Thousands of Vagars wanted to enlist and each one needed to be physically examined and questioned at length. In turn this led to massive lines of men, snaking out around the buildings, blocking thoroughfares. Ro had been summoned to create order from the chaos. At the first of the barracks he had found Rael and Mejana in heated debate. She wanted to know why fit young men could not merely sign their name and be assigned to a unit. Rael was struggling to explain the military ramifications of such a move. Neither was making an impression on the other.

Ro stepped in. "If I may speak," he said. Mejana was struggling to hold her temper. Rael also was ashen-faced. Both nodded. "Let me first sum up both points of view. The Questor General is concerned that our new army be disciplined and effective. You, lady, are worried about the need for such rigorous examination, fearing it may be some part of a secret Avatar plan to retain control of the army."

"Exactly," said Mejana.

"I am not, as Rael knows, a military man," said Ro. "But I do know certain principles that should always apply. Our army is small but it has, over the years, proved effective. Lines of communication are well drawn, officers and men know one another well. Orders, when given, are carried out with speed and efficiency. A huge influx of untrained recruits could prove chaotic. It is, I understand, the Questor General's plan to add one thousand new soldiers. This would almost double our force."

"We could put twenty thousand men on the field of battle," said Mejana. "We would outnumber the Almecs five to one."

"And watch them all slaughtered!" snapped Rael.

"With respect, lady," said Ro, soothingly, "and I do mean with respect, for I believe you to be a formidable woman, you are out of your depth in this matter. What I said about lines of communication is not just important, but utterly vital. In any battle a general must be able to formulate changes in strategy, give orders and see them carried out swiftly. What you are suggesting is that we face the Almecs with an undisciplined mob. We Avatars have fought such armies before. We always won. At the first attack hundreds of them are killed. The rest become demoralized. Some decide to run for safety. This causes confusion and, more often than not, panic. We do not have time to train a huge force. However, I think I know a compromise."

"It needs to be a good one," said Rael.

"There should be two forces," said Ro. "The first will be the army and we will continue our examinations as before, seeking only one thousand of the fittest, most able men. The second will be a militia force under appointed commanders in every district. These will be men who will defend the walls when called upon or who will fight on the streets if the walls are breached. Each district commander will appoint sub-commanders and they will organize distribution of weapons. How does that sound?"

"A recipe for disaster," said Rael.

"I like it," said Mejana. "My people will feel, perhaps for the first time, that their destiny is in their own hands."

"Then we are done here," said Rael. "Excuse me." He stalked from the room. Mejana turned to Ro.

"Will you assist me in organizing the militia?" she asked him.

"Of course, lady." Ro was silent for a moment, then he looked into Mejana's eyes. "He is a fine soldier. We could have found none better to oversee the defense of the cities."

"But?" she said.

"But he has nothing to fight for. If he wins, he loses. You understand?"

"The day of the Avatar is over," she said. "I would do nothing to change that, even if I could."

"I understand that," Ro told her. "That is not the point I am making. No matter what is done with the militia, or new Vagars drawn into the army, the fighting spearhead of the war will be the Avatar soldiers, with their zhi-bows. Men fight best who fight for causes. As matters now stand, why should Rael not gather the few hundred Avatars left, take control of the *Serpent*, and sail to a far land to rebuild?"

Mejana considered the question, and its ramifications. If such an event were to take place Egaru and Pagaru would certainly fall to the Almecs.

"I have nothing to offer them," said Mejana, at last.

"You could make it clear that there will be no retribution against my people should the war be won."

"Such an offer would be a lie," she admitted. "Hatred of the Avatar is so deeply ingrained that it would manifest itself very swiftly."

"I know," said Ro, sadly. "And so does Rael."

"What then can I do?"

Ro did not reply. He had sown the seed and could do no more.

The day had been exhausting, but by dusk the beginnings of organization could be seen. Twenty district commanders had been appointed and ten further training areas identified. The long lines of recruits had thinned and a sense of order was beginning to prevail.

An hour before midnight Ro had returned to his home, dismissed his servants, and requested that Sempes wait for the arrival of the Lady Sofarita. Ro himself had taken a long bath and retired to his bed.

Sleep would not come. His mind was in a whir. He thought of his lost wife and children, his years of work and study, his meeting with Sofarita, and the emotions that meeting had unleashed—emotions that would never be fulfilled. At first he had entertained hopes for the deepening of their relationship, but then he had seen how she looked at Talaban. How could he hope to compete with him? Talaban was tall and handsome. Such physical considerations should have had little to do with genuine love. But the reality was far different, Ro knew.

He climbed from his bed and filled a goblet with cool water. His door was open, and he felt a chill breeze. His gaze flicked to the open window. No draft was coming from there and the curtains were not moving. Walking to the door he stepped into the hallway. Immediately he began to tremble with cold.

This was ridiculous! Running back into his room he threw a woollen cloak around his shoulders and returned to the hall. It was dark, and yet he could see a faint blue light coming from Sofarita's room. Was she working some magic? Would he disturb her if he ventured in? He shivered. Then walked along the hallway. The door was open. Thick ice had formed on the walls and swirling snow filled the room. Ro stepped inside.

Sofarita was lying in bed, snow and ice covering her face.

Ro ran to her side. As he did so he caught a glimpse of movement from the corner of his eye. Swinging round he saw—just for a moment—the transparent figure of a young woman, white-haired and ghostly, with eyes of cold green. Then she was gone. Dragging back the covers Ro pushed his arms under Sofarita's limp body and, with a grunt of effort, lifted her clear of the frozen bed. Staggering out into the hallway he carried her to his own room. Her skin was icy cold, her lips blue. There was no time to light a fire. Ro laid her on the bed and tore off her frozen clothes. Covering her with a blanket he threw off his cloak and night-shirt and slipped in beside her, drawing her to him, allowing the warmth of his body to raise her temperature. Gently he rubbed at the cold flesh of her arms.

For a time he felt sure he would fail and that she would die in his arms. But then a soft moan escaped from her lips. Ro hugged her close, feeling the warmth seeping back into her body.

Sofarita's eyelids flickered. "She . . . tried to . . . kill me," she whispered.

"You are safe now," Ro told her. "Safe with me."

She gave a weak smile and snuggled in closer. Then she slept.

Ro drew the blanket over her shoulder. She was warmer now, and he could feel the heat beginning to radiate from her flesh. Ro became acutely aware of her thigh pressed close to his own. He lay back and closed his eyes. Sadness touched him, for he was now where he had dreamed of being, alongside the naked Sofarita, her arms around him. And yet he sensed there would never be another moment like this, never the physical closeness, the intimacy, the sheer joy of togetherness. Ro wanted it to last, and he lay without moving, holding to every memorable sweet and fleeting second.

• • •

Talaban lay still in the darkness, his hands lashed behind him, his head pounding from the blows he had taken. He could taste blood from a gash inside his mouth. Why he was alive he did not know. They had been riding for the rendezvous point with the *Serpent* when they had come across a hunting party of Almecs. Pendar, heady with the success of the last few days, had led his men in a wild charge. Talaban had galloped after them, shouting for them to turn back.

A larger force was hidden in the undergrowth and a vicious volley of shots ripped into the Vagars. Ten men were hurled from their saddles and the charge faltered. "Get back to the river!" bellowed Talaban. The survivors needed no second order. Wheeling their horses they had thundered back towards the Luan. Talaban swung on his reins. At that moment two Almecs came running from cover. One loosed his fire-club, the shot taking Talaban's mount in the skull. The horse tumbled forward. Talaban was hurled over its dipping head. Landing awkwardly he struggled to rise. Something struck him a wicked blow to the side of the head and he had opened his eyes to find himself tied hand and foot and travelling in the back of a wagon.

They had brought him to a deserted village and had thrown him into an empty grain store.

There were no windows and the Avatar did not know if it was day or night. Occasionally he lapsed into unconsciousness. Each time he woke he felt nauseous and cold.

The door was pulled open. Two men moved into the store, took Talaban by the arms and dragged him out onto open ground. Two other men stood waiting. One, dressed in breastplate of shining gold and a helm adorned with golden feathers, had a face which shimmered in the moonlight, like glass. The other was a hunchback holding a golden rod, topped with a circle.

Talaban was hauled before them, then kicked savagely in the back of the knees, causing him to tumble to the earth. Someone grabbed his hair and dragged him to his knees.

"You have been troublesome, Avatar," said the man with the glass face. "But no more troublesome than a bee sting. Tomorrow I begin my march on your cities. We know much about your defenses and the plans of your leaders. You, however, will tell me more."

"You will learn nothing from me," said Talaban.

"On the contrary. Everything you have ever known will be divulged to my servant. He has a particular skill—as you will discover." He turned to the hunchback. "Drain him," he said.

The hunchback tucked the golden rod into his belt and moved alongside the prisoner. His hands clasped Talaban's head, his fingers pressing into the temples. Fire lanced through the Avatar. It was as if a snake had entered his ear and was eating his way through the flesh of his brain. Talaban honed his concentration, moving into the first of the rituals, seeking a defense against the probing snake. The movement inside his head slowed. He threw up a mental wall, created from darkness. The snake's fangs ripped at it, shredding it like rotten silk. Talaban retreated, holding to his identity. The snake advanced. Talaban moved into the Second Ritual, then the Third. Utterly focused now he let the snake advance.

Then he counterattacked, driving his spirit into the snake like a spear. Instantly images began to form. A childhood spent in isolation and fear, bullied, beaten, mocked. Sold by his parents to a group of beggars, who used his deformity to earn coin. They scratched his skin and smeared it with animal excrement, causing terrible sores that made the hunchbacked child ever more grotesque and therefore more valuable.

The snake tried to draw back, but Talaban had him now.

He saw the hunchback's childhood, his adolescence, and his training by Cas-Coatl. Crystal-fed, he had developed amazing talents to read the minds of others. Suddenly the hunchback had power and he used it mercilessly for more than 300 years.

Talaban saw it all, and through the hunchback's thoughts relived the magical flight from their own doomed world, saw the magic used to achieve it.

Almeia, the glorious goddess, the Crystal Queen.

And, in one sudden, brilliant flash, he saw why Almeia needed so many deaths.

The snake was struggling now, desperate to pull clear.

"Your life has been sad," Talaban told him. *"Your youth saw you abused and hurt, your manhood saw you abuse and hurt others. I pity you."*

The snake ceased its struggle. *"I am what men made me,"* said the hunchback.

"May your next life be a happy one," Talaban told him.

Moving into the Fourth Ritual Talaban severed the head of the snake.

The hunchback fell dead to the ground. Talaban swayed but remained upright on his knees.

Cas-Coatl knelt beside his fallen servant. "How did you kill him?" he asked, conversationally.

Talaban looked up. "In the same way you would have, Cas-Coatl," he said.

"Ah, I see. You Avatars are truly similar to my people. Unfortunately for you this means I must resort to torture." He swung to the two guards. "Lock him away and send for Lan-Roas. Tell him to bring all his . . . tools."

The guards took Talaban by his arms and lifted him. "Torture will gain you nothing, Almec," said the Avatar.

"I suspect you are right," agreed Cas-Coatl. "Sadly we will have to find out. Lan-Roas is very skilled. He will begin by burning out your right eye, then cutting the fingers from your right hand. Then the hand itself. And that, my friend, will be merely the beginning. You will be amazed at what levels of pain he can inspire in his victims."

Talaban said nothing as he was taken away and then thrown to the ground inside the grain store. The door slammed shut, leaving him once more in total darkness. With an effort he rolled to his knees, then began to work at the binding on his wrists, tugging and twisting. The leather thongs did not give. Pushing himself to his feet he began to walk carefully until he reached a wall. Turning his back to it he inched his way along it, feeling for any rough edges against which he could saw through the bindings. There was nothing.

How long did he have before the torturer arrived to maim him?

Put such thoughts from your mind, he told himself sternly.

Moving along the wall he reached the doorway. The timbers had been set back into the stone, and once more he found no straight edges with which to work. Lastly he began to move across the floor, slowly sweeping his foot, seeking any piece of stone that might be lying close by. Again there was nothing. Despair touched him with an icy finger. Setting off once more he moved with even more care. His foot scraped against a small object. Sitting down he reached out, the tips of his fingers brushing the dirt floor. At first he could not locate the object, but then his fingers touched something hard. It was flat and irregular in shape, no more than an inch across. Lifting it carefully he ran his thumb across it. It was a piece of broken pottery.

The edge was sharp.

With great care he lifted it back toward the thongs, and began to saw at the bindings. After some minutes he managed to get his finger against the leather. He had made almost no impression upon it. This could take hours, he knew.

And he did not have hours to spare.

Moving back to the door he managed to wedge the shard into a crack. Then he pressed the edge into his left wrist above the bindings. The skin parted and blood began to flow, wetting the dry leather. He let the flow continue for some minutes until he could feel it dripping over his fingers and dropping to the floor. Then he bunched his muscles and pulled with all his strength.

The bindings held. Taking three quick breaths he tried again. This time there was a little movement. Steadying himself he twisted his left wrist, and pulled again from a slightly different angle. The bindings stretched a fraction more.

He could hear footsteps approaching. The sound gave him renewed strength and he dragged back on the thongs. The skin of his wrists was torn further open as he did so, further drenching the leather. As the footsteps reached the door the thongs parted. Talaban staggered, then lurched towards the opening.

He heard the bar being raised, then the door swung in. A tall man entered. He was carrying a shoulder sack and in his hand was a small saw. He froze as he saw Talaban waiting for him. The Avatar leapt, his right hand sweeping forward, fingers extended. The points of the fingers slammed into the man's throat, smashing the bones beneath. He fell back against the wall, gurgling and struggling for breath that would never come again. Talaban pushed past him. Three guards stood beyond the doorway.

There was no way he could defeat them all.

At that moment a dark figure leapt from the low roof. The small bright hand-axe sliced through the throat of the first guard. Talaban sprang at the second, sending a left hook that exploded against his chin. The third guard drew his sword and lunged at the Avatar. The blade took Talaban under the left ribs, ripping away the flesh. Talaban grabbed the sword arm, hauling the Almec forward—straight into Talaban's rising left elbow. The man half fell. As he righted himself Touchstone's axe buried itself in his skull.

"Better move quick," said Touchstone. "Horses beyond village."

A cry went up behind them. Talaban swung and saw Cas-Coatl and a dozen men running across the square. "Now be good time!" said Touchstone. The tribesman sprinted off. Talaban began to run after him. By the time the Avatar reached the outskirts of the village Touchstone was far ahead, disappearing down into a shallow dry gully. Talaban was close to exhaustion and could run no further.

He risked a glance behind and saw that the Almecs were gaining on him. He heard the thunder of hooves. Touchstone came riding out of the gully, leading a second horse. As he rode past, Talaban reached up, grabbed the saddle pommel and vaulted into the saddle. Fire-clubs sounded behind them, but no shots came near.

The two men galloped their mounts towards the west and up over the hills, riding fast towards the distant Luan. After a while Talaban could just make out the silhouette of the *Serpent*.

Half an hour later he was sitting in his old cabin, Touchstone stitching the wound above his hip. Methras was sitting opposite him. "I did not expect to see you again," he told Talaban.

"I hope you are not too disappointed."

Methras grinned. "Touchstone promised to cut my throat if I didn't give him the chance to track you down."

Talaban winced with the pain from his wounds. "They took my crystal," he said.

"Use mine," said Methras, opening the pouch at his side. Talaban looked into the man's blue eyes. Only a week ago Vagar possession of such an item would have brought about a swift death sentence.

"Can you use it?" asked Talaban.

"After a fashion. But I will learn."

Talaban accepted the gem, and held it over the hip wound. Instantly the flesh began to knit. "I will teach you the rituals," he said.

"I know them. But my Vagar blood holds me back," said Methras, with a smile.

"How long were you on that roof?" Talaban asked the tribesman.

"Long time. Too many soldiers close."

"How did you get there without being seen?"

"Plenty skill. Bet you glad see me."

"I'm glad I gave you that axe." Returning his attention to Methras he said: "We need to get back to Egaru as fast as possible. The Almec army marches tomorrow. They will be at the city in less than five days."

"The Questor General knows. There are three armies marching. Close to eight thousand men."

"Big number," said Touchstone. "We lose maybe."

Talaban grunted as he rose from the bed. "I need to rest," he said. "Where is my cabin?"

"This *is* your cabin," said Methras.

"No, not any longer."

Methras smiled. "I shall be spending most of the night in the control room. Rest here. I will wake you when we reach Egaru."

Too weary to argue, Talaban stretched out on the familiar bed.

As Touchstone made to leave Talaban reached out and took his arm. "You are going home, my friend. To Suryet."

Then he closed his eyes and fell into a deep, dreamless sleep.

Chapter Twenty-four

For Rael the events of the last month had been unremittingly bleak. Nothing seemed to have been right since the day Questor Ro returned with those four fully-charged chests of power. It was as if, at the point of greatest hope, the Source had turned against them.

Now three disciplined and deadly armies were marching on the twin cities, the Vagars were waiting to take control of their own destinies and the witch woman was growing in power daily. Rael was weary. Taking a white crystal from his pouch he held it to his brow. Cool, invigorating energy swept through him. He sighed, and his thoughts returned to Sofarita. Whenever he saw her Rael had to leave his crystals behind. Close proximity to her drained them. As a result he no longer invited her to the Council Chamber, but instead visited her at Ro's home.

Rael sat at his desk, staring down at the mass of paper there.

Lifting the first, he read of the food situation. From the day he had learned of the Almecs he had ordered massive imports of food and the grain stores of the twin cities were now bulging. Even so a prolonged siege would see the populations begin to starve within three weeks. Rationing would have to begin tomorrow.

Moving to his window he looked out over the bay.

The *Serpent* was at anchor there, with some fifty smaller Vagar vessels. They had been supplying the city for days, but now there was nowhere for them to sail. The grain villages along the Luan were deserted, the people fled or slain.

Returning to his desk he shuffled through the papers, coming at last to the report from the Crystal Treasury. Caprishan had taken a second chest to Anu, as requested. The third was in use now, re-powering zhi-bows. The last chest remained in the heart of the *Serpent*. Soon Rael would need to have it removed. Then the *Serpent* would sail no more.

In some ways *Serpent Seven* was like the Avatar—powerful but doomed.

Short of power, and short of men, Rael was in a grim mood. Talaban had called him the greatest strategist alive. Rael believed it. But there was little point in being a fine strategist if one did not have the means to execute those strategies.

Ideally Rael would have sent out several strong units to harry the advancing armies, cutting off their supplies, wearing them down. But with fewer than 200 fighting Avatars he could not afford such a move. And sending out lightly armed Vagars against the fire-clubs of the Almecs would have proved suicidal. Therefore the advancing armies could move at their own pace, dictating the course of the war.

The one advantage Rael possessed lay in the deadliness of the Almecs. Had their invasion been less bloody they could have used the captive population to keep them in supplies. As it was, they would need to take the cities with speed.

Rael pondered this. Pagaru's walls were not strong. They had been built fast in the early days of conquest. They would be breached, he was sure. Egaru, with a smaller perimeter, could be held far more effectively.

With this in mind he decided to dispatch more Avatars to Pagaru.

Then he turned his mind to Ammon. The king was in the apartments chosen for him on the second level of the Council Building. Soon Rael would have to meet with him. His 5,000 men could help turn the tide, but how sensible would it be to invite 5,000 essentially hostile warriors into the cities? If, by some miracle, the Almecs could be massively defeated Ammon would find himself in a position he had longed for. In control of the Avatar Empire.

Empire?

What empire? The thought depressed Rael. There was no empire any more.

The door opened and Viruk stepped inside. "What do you want, cousin?" he asked, irritated by the sudden intrusion.

"Don't cousin me, you whoreson!" thundered Viruk. "You send me from an Avatar city to rescue an androgynous sub-human and what do I find when I return? The city being run by Vagar dogs. I ought to cut your throat, you treacherous bastard!"

Coldly angry, Rael rose from his desk and moved to stand in front of the outraged warrior. "If anyone is guilty of treachery it is you, you arrogant fool," he said. "The village woman you bedded is the real power in the cities now. And do you know why? Because you broke the law and healed her, Viruk. She is crystal-joined. Surely even you will understand what that means. We tried to kill her. We failed."

"I could kill her," said Viruk. "There is nothing that lives or breathes that I cannot kill."

"It is not—at this time—an option. Her powers give us at least a fighting chance against the Almecs. But once Anu's pyramid is complete we may have a better chance."

"What then? Do we seize back power?"

"Of course," lied Rael, smoothly.

Viruk smiled broadly. "That is more like it."

"Now I must greet my guests." Rael looked at Viruk's travel-stained clothes. "I suggest you go to your home and bathe."

"You wouldn't happen to know if my marsh marigolds arrived safely?" asked Viruk.

"No, I wouldn't," the Questor General told him.

After Viruk had left, Rael walked down to the Council Chamber and sent a servant to request the presence of the Lady Mejana and Ammon.

Mejana arrived first, dressed in a voluminous blue robe. She nodded curtly at Rael, then sat down on his right without speaking. They sat in silence for several minutes before a servant announced the arrival of the king.

Ammon entered, dressed in a borrowed tunic of pearl-grey silk and silver-thonged sandals. His dark hair had been washed and perfumed and hung low to his shoulders, and his movements were languid and graceful. Moving around the table he drew up a seat close to Rael. "Charming apartments you offered me," he said, "but I would appreciate the talents of a tailor."

"I shall have one sent to you as soon as we are finished here," said Rael. "But first let me welcome you to Egaru. It pleases me to have been helpful in your rescue."

"No doubt there will be a price to pay," said Ammon. His violet eyes flickered towards Mejana. "And you are, lady?"

Rael cut in swiftly. "Allow me to present the Lady Mejana, my First Councillor."

Ammon bowed his head briefly. "Is this a new fashion among the Avatar, lady, to eschew blue hair?" he asked, mischievously.

"I am not an Avatar, sire."

Ammon assumed an expression of mock surprise. "Indeed? Then how, one wonders, have you achieved such remarkable status?"

"As you are well aware," said Rael, keeping his tone even, "Mejana is the head of the Pajists, an organization funded by yourself and your minister Anwar. However, that is of small consequence now. We are all facing a terrible enemy. What we must decide here is how best to combat them."

"My army should be here within a few days," said Ammon. "I would suggest we then defend the walls."

"Certain assurances must first be given," said Mejana.

"Such as?"

"Your promise that the soldiers will leave once the war is won."

"I do not need to offer assurances, lady. This land was once under the direct rule of the Erek-jhip-zhonad. It will be again. It seems to me that it is I who should be making demands."

The door opened and a servant moved across the wide room. He bowed to all three occupants then approached Rael. "A message, lord, from the Lady Sofarita."

Rael took it, read it, then leaned back in his chair.

"Good news, I hope," said Ammon.

Rael rose. "Your army was attacked in the Gen-el Pass. Three thousand dead, the rest scattered. Our conversation here is concluded."

"I think the Source must have come to hate me," said Rael. He had told her of the destruction of Ammon's army, and of the approach of the invincible Almecs. Taking him by the hand she led him to the roof garden. A long table had been set there, covered by soft towels.

Beside it was a smaller table, upon which sat vials of scented oil.

"Take off your clothes, Rael," she said.

"I have no time, Mirani."

"Do as you are told, husband," she said. Rael sighed and removed his tunic and leggings. She gestured for him to lie face down on the massage bed. Once he had done so she poured oil into her hands and gently began to knead the muscles of his shoulders. "They are like bands of iron," she told him. He groaned as she probed more deeply. "You think the Source hates you? If that is true he has a strange way of showing it. You and I have known more than a century of love. Arrogant man!" Her fingers and thumbs eased the tension from his upper back then moved down along the spine. "The Source does not hate you, Rael. But he must hate what we have become. Slave masters and tyrants. All our plans, all our ambitions, are for one purpose only: to retain control, to dominate. We live by stealing the lives of others. If the Source did not hate that, then I would have no time for the Source. Now do you understand why I refuse to join the Council?" He lay very still as her hands worked their magic. She continued the massage, using her elbow to stretch the long muscles above the hips. Rael groaned again.

"Are you trying to heal me or kill me?" he said.

"I am trying to make you see the truth," she told him. "Mejana is the bright light of dawn; Sofarita, the sunshine that follows rain. They are not evil, Rael, they are necessary. We were blessed with many children in the early days. All grew to adulthood. All died in the fall of the world. All except Chryssa." He closed his eyes against the pain of remembrance. "She lived for but a few years, and gave us great joy. Think of how Mejana must have felt when her daughter, the light of her life, was crystal-drawn. Think of her pain, Rael.

Yes, she murdered Baliel, and ordered the deaths of others. Yes, she hates the Avatar. But her cause is just. She has dedicated her life to ensure that no mother will ever see her child crystal-drawn again. Do not hate her, Rael. Admire her. Respect her.

"And as for these reverses you suffer . . . Did you expect all wars to be so easily won? You are the Questor General. You will find a way to win. I would expect no less of you. Now turn over."

He rolled onto his back. Mirani loosened the ties of her dress, and let it fall to the grass. Then she climbed to the table, straddling him.

He reached up and stroked her shoulders. "How did you get to be so hard?" he asked, with a smile.

"I married a soldier," she said. And kissed him.

"The dangers are too great," Questor Ro told Talaban. Sofarita sat silently on the grass, apparently lost in thought. The heavy scent of jasmine was in the air and the trio were sitting in the afternoon sunshine. Ro had not been pleased to see the tall officer arrive. He had noticed, with concealed dismay, the way Sofarita brightened with his presence.

"I think it is our only hope, Questor," said Talaban.

Sofarita glanced up. "Tell me again what you learned from the hunchback. Every detail."

Talaban smiled. "I could tell you his entire life, lady, but that would serve little purpose. The important fact is that the Crystal Queen did not intend to move a part of her continent to this world. What she was trying to do was, first, create a barrier over which the tidal wave would flow and then move her cities to a more clement part of their own planet. What she *actually* did was open a gateway between worlds. This, in itself, would be unimportant—save for the fact that she did not completely close the gateway. Tremendous forces are at play here, straining to draw her land back to its own place. She is using massive amounts of power merely to hold her continent in place. That is why she needs so many deaths. And why she fears you, lady. You can drain away some of the power she needs. But not from here. Rael tells me that he no longer dares to approach you carrying crystals. He leaves them back at the Council Chamber. Even there your power is drawing on them, but less so. It is my belief that if we travel to the west, and approach the realm of the Crystal Queen, you will be able to weaken her. Perhaps then the Almecs will be sucked back through the gateway."

"Only those still on the continent," said Sofarita, absently.

"You think I am wrong, lady?"

"No, not wrong, merely ahead of yourself. My powers are not yet great enough to attack her directly. First I must help Rael destroy this invading force. Then we can think of an assault in the west. Now let us talk of more pleasant matters. You have a beautiful garden here, Ro."

"Thank you," he said. "It is not as fine as Viruk's, but it gives me great pleasure. I have always enjoyed watching—"

"She is gone," said Sofarita, suddenly. "Almeia was watching us, observing and listening. She will return. We do not have much time to plan our journey."

"Then you think I am right?" asked Talaban.

"Yes, there is no other way. But as soon as we sail she will know what we plan. We will face many dangers."

"She is not all-knowing," insisted Ro. "She did not anticipate the Sunfire, and the destruction of her ships, nor the arrival of the Serpent to save Pagaru. Nor did she succeed in the ambush of Talaban at the pass."

"She *knows*," insisted Sofarita, "but she is limited by her need for others to carry out her commands. It is one matter to inform a general that a force is moving through a pass, quite another to direct the course of the subsequent battle. Her general, Cas-Coatl, communicates with her through the crystal he wears in his belt. She told him a small force was due in the Gen-el Pass. He sent two of his captains to oppose you. But they had no means of communicating with Almeia. Equally, Cas-Coatl was told of the Sunfire. He thought he could destroy it before the *Serpent* arrived. He was wrong. Trust me on this. She knows our every weakness. But our strength lies in the time it takes for her orders to be carried out. We will sail to the west. I shall choose a landing place, and tell no one my choice until we are almost upon it."

"I shall come with you, Sofarita," said Ro.

"You are not a warrior, my friend. What will you do there?"

"I have other talents," said the little man. "And you will need them."

"Then let it be so. We will sail at midnight."

Viruk sat back in the open-topped carriage, his arm around the shoulders of the potter. "Over there," he said, "is the Great Library." Sadau had never seen such a building. He had thought the King's Palace in Morak was astounding, but this made it look like a mud hut. The Library was massive, two 30-foot-tall statues supporting a colossal lintel stone at the front. Upon the lintel was a statue of a seated man, his hands outstretched. It was the tallest building Sadau had ever seen.

"Who is the king seated there?" he asked.

"The Fourth Avatar Prime," said Viruk. "Or the Fifth. I really don't remember. The building has over three hundred rooms." A line of carriages waited outside the building and scores of servants were carrying chests inside.

"What are they doing?" asked Sadau. "Moving treasure?"

"Of a kind," said Viruk. "It is the strongest building in Egaru. Avatar wives and children are being moved here for safety. Now, would you like to see something really special?"

"Special?" queried Sadau. "It doesn't involve killing, does it?"

Viruk smiled and patted the man's back. "Why would you think that?"

"Because I didn't deliver the head. Because I ran away and hid."

"So, you think your death is so important to me that I would hire a carriage merely to transport you to your doom? Come now, potter. Had I wished you dead I would have done it before now."

"Thank you, lord," said Sadau, remembering how Viruk had reacted when the travellers had first come across the man Boru. Viruk had smiled at him, then drawn a dagger, leapt to the wagon, grabbed the man's hair and wrenched back his head. The blade was poised above Boru's throat when the king's voice rang out.

"Do not kill him, Viruk, for he is mine!"

The Avatar had stood frozen for a moment, then he had sheathed his blade, sat down beside Boru and placed his arm over the man's shoulder. Almost exactly in the manner he was doing now. "Good to see you again, Boru," he said, with a wide smile. "How have you been?"

Sadau shivered at the memory. The Avatar was insane. And here he was riding with him to the gods only knew where.

The carriage continued along a wide avenue, then on up a tree-lined road rising to a wooded hilltop. There were few houses here but the ones he could see were grand indeed. Viruk's home—as Sadau had expected—was the finest in the hills.

The carriage drew up outside the marble-fronted entrance. Viruk climbed down, paid the driver, then led Sadau through into the rear of the building. Here the Avatar threw open the doors to the garden. "Behold!" he said.

Sadau gazed out over a landscape of exquisite beauty, of matching colors and sweet scents. There were flowers here he had never seen before. He stood open-mouthed. It was like a vision of paradise.

"Well?" said Viruk.

"Heaven cannot look this fine," whispered Sadau. Ignoring the Avatar he walked out onto the paved pathway. A set of wide steps led up to the rockery. On each side of the steps were large terracotta pots filled with flowers.

Viruk strolled out alongside him. "This is my world," he said. His voice had changed, and Sadau looked at him sharply. Gone was the menace, and even his grey eyes seemed softer.

A middle-aged servant came walking along the path. Over his shoulder was a sack made from straw. It was full of weeds. He grinned as he saw Viruk. "The marsh marigolds are thriving, lord," he said. "You must see them. They are wonderful."

Leaving Sadau standing Viruk and the servant disappeared along the pathway.

The potter kicked off his shoes and wandered around the rockery. The ground was luxuriously damp. Moving on, he came to a small stream. He sat on the grass and lowered his feet into the water. For the first time in many days he felt at peace. Stretching out on the grass he closed his eyes.

When he awoke it was growing dark. He sat up and

rubbed his eyes. Then he scrambled to his feet, gathered his shoes and made his way back to the house. A servant saw him. He was a tall thin man, long-nosed, with sharp small eyes.

"Can I help you?" he asked primly, staring with obvious distaste at Sadau's travel-stained clothing.

"The Lord Viruk brought me to see his garden," said Sadau. "We travelled together." The servant seemed unimpressed. "We rescued the king."

"Which king would that be, sir?"

"King Ammon. We brought him to Egaru. The Lord Viruk took me around the city in a carriage. I saw the Library."

"Well, sir, the Lord Viruk has gone to the Council Chamber. And he did not mention that he had a guest."

"I expect he forgot me," said Sadau.

"Where are you staying, sir? I shall send for a carriage for you."

"I don't know. I sat in the Council Chamber for hours. Then the Lord Viruk brought me here."

At that moment the gardener entered. "There you are," he said. "I have been looking for you. My name is Kale." He thrust out a large hand.

"Sadau," said the potter.

"The Lord Viruk says you are to stay with me tonight. I have a small house about a mile away."

Sadau started to speak, then hesitated. "What is it?" asked Kale.

"I . . . er . . . haven't eaten anything in two days. Is there some food at your house?"

The gardener chuckled.

"The Lord Viruk is a fine gentleman, but he does not entertain guests very often." He glanced at the servant. "We'll have the rest of that pie, and some bread and salted butter," he said. "We'll eat it in the garden. Fetch us some lanterns."

To Sadau's surprise the servant merely bowed and backed away.

"You must be a very important man," he said. "I thought he was going to spit upon me."

Kale smiled. "I am merely a gardener. But I am the Lord Viruk's gardener. And believe me, that is almost like being a king."

The first Almec army arrived before the walls of Pagaru just before dusk. Across the bay Rael watched the message from the flashing lanterns high on Pagaru's eastern watchtower. "Four thousand men," said his aide Cation, reading the lights. "But no siege towers or other weapons in sight. They are making camp just out of zhi-bow range." On the south side of the river there was no sign yet of the enemy. "The Lady Mejana is coming, sir," said Cation.

Rael turned and offered the Vagar woman a slight bow. She was wearing a heavy cloak against the evening winds and she looked older, more tired than Rael had seen her. "I received your message," she said.

"Best not to speak of it, for the reasons I wrote in my letter."

She nodded. "There are two thousand militia men to call upon in this district," she told him. "I have assigned runners to every two hundred yards of the wall. If any of your officers need reinforcements the runners will fetch them."

"You have worked well and efficiently, Mejana. I commend you," said Rael absently. Once more he was staring out at the low-lying hills.

Mejana leaned against the battlements and closed her eyes in exhaustion. For the first time Rael saw her not as the leader of the murderous Pajists, but as a woman, weary and bereaved, doing her best in an impossible situation. Taking a crystal from his pouch he reached out to her. She opened her eyes and backed away. "I don't want your damned magic!" she said.

Rael sighed. "I understand. But you will need all your wits about you, lady, in the hours and days ahead."

"That might be so, Rael. But I will do my best in this frail, aching body. It is mine. Its strength is mine and its weakness also. All mine. But I thank you for your offer, and hope you will excuse my sharpness of tone."

Her words surprised him. He leaned forward, placing his hand on her shoulder. "Perhaps the coming excitement will help to revitalize you. But, failing that, I suggest you go home and sleep for a couple of hours. Even when they come it will take time to set up their battle lines and their weapons. I shall send a messenger for you."

"No," she said. "Already I am feeling a little better. Would you mind if I wait?"

"Not at all." Turning away from her he slipped the crystal back into his pouch. He caught Cation's eye and knew the officer had picked up the emanations from the crystal use. Rael smiled at his aide. The signal lights flashed again from Pagaru. Rael missed the first part of the message but caught it when it was repeated moments later. From their vantage point across the estuary the Pagaru defenders could see the army approaching Egaru.

"Many wagons," said Cation. "Mounted bronze? What does that mean?"

"Bronze weapons are mounted on the wagons," said Rael. "Signal back. Ask how many they can see."

Cation moved away. Mejana touched Rael's arm and pointed to the east. The first line of marching men could be seen silhouetted against the skyline. Mejana glanced along the wall then looked back at Rael. "You cannot hold a two-mile wall with two thousand men."

"No, I cannot," he agreed. "But they cannot destroy

the whole wall. Where they breach it is where the hard fighting will be."

Hearing movement behind him Rael turned to see Caprishan climbing to the ramparts. The fat man was breathing heavily and his face was sweat-drenched. "Did you get through to Anu?" asked Rael.

Caprishan nodded, then took a moment to catch his breath. "We shouldn't have," he said at last. "We were seen by a group of Almecs. A large group, maybe two hundred strong. I thought we would all be killed. But they drew back, offering us no harm. What do you make of that, Rael? It makes no sense to me."

"Nor me," said Mejana.

"It makes perfect sense," said Rael bitterly. "Think of what Anu is doing. He is recreating the White Pyramid. It will draw power from the sun and feed all our crystals. As Sofarita has told us, the Crystal Queen has an insatiable hunger. A great need. Once the pyramid is complete she will feed from that."

"Then we must stop Anu," said Mejana. "He must not complete it."

"I couldn't stop Anu even if I wanted to," said Rael. "But there will be no more supplies to him now and no way to contact him. That is why he requested the second chest. He will feed his workers with crystal power. He is cut off from us, Mejana. We can only hope to defeat the Almecs before he completes the pyramid."

"There is other news, cousin," said Caprishan.

"Good news, I hope."

Caprishan shrugged. "The king of the Mud People has fled the city. He requested a horse for a ride through the parks. Then he fled. Is that good or bad news?"

"Neither. There is no time to rally the tribes. We stand alone."

Caprishan gazed over the battlements at the advancing lines of men. In the dying light they looked inhuman, moving in harmony. From this distance they could have been a line of ants. Caprishan shivered. He did not like to think of insects. It made him itch. "Well-trained soldiers," he said. "Look at the way they move. Perfect discipline."

Behind the defenders the sun dipped low into a blood-red sea.

And *Serpent Seven* slid from view over the horizon.

Methras had insisted that Talaban stay in his old quarters and the Avatar had accepted gratefully. Now he stood on the small deck of the captain's cabin and gazed back at the towers of Egaru. They were bathed in the light of the dying sun. He felt a shiver run through him as the city faded into the distance, a brooding sense of farewell that he could not shake. Talaban had few friends among his Avatar comrades, but this did not mean that he disliked them. There were some people he had known for almost 200 years, men and women he respected, or admired. Above all else they were family. Almost all the Avatars who had survived the fall of the world were related.

Now he was leaving them to their fate.

It did not matter that his mission was to save them. At this moment it felt like desertion.

"Yet it is not," said Sofarita. Talaban turned slowly. She was standing by the desk, a goblet of water in her slender hand, a blue robe covering her exquisite form. Her hair had been pulled back into a ponytail and her neck was sleek and joyous to behold.

"Eavesdropping is said to be rude," he told her.

"I cannot always control the power," she told him. "Especially when the emotions of people close to me are raised."

"When you say close . . . ?" He looked at her and smiled.

"I mean in close proximity," she replied, a blush coming to her cheeks.

"Since you have read my mind you know my feelings for you. Do they cause you concern?"

Now it was her turn to smile. "No. It is sometimes pleasant to be . . . held in such high regard. What is it you desire about me, Talaban? My body? My talent? Both?"

He took her hand and kissed it. "I wish I could tell you," he said. "I wish I could find the words. But the first moment I saw you it was as if lightning had flashed in my mind. Since then you are always in my thoughts."

Gently she withdrew her hand. "We cannot be lovers," she told him. He thought he sensed regret in her voice. "My powers are growing daily. If I made love to you I think you would die. It is not only the crystals which I draw upon. I am beginning to . . ." she faltered. "Let us not speak of that." She walked out onto the small deck.

Egaru was almost out of sight now. Moving behind her he placed his hands on her shoulders. She shivered at the touch. "Do not fall in love with me, Talaban," she warned him.

He laughed then. "As if I had a choice."

"We all have choices," she said, turning her back to the rail. He started to step in closer. She raised a hand and he felt a pressure on his chest pushing him back, even though she was some feet from him. "Think about what you are doing," she advised him. "You see a woman, but I am no longer fully flesh and blood. I am turning to crystal. Slowly, it is true. But crystal nonetheless. Did you learn nothing from loving Chryssa?"

The question shocked him. "This is not about Chryssa."

"How strange then that you should fall in love with two crystal-cursed women."

"That is unfair. I did not know you were so afflicted when first I saw you. And when Chryssa and I were betrothed she was also fully flesh and blood. Do not play mind games with me, Sofarita. I believe I would have loved you had I ridden into your village and seen you working in the fields. If you doubt me, read my mind. Look into my heart. Do you see anything base there?"

"No," she admitted. "Nothing base, Talaban. You are a good man. But I am no longer the village girl. I am something far more, and greatly less." She winced suddenly. "I must go and rest," she said.

"You are in pain?"

"A little. It will pass."

He watched her move across the cabin. The sway of her hips made him feel breathless. When she had gone he sat down at the desk, his mind in turmoil. What he would not give to be able to hold her close, to slip that blue robe from her pale shoulders.

He heard a tapping at the door. "Come in," he called. Questor Ro entered.

"Am I disturbing you, Talaban?"

"Not at all. May I offer you some wine?" Ro shook his head and sat down. He seemed troubled.

"How did Sofarita seem to you?" he asked.

"In what way?"

"Her health."

"Fine," said Talaban. Then he paused. "She is in a little pain, I think."

Ro nodded. "It will increase. We may have a problem."

"I'm listening."

"Her power comes from her ability to draw on crystals. There were thousands of them in Egaru. Not so here. There is the chest, the zhi-bows, and our own personal stones. Rael had the Sunfire moved to the city walls. I have warned her of the danger of this journey and she is trying to block herself from drawing on the power here in the ship."

"And the problem?"

"Think of the Vagars who become addicted to narcotics. When they are separated from their opiates they become agitated, sometimes violent. They are filled with cravings. Some have even killed to gain coin to satisfy their desires. Sofarita is suffering now, and we have only just left the city. It will take three weeks to cross the ocean. If she cannot fight the craving she could drain the ship. Or worse."

"What could be worse, Ro?"

The Questor tugged at his beard. "We feed the crystals with human life. The gems merely hold the energy. If Sofarita became desperate we could all be crystal-drawn by her."

"She would not do that," said Talaban. "She is a fine woman."

"It may prove beyond her control," said Ro.

"What then do you suggest?"

"How fast can we travel?"

Talaban considered the question. "We are already moving at speed. Sailing vessels would take two months to cover the distance." He paused. "However, if we do not concern ourselves with conserving power, and if there are no sudden storms, we could make the journey in twenty days. But there are perils, Ro. Travelling at such speed if we struck a whale, or a reef, we could suffer serious damage."

"Twenty days is too long," said Ro. "Sofarita's hunger will overcome her before then."

"What time scale are we talking of here?" asked Talaban.

"I would guess three days."

Chapter Twenty-five

*The demons were mighty, their weapons awesome
to behold. Those who lived in the Heavenly City
gazed upon the Hell Horde and knew fear. Ra-Hel,
the king of the gods, watched them assemble. The
Queen of Death watched also from afar. Oh, my
brothers, this is a tale of heroes and of war. The
demons were as many as the leaves of the dark forest, but Ra-Hel was the god of the Sun. And he
called upon its power.*

From the *Sunset Song of the Anajo*

In a battle, Rael knew, timing was everything. Sofarita had told him that the Crystal Queen could observe and listen to all plans of action. She could then
inform her commander Cas-Coatl, and he would take
appropriate measures. This required time. It was the
only advantage Rael had.

The Almecs had massed their men just over a quarter
of a mile from Egaru's walls—just out of range of the
zhi-bows. Behind them, even farther back, were more
than 40 firing tubes of gleaming bronze. Even the Sunfire could not hit them at this distance, and even if it
could Rael no longer had the power for 40 charges.
With luck he might manage three.

Mejana and Pendar had joined Rael on the battlements. "Why don't they come?" asked Pendar nervously as the morning wore on.

"They will," said Rael.

At that moment the bronze tubes loosed their fireballs. They sailed high over the battle lines, curving down to strike the wall at three different places. Stone ramparts were smashed, men hurled to their deaths. A gaping crack appeared and a section of wall fell away some 300 yards to Rael's right. Peering over the battlements Rael saw the Almec engineers recalibrating their weapons. Now all the fireballs rained down on that one spot. The 40-foot-high wall withstood twelve of the explosions. Then it collapsed, creating a 30-foot gap through which the enemy could invade the city.

Rael shouted instructions down to Goray and Cation below. A wagon was hauled into place and twenty men rushed forward to unload it. The bronze Sunfire from *Serpent Seven* was carried, in sections, up to the ramparts. Four soldiers hefted the base and gear wheels and these were set on a platform alongside Rael. Then the barrel was strapped into place, and lastly Rael and Cation connected the golden wires from the power unit. Rael swung the Sunfire to point at the earthworks barrier which prevented the Luan from flooding in the rainy season.

The machine began to vibrate.

Rael glanced nervously at the line of Almec firing tubes. They were silent for the moment, but engineers were recalibrating three of them. Rael knew that within minutes fireballs would be hurled in his direction. "You'd better get back," he told Mejana. "We will be the targets now."

She shook her head and stayed where she was.

The Almec army was marching forward in a broad line towards the hole in the city wall.

The Sunfire ceased vibrating. Rael sighted the weapon on one section of earthworks and, closing his eyes, pulled the firing lever. The massive bolt struck the earthworks. For a moment nothing happened. Then, deep within the barrier the bolt exploded. An enormous cloud of dust and earth billowed up. The freed waters of the Luan began to pour through the gap, gushing down over the plain. The power of the river tore away a 60-foot section of the barrier and the flood began.

The Almecs continued to march. The water flowed over their feet. Holding their fire-clubs high the advancing soldiers came closer and closer to the gap.

Rael swung the Sunfire again. "Lift the rear," he called out to Goray and Cation. With the barrel resting on the crenellated battlements the two men, and three other soldiers, grabbed the rear section and lifted it high.

To Mejana their actions seemed almost comical. Thousands of men were about to attack them and the Avatar General was wasting his time with a single weapon. Even if he struck the advancing lines it would kill perhaps twenty men.

Two fireballs were loosed. They sailed high then dropped towards the battlements. The first thundered against the ramparts, sending a tremor along the wall. The second flew over the defenders, crashing against the roof of a warehouse, and setting it ablaze.

Rael put his hand on the lever of the Sunfire and looked down on the men splashing their way towards the city. Mejana came alongside him.

"What is it you are planning?" she asked him.

The vibration in the weapon ceased. "Close your eyes," said Rael softly. Then he fired the weapon.

The bolt flashed down, missing the first line of marching soldiers and striking the water behind them. Mejana opened her eyes—and saw the horror that followed. Blue sparks rippled out from the point of impact, dancing across the water. Hundreds of Almecs began to jerk spasmodically. Blue flames spread over them. Their clothing caught fire, their weapons discharged. Everywhere men were dying. The advance faltered.

"Give me one more! Just one!" shouted Rael, gazing up at the skies.

Three more fireballs exploded close by. Mejana was hurled from her feet by the blast. Dazed, she struggled to rise. Two of the Avatars were down, their white cloaks blazing. Pendar, pulling off his own cloak, ran to them, smothering the flames. Rael rose up alongside the Sunfire. The left side of his face was horribly burned. With a grunt of pain and effort he swung the Sunfire. "Someone lift it!" he shouted. Cation, Pendar and Mejana ran to him. Together they grabbed the rear and hoisted the Sunfire high. Rael pulled the firing lever.

Another bolt struck the water, this time further back.

Once again the blue fire rippled out. Turning, the Almecs started to flee the field. More than 200 died in the second blast.

"There's time for another!" said Rael. His face was horribly disfigured, the flesh stripped away. His left arm was also badly blistered and black.

"No, sir," said Cation. "We will die if we stay here."

"You coward!" shouted Rael.

"He is not a coward," said Mejana. "Now do as you are bid!" Taking his right arm she pulled him forward. Rael sagged against her. Together she and Cation carried him to the rampart steps. Behind them Pendar was helping Goray to his feet. The Avatar had been blinded by the last fireball. Pendar got him to the safety of the steps just as the battlements blew apart. The Sunfire was sent spiralling into the air, its power chest destroyed.

Below the wall Cation and Mejana lowered Rael to the ground. Cation produced a green crystal, which he held to the General's burnt face. Mejana watched as the skin began to repair, the inflammation dying down. The swelling around his eye sank back, the blisters on his flesh receding. Rael sighed. Reaching up he took Cation's arm. "I am sorry for what I called you," he said.

"It was nothing," said Cation. "Lie back. Relax. Let the crystals do their work."

Just beyond them Pendar was holding a crystal above Goray's ruined eyes. Cation began the healing process on the General's burnt arm, then swung to Goray. He paused as he saw Pendar at work. For a moment there was anger, then it faded. Moving alongside the young Vagar he added his own crystal to the process. "Try not to think of healing," he advised him. "Merely concentrate on what *should* be. See good, clean skin. Picture him as he was. And let the crystal do its work."

"Thank you," said Pendar.

Goray groaned and opened his eyes. "I can see," he said. Lifting his hand he took hold of Pendar's shoulder. "You have my gratitude, boy," he said.

A soldier on the ramparts shouted down. "Someone is coming. Fetch the Questor General!"

Cation moved back alongside Rael, and helped him rise. Together they climbed the rampart steps, clambering over the fallen masonry.

Cas-Coatl was moving toward the wall, his hands clasped behind his back. He could have been out for a stroll, and showed no tension as he walked closer and closer towards the defenders, ignoring the zhi-bows trained upon him.

"What is it you want, Almec?" shouted Rael.

"We need to talk, Avatar. Do I have your permission to enter the city?"

"You do," said Rael. He, Cation and Mejana walked

along the ramparts, then down the last set of steps before the gaping hole in the wall. Water was ankle-deep here and Cas-Coatl waded through it to stand before the Questor General.

"Can we talk somewhere where it is dry?" he asked.

"Here is fine," said Rael. "Have you come to surrender?"

Cas-Coatl smiled with genuine humor. "We need to talk together, man to man," he said. "Just you and I."

"Very well," said Rael. "Follow me." The two men walked past the ruined wall to a building close by. Pushing open the door Rael entered the guard-house. Three Vagar soldiers were sitting in the narrow room eating a breakfast of flat-baked bread and mutton. They scrambled to their feet as the General strode in. "My apologies to you," said Rael. "But I would be grateful if you would allow us some privacy." Grabbing their food the men bowed, then left. "Sit down," said Rael.

Cas-Coatl did so. Rael stared hard at the man's glass-like brows and cheekbones. "How is it that you survived being crystal-wed?"

"The Crystal Queen needs me. She saved me, and for that I serve her."

"My daughter was crystal-wed. For her there was no savior."

Cas-Coatl said nothing, and the two men sat in silence for several moments. Then Rael spoke. "Why are you here, Almec?"

"You were right and I was wrong," said Cas-Coatl. "I did underestimate you. You are not merely talented sub-humans. You are, in fact, Almecs. Or perhaps we are Avatars," he said with a smile. "My queen believes we should unite. We have much to offer you, and you can enrich us."

"And, of course, I am to believe this?" said Rael.

"It is the simple truth, Rael. I have the weapons to destroy this city utterly. I do not need to lie to you."

"Somehow I do not see myself travelling the world merely to rip out people's hearts," Rael told him.

"Nor I. Some sacrifice is essential, in order to keep the lower orders in their place. But this slaughter does not sit well with me—nor with my queen. It is, sadly, necessary at this time. But once Anu completes his pyramid there will be no need of such mass extermination. We are brothers, you and I. I do not wish to see you Avatars die."

"And if we agree?"

"My troops will enter the twin cities. No Avatar will be harmed."

"The Vagars?"

"Anu's pyramid is not yet complete. And my queen is hungry. But do not concern yourself with sub-humans, Rael. If you have favorites among them, take them to your home. They will be spared."

"This is not a decision I can make alone, Cas-Coatl. I will need to call my people together."

"Of course. You have until dawn to make a decision. I urge you to make it a wise one."

Talaban was deeply troubled. Several times now he had gone to Sofarita's cabin. She had ordered him to leave her in peace, and he had heard her groans of pain. Ro had warned him she would not withstand a twenty-day trip, and Talaban now believed this to be true.

There was no way to increase the speed of the *Serpent*. Talaban sat in his cabin running the problem through his mind again and again, seeking a solution.

Ro came to him, and together they discussed methods of increasing the power, calculating the effect of reducing the weight by throwing overboard every unnecessary item. But even if they emptied the ship of furniture and weaponry, and ordered every crew member over the side they could not decrease the time needed by more than a day.

Touchstone arrived at dusk, but he could offer no solutions, and sat silently as they spoke.

"If Anu were here he could speed the Dance of Time," said Ro.

"And if the ship had wings we would not be in peril," snapped Talaban. He was instantly contrite. "I am sorry, cousin. I am tired and on edge."

"We bring him," said Touchstone.

"Bring who?" responded Talaban.

"This Holy One."

Talaban rubbed at his eyes and fought for calm. "Are you suggesting that we turn back and ask Anu to travel with us?"

"No," replied the tribesman. "Magic not in body. Magic in spirit. We fetch spirit."

"And how do you intend to achieve this . . . this miracle?" asked Ro.

"One-Eyed-Fox," said Touchstone, looking directly at Talaban. "Like before. We fly."

"The last time almost killed both of us," said the warrior. "But I agree. It is the only way."

Touchstone moved into the center of the cabin and sat cross-legged on the rug. Talaban sat opposite him. Placing their hands on each other's shoulders they lowered their heads until their brows touched.

Relaxing his mind Talaban flowed into the trance state, seeking focus without concentration, the melding of opposites, the closing of the circle. As before, he felt himself moving, spinning. Colors danced in his mind, swirling rainbows passing over, around and through him. And then again he heard the music, the drumbeat of the universe, the whispering of cosmic winds.

Once more he and Touchstone were as one, and together they called out for the One-Eyed-Fox, chanting his name in time to the drumbeat, creating a song that echoed out across the void.

Time had no meaning now, and the chant continued. The swirling colors brightened, merging into blue—the blue of a summer sky. Talaban gazed down and saw a forest below them. A swirl of grey smoke lifted from the forest, lazily drifting toward them. As it reached the floating figures it coalesced into the shape of a warrior. "What is it that you need, my brothers?" asked the One-Eyed-Fox.

Talaban told him. Reaching out, the figure of smoke took hold of their hands, and again the colors blazed around them. This time when they faded the scene which sprang into life around them was night dark. They were within a small hut, where an old man was kneeling on a prayer mat.

He glanced up as they arrived. Talaban was shocked at his appearance. He was incredibly frail and his hands trembled. A blue aura shimmered around him and the spirit of Anu rose.

"I know what you need," he said.

"Can you help us?" asked Talaban.

"I can, Talaban, but there is a high price to pay."

"What price?"

Anu's spirit hand reached out, touching Talaban's brow. The words Anu then spoke were heard by him alone. "The Music is incredibly powerful, and can be immensely destructive. I learned to control it during a five-hundred-year apprenticeship. I cannot leave here and create a second spell. I do not have the strength. You do and you can. I can implant the knowledge in you, and you can cast the Music into the *Serpent*. But the price will be your life. I cannot teach you in hours what took me five centuries. And so the Music will eat away at you like a cancer. Your life span will be measured in days. You understand?"

"I do."

"Are you willing to die, Talaban?"

The warrior thought of the woman in pain on the *Serpent*, and of the terrible perils facing his people. "I am," he said, simply.

"Then let it be so."

Heat flowed from Anu's spirit fingers, seeping into Talaban's mind. It was as if all the random, brilliant colors of the universe were exploding within his skull. He reeled back. Images flowered in his brain, then the Music began, a majestic symphony that flowed backward, millions of strands joining together, becoming ever more simple, until, in the end, he could hear only twelve notes, then five, then three and finally one. Anu spoke again. "When you return to the ship, find a flute. Almost every sailor will have one. Take it to the Heart Room. And let the Music flow over the chest. You will see the crystals brighten, as if flames had burst into life within them. Then the Dance will begin."

"How swiftly can we make the crossing?" asked Talaban.

"Two days."

"And how long will I live after that?"

Anu was silent for a moment. "Perhaps a week."

"I thank you, Holy One."

"We will meet again, Talaban. On the journey beyond life."

He removed his hand. The world twisted, rainbows blazing in Talaban's mind. He awoke with a start. Touchstone drew back from him. Questor Ro moved alongside. "Did you find Anu? Did you bring him back?"

"We found him," said Talaban, pushing himself to

his feet. "Now I must find a flute," he said. Slowly he walked across the cabin, opened the door, and left.

Ro swung towards Touchstone. "What happened?"

"Not know all. Holy One only spoke him."

"So when will we reach the coast?"

"Two days," said Touchstone.

"Yes!" shouted Ro, punching the air. Then he looked at Touchstone, and saw that the tribesman did not share his enthusiasm. "What is wrong?" asked Ro, speaking now in Anajo. "Is there something else?"

Touchstone shrugged. "I do not know, but my heart is heavy, my soul burdened."

Sofarita lay on the floor of her cabin, her knees drawn up, her arms hugging her body. She was trembling uncontrollably, her frame racked by a series of cramps that caused her to jerk spasmodically.

Never in her short life had she suffered such pain or felt such a terrible hunger. It was as if she stood starving at the center of a feast, fine food all around her, exquisite delicacies to melt with flavor upon the tongue. Sofarita groaned.

Another cramp struck her belly and she cried out. She felt suddenly cold and began to shiver. Struggling to her knees she crawled to the bed. The blankets were thick but they offered her no respite. Through her pain she recalled the attack by Almeia and how Ro had warmed her with his body.

This was different. Now she was under attack from her own starving system.

Ro had warned her of the dangers of such a journey, separated from the city's crystals, but she had not imagined the symptoms would be so severe. Her mind screamed at her to take just a little energy from the ship's chest. Just a tiny morsel . . .

She resisted the temptation, knowing that if she allowed herself to follow her desires she would drain the ship in an instant.

When the pain first started she had attempted to flee it by allowing her spirit to soar free. But she could not. The cramps cut through her concentration, trapping her within this hurting cage of flesh and bone.

Talaban had come to her cabin twice that day but she had refused to open the door. Even through the wood she could feel the sweet pulsing of his life force. Her flaring hunger terrified her.

She found herself thinking about members of the crew and how some of them were unpleasant or dishonest. As she had come aboard she had felt their thoughts. Base men, cruel to their families. No one would miss them, she thought.

No! Their lives are their own. I have no right!

You have every right. You are a goddess! You are needed. They are not. If their lives are lost so that the Crystal Queen can be destroyed, then they will have served a greater purpose.

The argument was compelling.

Sitting up she wrapped the blanket around her shoulders and began to plan how to reach the worst of the men. Another cramp struck her, this time with needles of fire that made her arch her back and cry out.

She was hot now, burning with fever. Throwing back the blanket she moved to the water jug and filled a goblet, draining it swiftly.

The door opened and Questor Ro stepped inside. "Go away," she said. "I have . . . work to do."

"What work, Sofarita?"

"Go away, I said!" Her hand shot up. Ro was lifted from his feet and slammed back into the cabin wall. He slid to the floor. Grabbing the door frame he hauled himself upright.

"I know you are suffering," he said. "But it will soon be over. Anu has shown Talaban how to speed the Dance of Time. We will cross the ocean in only two days."

"I need . . . to feed!" Walking past him she pictured the faces of the men she would destroy.

"Like Almeia needs to feed," said Ro. "Perhaps we should bring a child to you and bury it for you, alive and screaming."

Sofarita paused in the doorway. "Do not make me angry, Ro."

"Even if you drain Almeia and end her evil, it will be as nothing if you become like her," he said. "You are better than that, Sofarita. Stronger. But if you need a life, take mine. It is yours. I offer it freely."

She swung toward him. "Why? Why would you offer this?"

"To prevent you from murder."

She looked at him then and, for a moment, the pain eased.

"Evil is like a poison," he said. "That is why we cannot use it. To defeat evil with its own weapons, only replaces one evil with another. I believe the Source has blessed you with power. It must not be stained or sullied."

"What can I do? The yearning is tearing at me."

"We will be there soon. You need to be strong."

"And what happens when—and if—I drain Almeia's power? What will become of me then?"

"Anu's pyramid will be complete. That will feed you."

She laughed at him, the sound bitter and derisive. "Anu's pyramid will kill me!" she shouted. "It will rip my soul from me." As soon as she had spoken the words she blanched. "No!" she whispered. "What have I done?"

Ro stood by silently, staring at her stricken face.

"I have doomed them all," she whispered. "Almeia was here. She heard me! Oh sweet Heaven!"

"She knows what?" asked Ro.

"Anu's pyramid is not intended to feed the crystals but to drain them utterly. He is building a weapon against Almeia. This journey was merely a distraction, to keep her energies focused on me." Suddenly she cried out, as another spasm of pain tore into her. "I cannot . . . survive . . . without feeding, Ro!"

Tenderly he took her hand. "Sit with me on the floor. Link with me as I move through the Six Rituals. We will find calm. We will win, Sofarita. Let your pain and your need flow into me and we will fight it together."

"It will destroy you," she whispered.

"We will see," he said.

They sat together on the rug, hand in hand.

The Great Hall of the Questors was rarely used, save for ceremonial functions or the funeral orations—thankfully rare—of those Avatars who died after centuries of service. Situated beneath the Great Library the vast circular hall had high arched windows and banks of seats around the walls. It had been built to stage plays for guests of the ambassador to the Avatar Prime and could accommodate 800 people.

Now it was scarcely half-full as all of the surviving Avatars and their families gathered to listen to the words of the Questor General. Rael stood in the center of the hall, gazing at the people as they took up their seats. Rarely were all of the Avatars gathered together, and only at times like this did it come home to him how few they were. Six of the women held newborn babes. A mere six. Elsewhere the younger children were playing in the high gallery watched over by two of the mothers.

When at last all were gathered—save the twenty men sailing with the *Serpent*—Rael called for silence. Then he told them all of the offer made by Cas-Coatl. Unity with the Almecs. A new life with a brother race. He made it clear to them that he believed the assurances given by the Almec. Then he fell silent for a moment.

"I shall speak again at the close of the debate," he said. "But now I shall take questions."

"What changed their minds, Rael?" asked Niclin.

"I believe the most significant factor is the work of Anu. The Crystal Queen learned of his talents and knows that by absorbing his wisdom and his knowledge she can assure herself of life eternal."

"What was it that stopped you agreeing at once?" asked Caprishan.

"As I said, I shall speak later."

High at the back of the hall Mirani raised her hand.

"I recognize the Lady Mirani," said Rael.

"What are the Almecs' intentions toward the peoples of the twin cities? It is my understanding that these killers leave only destruction in their wake."

"They intend to kill all of the Vagars," said Rael, his voice even. "Cas-Coatl maintains that the Crystal Queen needs this sustenance until such time as Anu's pyramid begins to generate power."

"So they are offering us our lives in return for utter betrayal?"

"Indeed they are," said Rael. Mirani met his gaze, and fell silent.

"Has Anu been apprised of the situation?" asked another man, sitting close to the front.

"We have no way to contact him," said Rael.

The blue-bearded Goray raised his hand. Rael gestured for him to speak. "As you know," he began, "I am one of the oldest here. I have seen many wars and a

host of battles. My question is this: do you, Questor
General, believe this war can be won?"

"I believe it can be won," said Rael.

"Then I have a second question. What becomes of us
if we do win? Where do we go?"

"I cannot say, Goray. For I do not know. Are there
any other questions?"

Niclin rose. "Can we win back power once Anu's
work is completed?"

"I do not believe that we can," admitted Rael. "Our
days of pre-eminence here are over. Worse still, I do not
believe the Vagars will allow us to merely go on as immortals in their midst. There will be those who seek revenge against us for what they perceive as past wrongs.
There will be others who envy our immortality. No. If
we do win this war we must make our home elsewhere."

"Unless we join with the Almecs," said Caprishan.

"Indeed so," agreed Rael.

No one spoke, and Rael waited for several heartbeats. "Now," he said, "it is time to debate the question
facing us. As is our custom I shall ask two of our number to address us, one in favor of joining with the
Almecs, one against. I will ask Questor Caprishan to
put forward reasons in favor of accepting Cas-Coatl's
offer."

Caprishan stood, walked out to the center of the
floor and turned to face his fellow Avatars.

"It seems to me," he said, "that there is little need to
debate this issue. We are no longer fighting for our
homes and our land, for we have no land and our
homes and possessions will be forfeit should we succeed
against the Almecs.

"But let us put aside thoughts of the war and the
loved ones we have lost since it began. Let us look instead at our first thoughts concerning the Almecs. Since

we first learned of them we knew they were Avatars like ourselves. We hoped that they would accept us as brothers and join with us in maintaining control of this savage world. That was our hope then. Why should that be changed? What prospects have we if the war goes on? To become an exiled people—if indeed the Vagars do not seek to murder us when the war is won? To sail the seas and set up dirt camps on some foreign shore? To grub in the earth like farmers? How many of us know how to plant crops and gather them? How many can raise cattle, and butcher them? Does anyone here know how to build a house, or weave a cloth, or make a chair?

"We are gods, my friends. Gods do not have to concern themselves with such grubby detail. We have servants to minister to us and serfs to farm the land.

"So, the Almecs need to kill a few Vagars. Why should that concern us? Their lives are measured in a few heartbeats. Ours are almost eternal.

"The simple truth is that if we defeat the Almecs we defeat ourselves. Therefore we should join with them."

He was widely applauded as he strode to his seat. Rael moved back to the center. "I ask Viruk to speak in rebuttal," he said.

Viruk, sitting two rows back, looked startled. He rose and walked down the steps to where Rael waited. "But I agree with Caprishan," he whispered. "Why choose me?"

"Because you are a gardener," said Rael, moving away.

Viruk stood in the center of the hall looking at the silent Avatars in the bank of seats before him. He had sat listening to Caprishan and had agreed with every word. Debating the issue seemed pointless. And yet Rael had asked him to speak in rebuttal. The Questor

General had chosen him. Viruk felt honored, for Rael was the one man he respected above all others. In many ways he loved him as he had never loved his own father. And it was important to Viruk that he did not let him down.

They were waiting for him to speak and he had no idea what he was going to say. Rael's words meant nothing to him. What did gardening have to do with an Almec—Avatar alliance?

"I think our cousin is a little tongue-tied," said Caprishan. Nervous laughter rippled out. Viruk gave a wide smile. And in that moment he knew what Rael required of him.

"I was thinking of my garden," he said. "Of all the plants and shrubs and insects and worms. Did you know that the humble worm is vital, for its tunnels allow air to penetrate and feed the earth? The flying insects which plague us in the city during the heat of summer pollinate the plants, allowing them to seed and enchant future generations. Everything in my garden speaks of harmony and of continued life and growth. Each has its purpose in the great scheme. But I am a ruthless gardener. Those plants which fail to flower are ripped out with the weeds. Thus my garden thrives.

"Every plant has its role to play, a scent to draw butterflies and aid pollination, a wide leaf to gather moisture and provide shade for the earth. And when their leaves and petals wither, they go down to the earth to feed the ground for future generations of blooms."

His voice rang out. "This land, this planet, is a garden. We are like plants upon it. But what kind of plants are we? Two thousand years ago an Avatar developed a script through which people could communicate without speech. Fifteen hundred years ago another Avatar discovered the link between certain crystals and sunlight. Twelve hundred years ago three mathematicians,

seeking the secrets of the stars, discovered the Great
Song. Its music helped build the wonders of the lost
continent. We were valued plants in the garden then,
my friends. We taught the world to write and farmers
how to feed the land and grow better crops. We conquered disease and finally death itself. We were like
fruit trees growing from naked rock. We fed the world
with our knowledge." He paused, and scanned his audience.

"But that was then. What are we now, we innovators,
we inventors, we *Questors*? For what do we quest?
What do we offer this garden? We stand facing annihilation, and the only argument that my cousin Caprishan
can offer for joining with the enemy is that we are now
so useless that we cannot possibly survive alone. We,
who gave the world its civilization, cannot make a
chair. We, who clothed the tribes with knowledge, cannot weave a cloth. What then is our purpose in this garden land? We are no longer fruit, nor even flowers. We
are straw, long dead and dried out.

"And make no mistake, Avatars. The Almecs are the
same. They do not give to the world. They take. They
do not feed, they hunger. Yes, they are like us, and like
us the Gardener will weed them, casting them out.

"And I have an answer to Caprishan's questions. Yes,
I can grow crops, and yes, I can raise and butcher cattle.
And I *have* made chairs and tables and even a bed to
sleep upon. No, I cannot weave cloth. But if I need to I
will learn.

"I put it to this gathering that we reject the Almecs'
offer."

The audience sat in stunned silence as he returned to
his seat.

Rael returned to his place in the center. "My thanks
to my esteemed cousins. It is left now for me to speak as
the Questor General. We have, through these past de-

cades, managed to convince ourselves that the Vagars
are sub-humans and natural slaves for us. We have seen
ourselves as benevolent parents, overseeing a land peopled by unruly children. The first point, as I have come
to realize during these past days, is a fallacy. The second
is a conceit. But it is that second point on which I would
like to dwell. If we are, indeed, benevolent parents, then
do we allow our children to be slaughtered? I think not.

"Despite their knowledge and their advanced civilization the Almecs have descended into evil. They do not
see themselves in this light, I am sure. But that is what
they are, nonetheless. To join with them would be to
embrace that evil, to accept its validity in our lives. I
cannot in all conscience consider such an action. It is
my intention to fight them, and to defeat them. If this
gathering votes to join with the Almecs I shall renounce
my Avatar heritage, surrender my crystals and fight
alongside the Vagars." He fell silent for a moment, then
took a deep breath. "This gathering is suspended for
three hours to allow you all to discuss the matter
among yourselves. We will assemble again at midnight
and a vote will be taken.

"In the meantime would those among you who remain soldiers of the empire walk with me to the Museum armory."

One hundred and twelve Avatars rose from their
seats. Mirani moved to stand beside him. Taking his
arm she said, "I am so proud of you, Rael. I have never
loved you more than I do at this moment."

Leaning down he kissed her. "As long as you are beside me I fear nothing," he said.

"Then that is where I will always be," she promised.

The armory was a dank cold place, windowless and
deserted. Dust-laden cobwebs hung on the arches and

upon the suits of armor flanking the grey walls. Dust was also heavy in the air as Rael led his soldiers down into the depths of the building. Lanterns had been lit in the stairwells and in the armory itself, and the silver armor on display glittered in the dull red light.

"These battle suits were once worn by the royal guards of the Avatar Prime," said the Questor General. "They were crafted two thousand years ago and last used in the Crystal Wars." Viruk strode to the nearest suit of armor. It had been set upon a wooden frame, the silver-winged helm perched on the top. Lifting the helm clear he brushed away the webs and examined it. It was lighter than he expected and crafted from a metal unknown to him. It had a curved visor that slid down to shield a warrior's face and a long, curved neck guard at the base. The breastplate was created using bands of silver over a leather undershirt, and thigh guards and greaves were fashioned over leather leggings.

"They are too bulky for the men to wear," Viruk said.

"I was not intending them for use in defense," Rael told him. The Questor General climbed to a table and turned back towards the gathered men. "The Almecs' superiority rests in their thunder clubs and the tubes which unleash the fireballs. We know that they are powered by black dust. Great amounts of it. If we can destroy that power source then the Vagars will merely be facing eight thousand warriors with swords."

"Merely?" put in Viruk. "And you say the *Vagars* will be facing. What is it you are suggesting, cousin?"

"I intend to repeat the strategy used by Banel in the last battle of the Crystal Wars." A murmur started up among the soldiers. "Do not speak of it aloud," he warned them. "We cannot know whether the Crystal Queen is observing us."

Goray stepped forward. "You say you intend to repeat the strategy, Rael. But what if our people vote to join the Almecs?"

"Do you think they will?" countered Rael. Goray was silent.

"Of course they will," said Viruk. "You think the fatted calf would vote for slaughter?"

"I am hoping that my people will act with honor," said the Questor General.

Viruk laughed. "I love you, cousin," he said, "but you have become a romantic. Fear not, I will follow you on Banel's path."

"And I," said Goray.

No one else spoke. Rael looked at his soldiers' faces in the lantern light and realized that Viruk had accurately gauged the feeling of the Avatars. None of them was willing to continue the battle. Fat Caprishan stood silently at the back. "I will not need the armor," he said.

"None of the suits would fit you, you fat bastard," said Viruk.

At that moment the sound of thunder echoed high above them, followed by a series of explosions that caused huge cracks to appear in the ceiling of the armory.

"Sweet Heaven, we are under attack!" shouted Goray.

"Stand fast!" bellowed Rael. "We are under the building here. Nothing can reach us!"

Scores of explosions sounded, one after the other, as if the world were ending above them in fire and death.

After what seemed an age the noise subsided.

Rael led his men up the stairs. They were blocked by fallen masonry. Working steadily the Avatars dragged clear the stones. Above them they could see moonlight. Rael was the first to push himself out into the ruins of what had once been the Great Library. The statue of the

Avatar Prime had fallen, the head smashed into a dozen pieces. Fires were burning all around and bodies were scattered among the broken rocks.

Vagar troops appeared, led by Mejana and Pendar. Rael walked out to meet them.

"It was so sudden," said Mejana. "The Almecs began to move their fire tubes about two hours ago. They concentrated them then began loosing their fireballs. We thought they were attacking the walls, but every missile was aimed at the Library. There was nothing we could do."

"Did anyone get out?" he asked her.

"Three children were carried clear. One died, the others are only shocked." Rael said no more, but ran into the ruins with the other Avatars, and began tearing at the fallen rocks.

As the night wore on more and more bodies were pulled from the wreckage. By dawn the scale of the massacre became known. Two hundred and seventeen Avatars had died, or were still missing. Only four of the women and two of the children had escaped.

Rael found Mirani just before dawn. She had tried to shield two children from falling masonry. Their bodies were beneath hers, her arms around them. Avatars and Vagars worked together to clear away the stones. Rael lifted her body clear and sat back on the rubble, cradling her to him. He did not speak, and his soul was too heavy for weeping. He just held her close and rocked to and fro.

Some distance away, exhausted, Mejana sat and watched his silent grief.

Two stretcher bearers stood by nervously, afraid to approach Rael. Mejana walked across to the Questor General. "It is time to let her go," she said. Rael looked up at her. He did not speak. Then he kissed Mirani one last time and carried her to the stretcher.

With the rising of the morning sun Rael gathered his last soldiers, and together—all save Caprishan—they returned to the armory and clothed themselves in the silver armor of the Crystal Wars.

For Ro it was a different kind of pain. There was no longing involved in it, no yearning to draw the life from others. For him it was the pain of despair, of bereavement and loss, allied to an aching of the limbs that made him feel his muscles were slowly tearing themselves apart.

He sat cross-legged upon the rug holding onto Sofarita's hands. His fingers were numb now, his thoughts almost desolate. Tears fell from his eyes and he would have welcomed death like an old friend. She sensed his increasing despair and allowed the pain to flow back inside her. Ro sighed with the release from agony.

And so, locked into the rituals of the Avatar Prime, they endured the journey, sharing the pain, each holding to it for as long as possible, then allowing the other to take up the burden.

On the evening of the third day, as the *Serpent* approached the land mass of the western continent, Sofarita felt the power returning to her. It came like a breath of sweet breeze, faint crystal energies flowing over her. She drank them in. They tasted of life.

Drawing in a deep breath she released Ro's hands. He opened his eyes, smiled at her, then slumped to the floor, exhausted. Reaching forward she tenderly stroked his cheek, then she rose and stretched. Moving from the cabin to the central deck she stood in the last light of sunset and watched the gulls wheel and dive over the ship.

Talaban saw her there and moved alongside her. "How are you faring, lady?" he asked her.

"Ro saved me," she said.

"I know. I came to your cabin many times and saw the two of you sitting there. He is a good man."

"The very best," she said.

Without another word she moved away and sat on a coil of rope by the port deck rail. Releasing her spirit she soared high over the distant bay, across the darkening land and its forests and plains, seeking out the One-Eyed-Fox. The encampment she had first encountered was in ruins now. Blackened tent poles flanked the river and several bodies lay on the ground. But there had been no wholesale massacre. The Anajo had largely escaped the attack. She searched the area, and found a mass grave near the tree line. Allowing her spirit to sink beneath the earth she found the grave contained around forty bodies of Almec warriors.

The Anajo had not only survived, but had inflicted heavy losses upon the enemy.

As high as a hunting eagle Sofarita flew in a wide circle over the land seeking sign of movement. She saw an Almec column of close to 500 men moving toward the east. As she flew toward it she saw a second, smaller force running through the trees two miles ahead. Sofarita sped over them. They were Anajo, seventeen men and three women. Their faces were smeared red and blue and they carried short hunting bows and quivers. In their belts were battleaxes made of flint.

As she came closer the first of the twenty runners paused and looked up. He was a middle-aged man, with deeply tanned skin and deep-set brown eyes. He raised his hand, palm outwards toward her, and smiled. Then he knelt, folded his arms across his chest, his spirit rising from his body.

"It is good to see you, my sister," he said.

"Your enemies are close behind," she told him.

"They will not catch us until we wish them to. Is Touch-the-Moon with you?"

"Yes. And Talaban."

"Aiya!" he said, his tone triumphant. "That is good. I have my wolf soldiers with me. Come ashore in the bay and head southwest towards the highest mountain. We will meet you there. We will fight the last battle, yes?"

"There is no need," she told him. "The Crystal Queen knows about Anu and his pyramid. My journey here is now futile."

"Not so, my sister. I have walked the Grey Road. I have seen. She is trying to pierce the magic around his encampment. She seeks to stop him before he completes his work. You can drain her power. You can give Anu time. Nothing is futile. Go to the mountain. We will draw the Almecs away from you." He paused and sorrow touched his face. "First, though, fly to your city of stone. Much has happened there. The Spirits of Death fly over it and the Ravens wait for the heroes to ride. I will see you on the mountain." Fading back into his body he waved a farewell, then led his runners away to the north.

Sofarita returned to the ship, told Talaban to head for the bay, then journeyed again to Egaru.

When she returned less than half an hour later she found Ro and Talaban and Touchstone waiting. The *Serpent* was at anchor in the bay, and from here she could see the tall mountains to the southwest. "That is where we must go," she said. "The One-Eyed-Fox awaits us there."

"How many warriors does he have?" asked Talaban.

"Twenty."

"Did you see any Almecs?"

"Hundreds," she said. Talaban swore softly.

"I promised Rael to send the ship and its crew back to Egaru. But we will sorely need the ship's twenty

Avatar bowmen. Is there time for you to contact him and request them?"

"No," she said, her voice hard. "But they will be neither needed, nor welcome, at Egaru. Use them as you will."

"What does that mean?" he asked her.

"I do not wish to speak of it yet. Let us get ashore."

"You think they are going to betray us?" asked Pendar, as the 112 Avatars rode through the southern gates heading along the coastal road. Mejana leaned on the parapet and watched the riders. She did not answer. How fine they look in their silver armor, she thought, like heroes of legend. It was confusing to see them like this. These were the evil men who had dominated her people, extending their own lives by draining the life force of others. The same men who had taken her daughter, leaving her senile and spent. Yet now the sun glittered upon them, and they were riding to their deaths to save the cities. Mejana no longer knew what to think or feel. She had plotted their downfall for so long, so many lonely bitter years.

And here was the day.

There was no feeling of triumph in the air, no heady joy. This was not as she had imagined it.

"They'll make a pact with the Almecs," said Boru. "They cannot be trusted. We will all go to our deaths."

"You may be right," said Mejana, at last. "But I do not think so. Their wives and their children are dead, their power almost gone, their day over. We will follow the last orders of the Questor General."

The area to the east of the city was still flooded, but to the south the ground rose and she could see Rael in his silver armor leading his riders up a low hill. Glancing back she looked down at the hundreds of militia

men waiting nervously behind the gates. Some were
armed with swords and spears, but most carried knives
or rough-made clubs. They had no armor and there
were few bowmen among them. She swung to Pendar.

"Go now to the Third Gate. When Rael attacks lead
out the army. The militia will follow."

"There will be fearful losses, grandmother," he
warned her.

"Try not to be among them," she said. Pendar
bowed, then ran along the ramparts to where the Vagar
soldiers were waiting. Turning to Boru she looked into
his hard blue eyes. "You may stay here with me, or fight
alongside the militia. Your choice," she told him.

"Do you hate me?" he asked her.

"This is not a day for hate," she said. "This is a day
for regret."

Drawing his sword he gave a cold smile and walked
back down the rampart steps to stand with the men
there.

Out on the battlefield the Almecs had seen Rael's
troop moving across the hills and a column of soldiers
marched out to intercept them.

Mejana was weary. She had spent the night helping to
search for survivors in the ruined Library. They had
found two people alive. One died as she was being lifted
clear, the other had lost both legs and bled to death as
they lifted the roof beam that had crushed her. The res-
cuers had removed scores of corpses.

Through that long night Mejana found her hatred of
the Avatar evaporating. Whatever revenge she had
planned seemed small and petty compared to the grand
tragedy all around her. And she had wept when they
discovered the children, their tiny bodies broken by
falling rocks, their lives extinguished by fire and death
from the skies.

But the last of her hate had vanished as she saw Rael holding the broken body of the wife he loved.

Yes, the Avatars had been evil, and the Great God had punished them. It was not for Mejana to harbor further thoughts of revenge.

Rael had come to her before the last ride. He had stood silently for a moment, then he had offered his hand. She took it. "I wish you well," he said. "You Vagars are now the guardians of the twin cities. You will write the histories. It may be that you cannot speak well of us and our rule, but I urge you to remember the manner of our passing."

"You do not have to do this, Rael," she said.

He shrugged. "I do if we want to win."

He had turned away then and mounted a huge gray war-horse.

Pulling her cloak tightly about her she transferred her gaze to the distant hills. The Avatars had formed into a fighting wedge, like a great silver spearhead.

Then they charged.

Rael had not looked back once since he left the city. In all his long life, he realized, he had spent too long doing just that, staring back into the past, fighting a vain battle to keep it alive. The city would survive or it would not. It was no longer his duty to guarantee its future.

Sofarita had come to him and told him exactly where the Almec supplies were based, and how strong the defenses around them. The chances of the Avatars fighting their way through were slim. But Rael no longer cared. Mirani was dead, his dreams buried with her. If his death could cause the fall of the Almecs it would be a small price to pay.

There was no need now to give orders. Every man riding with him knew the objective, and knew further that this was to be the last ride of the Avatars. No one spoke, each lost in his own thoughts, remembering families and loved ones.

Rael led his silver-clad riders up the eastern slope. To his left he could see a regiment of Almecs moving to intercept. "Fighting wedge!" he yelled, galloping forward to create the spear point. His riders closed in around and behind him.

"Forward!" he bellowed. Pulling down his visor he urged his grey war-horse, Pakal, into a run. Rael's zhi-bow was in his hands and he sent a bolt flashing into the advancing Almec foot soldiers. They were still just out of range of the fire-clubs and the Avatars unleashed a deadly volley of light bolts into the massed infantry. Scores of men were hurled from their feet. The horses were at full gallop now, the thunder of hooves filling the air. Again and again the zhi-bows loosed their deadly shafts, and a gaping hole showed in the ranks of the Almecs. Yet they did not break. The fire-clubs came up—and thundered. Lead shot smashed into the advancing horsemen. Twelve horses went down, ten more were hit, but kept on running. Rael was leading a charmed life at the point of the wedge as shots hissed by him.

Just behind him Cation's horse tumbled, throwing the officer to the ground. He rolled to his knees and calmly sent bolt after bolt into the defensive line. A shot took him in the cheekbone, smashing up into his left eye socket and into the brain.

Still the charge continued.

The lead riders struck the line. The Almecs scattered before them. Shots were more sporadic now as the Avatars clove on, shooting as they rode. Rael was hit in the shoulder and hip. He swayed in the saddle, but did not fall. Another murderous volley struck the Avatar left flank, and a score more horses fell.

Rael rode on, shooting to left and right. Beside him now Goray's horse was shot in the head. As it fell Goray leapt from the saddle, killing four Almecs before they struck him down with swords and daggers.

The Avatars had advanced more than a hundred yards into the mass of the enemy.

Rael cast a swift glance back towards Egaru. The gates were open and Vagar soldiers were streaming out over the flooded fields, followed by a swarming mass of militia men.

Something struck Rael in the side of the head. He toppled from the saddle. Three Almecs ran at him. The great grey, Pakal, reared up over them, lashing out with his hooves. Two men fell. Rael rolled to his feet. He was still holding his zhi-bow. His fingers flickered on the light strings. One after another six bolts flashed into the Almec line, blasting men from their feet. Rael grabbed at the saddle pommel and got his foot into the stirrup. A lead ball smashed into his helm, tearing it from his head. A second shot struck his face, snapping back his head. In agony now he hauled himself into the saddle and fired four more bolts. Some of his riders were milling around him, but at least thirty more had continued their charge deep into the enemy ranks. Rael spurred the grey after them, shooting as he rode. There was no need to aim now. The enemy was all around him.

A man rushed forward, thrusting his fire-club up at Rael. The explosion was deafening. Smoke and flame belched out, the shot punching a hole through Rael's armor and ripping into his belly. His zhi-bow spent, he hurled it aside and drew his saber, slashing it down into the man's head. The Almec jumped back, his face streaming blood. A fusillade of shots tore into Pakal. The great horse reared and fell. Rael struggled to rise. Two shots spun him and he fell onto his back.

The noise of the battle receded from him. Struggling

to his knees he tried to focus. But all he could see was a distant bright light at the end of a long dark tunnel. The light beckoned him and he recalled a time when he had, as a child, been lost in a forest. Night had come on swiftly and Rael had blundered through the trees in growing panic. Then he saw a golden light, like a candle in the distance. It was the lantern-lit window of a crofter's cottage. His young heart had soared then, for the light meant safety and life.

It was soaring now—and his spirit soared with it.

From the rear of his force Cas-Coatl watched the last ride of the Avatars with a sense of foreboding and deep regret. He had been honest with Rael. Cas-Coatl sincerely wished for union with the Avatar. He felt a kinship with them and, in a strange way, wished that he too could be a part of that glorious death ride.

But Almeia had come to him last night and told him of the reality of Anu's pyramid, and of the decision by Rael to fight to the last. She had ordered the destruction of the Great Library and with it the annihilation of the Avatar families. As always, Cas-Coatl had obeyed.

Now he watched as the Avatars thundered on. Half their force down, their leader dead, the riders were hurtling towards the hidden trip wires and spiked trenches prepared by his men under cover of darkness. It would be an ignoble end to such a valiant effort, but Cas-Coatl could not allow the destruction of his powder supplies. Without powder the mortar tubes and guns of his men would be useless.

The huge emerald on his belt began to vibrate. Touching his hand to it he heard the voice of Almeia. "Your men have almost broken through the mist. Go and join them. Take Anu alive. What he has done, he can undo. He knows the Music."

Cas-Coatl transferred his gaze to the battlefield. The

front lines were under heavy attack from the Vagars and city dwellers, the Avatars were still riding hard, and inflicting murderous losses on his troops. "We could still lose here, my lady," he said.

"We are lost anyway if Anu completes his pyramid. The woman Sofarita is drawing on my power. Our defenses are weak. Anu must be taken. Go now!"

Cas-Coatl turned to his aide. "Maintain our position here, and when the Avatars are all dead lead a counterattack from the left flank. The city should be ours by nightfall." The man saluted and Cas-Coatl threw one last glance at the charging Avatars, then made his way down the slope to where the three golden ships were anchored.

As he moved away he realized he was glad to be avoiding the moment the charge ended, as the horses struck the trip wires, their riders hurled into the sharpened spikes dug into the hillside.

Chapter Twenty-six

For a hundred days and a hundred nights the battle raged in the sky. And great was the slaughter. At last only one of the heroes remained alive, and that was Virkokka. All around him the demons gathered, a forest of spears confronting him. Virkokka killed the demons in their thousands, but still they came. And at the last even he grew bored with the endless fighting, and, plunging his sword into the ground, he called upon the Earth Flame to aid him.

From the *Evening Song of the Anajo*

When Rael fell Viruk took up the point. Intoxicated by battle fury he was in ecstasy. Niclin rode to his left, the surviving thirty Avatars closing up in formation behind. As he rode, bolts flashing from his zhi-bow, Viruk saw the concentrated mass of bronze fire tubes to his left. Forgetting the mission he angled his mount toward them. The Avatars followed him. "The supplies!" shouted Niclin. "We must get to the supplies!"

Viruk ignored him—and in doing so unwittingly turned the charge away from the hidden wires and trenches. Almecs were scattering before them now and Viruk took aim at a barrel resting near the base of the closest fire tube some 60 yards ahead. The zhi-bolt flashed into it. The barrel exploded in a rush of flame and smoke, igniting two others close by. The resulting blast lifted the bronze weapon high into the air. It landed on a second tube, tearing it from its base. The Almecs around the weapons fled as the Avatars bore down upon them. There were more than 50 fire tubes clustered together. Viruk and his riders sent a volley of bolts into the barrels around them.

A series of blasts followed. Smoke and fire belched up towards the skies and a thick grey fog seeped out across the battlefield.

Niclin rode in close to Viruk. "The supplies, you fool!" he shouted. "We must destroy the black dust!" Kicking his horse into a run Viruk swerved toward the hills once more. A company of Almec soldiers ran into position. Their fire-clubs boomed and a dozen Avatars went down.

Viruk urged his tired horse up the hill, Niclin and the sixteen survivors behind him.

Once over the crest he saw the enemy base camp, their supplies covered by sheets of canvas.

Spread out in a half-circle, protecting the camp, were a hundred krals.

Viruk did not hesitate. Spurring his mount he galloped down the hill.

On open ground now the Avatars spread out. Behind them Almec soldiers had run to the crest and were shooting down the slope. Five horses were hit in the first volley, the riders pitched from the saddles. Seven went down in the next. The six remaining riders bore down on the krals.

The huge beasts ran at the Avatars. "Flanking run, left and right!" bellowed Viruk. Niclin dragged his horse to the right. A single Avatar followed him. Three more riders broke to the left. The krals split into two groups to cut them off.

Viruk charged at the gap opening in the center.

Three krals lumbered back to block the opening. Viruk shot two and leapt his horse at the third. The kral's talons flashed out, tearing open the gelding's throat. The horse fell. Viruk rolled clear—and sent a bolt into the face of the kral.

More of the beasts were moving towards him now. Spinning on his heel he began to run for the camp some 300 yards distant.

More than a dozen soldiers moved from hiding places at the camp's perimeter. Viruk hurled himself to his right as shots rang out. He was not quite fast enough and a lead ball tore into his thigh.

Rolling onto his back he saw the krals were almost upon him. Surging to his feet he shot three of them. Then he heard hoof beats. Swinging to his right he saw Niclin galloping towards him.

Another volley of shots boomed. Niclin was smashed back, his body toppling from the saddle. Viruk ran to intercept the panicked horse, grabbing the pommel of the saddle as the gelding ran by. Viruk vaulted to the saddle and ran the horse at the Almec soldiers. Most were struggling to reload. Two fired their weapons. One shot missed, but the second took Viruk high in the chest.

The horse galloped into the camp. Viruk steered it past the supplies and on to the river wall. Here he dismounted and scrambled up to the steep slope. The krals were close behind. Dropping to his knees Viruk waited calmly for the beasts to reach the foot of the slope. He had known, as had all the Avatars, that he would die today, and he found himself thinking of his garden. He smiled as he pictured the surprise on Kale's face when he discovered that Viruk's house, grounds and wealth had all been willed to him.

He hoped he would make a home there for the little potter.

Then he took aim. And sent a bolt of lightning into the hundreds of barrels clustered below.

The explosion was colossal and a gigantic pillar of fire blasted into the sky. Viruk was lifted from the top of the river wall, his body hurled high into the sky.

Such was the noise that for a moment all fighting on the battlefield ceased, as men looked up at the billowing smoke, swirling higher and higher. The disciplined Almecs reacted better, shaking off their shock and sending a volley into the massed stunned ranks of the Vagars.

Once more the Vagars hurled themselves at the Almec line. At the center Pendar urged his soldiers forward. He was bleeding from a cut on the brow, but he felt no pain. The few lessons Talaban had given him in the art of sword play had kept him alive, and he had already killed two Almecs. His soldiers swept around him, giving him a short breathing space. He glanced left and right. The Vagars outnumbered the Almecs by at least three to one, but they were mostly untrained and the defensive line was holding.

Even though he was unversed in the ways of battle Pendar was still an intelligent man. He could sense the battle shifting. Vagar losses were rising and it would not be long before the fighting citizens were driven back.

Even as the thought occurred to him he saw a regiment of Almecs moving out in a flanking maneuver.

Once they had formed a battle line they would be able to send volley after volley into the unprotected right flank of his force.

Then he heard a series of trumpet blasts from the east.

Over the hills came a line of marching men, dressed in armor of bronze, and carrying long shields and spears. Hundreds of them came into sight. The trumpets sounded again, and the soldiers formed into four lines and rushed at the flanking Almecs. The fire-clubs boomed, but the shields of the advancing force took most of the impact.

The long spears dropped into the horizontal attack position. The Almecs tried to stand firm, but the spears tore into them. Then the attacking line opened and hundreds of swordsmen charged the defenders, hacking and slashing. Within moments the Almec regiment had been cut to pieces, the survivors fleeing back to the main force.

Pendar felt a surging sense of joy. The battle had shifted once more and now the Almecs were fighting for their lives, slowly retreating back up the hill, attempting a fighting withdrawal to the safety of their ships.

All along the line the almost demoralized Vagars found new heart.

Pendar shouted for the charge and his soldiers followed him, cutting a path into the fleeing Almecs.

The retreat turned into a rout, the enemy spinning on their heels and running for the transient safety of the river. Small groups of Almecs formed fighting circles, but these were soon overrun.

On the city walls Mejana, realizing that victory was close, ordered the last of the militia companies to race out and join the battle.

The bronze-armored newcomers, in perfect formation, marched across the battlefield to the beat of a score of drums. The Almecs fell back before them, throwing aside their weapons. Some threw themselves to their knees begging for mercy. None was forthcoming.

At the river the dismayed Almec force found the golden ships had deserted them. Milling and confused they offered no real resistance to the swarming, murderous attacks the Vagars launched against them.

Immediately weary now, Pendar stood back from the slaughter. He made no attempt to stop the massacre. This was, he considered, a day of reckoning.

A figure in bronze armor walked up to him. "Are you in command?" he said, lifting off his helm.

"Loosely speaking," admitted Pendar. The man was incredibly handsome, his hair dyed gold at the temples, his eyes large and violet.

"I am Ammon. I trust my arrival was timely?"

"It was indeed, sir. However, there is another army besieging Pagaru. Your aid would be most welcome."

Ammon gazed about the battlefield. "Where are the Avatars?" he asked.

"All dead. They charged the enemy and destroyed their base."

"That was the thunder we heard," said Ammon. "I thought the skies had fallen. All dead, you say?"

"It was a valiant charge. Glorious to behold."

"I am sorry to have missed it," said Ammon. "This means then that the Lady Mejana controls the city?"

"Yes and no. She holds power until we can elect a ruling council."

"I think you will find you need a king," said Ammon. "But such thoughts can wait for another day."

Sofarita called Methras to her as the first then of the Avatar soldiers, along with Questor Ro, climbed into the silver longboat and headed for the moonlit shore. "You must sail back as swiftly as we came," she warned him. "If all goes well this will be the last voyage of the *Serpent*."

"The last voyage? I don't understand. There should be power in her for years yet—even with the Music."

"Not for much longer. Anu's pyramid will not feed

the stones, but draw the power from them. That is its purpose. He foresaw the coming of the Crystal Queen. If the *Serpent* is still at sea when the pyramid is complete she will wallow and sink."

"How then will we come back for you?"

"You will not."

Turning away from him she walked to the deck rail and stood beside Talaban and Touchstone. The tribesman was scanning the shoreline. The silver longboat returned. Talaban climbed down the rope ladder, followed by Touchstone and the remaining ten Avatar bowmen. Sofarita climbed last. Her joints ached with the effort and there was a flaring pain in her left hip.

Talaban helped her down.

The longboat swung and headed for shore. "Will you tell me now what has happened in Egaru?" said Talaban.

"They have defeated the invader," she said. "But at great cost."

He gave a grim smile. "Damn the cost. Rael is a fine strategist."

"*Was*," she said. "He is dead. And the cost was greater than you could imagine. All the Avatars died with him."

The men in the boat were silent as she told the story of the destruction of the Library and the last charge, and of how Viruk had galloped his mount through the line of beasts, drawing them into destruction. She told them also of Ammon's flight from the city to gather the remnants of his army, and how they had arrived in time to turn the battle.

The longboat came to a stop at the shore, but no one moved. "We are the last of our race," said Talaban. Sofarita gazed at the faces of the men in the boat. The expressions were thoughtful and heavy with sadness. There was no arrogance in them now. They were no longer the god-race, merely men who had lost their families and their loved ones.

Touchstone broke the silence. Laying his hand on Talaban's arm he said, "Kill Almecs now. Yes?"

Talaban did not reply, but he stepped over the side of the boat and waded to the shore. The other Avatars followed him, joining the first group and telling them of the disaster. Questor Ro ran to the boat and took Sofarita's hand.

Once ashore she took a deep breath. "There is no going back, Questor Ro," she said.

"I am where I want to be," he told her. "Is it true they are all dead?"

"Yes, it is true."

He stood silently for a moment. "We became selfish, but it was not always so. We gave the world civilization, the written word, architecture, poetry, learning. I hope when men remember us they remember the good with the bad."

"They will not remember you, Ro," she told him. "Not as men. You will first become legends, and then the gods you dreamed of being. That is, if we win."

A slim figure moved from the shelter of the trees and stood waiting.

Sofarita saw that it was a woman, and one of the wolf soldiers. Her face had been smeared with red lines, her brow painted black. Touchstone gave a wild whoop and ran towards her. The woman stood very still. Touchstone halted before her.

"All is complete," he said. "The winter of my soul is over."

She did not smile, but she reached out with her left hand. Touchstone took it in his right, and held it to his heart. "Did you hear my prayer-songs?" he asked her.

"Every one," she replied. "Did you feel my heart reach out to you?"

"I felt it. Aya! But this is a good day!" Still holding her hand he led her to Talaban. "This Suryet," he said proudly. "This wife of heart. Die happy now." Then he spoke in Anajo to Suryet. "This is the Lord of the Black Ship, who promised to bring me to you. He is a good man, a fine warrior, and he has come to aid the People against the invaders. Greet him as a brother of my soul."

Suryet stepped forward and placed her hand over Talaban's heart, then transferred it to her own. This done she spoke a swift sentence to Touchstone and swung away, walking swiftly toward the trees.

"She say we go," said Touchstone. "Enemy close."

Talaban nodded and led his men after her. For an hour they followed Suryet along deer paths and narrow trails through the trees. Sofarita found the journey increasingly difficult and began to fall behind. Questor Ro called out to Talaban. The warrior loped back. "What is the problem?" he asked her.

"My joints are crystallizing," she said. "I cannot walk much farther." Tossing his zhi-bow to Ro, Talaban swept her into his arms. She was lighter than he expected. Ro looked crestfallen as the warrior moved back toward his men. Being small and slight he could never have carried her far, but the sight of her in the arms of another man was hard to bear.

For Sofarita the relief from pain was more than welcome and she nestled her head on Talaban's shoulder.

The moon was bright in the sky, its light bathing the forest in a spectral glow. It was silent and ghost-like, not a breath of wind disturbing the trees. At the head of the column Suryet walked with Touchstone, neither of them speaking.

Towards dawn Suryet threw up her hand, then crouched low. The Avatars halted. Setting Sofarita down, Talaban moved alongside Suryet. She touched a finger to her lips then pointed away to the right. There were campfires in a large hollow by a stream. Suryet indicated that the column should swing to the left and move around them. Talaban nodded, and the journey began again. Talaban was tired now, and ordered an Avatar soldier to carry Sofarita. Talaban himself walked at the head of the column, alongside Touchstone and Suryet.

With the coming of the dawn they emerged from the tree line. Ahead of them was a range of mountains, but it was not the mountains that caught the eye and made the breath catch in the throat. Beyond the range was what appeared to be a black wall across the world, gigantic and dark, and stretching as far as the eye could see.

"Almec land," said Touchstone.

It was alien and unnatural and Talaban could not tear his gaze from it. "It stretches for hundreds of miles," said Sofarita.

"Open ground now," said Touchstone, pointing to the narrow plain between them and the mountains. "Big danger."

Talaban alerted his Avatars. All along the line string of light appeared on the zhi-bows. "Time to go," he said.

Moving out onto the slope the Avatars spread out, bows ready. There was at least a mile of open ground to cover before they would reach the foot of the mountains. They were halfway across when one of the Avatars shouted a warning. Behind them they could see armed men emerging from the trees.

The chasing group was a half-mile back, but carrying Sofarita was slowing the Avatars, and Talaban knew there was little doubt that the Almecs would get into range before they reached the shelter of the slopes.

Sending half the men onward Talaban and ten

Avatars dropped back. The range of the fire-clubs was around one hundred yards—half that of the zhi-bows. Talaban hoped at least to slow the pursuit.

The Almecs were running now and the gap was closing. Five hundred yards. Four hundred. "Ready!" yelled Talaban. There were at least 500 men in the chasing force.

Three hundred yards. Two hundred.

Talaban loosed a bolt, then another, and another. The zhi-bows sang and more than thirty Almecs were blasted from their feet.

The charge continued. "Once more!" said Talaban. Twenty more Almecs died. Still they came on.

The fire-clubs boomed. Shots slashed all around the Avatars. One man was struck in the forehead and dropped without a sound.

"Back!" yelled Talaban. The Avatars began to run across the grassland. Another man was hit, but he kept running.

"All Avatars to me!" shouted Talaban. Up ahead the soldier carrying Sofarita lowered her to the ground, retrieved his zhi-bow from Ro and turned, with the other nine bowmen, to run back to join Talaban. Forming a wide line the Avatars began to shoot into the oncoming Almecs. More than a hundred of them died before the charge broke, the remaining enemy warriors dropping to the ground and discharging their fire-clubs. Three Avatars were hit, but only one killed.

On the mountain slopes Touchstone was now carrying Sofarita, and they were almost at the tree line. Talaban waited until they were safely out of sight then led his men onto the slope. The Almecs rose from the ground and sent a volley after them. Another man was hit in the leg. He stumbled, but carried on running.

Twice more Talaban swung the Avatars to send more zhi-bolts into the enemy.

And then the Avatars reached the transient security of the trees. From here they unleashed their bolts to terrible effect on the Almec warriors exposed on the slope. More than half the enemy force had been killed before they were forced to fall back.

"One has to admire their courage," said Questor Ro, moving alongside Talaban.

The warrior nodded. "They certainly do not lack bravery," he admitted. "Where to now, Questor?"

"Sofarita says we must continue to climb. She needs to be higher than the land mass of the Almecs. Then she can really attack the Crystal Queen."

Talaban and his men faded back from the tree line. The two wounded men volunteered to stay behind and harass the enemy. Talaban agreed, shook their hands, and moved off.

"They will die there," said Ro.

"And they know it," said Talaban.

Slowly they climbed on. The sounds of fire-clubs came from behind them, and the screams of dying men.

Up ahead Suryet and Touchstone had stopped near a waterfall. From the undergrowth around them rose Anajo warriors. The One-Eyed-Fox hugged Touchstone, then moved beyond him to Sofarita. "We will hold them here," he said. "You must go on."

Reaching out she took the One-Eyed-Fox by the arm. Power coursed through him. "My thanks to you," he said with a wide grin.

"And mine to you," she said. "It is a small repayment for saving my life."

Talaban came up. The One-Eyed-Fox spoke to him, but the Avatar could not understand a word. "He say you welcome," said Touchstone. "He also say second army coming from north."

"We need a defensive position," said Talaban. "Somewhere narrow that we can hold." Touchstone translated for the One-Eyed-Fox. The two men spoke swiftly. "He say there is such a place. But with so few men we not hold long. Maybe day."

"We need two days," said Sofarita. "At the very least."

"If it is possible it will be done," promised Talaban.

As the *years* passed within the Valley of the Stone Lion the workers grew ever more close knit. This had, at first, surprised Yasha. It was one thing, with the promise of riches, to commit oneself to a twenty-year contract, quite another to labor through the endless years in bleak monotony. Yet it had not been bleak. In the main the work had been joyous, as course after course of the pyramid was completed. An added advantage was the perennial youth and strength of the workers. The years passed, but not a gray hair was seen among them. The men felt vibrant and always full of energy.

All save the Holy One. He aged by the day, growing ever more frail.

It was as if he alone had accepted the burden of their passing years. At first the workers had found the change in him disconcerting, but slowly they had come to love him for it. His physical deterioration made a powerful contrast to their perpetual youth.

When news reached them of the terrible war raging beyond the mist they felt safe here, and when Anu assured them that the building they were constructing would save the cities, and their families, they worked even harder and with greater zeal.

Now it was almost over, Yasha felt curiously bereft.

He stood in the deserted camp staring up at the golden pyramid. One million two hundred thousand blocks of limestone and granite weighing three million tons and standing 250 feet high. One hundred courses of stone, some blocks weighing in excess of 25 tons.

It was a monumental achievement.

Anu had earlier thanked his workers and sent them towards the north to hide in the hills above the stone quarries. "The enemy is coming now," he said, his voice so weak that the closest to him had to echo his words for the men behind who could not hear them. "The enemy will not seek you. They will come to the pyramid and then they will depart in their golden ships. I promise you this. You will return to your homes, and you will receive every part of the fortune promised you. Go now with my blessing."

Yasha stood alone now outside the hut of the Holy One. Anu had asked him to wait while the others fled. The burly foreman cast his gaze over the deserted shacks that had housed the whores and idly wondered how many women he had enjoyed during the timeless decades that he had worked in this place.

The door of the hut creaked open and Anu moved slowly and painfully into the light. He was carrying several rolls of papyrus. "Thank you for waiting," he said.

"We must be going, Holy One," said Yasha. "I will carry you."

"I am not leaving, Yasha. But you can carry me." With a trembling hand he pointed to the pyramid. "Take me there. To the peak."

The ladders were still in place and Yasha lifted the old man and carried him across the open ground. Then he took Anu on his back and slowly climbed to the top of the pyramid. The peak was flat, for Anu had insisted there be no capstone. Yasha found this strange, for the pyramid was perfect in every other detail.

Anu sat down on the golden stone and together the two men looked around the valley.

"A long time ago I made you a promise, Yasha," said Anu. "I said that this pyramid would not be just for the Avatar, but for the world. When it sings its song it will deliver us from evil. The enemy will be no more."

"It is a beautiful building," said Yasha. "It will stand for eternity."

"No," said Anu. "It will stand for less than a year. The Music I have made is very powerful. Once begun it will eat away at the blocks, turning them to dust. The winds will scatter that dust over the earth. Nothing will be left."

"Why, Holy One?" asked Yasha, appalled.

"We sit upon a vast and wondrous source of power, Yasha. And as with all power it can be used for good or evil. If I had left it standing there would have come a man—or a woman—who could reshape the Music." He smiled sadly. "As it is there will be many attempts in the centuries to come to duplicate what we have achieved here. Perhaps one will succeed. I am not so arrogant as to believe I am the only man who will ever be blessed by the Source." He patted Yasha's arm. "Now, time is slowing down, Yasha, and there are matters we must discuss. There are few Avatars left in the cities and control has passed to a Vagar council. With the terrible destruction they have suffered they will not feel inclined to honor an Avatar promise. Especially one that would empty the Treasury. The workers will arrive back in the city to discover there is no payment for them. My man, Shevan, is telling them this even as we speak. He is also telling them that you will see to their payments. That you will honor my promise."

"And how will I do this, Holy One?"

Anu passed him the two scrolls he held. "The first is my will, and I bequeath all that I have to you. It may be that this also will not be honored. I cannot say. The second is a map, showing where I have buried twelve chests full of gold coin. Enough to pay every man who worked here. And every whore who still carries tokens."

"You would be a fool to trust me with all that gold," said Yasha. "Why did you not give it to Shevan?"

"I have been foolish in my life, Yasha. No man who draws breath can say otherwise. But in this I am right. You are a proud man and an honorable one. I might not trust you with my wife or my daughter, but this is only gold. You will see it paid, and you will do it with scrupulous honesty."

"Aye, I will," admitted Yasha. "I will do it for you, Anu."

Tucking the scrolls into his shirt he sighed. "Why is it that you wish to remain here?"

"I must. I am the capstone. I am the last of the Music. And now you must go, Yasha. Leave me."

The big foreman rose, then leaned forward and kissed the old man's brow. "You will not be forgotten, Holy One."

"Yes I will," said Anu, with a smile. "All men are. Go now!"

Yasha moved to the ladder, took one last look at the white-bearded old man sitting on the stone, then climbed back to the valley floor.

Talaban, his zhi-bow completely discharged, leapt from the boulder into a group of Almecs. His sword slashed out, slicing through the neck of the first man, his dagger plunging into the chest of a second. Touchstone ran from hiding with several Anajo warriors and together they tore into the Almec ranks.

The suddenness of the attack dismayed the Almecs, who fell back down the trail. Talaban swept up a fallen fire-club and discharged it into the fleeing group. Then he flung it aside.

Glancing up at the sky he saw dusk was approaching. They had held the Almecs for almost a full day and a night. Only three Avatars remained alive and fifteen Anajo. The defenders had been pushed further up the mountain and almost forced out of the narrow trails. One more push and they would be on the exposed flank where they would be swiftly overrun.

Blood was running into Talaban's left eye, seeping from a cut on his brow. He wiped it away and moved forward to the line of boulders that marked the end of the trail. As he peered round them several shots rang out, smashing into the stone close to his head. Talaban swore and ducked back. "They are massing again," he told Touchstone.

One-Eyed-Fox moved alongside them. He spoke to Touchstone. "What did he say?" asked Talaban.

"Need hold till dawn."

"Dawn is a long way off."

"Time for new plan," said Touchstone.

Talaban gave a grim smile. "That's true. What do you suggest?"

"Attack!" said Touchstone.

Chapter Twenty-seven

*And so Star Woman and the Goddess of Death
came face to face on the Last Day. The Goddess
was powerful, but Star Woman had with her
Storro, the Speaker of Legends, to guard her heart,
and Tail-avar, the god of wisdom, to defend her
body, and Touch the Moon to protect her soul.
Aya! When will we see such heroes walk again?*

From the *Sunset Song of the Anajo*

High on the southern flank of the mountain Sofarita
pulled herself over a wide ledge then sank to her
haunches. Ro hauled himself up alongside her. The
wind was bitter here and he wrapped his cloak around
Sofarita's shoulders. They were finally above the towering black wall stretched across the land, and Ro could
see the lights of a distant city flickering in the distance.

"Can you feel her power?" he asked Sofarita.

"I can feel it." Throwing back the cloak she stood
and stretched her arms out wide. It seemed to the
Avatar that she began to glow. Within moments he
could feel heat radiating from her. Her limbs stiffened.
She was like a statue now, her skin gleaming as if coated
with ice. He reached out for her, but her voice sounded
in his mind.

"Do not touch me, Ro. This is my destiny. I will die here."

Her words were a dagger in his heart and he slumped to the rock wall, his head in his hands.

With a hundred men Cas-Coatl stood at the northern edge of the mist barrier. His engineers were working furiously to find ways to break through. All had failed.

Cas-Coatl waited calmly. The army besieging Pagaru had been evacuated to twelve golden ships, which were now heading back across the ocean, their holds packed with chests full to the brim with charged crystals. Once these had been fed to Almeia her strength would return and she would sever the spell that sought to drag them back to an icy doom.

The setbacks here in the east were temporary. When next he came there would be no Avatars to destroy his supplies. But first he must capture Anu and force him to reverse the magic of the pyramid. Failing that he would destroy the pyramid itself. He glanced back at the score of wagons containing the last of his powder.

A cool wind whispered across the valley. Cas-Coatl shivered. His face always ached with the cold. Lifting his hand he stroked his fingers across the smooth hard glass of his cheekbones.

Crystal-wed.

He had been horrified when the disease took hold. His parents had taken him to Almeia's resting place and had prayed for him throughout the day. Almeia herself had appeared to him in a dream, promising to save him. The promise had been kept and, with joy in their hearts, his parents had sacrificed sixty slaves to the goddess.

Cas-Coatl's hand rested on the huge emerald set into his belt. It linked him to the goddess in a special way and its power held at bay the onset of crystal death.

There had been a price for salvation. Almeia had never allowed Cas-Coatl to take a wife or sire children. He was to be hers alone for all eternity. Cas-Coatl had paid that price willingly.

He was less sure of his actions now. The Almecs had always taken some prisoners to the Ziggurat for sacrifice. It was pleasing to the goddess. But never before had Cas-Coatl been instructed to butcher entire populations. Yet even this he had done, in the expectation that with the completion of Anu's pyramid the slaughter would cease.

What now, he wondered? Is this to be my life, scouring the earth for fresh victims to murder?

"Lord," shouted an engineer. "The mist is lifting!"

"What did you do?" demanded Cas-Coatl.

"I would like to take credit for it, lord. But it was not my doing."

The breeze picked up, dispersing the mist. Now Cas-Coatl could see the valley beyond and, at its center, the towering pyramid. Ordering his men forward Cas-Coatl marched into the valley.

As he came closer to the deserted site he saw a movement at the pyramid's peak. A bearded old man was staring down at them. Turning to his soldiers he sent two to apprehend him. From a pouch at his side he drew a large green crystal. Attuning himself to it he held the gem towards the pyramid. He could feel the energy being drawn from it. But the process was incredibly slow, the loss of power infinitesimal. Moving back some fifty yards he tested the crystal again. There was no loss now.

Cas-Coatl laughed. All his fears concerning Anu's pyramid vanished like the mist in the breeze.

There was no threat from it.

Relief washed over him. Was there any point in locating Anu, he wondered? The man was a failure. He had built a golden mountain that could not drain a single crystal. And yet . . . Almeia had been so sure of his talent. She had observed the construction and had told Cas-Coatl of the movement of giant blocks as if they weighed no more than a hollow box of wood. Surely someone with that degree of skill could have created a more potent weapon.

The sound of music filtered down to him. The old man on the pyramid was playing a flute, the music sad and wistful. Cas-Coatl felt the emerald at his waist begin to vibrate. With a shock he realized the old man was Anu and he was still casting his spell.

"Kill him!" he bellowed, his voice ringing out. The two climbing soldiers glanced back at him. "Kill the old man. Do it now!" The men steadied themselves on the ladder and lifted their fire-clubs from their shoulders. At that moment the music stopped, the old man stepping forward to the rim of the peak and standing, arms outstretched, as if beckoning death. At first Cas-Coatl was relieved, for the climbers still had some way to go to reach the summit and who knew what magic Anu could still summon. But as he watched the holy man greet his killers with open arms a terrible fear struck him. Cas-Coatl was a man raised in the principles of blood sacrifice and the power it could bring.

In that one dread moment the Almec general knew that death was what Anu required. He needed his blood to fall upon the stones. He sprang forward and screamed out a single word.

"No!"

The fire-clubs boomed. Anu crumpled and fell back. For several heartbeats nothing happened. There was almost time for Cas-Coatl to wonder if he had been wrong.

Almost.

The crystal at his belt began to tremble and shake. Then it shattered into a thousand pieces.

The Almec stood stock-still, his joints stiffening, his skin pulling tight. Terrible pain smote his chest and belly, as if red spiders were inside his flesh tearing at his organs. He wanted to scream but his face had set. His left leg shattered and he fell to the grass. His right arm broke off. After that Cas-Coatl ceased to exist as a thinking living creature. The silent music of the pyramid swelled over his crystal corpse. Cracks appeared all over his body, widening, growing like spiders' webs. Then he imploded, and all that was left upon the ground was the hollow shell of his armor, his helm, leggings and boots.

Bereft of leadership the Almecs moved back from the pyramid, frightened lest it should turn its wrath upon them.

Leaving the powder wagons behind they fled for the river and the ships that would take them home.

The One-Eyed-Fox gathered his men about him, moving to each and laying his hands over their eyes. With each man he chanted a few words before moving on. At last he came to the Avatars. Talaban guessed the tribesman was singing a prayer song of power to aid the warriors.

He was right—but not in the way he expected. The darkness around them was almost absolute, thick clouds obscuring the moon. But when the One-Eyed-Fox lifted his hands from Talaban's face the Avatar found he could see as clearly as if it was noon. It was bizarre. There was no color around him, merely a sharpness of black, gray and white.

The shaman summoned the men to him. "The blood

seekers will try to attack us in the dark. But we, like mountain cats, can fall upon them. They will be as blind men."

The fourteen Anajo men and Suryet hefted their bows and their arrows of flint and melted away into the undergrowth. Talaban made to follow them, but the One-Eyed-Fox stepped in front of him. Touching Talaban's brow he closed his eyes. His voice echoed inside Talaban's mind. "You make too much noise, my friend. Wait here with your brothers and kill any who reach the end of the trail."

Then he was gone.

Talaban drew his sword and dagger, signalled his three men to stand with him, and positioned himself at the crest of the trail. More than a hundred of the enemy would be climbing the mountain. Even with the advantage of superb night vision the Anajo could not stop them.

I am going to die here, he thought suddenly. I do not even have the week that Anu promised me. Fear struck him and he felt suddenly nauseous. I don't want to die on this foreign mountain, he thought. I have no sons to carry my blood like a gift into the future, and no wife to mourn for me. He thought of Sofarita. He had accepted Anu's warning of death, but had hoped that Sofarita's power could save him. But she was not here. For the first time in his life Talaban found himself wanting to run away. Yet he did not. Could not. He looked at the man to his right. The shock jarred him from his melancholic thoughts. The Avatar's eyes were wide, the pupils slitted like a cat. He saw from the surprise on the soldier's face that he too must look equally sinister. Talaban grinned suddenly. The man responded, then reached out his hand. Talaban gripped it, then turned and shook the hands of each of the warriors.

"Not as glorious as the last ride," he said. "But we

lived like gods and we'll die like men. It is enough, I think."

The screams of wounded men sounded from down the trail, and several fire-clubs were loosed.

Talaban hefted his sword.

Back in the city of Egaru fat Caprishan knelt in his luxurious bed-chamber emptying bags of fully charged crystals into two chests. He had declined Rael's invitation to ride out against the Almecs and was now trying to estimate how much life these crystals would allow him. Like all Avatars his mind was skilled in calculation. There were over 2,000 crystals, each one capable of keeping a normal man healthy for months. Caprishan was not a normal man. His immense weight and his prodigious appetite had weakened his heart, and he could exhaust a fully charged crystal within six days. Twelve thousand three hundred and sixty days. Less than thirty-four years!

Disappointment seized him. "Better than being dead and rotting on a field of battle," he told himself. "And who knows, perhaps there are more crystals to be found?"

He sat staring into the chests, watching the light glitter on the gems. Much could happen in thirty-four years.

A crystal vase on his windowsill suddenly shattered. The sound made him jump. Pushing himself ponderously to his feet he waddled to the window, looking out to see who had thrown a stone. There was no one in sight. A strange popping sound came from behind him. He swung, and saw green dust spraying out from the chests. He stumbled back and fell to his knees. The crystals within were writhing and splitting. "No!" he shouted, digging his fat hands into the first chest, closing his fingers around the few remaining gems. But even inside his grip he felt them shatter and turn to dust. The red gems in the rings on his fingers exploded.

Caprishan began to weep piteously. One of his servants ran into the room.

"What is it, lord?" he asked.

"Leave me alone!" shouted Caprishan. The man backed away. Caprishan pushed himself to his feet and walked to the balcony.

He could wait for the six days to pass, and die slowly and horribly.

Or he could . . .

His fat body sailed through the air and smashed onto the stone path beside a fountain.

And the music of the pyramid swept out over the ocean.

Serpent Seven was close to the shore when all power vanished. For a little while the black ship struggled on, carried by her momentum and by the inrushing tide. But then she began to wallow in the waves, tipping and rolling.

On the journey back Methras had ordered the crew to strip the cabins and holds of everything that would float. Several rafts had been made, and makeshift oars. The men had thought the orders strange, but they had obeyed them.

The ship swung broadside to the land and tilted perilously. "Over the side!" yelled Methras. The crew began to throw empty barrels into the sea, then the rafts were hurled after them. One by one the men jumped into the ocean. The strongest swimmers set out for the shore. Those unskilled in the water clung to the rafts or other floating debris. Methras saw a crewman go under. He dived and grabbed at the man's collar, hauling him up. The Vagar struggled and almost pulled them both down, but Methras spoke to him calmly, then helped him to a floating barrel. "Hold on and kick out with your feet," he advised the man. "The tide will carry you in."

Methras swam to a raft. Several men had clambered aboard and they pulled him up.

He sat down and turned to watch the *Serpent*. Like a sick whale it rolled and pitched. Then it tipped completely and sank beneath the waves.

"What happened?" asked a Vagar seaman.

"Anu's magic," he said.

"I thought he was on our side."

"He is," said Methras. "The golden ships will be sinking just as we did."

"He could have waited another hour," grumbled the man. "We'd have been in port by then."

As the dawn rose over the sea Ro felt a strange sensation rippling through him. Attuning his mind he focused on it. It was music, whispering on the wind. It was discordant and yet . . . it made him feel a part of everything, the earth, the sky, the rock beneath his feet.

A strangled cry came from Sofarita. He turned to her and saw her begin to tremble. Rising he threw his arms around her, holding her stiff body close. She fell into him, almost carrying them both from the ledge. Ro struggled to stay upright. Sofarita's arms were outstretched, still stiff, her joints locked. She was trying to speak, but her tongue could form no words. "I am here," he said. "I am with you. Remember the rituals. Join with me."

At first there was nothing, then a terrible pain swept over him. His body was shattering like glass. Ro fought down panic and instinctively concentrated on the reality of flesh, the softness of the wet tissue that bonded into strong muscle, the flowing of rich, warm blood.

The Music in his mind expanded, a magnificent symphony, a song as large as the universe. It flowed over them both.

Sofarita's head lowered to his shoulder, her arms dropping. Ro could feel her flesh beneath his hands, soft and warm. He laid her down on the ledge and knelt beside her. "Speak to me," he said. "Show me you are alive."

Her eyes opened. "The power is gone from me," she said. "I am a woman again. How did you make the Music?"

"It was not mine."

She sighed and struggled to sit. "I am no longer a goddess, Ro. I am just a Vagar woman."

"You are the woman I love," he said, surprised as the words rushed out. He waited for her rejection, knowing it would be kind and burn him like fire.

"I love you too," she said. "I've known it since the night you saved me from Almeia, when you lay beside me and warmed me with your body."

A fierce wind swept across the ledge. Ro clung to a rock. Sofarita was thrown against him.

A brilliant light blazed in the sky. Ro looked up, to see a second sun shining brightly through swirling clouds. A terrible groan came from the wall across the world. Boulders began to rain down from it. Then, with an awesome wrench the wall, and the land beyond it, broke away and lifted into the sky, tipping as it rose. A huge earthquake rippled across the floating land mass and it split into two. Both parts continued to rise towards the second sun. Something glittered in the air like a golden bird. Ro saw that it was a ship, spinning through the air to crash into the airborne land. More ships appeared, as if being drawn up by an invisible whirlwind.

A ring of fire hundreds of miles in diameter flared in the sky. The broken land floated towards it, entering the circle of flames. As Ro watched, the land of the Almecs disappeared. The fire ring began to close, shrinking smaller and smaller.

Then it was gone.

There was no wall now, no dark and threatening land. A vast and ruined plain lay before their eyes.

"The grass and trees will grow again," said Sofarita, "and streams will flow. Life will flourish again."

Ro stood and, holding Sofarita by the hand, walked back along the ledge.

Further down the trail they met the One-Eyed-Fox and Touchstone and Suryet. Four other Anajo tribesmen were still alive.

At the mouth of the trail Ro saw a mound of bodies. Just back from them Touchstone was kneeling beside the fallen Talaban. Ro ran forward, thinking the Avatar merely injured. But as he came close he saw the terrible wounds and the cold, still face. He sighed and felt deep shame at the surging joy he had experienced when Sofarita told him she loved him. Talaban had given his life so that he could hear those words.

Moving to the fallen Avatar he knelt by the body.

"He and the others killed more than twenty," said Touchstone in Anajo. "They did not give way. Talaban was the last to die. I tried to reach him, to help him. I wanted to save his life as he saved mine. He saw me running forward. They were all around him. He died just as the sun rose." Drawing his dagger Touchstone cut a lock from Talaban's hair. "I shall make a prayer song for him. It will reach all Anajo spirits. They will make him welcome."

"I am glad you survived," said Ro. "That would have pleased him."

"I thought I would die. But when the second sun rose the Almecs fled. What will you do now, Questor Ro? Will you try to go back to your place of stone?"

"No. I will stay here if you will have me. I will teach and I will learn. I will find a way to make a history of these events."

Touchstone laid his hand on Talaban's brow. "He will live in my heart always. And my sons shall learn of him. And their sons. He is a part of the People now. We will not forget." Sofarita came alongside and Ro took her hand. She gazed down at the dead Avatar, and Ro felt no jealousy at the sorrow in her eyes.

Epilogue

On the day that men call Reshgaroth the gods went away to continue their war in the heavens, leaving the fields and the forests, the mountains and the valleys. They journeyed far beyond the bright stars, lifted on the backs of silver eagles. All vanished, save one. Virkokka knew that the Frost Giants would return. He alone remained among the People to protect them from the cold of death.

From the *Evening Song of the Anajo*

On the shores of the Luan work was underway clearing the bodies, for disease was an ever-present threat after a battle. Vagar and Avatar corpses were carried away for burial, while the Almecs, stripped of their clothing, were burned on huge pyres.

Three Vagar workmen had paused for a noon break. They walked down to the Luan and splashed their faces with cool water. One, a young carpenter named Leshan sat down and glanced toward the north. "Another body there," he said, pointing to a blackened corpse half out of the water.

"Leave it. I'm exhausted," said another.

"I like to do what I'm paid for," said Leshan, rising and walking across to the body. It was lying face down, the clothes singed, the shirt in tatters. The flesh beneath showed black and red burns. Leshan could not tell whether the corpse was Vagar or Almec. With an effort he rolled it onto its back. The man's chest was badly scarred and most of his hair had been burnt away, but his face was unmarked. Leshan knew him. Who did not? He was the deadliest and most hated of all the Avatars.

Viruk's eyes flickered open. They were pale, and gray and cold. Then he groaned.

"He's alive," shouted Leshan.

"Of course I'm alive," grunted the wounded man. "I'm a god, you moron!" Viruk closed his eyes and gritted his teeth against the pain. Leshan's hand slid down to the knife at his belt. With one thrust he could destroy this man, plunging the blade deep into the heat-blistered neck.

He saw Viruk's eyes were open again, and that the Avatar was watching him. "You deserve to die," said Leshan.

Viruk grinned, and levered himself to one elbow. "I don't know why you sub-humans cannot grasp simple realities," he said. "We don't get what we deserve, idiot. We get what we get. Now if you are going to stab me, do it. If not, call for a surgeon. I may be a god, but I am a god with a broken leg."

Leshan shook his head and smiled. Viruk was in terrible pain, and at his mercy. Yet still he could hurl casual insults and defy death.

Who could kill such a man, he thought?

And when the last of the Frost Giants had been slain Virkokka grew bored. Then Storro, the Speaker of Legends, journeyed across the star-filled ocean of the night sky to the Stone City and told

Virkokka of a great war brewing, of sorcerers and chieftains and armies hungry for blood. Virkokka laughed with relief as he heard this. And he took up his sword of fire, and went forth once more, to battle evil.

From the *Evening Song of the Anajo*